I0637160

I Can't Even

Jenn McKinlay

Published by JMO Ink, 2025.

I CAN'T EVEN

First edition. April 8, 2025.

Copyright © 2025 Jenn McKinlay.

ISBN: 979-8986503455

Written by Jenn McKinlay.

Dear Reader,

I originally started writing the romantic comedy I CAN'T EVEN in 2016, following the passing of my father. We had a complicated relationship and I channeled my grief into this story. Last year, in an effort to finally finish the manuscript, I published it on Kindle Vella (now defunct).

I'm glad I did. It was nice to wrap up the lives of the characters I had come to care for and it helped me work through some leftover childhood issues.

This book includes the following subjects: loss of a parent, grief, alcohol use, childhood trauma, and diversity, including LGBTQ+ characters. There are also some explicit love scenes. If these are tender topics for you, please read with care.

XO. Jenn

Chapter One

"Jules, you have to come home. It's Mom." Sophie, my older sister, spoke with the gravity of someone imparting dreadful news.

"What about her?" I frowned at the coding on the computer screen in front of me as I gave my sisters, who were on speaker phone, half of my attention.

"She's...she's dying," Emily, my younger sister, said. There was a catch in her voice as if she had to force the words out.

"Again?" I asked.

"Jules!" My sisters wailed together, sounding perfectly horrified by my callousness.

"What? You know it's true," I said. "This is seasonal for her, like allergies but so much more dramatic."

I deleted some bad code and retyped what I thought the program needed. The pictures I wanted to use on the webpage I had designed were too big so I typed in a smaller ratio hoping to make them fit.

"Not this time." That was Emily, the closest to our mother, probably because she still lived at home despite being twenty-five years old.

"Puleeze, the last time I fell for Babs's overwrought death summons, I dropped a client and raced home only to have her blind date me with a podiatrist."

I heard one of them snort. My money was on Sophie. As the oldest of us Blumer sisters, she was delightfully snarky, although she pretended she wasn't.

"Three hours spent talking about feet. It was the worst dinner of my life. I still can't look at a crouton and not see a plantar wart." All true.

"Oh, ergh, I think I just threw up a little in my mouth," Em said.

"Jules, I know Mom can be a meddler," Soph began.

"You think?" Fearing I would get distracted and forget, I saved my work. "Or have you forgotten that she went to the furniture store where you bought your new living room set, canceled your order, and replaced it with one she liked better?"

"No, I haven't forgotten," Sophie said.

"She means well," Emily protested.

In addition to being the closest, Em was also the most loyal to our mother, Babs. I had no idea why since Em's life was by far the most stifled by our mother's overbearing manipulative interference.

"Em, she hasn't let you cut your hair or buy your own clothes without her approval since...oh, wait...that would be ever in this lifetime."

"I value Mom's opinion," Emily said. I huffed out a breath and she insisted, "I do. She has excellent taste."

"Oh, my god," I argued. "Mom dresses you like you're a librarian and not one of the cool ones."

"She's got you there," Sophie said.

"You have no cred here, Soph," Em disagreed. "Mom has been overreaching in your parenting of the twins since you got knocked up your freshman year of college."

"Hey!" Soph protested. "That's a low blow."

"And yet, also true." I exited the software program I was using.

"Shut up!" Sophie snapped.

See? This was why we didn't speak very often. It rarely stayed civil for more than a few minutes.

"Babs treats both of you like puppets on a string." Yes, I was a bit smug, but that's what happens when you're the smarter middle child.

I stood up and stretched, putting my fist into my lower back for that little extra pop. My tiny studio in Brooklyn was not big enough to pace end to end, so I lapped the futon that folded out into a bed in the center of my apartment.

Spaghetti and Meatball were sacked out on their cat tree, ignoring me. Why Spaghetti and Meatball? Because I rescued them from an alley where they'd been dumped in a plastic bag behind Decusati's Italian Ristorante. Spag was a long and lanky orange tabby while Meat was a round black blob, so it had made sense at the time. Actually, in the five years they'd crashed with me, their shapes had not changed an inch so still accurate.

"You're one to talk, Jules," Soph said. I could tell her dial was turned to maximum peeved as her words were as clipped as the bangs she'd cut too short on me when I was six. Yep, still scarred.

"How's that?" I knew I shouldn't open that door, but I foolishly did anyway.

"You moved three thousand miles away from home and you rarely come back," Em said, interrupting whatever Sophie was about to say. "Who does that?"

"People who choose not to live with their mother when they're a grown-up," I assumed the hatha yoga asana of tree pose in an attempt to maintain my Zen.

"Don't be so judgy," Emily said. "I'm happy."

"You need to upgrade your definition of happiness," I argued. "Like, you might want to include miniskirts and some orgasms on that list."

There was a beat of silence. Okay, maybe I'd gone too far given how naïve Em was.

"I have a...a...miniskirt," Em said, flustered.

I burst out laughing. I know it wasn't nice and I should have held it in, but she sounded like an angry kitten who hadn't quite mastered the hiss and spit yet. Seriously, she could take lessons from Spag and Meat.

"It's not funny!" Em oozed hurt.

I knew I had to rein it in, but I could hear Sophie trying not to laugh, which didn't help my control issues.

"You guys are such jerks!" Em growled.

"I'm sorry, Em." I switched my yoga position to the other side. "Really, I mean it. Forgive me?"

"No."

"Ah, come on," I protested.

"Nine words," she said.

"Really?" I asked. "Is this really a nine-word offense?"

I could picture Em with her straight honey-colored hair hanging halfway down her back, chin tipped up, and arms crossed over her chest in a stubborn stance as clearly as if she were standing beside me.

"You might as well say them," Sophie said. "It'll be good practice for when you come back here and have to say them to Mom every day."

"I'm not coming back, but okay, fine, here's your nine words." I rolled my eyes. "I am sorry. I love you. Please forgive me."

This was a Babs thing. When we were young, she'd thought that making us simply say "I'm sorry" did not get the point across sufficiently, so she'd instituted the nine words. We had to say all nine words and sound like we actually meant our apology in order to get forgiveness. It just goes to show that even the worst mother has her moments.

"You are forgiven," Em said, her tone mollified.

"And now back to the reason that we called," Soph said. "You really do need to come home, Jules. Something is wrong. Babs, er, Mom, is not herself."

"Really?" I asked. "Has she quit drinking?"

"No," Emily said.

"Quit snooping?"

"No." Sophie sighed.

"Quit shopping?" I asked.

"Yes!" they answered together.

Okay, that gave me pause. Babs was a shopper of the first order. She had a credit card for every department store in southern California and she liked to workout with them regularly.

"In fact, I asked her if she wanted to go to the mall yesterday, and she said no," Em said.

"No?" I couldn't imagine my mom turning down a trip to the mall.

A small fission of alarm rippled through my belly, my early warning signal that something was amiss. My mother, Barbara "Babs" Blumer, had to date only missed one sale ever and that was when an El Nino weather system hovered over the county for several days and the store having the sale was flooded to the rafters.

"See?" Soph said. "We're serious. Something's not right. You have to come home."

I frowned. It was easy for her to say, it wasn't like she lived three thousand miles away and would have to catch a very expensive flight out of New York City to go home to Gull's Harbor, California, to sit at the bedside of that bitter pill we called Mom. Well, I called her Babs, mostly, but not to her face.

"Jules, she's...she's asking for you." Emily's soft voice was barely above a whisper.

My heart pounded hard in my chest, and I had a hard time swallowing. I had to take a steadying breath. My mother, the one and only—thank Christ—Babs Blumer, had asked for me. Well, in ten years, that was a first.

"I'll be on the next flight." I ended the call.

I arranged for my friend Jessie to watch the furry kids for me and by ten that night, I was on a flight out of JFK International. I spent a brain numbingly long layover in Chicago, which not even a Chicago dog could make better, and landed in San Diego at seven the next morning where Sophie picked me up just outside baggage claim.

Her smile, wide and warm, was the first thing I saw as she parked her SUV at the curb and dashed out of her car to greet me. It hit me then how much I'd missed her. Eight years older than me, I had spent most of my life trying to catch up to Sophie until at nineteen, she'd found herself married to medical student Stan Timmons and the mother of twins, a boy and a girl. *Surprise!*

At eleven, I had struggled with the abrupt loss of my big sister to her own family. She had always been the buffer between me and Babs and without her, well, things got pretty dicey.

Soph's honey-colored hair was neatly trimmed and styled, just brushing her shoulders in the perfect mom bob, and her outfit, khaki capris and an aqua knit top, was without a wrinkle or a smudge. So much more grown up than my skinny jeans, black Converse kicks, and baggy hooded sweatshirt. In my defense, I'd been in a rush to leave New York. Yeah, total lie; I dressed like this every day.

Sophie hugged me tight and I noticed she was thinner than the last time I'd seen her. It took my sleep-deprived cabeza a second to do the math. Had it really been over five years since I'd been in Cali? Guilt began to nibble at my edges, leaving me frayed.

"How was your flight, Jules?" Sophie released me, grabbed my carryon and tossed it into the back of her SUV.

"Fabulous," I said. "I scored a seat next to a teenage boy who smelled like rancid bologna and played his music so loud I now know all the words to Post Malone's latest album."

"Sorry," she said. "You would have preferred Taylor Swift?"

"Hey, step away from the Swift," I said. "The Eras tour was epic."

Soph wrapped me in another hug that strangled. "Oh, God, I've missed you. Come on, you can power nap on the ride up the I-5."

"You mean I'm not asleep now?"

Sophie smiled as she opened the passenger door for me. I climbed onto the seat and relaxed, hoping to catch a few Zs before facing Babs.

It's not that I don't love my mother—I do. It's just that loving Mom is sort of like loving a cactus; it's best done from a distance...of miles.

Of course, having her ask for me, well, that was a game changer. I wondered if, after all these years at odds, she had finally mellowed. Maybe she had come to love me for who I was and maybe this time we would have the tender mother-daughter moment I had always longed for. I barely acknowledged the tiny flickering flame of hope that burned low and deep inside of me for fear it might smother under the weight of my expectations.

I dozed as we made the forty-five-minute drive to Gull's Harbor, a hilly seaside community nestled on the California coast halfway between San Diego and Los Angeles. It was tucked amidst the uber wealthy towns surrounding it like a sprig of baby's breath in a bouquet of red roses.

Gull's Harbor was a bit too blue-collar quirky and off-the-wall artsy to be considered picturesque like its more well-known neighbors, La Jolla and Oceanside; also its beaches were guarded by rocks, temperamental surfers, and pungent barking sea lions so tourists were discouraged.

With a population of less than six thousand, Gull's Harbor boasted a town square with the requisite gazebo, which held brass band concerts by the local veteran's group every Friday night in the summer. It had been a long time since I'd been to one, but I vaguely remembered a lot of discordant squeaking culminating in a finish that sounded like someone stepping on a goose. Good times.

Local shops circled the petite town green. The small independent businesses survived here but would expire like road kill if they were to try and make a go of it anywhere else—including Liam's Coffee Shop.

We were stopped at an intersection. I blinked fully awake to find the enormous coffee cup denoting Liam's looming over me as if beckoning me to come inside. I averted my gaze, not wanting to confront my past just yet. I had managed to duck and weave for nine years; I did not want to take it on now when I'd had less than four hours of sleep and probably looked like something found growing on the crust of an old loaf of bread.

Sophie glanced at me as she drove on. "How are you doing?"

I sat up straighter. "Good. Great. Terrific."

"Who are you trying to convince?"

I sagged back against the seat. Sophie was right. Who was I kidding? I was exhausted.

"That bad?" I asked.

My older sister handed me her purse. "Lipstick and a comb in there."

"Okay." I could take a hint.

I flipped down the visor and stifled a small shriek. My curly brown hair, I did not get the honey-colored tresses of my sisters, was a frizzy mess while remnants of my mascara were flaked all over my face. I had bags under my eyes big enough to replace the carryon I'd used for luggage and the beginnings of chapped lips. Lovely.

"What did Babs say when you told her I was on my way?"

Sophie bit her lip. She gave me a sideways glance and my eyes widened in surprise.

"You didn't tell her I was coming? Why not?"

"Em and I thought about it, but..."

"You were afraid I'd flake?" I finished for her.

Sophie did not immediately confirm or deny. I tried to comb my curls down but with the Pacific morning mist at full blast so was my hair. Giving up, I found a hair band in Soph's purse and braided my hair into one thick plait that I let dangle over one shoulder. I waited for Sophie to answer.

"Well..." She shrugged. "After your last visit..."

"Visit?" I asked. "You make it sound like it wasn't the equivalent of falling into a hell mouth."

"The Christmas of twenty-seventeen," she said. "Em and I have dramatic reenactments every holiday."

I sighed.

"Lipstick," Sophie reminded me. "And don't worry. I'm sure Em will tell her you're on your way. Mom will be thrilled to see you, you'll see."

I dropped the comb into her bag and fished out her lipstick. Like a sacred commandment, Babs believed that no woman should ever leave the house without her hair and make-up done. Woe be to the woman who showed up at Bab's house without her face on.

Being a tree climbing, freewheeling tomboy, this might have been the rule that about broke me during my formative years. More battles had been fought in our front room over my wild mane and lack of make-up than any other subject save one. Liam Mahony, the hot boy next door, had trumped all other arguments combined. And it was my relationship with Liam that had finally driven me away from home without a backward glance.

I swiped the coral lipstick over my lips and pressed them together. I hadn't worn lipstick regularly in years, being more of a cherry ChapStick sort of gal. Funny how old habits don't die, however. I grabbed a tissue out of the pack in Soph's purse to blot my lips just as Babs had taught us. I knew I still looked exhausted, but perhaps the tamed hair and lipstick would be enough to appease the old cranky pants.

We left the center of town and wound our way up the hill into the residential section. Midcentury modern was what the hip kids were calling it now, but back in its heyday, the fifties, it was just considered modern. The houses on the street where I grew up were all about squared edges and big windows, the better to appreciate the view of the ocean, and the yards were small, tidy, and fenced. A few stucco houses with red tile roofs and some rectangular gray ultra-modern houses peppered the neighborhood but for the most part, Gull's Harbor clung to its Brady Bunch split levels with a tenacious grip.

Soph parked in front of our childhood home and I felt a clutching sensation in my chest. The house looked exactly as I remembered it; rough cut stone on the bottom with pale yellow on the wood above, the roof peaked over the double front doors which were painted white like the trim. Rectangular planters loaded with succulents lined the short walkway to the door, and I took a deep breath realizing I was now going to have to make that walk and face the dragon within.

I climbed out of the car and glanced behind me, down the hill, over several rooftops and the center of town until I could see the blue of the ocean all the way to the horizon. I took another deep breath of the briny sea air and held it in my lungs.

Whenever life seemed to be too much, I took comfort in the constancy of the sea. It was here before me and it would be here long after I departed this earth. For some reason that awareness always helped me get my perspectacles on and focused. There were things in the world so much bigger than me and my petty problems.

"All right?" Soph grabbed my bag and joined me on the walkway.

"Yeah, I'm good," I said.

The front door wasn't locked so I gave it a gentle rap with my knuckles before walking in. "Hello?" I called.

No one answered as we walked through the small entryway and turned left into the great room that boasted floor-to-ceiling windows with the same spectacular view I had been taking in from the walkway outside.

"Who's there?" Babs sounded grumpy.

"It's me, Julia." I stepped fully into the large living room, giving my mother a small smile. She was seated on her favorite burgundy velvet divan, which had always reminded me of a throne. It was placed on the far side of the room and gave her an optimal view of the goings on in the house and outside. She had a pretty aqua afghan draped over her legs and an untouched breakfast tray on the coffee table beside her.

Her hair, styled in a pixie cut and dyed the color of champagne, was expertly arranged and her make-up was perfection. No one would ever guess she was sixty-four years old. Her pale blue eyes raked me from head to toe and her lip curled up on the right side just the teensiest bit so it was sort of like smile, you know, if she was paralyzed down one side and giving it her best effort. She wasn't and it wasn't.

"Julia, what are you doing here? Dear god, did you wear that outfit in public? You look like a homeless person," Mom snapped. Before I could open my mouth to answer, she continued, "Did you run out of money? Is that why you're here? Oh, hell's bells, you're not pregnant, are you?"

My head lowered toward my chest. Had I really expected a different greeting? I was an idiot.

Chapter Two

"I'm sorry, so sorry." Em apologized for what had to be the fifth time in as many minutes.

"It's fine," I said.

After kissing the cheek my mother grudgingly turned in my direction and giving her a hug, which was not returned, I decided it might be best if she was given some time to get used to the idea of my being here and escaped upstairs to my old room.

"I should have told her you were coming once Soph texted me from the airport, but I was trying to get her to eat some breakfast and first she wanted eggs, and then she wanted toast, but then it became pancakes, and, well, I forgot."

We were standing in my childhood bedroom on the second floor of the house. I glanced around the room. Not much had changed since I'd fled into the night nine years ago. The one time I'd been back five years ago, I'd stayed at Sophie's house as it was less stressful for everyone concerned, but this trip I'd planned to stay with Babs, so I could better assess the situation.

My old queen-sized bed with its matching desk and dresser was still here. The paint on the walls was the same sage green that I had spent endless hours staring at as a teen. A cream-colored comforter set decorated the bed, that was new, but the room still had all the personality of a motel.

That had been life with Babs. No boy band posters on the walls, no stuffed animals decorating any surfaces, no toys or books or games were to be visible. She was a big believer in a place for everything and everything in its place. Basically, there was never to be any indication of the personality of the resident of the room—ever. I had often wondered if Babs had hoped for generic children. She did not get her wish with me.

I strode over to the closet and slid one of the double doors open. The closet was mostly empty, just some extra pillows and blankets on the shelves, but if a person knew where to look, like the backside of the sliding doors, they could find all of my teenage personality stapled right there.

Moving my carryon into the closet, I stepped inside and turned around. Then I grinned. My Green Day and The Killers posters were exactly where I'd stuck them, as well as my collection of surf brand stickers from Lightning Bolt. I smiled. It was as if I had stepped into a time capsule.

My fingers ran over the frayed edges of the stickers, and the yellowing tape on some of the song lyrics I had written out on notebook paper and taped to the door. Then I saw the strip of photographs taken in a photo booth of me and my then boyfriend Liam Mahony, faded but still there. Just the sight of us smiling at one another, giddy with the infatuation of first love, felt like a punch in the feels I hadn't braced my feet for.

I stepped out of the closet, slamming the door shut behind me. Em was frowning at me, but I didn't explain. Liam Mahony was old news, the oldest news. I hadn't seen him in nine years and had no plans to see him ever again. I couldn't...not after what I'd done to him.

"You okay?" Em asked. "You look weird."

Clearly, she had no idea about the adolescent artifacts that existed on the inside of my closet doors; no one did.

"Weird how?" I asked. "Weird as in my mother just rejected me, again, or just weird in general?"

Em twisted her fingers together and I could tell she felt awful, which being her older sister by two years meant I should have alleviated her angst. I was the person who was supposed to comfort her not make her feel lousy. But I wasn't there yet.

"I'm sorry, Em. I'm bitchy because I'm really tired. Maybe if I nap, I'll be less of a jerk."

"You're not. It's okay. That's a good idea." Em stammered. "You rest. I'll be downstairs with Mom and Sophie if you need anything."

"Cool," I said. Before she could bolt, I stepped forward and hugged her. It was awkward. I went high and she did, too. I adjusted at the same time she did and we ended up in a slanted hug that felt unnatural. I let go first. "It's really good to see you, Em-cee-squared."

She smiled at the old nickname; I'd had a million of them when we were kids.

"You, too," she said. "Everything will be okay now that you're here."

My eyebrows went up, and I opened my mouth to ask what she meant by that but she slipped out the door, closing it behind her. As the youngest, Em had lots of practice listening in on the grown-ups, gathering information like a squirrel hoarding acorns and never getting caught. In short, she could be slippery.

I wondered why she thought my being here was going to make anything better when historically speaking, I was the one who typically made everything worse by being at constant odds with Babs.

I climbed onto the bed. The mattress was harder than I remembered. The last time I'd slept in this room had been nine years ago. I didn't miss it. I told myself this was temporary and as soon as I knew what was going on with Babs, I'd scuttle back to New York with all the speed of a cockroach escaping the light.

I had my own life in New York, and as much as I missed my sisters, I had a full and rich existence that they just weren't a part of, much like I wasn't a part of their lives here. Besides, I hated the way Babs made me feel when I came home, like I was a disappointment because I hadn't lived up to her expectations of me.

It might've helped if I'd understood what her expectations were, but Babs was the master at never really telling you how she felt so that you were always left dangling, swinging in mid-air by a thread that you knew she would cut at any moment.

I kicked off my shoes and rolled myself up in the comforter like a caterpillar in a cocoon. A yawn escaped me and I let it stretch my whole face wide, leading the way for the rest of my body to relax. I planned to take a power nap. Twenty minutes of rest and I'd be fine, ready to conquer the world or Babs's incessant criticism at any rate.

I woke up ten hours later as the sun was setting over the Pacific. Damn it! "No, no, no," I cried.

Lurching upright, I stretched, fingers tingling in the hand that had been trapped under my head while I'd slept. I shook out my arm, trying to get the blood flowing. I scowled at the window where the sky was just turning the color of a sun-kissed peach.

Why hadn't anyone woken me up? This was so bad. I was never going to sleep tonight and tomorrow would be even worse than today had been. If things kept up this way, by the end of the visit I was going be on the same sleep schedule as the area bats.

Climbing off the bed, I crossed the room and glanced in the mirror. Ye god, my hair had woven itself into some sort of funky hair hat. The corkscrew curls that were the bane of my existence had broken free of the braid I'd wrestled them into and now looked like individual antenna desperately seeking life out in the cosmos. I slapped a hand to my forehead, dreading my next meeting with Babs.

One of my earliest childhood memories was of my mother coming at me with a straightening iron, determined to tame my dark curls once and for all. Four-year-old me had sobbed and cried, terrified that she was going to burn me. Of course, now I realized she wouldn't have but at the time the fear was a very real thing.

It was one of the more significant instances of my childhood. My father had stepped up in a rare moment of parenting and told Babs to leave me alone. I had inherited his wild curls, and I knew he liked seeing that trait in one of his girls. He had unplugged the straightener and told my mother to back off—yes, in those exact words. To me, he was my hero, my shining knight, the slayer of my dragons. To Babs, he had crossed a line and she'd looked at him in shock, as if he had slapped her. In retrospect, that was most likely the moment where her intense dislike for me began, shaping our relationship for years to come.

My father, who had always called me *Peanut*, died when I was ten. My larger than life dad with the big booming laugh, gentle hugs, and a charmer's smile left me. He'd been the one person who was always on my side and who loved me unconditionally. The day he died my entire world crumbled. Dad suffered a cardiac arrest at his corporate muckety-muck job and was dead before the ambulance arrived. Luckily for Babs, who had never worked a day in her life, he had left her a very, very wealthy woman.

Babs would argue, of course, and say that being a good wife to my father had been a full time job. This I had difficulty believing, given that she had a housekeeper, a gardener, and for the big life events, an entire catering staff.

Babs had bagged my father with her va-va-va-voom figure, her thick honey-blond hair, her cute little upturned nose and her big blue eyes. That was the only feature of hers which I had inherited, a variation of her eyes. Hers were a pale blue, mine were darker, but we were the only ones in the family with blue eyes so I always felt it was a bond of sorts. You would think this would give me a pass with her. No.

In deference to Babs, I took my straightening iron out of my bag and plugged it in. It would take a while, but maybe I could tame my wild mane enough to mollify her. Although, why I cared what she thought I had no idea, thus the hours spent in my therapist's office talking about the crazy train breaking down at the dysfunction junction which was my childhood.

While I waited for the iron to heat, I unpacked, putting my meager clothing into two of the four empty dresser drawers. My laptop bag which also functioned as my purse was next. I set up my computer on the desk in front of the window, plugging it into the outlet below.

I sat at my old desk, wondering how much my back was going to hurt with the crappy ergonomics of this situation. Since I designed websites for a living, the amount of hours I spent hunched over a keyboard was significant. Truly, it was a small wonder that I didn't already resemble a one hump camel.

I popped open my laptop, planning to check my email and see if any of my clients were having a meltdown due to my surprise unavailability today. While I waited for my computer to boot up, I glanced over the top of the monitor at the neighbor's house. Much like putting on lipstick to appease Babs, memory was guiding my actions, reminding me of how I functioned in this space.

How many hours had I spent sitting right here, dreaming of the boy next door? Countless. Endless. Years worth. Liam Mahony was my first crush or "Trouble" as Babs called him. She'd been right. He was trouble in the best possible way.

I'd been fifteen when this brash, wild new boy had appeared in the window across the yard. He had a thick thatch of dark brown hair, a ridiculously ripped torso from hours spent taming the surf, and a smile that literally melted my shorts.

Our houses mirrored each other and California real estate being what it was with houses built spitting distance from each other, our rooms were only fifteen feet apart. Plenty close enough for a teen girl to get her fill of teen boy eye candy.

The tomboy in me had no idea what to make of the feelings the guy with the killer smile caused to flutter up inside of me like bubbles in a soda pop. One part of me wanted to run away from him as far and as fast as I could, but another part of me was fascinated like a diver facing a shark. I was both attracted by the mystery of this unknown species of boy and terrified of the same.

It took a few days for Liam Mahony to notice that we had the same walking route to school, sat in the same algebra class, and surfed the same waves in the afternoons and on weekends. When he stopped in front of me and introduced himself one afternoon, I panicked. We're talking full-on brain stutter, tripping over my own feet, complete neuro shut-down mother fluffing panic.

I'd probably looked like I'd been hit with a Taser. It sure felt like it and I was forever grateful that I didn't start to slobber and drool on the spot or even worse pee myself. Terrified, unable to speak, and at a loss for any coolness I might ever have possessed, I nodded at him once and fled the scene on foot like a criminal trying to outrun the law.

I spent the next two weeks avoiding him while covertly spying on him. I surfed different beaches, rode my skateboard to school, and refused to look at him during class. I couldn't handle the sizzle and zip I felt whenever he was near me. Even when he started hanging around with one of my closest friends, Jessie Lopez, I still couldn't be near him without being rendered utterly stupid.

It did not stop me from watching him when I thought he wasn't looking, however. From the cover of my darkened bedroom, I studied him in his room across the way. He did his homework at a desk in front of his window just like me. He also paced a lot, cranked his music, and, lord-a-mercy, lifted weights. The boy worked out every day, and I spied on him behind the cover of my sheer curtains, every day. Still, I never spoke to him and avoided any sort of contact, even ditching my friend Jessie if it meant I'd have to be in the same orbit as Liam.

And then everything changed. On a rainy Saturday, I took my board to one of the less popular beaches. It was called Devil's Backbone because there was a line of treacherous rocks hidden below the surf. Only the locals knew how to navigate the area, but the waves were decent, no ankle busters, and it was worth the risk if you knew what you were doing.

I was out alone for most of the morning, enjoying the rides I'd caught, the sound of the waves, the pelicans flying overhead while they fished for their lunch with dramatic diving catches. It was all very peaceful and Zen, until *he* showed up. Jogging out into the surf with his board tucked under his arm, I recognized him right away. Liam Mahony.

I glanced behind me, praying for a wave to appear that I could ride in to get away from him. The sea was as calm as glass. What the hell?

Liam climbed onto his board and paddled right for me. My heart started to pound in my chest and I was sweating despite the chill of the sea water my feet were dangling in. I could paddle back to shore to avoid him, but that would probably look weird, and I desperately did not want him to think I was any weirder than I was sure he already thought I was.

When he slowed alongside me, I glanced in both directions. There was a vast open ocean out here. He could surf anywhere. Why was he in my space, making my insides melt and my outsides shiver? I sent a silent prayer of thanks to the laundry goddess, also known as Helena our housekeeper, that I was wearing my best bikini, the purple one that made my bazooms look way bigger than they actually were.

"Hi, Julia." Liam's voice was low and gravelly. It hooked into the center of me, and I realized I really liked hearing my name on his lips.

He hauled himself up to straddle his board, and I watched as the water poured off his body. I wasn't positive but I was pretty sure I went momentarily cross-eyed at the sight.

"So, what's a nice girl like you doing in a place like this?"

"Huh?" I had to drag my gaze away from his chest to meet his warm brown eyes.

He grinned at me and the slash of white teeth against his full lips made my throat go dry and this time I knew I went cross-eyed and saw spots. Have mercy!

It was then that an enormous wave came and plowed us into the surf. I went down with a yelp and lost sight of Liam. We were on top of Devil's Backbone and I was terrified that he'd been slammed into the rocks below. I popped up out of the water as another wave hit, dragging me down. My shoulder scraped a rock but I was able to push off of it and swim to the surface.

When I came up again, I saw Liam face down in the water. His board was loose and being carried on the crest of a wave toward the beach. Meanwhile Liam was headed straight for the rocks. I climbed onto my board and paddled toward him. Another wave separated us, but I kept track of the bright yellow swim trunks he had on and used them to spot him. I grabbed him by the arm before he was pushed into a worse section of rocks and hauled him onto my board. With him unconscious but safe, I turned us toward the beach and paddled as hard as I could.

It took all of my strength to maneuver us in. Once we reached the sand, I ripped off my ankle harness, grabbed Liam under the arms, and dragged him up the beach until we were half in and half out of the surf. His eyes were closed and I couldn't tell if he'd hit his head on a rock or his board or if he'd just taken in so much water he couldn't breathe.

"Come on, new boy," I begged him. "Wake up and open those pretty eyes for me."

I knew basic CPR as Babs had insisted that I learn if I was going to spend my days on the beach. I think she had grand visions of me being the next Pam Anderson. Yeah, no.

Instinct took over and I went through all of the things I remembered a first responder was supposed to do. I listened to his heart and tried to see if he was breathing. I was so freaked out, I couldn't tell. I checked his mouth for an obstruction and his eyes to see if they were dilated.

Seeing no other recourse, I figured mouth to mouth was in order. I tipped his head back, closed his nose, took a deep breath and blew into him, trying to inflate his lungs or push out the water or whatever it was this was supposed to do. He remained terrifyingly unresponsive.

I was going in for the third time when I became aware of his hand in my hair, holding me in place while his tongue ran over my lips and he fit his mouth against mine, kissing me with a wicked thoroughness that left me, who had never been kissed before, stunned.

When he ended the kiss, he sat up and pressed his forehead to mine, each of us short of breath as if we'd both nearly drowned.

"I knew it," Liam said. His voice was gruff. "I knew it would be like that between us."

After a couple of moments, I sat back on my heels and studied him, uncertain about what had just happened but crazily wanting it to happen again.

"So, it looks like you're going to live." I was pleased my voice sounded so much calmer than I felt.

"Yeah." His deep brown eyes were fixed on my mouth and a flash of heat lit up my insides like a tiki torch.

I didn't know what to make of that, so I latched onto the much more familiar feeling of anger. My terror about what could have happened came roaring up out of me like a geyser. I punched him on the shoulder. Hard. It barely rocked him.

"Damn it, Liam, you scared the crap out of me!" I cried. "You could have been killed. We both could have."

He tipped his head and batted his ridiculously long eyelashes at me. "Aw, don't be mad, surfer girl. Look at it this way, since you just saved my life, you own it now."

"Huh?" I blinked at him.

"It's true," he said. "When you save a person's life, they are forever in your debt. They belong to you."

I stared at him for a moment and then I threw back my head and laughed. It was a great big belly laugh, a guffaw if you will, and much to my relief he didn't look offended so much as amused.

"I'm serious." He winked at me, then lowered his voice and added, "Now you can do whatever you want with me."

Well, didn't that just send a delicious shiver through me. Sadly, for him, I wasn't an idiot. I shook my head at him and grinned. I could not believe he would waste a move like this on me.

"So, new boy, this fake drowning thing," I said. "Is that your move? And if so, how's it working out for you?"

"That depends, surfer girl," he said. "Will you go out with me tonight?"

My chest constricted and my breath was short. Liam Mahony, Liam hot-as-shit Mahony, was asking me out, not only that but he had feigned drowning to do it. There was clearly only one answer to be made.

"Yeah, sure, I could do that," I said. I shrugged as if it was no big deal, when, *ermagawd* it was a big freaking deal!

His grin was blinding. "Well, then I can tell you that since I have only used the faked drowning technique to ask out one girl, *you*, it's success rate is one-hundred-percent."

"You know you could have gotten hurt for real," I said. The fear came back as I remembered seeing him face down in the water, headed for the rocks. "Devil's Backbone is out there and it's a gnarly stretch of rock."

"Well, I've been watching you, and I knew you could get us out of there. I believed in you."

Yep, my heart pretty much took flight right there.

"Besides," he continued, "given that you've been avoiding me like I'm a carrier for the plague, drastic measures were required. And after that kiss, I've got to say a concussion or near drowning would have been totally worth it. I like you, Julia Blumer. I have from the moment I first saw you."

Probably, I should have dropped dead on the spot, like I was pretty sure I was going to, and our story would have had a happier—okay, not so much for me—ending. But I didn't and we didn't. Pity.

I continued staring at the darkened window across the way, tasting the bitter flavor of regret on my tongue. There was no point in dwelling on the past I told myself. It was dusted and done, and I couldn't go back. Sadly, one of the first lessons learned when leaving childhood behind was that in real life there are no do-overs.

Suddenly, a light snapped on in the bedroom across the way. Curious, I watched and, as if he'd been ripped right out of my daydreams and thrust back into my reality, Liam Mahony strode into the room, shirtless. *Oh. My. God.*

Chapter Three

My heart stopped, literally stopped, and then as if remembering its purpose, it pumped doubly hard for three beats almost sending me into a dead faint. Okay, no, that was more likely due to the man I was staring at like a prime rib at an all you can eat buffet.

His thick dark hair was still unruly, like he'd just climbed out of bed but not a bed in which he'd been sleeping. His bare chest was even more muscled than I remembered with broad shoulders, roped forearms, and a sculpted V. Sweet baby Jesus, the man had an abdominal V, you know those muscles that frame the six pack abs and lead down to a guy's equator, yeah that V, that made me want to lick it and then bite him...it...no, him...everywhere.

I put my hand to my forehead and closed my eyes. Clearly I was having some sort of fit or hallucination, because while I hadn't seen Liam in years, I had gotten sporadic updates from Babs, usually when she was feeling particularly cruel, and the last I'd heard he was living in the apartment above his coffee shop in the center of town. Obviously, my little jog down memory lane as I sat here in the dark had caused me to conjure something that was not there. *Right?* Right.

I opened my eyes fully expecting to see a dark window across the way. Nope. Instead, Liam had his back to me and was working on some sort of freestanding apparatus doing pull-ups, which for the record, completely defined his back. I felt a trickle of saliva slide out of the side of my mouth and realized I was drooling.

I wiped my chin, never taking my eyes off the man as he hauled himself up and down and up and down and up and, well you get the drift. Lost in my appreciation for his scorching hot body, I didn't realize he was done until he dropped from the bar and grabbed a nearby towel to wipe the sweat off of his face. At which point, I moaned, out loud.

"Hey, Jules, are you going to..." Sophie burst through the bedroom door and then stopped as she took in the view. "Oh my..."

She perched behind me with her arms on the back of my chair and we watched Liam move to the free weights. When he started curling the barbell in toward his torso, I noticed he had several lines of ink on his left side, a tattoo. I wished I could read it, but I was too far away. I found myself wondering when he got it, what it said, and why he'd put it right there. Then he braced himself with one arm while flexing the barbell in toward his chest with the other. Soph and I both sighed deeply and appreciatively.

"Guys, what are you doing here in the dark?" Em strode into the room snapping on the light.

"No!" I yelped as my pupils contracted. Thankfully, I had the presence of mind to drop to the floor before Liam, who would now be able to see into my room with the light on, got sight of me.

"Ah!" Sophie dove away from the window, shouting to Em, "The light! Hit the light!"

"What? Why?" Em glanced out the window and then yelped. "Oh! Oh, shit!"

Em slapped the switch, and the room was plunged into darkness. She dropped to her knees and crawled over to where Sophie and I were crouched on the floor in front of the desk.

"It's okay, I don't think he saw me," Em said.

"'Lucy, you have some 'splainin' to do,'" I said in my best Ricky Ricardo accent.

"Yeah, um, I meant to tell you about that, er, him," Em said. I could just make out her face in the shadows and she cringed. "But I forgot. He's such a quiet neighbor, I forget he's there. Of course, my room doesn't look into his so not having a front row seat to the show, well, that could be why I forgot. I mean, wow, just wow."

"No problem," I lied. "He's back, Liam's back, living at home. These things happen. Maybe it's a failure to launch sort of thing, like his coffee shop tanked, and he had to move back in with the Prof. and Mrs. Mahony?"

Liam's dad was a professor of marine biology at Scripps Institution of Oceanography in La Jolla, so he was never Mr. Mahony to us growing up but always the Prof. Even though he had retired a few years ago, his title never changed.

"Not even," Sophie said. "Quite the opposite, actually. His coffee shop is so successful, he's opened two more, one in San Diego and one in Los Angeles."

"He actually bought the house from his parents so that they could move into a retirement community up the coast. His mom was super excited because they have bingo every week. She bought a swank set of daubers with their own carrying case. Doesn't that sound fun?" Em asked.

Sophie squinted at her. "You have got to get out more."

"Focus, people." I clapped my hands twice to get their attention. "So, he's been living next door for how long exactly?"

"About two months, give or take a week," Em said.

"Does Babs know?" I asked.

They both looked uncomfortable.

"She does, doesn't she?" I persisted.

They nodded.

"And she still hates him, correct?"

Again, they nodded.

"And yet you didn't tell me?" I asked. "You really didn't think this was something I might want to know to prepare myself in case I ran into him? Or worse, if Babs decided to drop this A-bomb on me over the phone?"

"Well, gees, Jules, you guys broke up like a million years ago," Em said. "I didn't think it was still that big of a deal."

I rose up on my knees and peered over the desk into Liam's bedroom. I motioned for her to follow me. Both Em and Soph popped up next to me, so the only things visible over the edge of the desk were our noses and eyes.

"Look at him," I hissed. "That is the man I gave my virginity to, the man I thought I would marry, the only man who has ever brought me to orgasm with just a glance. In a hundred years, running into him would still be a big deal."

"I can see that," Soph said. "My goodness, he has muscles in places I didn't even know you could have muscles. Sheesh, is it hot in here?" She began to fan herself with her hands.

"Um, you're kind of oversharing, Jules," Em said. Even in the dark I could see she was blushing. "But, yes, I see that he is a fine specimen, not obnoxiously bulky but just right, and, like super defined. It's almost as if he's in high def."

"Yeah," I said. "High def enough to make me want to lick the window."

Soph snorted and Em looked confused. It occurred to me that we'd failed our baby sister spectacularly in the appreciation of the male form department. Good thing I was here to correct the error.

As much as I loved ogling my ex-boyfriend with my sisters, I didn't think my poor heart could take much more. The riot of emotions coursing through me made it difficult to function. I needed to compartmentalize.

With one last lingering glance at Liam, okay, more accurately Liam's butt, I forced myself to turn away. "All right, so why did you two come up here?"

Soph and Em exchanged confused glances before saying in unison, "Dinner!"

It was then that I heard the very distinct sound of thumping coming from downstairs. Babs!

I dove for my hair straightener. Sophie unplugged it from the wall, grabbed my hand, and pulled me into the hallway.

"But—" I protested.

"No time," she said.

Em led the way. We barreled down the stairs and jogged into the great room where Babs sat with her afghan on her lap and her face squinched up on one side like she'd just bitten into a something sour. There was a cane beside her that I hadn't noticed before and I suspected was the source of the thumping noise I had heard earlier.

Mom glanced at the three of us, her disapproval obvious in the tight line of her lips. "Are we planning on eating tonight or are we on a newfangled starvation diet?"

"Dinner's ready, Mom," Em said patiently. "I'll set the table...unless you'd rather eat here instead?"

Babs simply stared at each of us as if considering how difficult it would be to share a meal with all three of her daughters. I tried not to take it personally, suspecting it was my presence that put her off. Finally, she gave Em a sharp nod. "Dining room."

Equal measures of relief and dread surged inside of me.

"I'll help with dinner," Sophie said.

"Me, too—" I began but Babs cut me off.

"You, sit," she said.

Mom pointed a bony finger at me and then at the armchair beside her. I sat. Twenty-seven years old and I still jumped when she spoke in that commander-in-chief voice. Seriously, Babs had untapped potential; she could easily have been a world leader, devouring smaller nations and leaving death and destruction in her wake.

"Did you sleep well?" she asked.

Well, that was...civil. I studied her. Now that I was rested, I could see that her face was thinner and more lined than I remembered. Her eyes were glassy and her skin crepe-like. For once my sisters had not exaggerated. Babs looked distinctly unwell. It made me uneasy.

"Yes," I said. "Longer than I intended, actually."

We were silent for a few moments. I heard the clock ticking in the corner, the rattle of silverware and plates as my sisters set the table in the dining room, and the quiet rasp of Babs's breathing. That was new.

"Enjoy sleep when you can." She glanced away from me and out at the dark night sky. "I don't sleep well anymore."

This seemed like a solid opportunity to ask her what was going on. I took it. "Ba...er...Mom. How are you, really?"

Her frail body stiffened and she turned to me with one of her frostiest expressions; her pale blue eyes looked positively wintery and I half expected snowflakes to shoot out her nose. "I'm fine, Julia, just fine. Thanks for asking."

May in Gull's Harbor was generally around seventy degrees during the day and in the fifties at night. The town maintained a perfect year-round temperature which was the reason so many people loved it, except for right now. As if Babs could control the atmosphere, I swear the temperature in the room dropped to freezing.

"Obviously, you are *not* fine," I persisted, surprised I didn't see my breath when I spoke. I tried to sound reasonable but when she rolled her eyes like a moody middle schooler, I lost the battle. "Listen, I didn't come all this way—"

"Stop!" Mom held up her thin, age-spotted hand as if she could physically ward off my words. "This isn't about you. It's about me. And I say the status of my health is between me and my physician, no one else."

Seriously? Babs was really going to play it that way? With her obviously wasting away and the three of us, her *daughters*, uselessly flapping our hands in dismay because we had no freaking idea what the hell was going on?

My temper spiked. This was likely the only other thing I had inherited from her besides her blue eyes. We were both a tad hot headed.

"You have got to be kidding me," I snapped. "I raced all the way here—"

"Again, I fail to see how this is about you." Mom made a *tsk* noise. It was her go-to sound when she was displeased. It had followed me around my entire life and still had the power to make my insides twist. I shook it off.

Her voice was infuriatingly calm but the two spots of color on her cheeks gave away her agitation. I probably should have felt bad that I'd upset her, but, yeah, not so much.

"Mom," I said.

Sophie charged into the room right then and announced, "Dinner is served."

I had no choice but to table the discussion. Damn it.

It became clear when Babs struggled to stand that she was weak and frail, using her cane to push herself up. It was jarring to see. The woman who had always dominated every room she entered with her natural grace and style was now hunched over, her posture that of a question mark.

Babs held out her hand and Sophie offered her arm to lean on while our mom also used her cane to cross the room. Shocked, I felt my throat get tight as I walked behind them and my eyes burned. As if sensing my distress, Sophie reached behind with her free hand and squeezed my fingers in reassurance.

It hit me then, all at once, that Babs really was dying and like everything else my mother had ever done in life, she was going to do it on her own terms and to hell with what anyone else thought.

Over the next few days, we settled into a rhythm. Dr. Patel, my mother's physician for the past twenty years, stopped by daily to check on her. When he did, she always shooed us out of the house.

I balked but both Em and Soph took Babs's side. They felt that as long as she had the wherewithal to be in charge, then we should respect her wishes. It chafed. Because I was outnumbered and had no choice, I fell in line.

Sophie had her own family to care for but as soon as Harry and Hannah left for school, she arrived at the house to sit with Babs. My older sister took the morning shift, staying most of the day until Em came home from work, when she left to make dinner for her family.

Em had cut to part-time at her insurance job and worked mornings, spending the afternoon and evening to fetch and carry for Babs. This meant the night shift was all mine, so I slept in and managed my online clients in the afternoon. I clocked in with Babs at eleven o'clock and stayed through until Soph arrived at seven in the morning. I wasn't sure who was less thrilled with me on nights, me or Babs, but I had the most flexible work schedule, so it only made sense.

As Babs's breathing became more of a struggle, Dr. Patel put her on oxygen. The steady hiss of the machine became the background noise to which I dozed in the recliner beside her divan. She drifted in and out of sleep, waking only when I had to give her the pain medicine the doctor had prescribed.

Once in the wee hours of the morning, she woke with a start and peered around the room as if trying to remember where she was. I took her withered hand in mine and gave it a gentle squeeze. "It's all right, Mom. I'm here. I've got you."

Her pale blue gaze latched onto my face, flickering over my features. With a curl of her lip, she yanked her hand free, shut her eyes, and turned her head away.

Instantly, I was seven years old again, bringing her a bouquet of Queen Anne's lace and black-eyed Susans that I'd picked in a field up the hill. She accepted the wildflowers, looked at them and then at me without a hint of a smile when I'd dared hope for a hug. She'd opened her hand and dropped the flowers into the dirt. "There's a bug on them." She'd walked away, leaving me gutted.

Tears coursed down my cheeks, just like they had that day, as I gazed at her frail back. I rubbed my eyes with the heels of my hands. Why was I here? Why was I putting myself through this? It wasn't worth it. She wasn't worth it.

"Why?" I asked. "Why do you hate me so much? And why did you ask for me to come?"

I thought Babs was asleep. I didn't think she would answer. Instead, she turned and glanced at me over her shoulder. In a tired voice that was no less scathing for the exhaustion in it, she said, "I never asked for you."

She closed her eyes again and fell into a deep medicated slumber. I slumped back in my chair, feeling as if she'd taken a scalpel and cut my heart out with a surgeon's precision. She hadn't asked for me? Then why had my sisters said she did? It didn't require a genius IQ to puzzle it out. Babs didn't need or want me here but my sisters did.

I pondered my options. Because the miserable old bat wouldn't tell us or let the doctor share what was wrong with her, we had no idea how long this could go on. Days, weeks, or god forbid, months. Could I endure this? Could I come out on the other side emotionally intact if I had to put up with her brutality for weeks? I didn't think so.

I opened my phone and checked for flights back to New York. It would be pricey but I could be home in a matter of hours. I found the flight. I chose my seat. I was about to click buy when a noise sounded from the stairs. I glanced over to see Emily tiptoeing down the stairs.

She'd skillfully avoided the one creaky step in the middle and then she was beside my chair. Her long blond hair was loose, and she wore a set of pink-and-blue striped pajamas that had a collar and buttoned down the front with a matching set of long pants. They made her look fifty instead of twenty-five and then I thought, no, even a fifty-year-old wouldn't wear anything that buttoned up. She was pale and her eyes had dark circles under them.

"How is she?"

"As bitchy as ever," I said. I thought Em would chastise me, but instead a small smile tipped her lips.

"That's good, right?" Em's eyes were locked on our mother's sleeping form. She reached out and adjusted the plastic tubing that hooked into Babs's nostrils, giving her a steady stream of oxygen.

"Depends whether or not you're on the receiving end of the comments." I turned my phone display side down.

My youngest sis glanced at me with sympathy. "What I meant was that if Mom's feeling feisty maybe she'll be able to beat this thing."

"Oh, Em." I looked at her face and saw the hope shining in her brown eyes and just couldn't do it. I couldn't tell her we were on borrowed time. Instead, I sent her a small smile. "That would be great."

I realized I wasn't going anywhere. Losing Babs would be a crushing blow for Emily, and even though I hadn't been the greatest big sister, okay, I was absentee at best, I knew I couldn't leave her to deal with this alone. Not this time. I took her hand in mine and gave it a gentle squeeze much like Soph had done for me when the reality of this situation had punched me in the face.

"You should get some rest," I said. "I'll take good care of her, I promise."

Em looked at me with gratitude and squeezed my fingers in return before letting go. "Thanks, Jules, I'm so glad you're here."

The bloody welts left by Babs's rejection healed a bit as I met Em's gaze. Perhaps I couldn't change things with my mother, but I could be here for my sisters. I closed the app on my phone as I watched her slip back upstairs.

One of my old habits returned with force during my days at home. Much like the sixteen-year-old girl who had been infatuated with the new boy next door, I found myself spying on Liam Mahony again. I learned his routine, fifty laps in the pool just after sunrise, and hour-long workouts in the evening in the room across from mine. Occasionally, there was a bonus sighting of him doing yard work, taking out his trash, or sitting on his back deck while he read a book and enjoyed a beer.

I told myself it didn't mean anything, that I was just appreciating the view, but the heat that licked up inside made a liar out of me. I don't care how pretty the sunrise was in the morning, it sure as shit never made me want to touch myself the way spying on Liam did.

It was on the sixth evening since I'd returned home that I got caught. Busted. Bagged and tagged. Nabbed. Nailed. Well, maybe I just wanted to be, nailed, really, really badly.

Em was downstairs with Babs while I caught up on clients in my room. It was an unusually overcast day, so I had the light on. I figured it was okay since Liam didn't generally work out until six o'clock. I had hours before he'd show, hours before I had to snap off the light and hide in the shadows to enjoy the guilty pleasure that was watching him exercise.

Like jumping into a rabbit hole, however, my understanding of the space-time continuum vanished while I tried to fix a glitch on the website I was creating for a bakery in Brooklyn. For some inexplicable and maddening reason, the links I'd put up to showcase their products kept yanking me out of the website, tossing me into cyberspace like a bouncy ball with no sense of direction. So annoying.

My back started to ache and my butt had gone numb, but those twinges weren't what pulled me from my work. Oh, no, the overwhelming sensation that someone was watching me, was what finally made me glance up.

When I did, I gasped. It was him, Liam Mahony, standing framed in the window across the way. He was wearing just a pair of basketball shorts, his skin was slick with sweat and his arms were stretched up as he gripped the windowsill overhead as if he had to visibly restrain himself from coming through the window to get at me. Oh, my.

His brown laser-like eyes focused on my face, studying me as if he didn't really believe I was there. It occurred to me that if he did reach me, he was more likely to throttle me than do the wicked things I had been imagining for the past few days.

Inexplicably, Adele's song "Hello" began to play in my head, my breathing became shallow, and I thought I might pass out but no—if I fainted I couldn't drink my fill of him and I desperately wanted to look until my eyeballs dried right the fuck out.

He did not smile, but instead seemed caught on the razor's edge between furious and aroused. The heat in his gaze made my insides liquefy and I nervously licked my lips and swallowed, trying to grab any sort of moisture to cool the heat of the slow burn that raged inside of me.

His gaze moved to my mouth and his nostrils flared; clearly aroused was beating out furious on his side of the glass. He dropped his arms to the waistband of his shorts. I sat riveted, not even blinking, when he slowly, oh, so slowly, pushed his shorts off and stood there completely naked. I knew exactly what he was doing, he was letting me see what I'd walked away from so many years ago. It was a gut punch, but I didn't look away.

The edges of my vision started to blur, and I was pretty sure that, yes, I was going to faint after all. I gripped the edge of the desk, taking in the sight of his cock, locked and loaded, his fists on his hips, and the hot hungry expression on his face.

My mouth opened to form a small o and I made some sort of female-in-heat yowl that in any other species would have been attractive but I'm pretty sure coming out of me was just scary. Thankfully, he couldn't hear me. I released the edge of the desk and pressed one hand to the window, as if I could push the glass aside to get to him.

We stared at one another for several long moments. Was he also trying to understand this new reality where we were once again the boy and girl next door?

Liam shook his head—rejecting the idea, rejecting me, and turned his back. For what it was worth, the rearview was just as captivating as the front, and I swallowed hard as he picked up a towel and draped it over one shoulder. Without another glance in my direction, he strode from the room leaving me to watch him walk away much as I had left him all those years ago.

Chapter Four

"Shut up! No, he didn't!" Soph cried. She had been here most of the day and I should have gone to my room to rest, but I couldn't sleep a wink.

"Yes, he did," I said. "Believe me, the sight of Liam in his altogether is forever burned on my retinas."

The two of us were in the kitchen hunched over mugs of Soph's banana tea while Em visited with Babs. With my sleep rhythm wonky from night duty, and now with the added vision of sexy, naked Liam in my head, there was no way I was ever going to sleep. Ever.

Soph had cut the ends off a banana and then boiled it, peel and all, in water for about ten minutes. She then strained the hot liquid into a mug and topped it with a sprinkle of cinnamon. She assured me it would knock my ass out. I was so tired I'd have taken a fist to the temple if it meant I could be blissfully unconscious, but this seemed worth trying first.

"Was he, you know, happy to see you?" Soph asked. "He was, wasn't he? No, don't tell me. I'm married. I shouldn't even be thinking about another man's magic wand."

"Magic wand?" I snorted and very warm banana tea shot into my nose, making me cough and hack. The cinnamon stung.

"Sorry—the twins and I had one of our annual Harry Potter movie marathons the other night," Sophie said. "Wand sounded much more genteel than dick."

"Seriously?" Em strode into the kitchen. "Is that all you two talk about? Dude parts?"

Two spots of color blazed on my baby sister's cheeks and again I felt as if we had let her down by not making sure she was properly educated and appreciative of masculine anatomy.

"Jules got to see Liam's bits," Soph said.

"Ha! Trust me when I say there was nothing bitsy about it." I smiled into my mug as I took a sip.

Em's eyes went wide, like tennis-ball size, as she stared at me in complete horrified amazement.

"Explain," she said. "How did this happen? It's not like a girl just stumbles upon a guy's compass point and gets a good eyeful."

"Tried that have you?" Soph asked and Em's face went rashy.

"No!" Em said. "I would never!"

"Calm down, Em," I said. "She's just teasing."

Em glared at Sophie who ignored her, which compelled me as the middle child mediator to divert Em's attention by telling her what had happened between me and Liam.

"Well, that was pretty aggressive, don't you think?" Em asked. "I mean, he just dropped trow right there in front of you, knowing you were watching?"

"Yeah," I said. "I'm sure my watching was the whole point of him letting the man cannon loose."

This time it was Soph who snorted banana tea up her nose.

"Whatever for?" Em asked, clearly not appreciating my witty way with words.

"I suspect to remind me of what I've been missing for the past nine years." The memories hadn't faded and nobody else compared.

"Thinks pretty highly of himself there, doesn't he?" Em asked, as if indignant on my behalf.

"As he should," I said with a deep sigh.

"I knew it!" Sophie banged her hand on the table and we all jumped.

Em shot her a dark look and tiptoed to the door to see if Babs was still sleeping. Thankfully, she was.

"I still say that was a pervy thing to do," Em said. "Downright hostile, in fact."

"Maybe." I traced the grain of the wood table with my finger while I considered the different angles of what had happened upstairs. "But since the last time he saw me was right before I skipped town with his best friend, well, I can't really say that I blame him."

Silence reigned. The night I had fled our childhood home at the age of eighteen, without saying a word to anyone, was still one of the worst nights of our collective lives.

Babs and I had had the mother of all fights, and in a fit of hysterics only an eighteen-year-old can manage, I jumped into my friend Jessie Lopez's Jeep and drove all the way across the country to New York City to attend school at my father's alma mater, Columbia University.

It had been the plan all along, but I'd arrived a month early without a dime to my name and my poor heart all shrunken up like an apple head. Leaving like that, with no goodbyes, was not one of my finer life moments. Jessie and I found a crap two-bedroom apartment in Brooklyn that we shared with three other impoverished students, and jobs waiting tables at a Mid-Town restaurant. I hated everything about it, especially the way I'd left home, because I knew there'd be no going back.

"I remember the night you left." Em's voice was soft and sad. "I don't think I've ever seen Mom so angry."

"Yeah, well," I said. "That makes two of us but it was a long time ago."

"Sounds like it's still pretty fresh for Liam," Soph said. I frowned at her and she shrugged. "He showed up at my house the next day, looking for you. He was wrecked. Judging by his reaction to seeing you now, I'm guessing he's still not over it."

"You never told me he came to see you," I said.

She gave me a tender look; the sort a mother gives a child. "No, you were hurting so much and Liam was a mess. I couldn't bear to make it worse for either of you and I figured if you were going to work things out, you'd contact each other and not through me as a carrier pigeon."

I flashed back to the intense pain of those first few weeks after I'd run away. The hurt, the longing, the desperate sadness, all of it. There were times I had been so sure I would actually die of a broken heart.

My feelings must have shown on my face because both Em and Soph reached for me at the same time, wrapping their arms around me and holding me tight as if they could buffer the storm that was raging inside of me.

A single silent tear dripped down my cheek as I clung to them. It hit me then how much I missed them, my sisters, how much I missed the girl I used to be, feisty and fiery, and how much I missed the boy I had run away from, the love of my life.

"It's all right, Jules," Soph whispered against my hair. "We're here. We've got you."

It was so reminiscent of what she used to say to me when I was little and in trouble with Babs for one reason or another that it made my throat tighten. I pushed past the knot and said, "Thanks."

My sisters released me just as we heard a moan come from the other room. Babs. I glanced at the clock. The doctor had put her on a schedule for her pain meds. She was due for another dose now.

"I've got it," Soph said. "It's Friday, so Harry and Hannah don't need to be up for school tomorrow. I can take the night watch and then go to Harry's soccer game since Stan can't make it. You two go get some sleep."

I was too wrung out from memory overload to argue.

"Come on," Em said. "I'll walk you up and make sure no man junk jumps out at you."

I barked a laugh and wrapped my arm around her shoulders. "I appreciate that, Em. But what would you do with it if it did?"

She turned a hot shade of red when I gave her side-eye and Soph laughed.

"I hate being the little sister," Em said. "I'm always the butt of the joke."

"Don't say that." Soph's expression turned serious as she smoothed Em's hair back from her face. "You're the best of us. Never forget that."

Em shook her head as if shaking off the praise. The three of us left the kitchen and walked into the great room. I paused beside Babs to kiss her while she dozed, just a gentle peck on her perfectly coifed hair before heading upstairs. Since yesterday, Babs resisted leaving her favorite divan to sleep in her bedroom on the first floor, and we all agreed that it wasn't worth the fight to make her move. If the divan was the hill she chose to plant her flag on, who were we to deny it?

Babs blinked at Em with a wan smile, but as soon as Soph gave her the pain meds, she eased back to sleep. Soph settled into the reclining chair beside her.

"Come get me if you need me," I said.

Soph waved me away and Em and I continued to our rooms. When we reached my door, Em strode inside and looked across the yard at Liam's window. The light wasn't on. She stared for a moment as if she expected him to appear. He did not. Satisfied, she lowered the shade.

"You know, we could switch rooms if you want." Em's lit up as if she really liked the idea. "That'd teach him."

"Yeah, but it might scar you for life," I said. She frowned. "It's okay, Em. I think he made his point, as it were, and I doubt I'll be seeing any more of him."

"Oh." She considered this with a frown. "That's for the best, right?"

"Yeah." I made it sound as if I meant it. I totally didn't. I was the lyingest liar of all pants-on-fire liars.

"Okay, then, sleep well," she said.

After our last awkward hug, we hadn't attempted another embrace and Em didn't now, sending a nod before she disappeared out of my room. I was left alone, staring at the drawn shade, and wondering what it said about me that I was going to open it and hope I saw Liam again. It didn't require much thought; I knew what it said about me. I was pitiful, straight up pitiful.

I took the day watch with Babs, so that Soph could attend her son's soccer game. Much like the prior shifts, I worked, Babs napped, and we watched the fashion channel. She looked smaller than she had the day before, and I couldn't shake the feeling that we were watching her shrink into nothing. The realization made my chest ache. Now that I knew she hadn't asked for me and didn't care if I was there or not, I supposed I should have cared less. I didn't.

No one said the C word aloud, as if it would get worse if we mentioned it, but the disease that must not be named was clearly killing Mom. Dr. Patel, when pressed, would not confirm or deny that it was cancer but he did tell Sophie, when she had a complete meltdown on him, that there was no treatment that could help Babs's condition at this stage. The most we could do was keep her comfortable and say whatever we had to say to her now before it was too late.

When we told Em what the doctor had said, she blinked at us as if uncomprehending. Then she sat on the floor, right in the middle of the kitchen, drawing her knees up to her chest. She looked like she was five instead of twenty-five.

"But I'm not ready," Em whispered. "I'm not ready to be in a world without her."

Soph held her while she cried, while they both cried. My world hadn't had Babs in it for a long time. But I understood. Even I wasn't ready to see the sun rise without Babs telling it how brightly to shine. It seemed inconceivable.

When she'd calmed down, Em took the early evening shift as Soph was leaving and coming back later since she had an event to attend with her husband. I hadn't seen her husband Stan since I'd been back. Hannah and Harry had come by a couple of times to see their grandmother and me since I hadn't seen them since their last visit to New York. Stan hadn't bothered.

I knew he and Babs had never gotten along, but I would have thought that being a doctor, Stan would take an interest in his mother-in-law's care. Soph had mumbled something about him feeling that as a dermatologist he couldn't really be of any help. I would have argued that since Babs refused to tell us what exactly was wrong any medical input would have been welcome, but I sensed it would hurt Soph and, really, we were suffering enough.

As I climbed the stairs to my room to catch up on some work, I wondered if the window across the way would remain dark. I glanced at my phone. It was ten minutes until Liam's usual work out time, but he'd been absent since our last encounter, so I had no idea if he had decided to work out elsewhere.

Anticipation, or maybe hope, thrummed through me, although judging by its point of origin, it was more likely lust that ricocheted around my insides like a pinball lighting up targets and ringing bells. I forced myself to walk rather than run to my room.

Given that the jig was up, there was no reason not to turn on the light. Still, I stood by the door, debating. Did I flick the lights on and potentially frighten Liam away? Or did I lurk in the dark like a creeper and hope for another eyeful of man candy?

Feeling bold, I snapped on the light. I strode across the room toward the desk, trying not to glance at his window. If he was there, I wanted to appear cool, casual, collected. In other words, the exact opposite of how I felt.

I kept my eyes down, knowing the disappointment of him not being there would be deep. Finally, when I had turned on my computer and futzed around my desk as much as I could, I glanced up.

Liam's window was dark. I felt myself deflate all the while realizing this really was for the best. Damn it. Using his hotness to distract myself from the familial misery I was drowning in was bad form. I knew that. Still, I longed for the sight of him just like I had longed for dandelion fluff wishes to actually come true when I was a kid.

Just then his light snapped on, and there he was, standing there with his arms crossed over his chest, almost as if...as if he'd been waiting for me, too.

My heart did its usual stop-stutter-start thing and I leaned against the desk to keep myself upright. He was shirtless, again, and he didn't uncross his arms as he stared back at me.

The intensity in his eyes reminded me of the first time we were together, yes, in *that* way. Liam had held my gaze as he'd slid into me that first time, never looking away, making sure I was okay with every millimeter of me he conquered, never leaving me to find his own release, never letting me go. Instead he had kept his gaze locked on mine, absorbing every bit of emotion I offered and returning it with his own. In all my life I had never felt as powerful a connection as I did in those glorious moments with him.

The memory made my insides clench with longing and not just for the physical but for the soul connection we forged in blood, sweat, and tears. I had never managed to replicate it with anyone else, not once, not ever. How could nine years have passed and with one look he reduced me to a void of desperate aching need?

As I stared, incapable of looking away or moving, he gave me one brusque nod. I raised my eyebrows in question. What did he want? He didn't make another move but just stood there, patiently waiting for me to figure it out.

With his hot gaze moving all over my body, I caught on pretty quick. Without moving a muscle or saying a word, Liam Mahony made it clear that he expected me to strip for him.

Chapter Five

I sucked in a breath and put my hand on my chest. Not a chance in hell, buddy! Well, that was my first response. My second was to tip my head to the side, considering. Yes, considering.

He mirrored my move and raised one eyebrow at me. It was the same look he used to give me when we were teens and he was daring me to do something, like beat his ass in air hockey, apply to my dream school, Columbia, tackle a curb grind on my skateboard, or admit that I loved him, you know, out loud with words.

I remembered how much bolder and braver Liam had made me. Well, maybe he didn't make me that so much as he'd loved me enough that it freed me to take risks I never would have taken without him as my landing mat.

If I refused, if I walked away from him right now and snapped out the light, I knew with absolute certainty that I would never see him again. I didn't think I could live through that a second time. I had no idea what would happen while I was here, but I knew I wanted to try to find some closure with Liam.

I glanced down at my outfit. I was wearing Em's clothes because I had run out of clean laundry two days ago and laundry just wasn't a priority for me right now. Since Babs had never stopped being in charge of Em's wardrobe, it was all high-end dresses, skirts, cardigan sweaters, button-up blouses, and slacks, you know, like a grown up. I missed my jeans and baggy thermal tops, but the blue shrug, white blouse, and Capri pants I had on would work so much better for what I was about to do. Oh, yes, I was all in.

Without overthinking it, I met Liam's gaze as I reached up and pulled the shrug off my shoulders. I twirled it over my head a few times before launching it across the room. His head jerked upright and even from this far away I could see his entire body stiffen. Obviously, I had surprised him. Good.

I put my hands on my thighs and did a very Marilyn Monroe, maybe more Betty Boop, booty pose. I slowly dragged my right hand up my body, across my abdomen and up to the top button of my shirt. I unbuttoned it and pushed my chest out, trying to use what I had. It was a challenge. I glanced at Liam from under my eyelashes. His jaw was clenching and unclenching and his nostrils were flared. Well, okay then.

It occurred to me as I worked my way down the row of buttons that he might be filming me, planning to put the striptease on the internet to shame me. It would be an epic payback for the humiliation I had dealt him, however unintentional, so many years ago.

The thought made me pause at the last button. If he did that then he wasn't the man I thought he was, and it sure would be a lot easier to get over whatever this thing was that still sparked between us like an ember in a forgotten fire. I glanced up. He hadn't moved. Was he even breathing?

I owed him this. With all the pain I had caused him in the wake of my departure, I owed him my trust one more time. I slid my shirt half off my shoulders and turned my back to him. I pulled the tie out of my hair, letting my wild curls loose, and tipped my head so my hair draped down my half naked back before I dropped my shirt.

I was relieved I wasn't wearing my usual sports bra. This was white and plain but thankfully had a little bit of a peekaboo see-through mesh thing going, keeping it from being too much like something you'd find under a nun's habit. I thought plain might be the sort of intimate garment nuns would wear, but who knew? Maybe they were all about red satin and leopard print undies hidden beneath their black garb. The thought made me smile and helped with my nerves.

Having dropped the shirt, I glanced over my shoulder to look at Liam, and then I whirled my head around, making my hair stream out in a circular motion like a stripper on the catwalk. Then I turned back around so I was facing him. He had one hand pressed to the window, his palm flat against the glass. Every bit of girl power I'd ever had was surging through me—I felt like a badass.

Dragging my hands over my sides, I unfastened my pants, planning to shove them down my hips, but the head twirling had made me dizzy and I staggered, probably looking as graceful as the town drunk.

I stepped wide to steady myself and stubbed my toe on the desk. Ouch! I hopped back a step and my pants dropped, tangling my legs, causing me to windmill my arms in a desperate bid to regain my balance. I failed and did a loud face plant onto the floor taking the desk chair with me. I laid there for a moment, stunned, the breath knocked out of me, my butt in the air—not my best side.

"Jules, are you all right?" Em cried as she barged into the room.

"I'm okay," I mumbled into the carpet beneath my cheek. And I was, you know, minus my dignity and all that pesky other stuff like self-esteem and pride.

"What are you doing on the floor?" My baby sister grabbed me beneath the arms and hauled me to my feet. I stood half dressed with stars moving around my head in a circular motion—oh wait, maybe only I could see those—slowly coming to the realization that I had probably just made a complete ass of myself.

I glanced at the window to verify. Yep. Liam was doubled over, his entire body shaking with laughter. He looked like he was having a seizure; every time he seemed to get it under control, he lost it again. I was really glad I couldn't hear the guffaws that were coming out of his face hole.

He must have felt me staring because he straightened and caught my eye. He tried to iron out his smile, yeah, that didn't work. First his shoulders started shaking, then his lips looked like they were wrestling with his cheeks to keep from turning up, and finally he had to wipe the tears that streamed out of his eyes with the heels of his hands. Yeah, Liam Mahony was having a good old laugh at my expense. Jerk!

Em glanced from him to me and back again. She studied me with consternation, taking in my half-dressed state and my hair gone wild.

"Oh, Jules, tell me you didn't," she said. "Tell me you did not let that man see you get undressed."

I sighed, knowing there was really no point in fibbing.

"Well, he didn't see me naked, because I didn't finish my striptease," I said. "I might've broken my toe."

Em reached around me and snapped the window shade down, sending Liam a dirty look as she did so. She scowled at me as if I'd lost all sense of common decency...I couldn't really blame her for that.

"What is wrong with you?" Em asked. "We have bigger stuff going on here than your old boyfriend living next door. God, Jules, get your shit together."

With that she slammed out of my room as if I'd lit her backside on fire. I waited until I heard her bedroom door open and close and then I peeked beneath the shade to see if Liam was still there.

He was and he was working out—yay, me—but every now and then he would pause with his weights half raised and he would have to put them down so he could laugh. I had no doubt he was laughing at me and I was surprisingly okay with it. In the grand scheme of things, it seemed like he'd received a solid karmic payback. I could live with that.

I dropped the shade. Maybe now that I'd humiliated myself in front of him, he'd see his way to not glaring at me like he had before. Oh, I didn't have any illusions that we'd ever be friends or lovers, but maybe we could be civil. You know, the sort of neighbors who saw each other, waved, and shouted out a "good morning," but who never stopped to chat.

The picture wouldn't form in my head, and I had the feeling it was because I could never envision a time where Liam would look at me with anything but anger. The thought made me sad.

Babs's condition deteriorated more the next day. She had stopped eating and getting her to drink was a battle of wills. A hospice nurse named Ashley arrived and admitted our mother into their care. Tense meetings were held in the kitchen as her medications were all but suspended, everything but the pain meds.

Sophie and I understood what this meant. I feared that Em wasn't really grasping it, but she surprised me when she asked Ashley, a sturdy woman built for giving hugs, "How long do you think we have? You see people like this all the time."

Ashley didn't flinch from the question, though her voice was soft when she answered, "A day or two at most is my best guess, but sometimes..."

Em nodded. She didn't cry or wail or breakdown. She stiffened her spine. "I'll be sitting with Mom from now on then."

"Me, too," Sophie said.

"And me," I said.

The nurse gently admonished us to take care of ourselves and we agreed, but I knew we were all just giving her lip service so she'd go away and leave us alone with our mom. Ashley seemed to get that and left, telling us to call her any time for anything.

Babs woke up to find the three of us staring down at her, hovering as if we were trying to memorize everything about her, so that we would never forget this complicated woman who had given each of us life.

She held her hands out to us, and Sophie took one while Em took the other. We all sat down on the divan, with me by her feet. Her voice was just a soft rasp now, and we had to lean in to hear her.

Mom looked at Sophie. "You've given up so much of yourself to take care of others, don't be afraid to go after what you want. I never did and I've always regretted it."

"I will, Mom," Sophie said. Her voice wavered a bit but, she kept her emotions in check. "I promise."

Babs turned to Em, her baby. Her eyes softened. "Thank you for taking such good care of me. You're free now. Live boldly, darling, you deserve it."

"I will, Mom." Em sobbed. "I promise I will."

Babs closed her eyes and exhaled. She appeared drained as if she didn't have enough strength left to breathe. I figured since we had a rocky history at best there really wasn't anything left for her to say to me. It hurt, much like all of my interactions with her, but perhaps that was just who we were.

"I'm sorry," Babs said. She opened her eyes and I noticed that the pale blue of her irises seemed to have faded over the past few days. She looked at each of us in turn, even me. "So sorry."

"There's no need, Mom," Em said. "It's no trouble taking care of you."

"No, trouble at all," Sophie said.

"No, not that," Babs said. Her gaze locked on me, and a tear spilled down her cheek. "I wanted more time to make it right."

My throat grew tight and my hand shook as I moved forward and wiped the tear off her face. Her skin was soft to the touch and delicate, almost papery thin.

"It's all right," My voice was thick with all of the conversations I knew we were never going to have. "I know you did your best."

"I wish I could have loved you..." Her words trailed off.

There. She'd finally said it. After all these years, my mother had finally admitted that she had never been able to love me. It really wasn't news. I could feel my sisters staring at me, but I kept my gaze on Babs. I supposed she was getting it off her chest before she died. It shouldn't have hurt as much as it did, but, oh, it cut deep, and the scars were going to be ugly.

"It's okay," I lied. I didn't mean it. It wasn't okay. In fact, it hurt so bad I thought I might die but what was I supposed to say when this was likely the last conversation we'd ever have?

"I'm sorry," she gasped. Another tear splashed down her weathered cheek. "I wish I had been more for you."

The tears I'd been fighting streamed down my face. Sophie took one of my hands and Em the other. They both squeezed my fingers with theirs, letting me know that they were with me. I wasn't alone Well, at least Babs had apologized. This was it then, the moment Babs and I made peace. I was surprised at the gratitude that filled me for this chance to let the past go, to let her go. Maybe I could finally stop feeling so hurt all the time.

"It's all right, Mom," I said.

She looked at me with gratitude before her thin lids fluttered closed.

"I love you, Mom," Em whispered. Her voice was choked with sobs.

Babs opened her eyes. It appeared to take quite an effort.

"I love you, too, Mom," Soph said.

"And I love you." Babs's voice was a rough rasp. "I'm so proud of my girls. I have the best girls in the world. Promise me, you'll take care of each other."

"We will," Soph said, speaking for all of us.

Babs smiled at us then. It was a sweet smile, unlike any I'd ever seen from her before, and then she slipped into an exhausted slumber. We didn't move but sat with her for another hour just watching her, wondering if this was the last of our moments with her.

It wasn't.

A few hours later, Babs stirred. She blinked awake, and Em sat up straight from where she'd been slouched.

"Mom, are you all right?" Em said. "Are you in pain? Can I get you anything?"

Babs blinked at us. A deep wrinkle formed on her brow as she scanned each of our faces, not in the adoring way of a loving mother, but in the irritated way a person in line at the DMV glares at everyone between them and the service counter.

"What am I still doing here?" she snapped. "I said what I had to say. I'm ready to go."

She looked exceedingly put out and I wondered if she really expected us to answer her question. The snort that came out of me was matched by a snicker from Sophie and a surprised chuckle from Em. Good old Babs, even at the end, she wanted what she wanted when she wanted it.

Chapter Six

After several days of not eating, Babs suddenly needed chocolate ice cream in the middle of the night. Soph made the store run while Em and I propped Babs up. And so it was we had a mini ice cream social in the living room at one o'clock in the morning. Babs only managed two small mouthfuls but the smile on her face when she swallowed was the happiest I had seen her since I arrived.

Soph, Em, and I camped out in chairs around her divan. At some point, we all drifted off to sleep. I wasn't sure what woke me, but I think it was the absence of sound rather than a sudden noise. The rasping wheeze of Babs's breathing that I'd been listening to for days suddenly wasn't there. Instinct had me up and moving to her side.

We kept one light on beside her lounge chair, and it was by this light that I examined her. I took her hand in mine, it was still warm but I couldn't see if her chest was rising and falling. I put my hand over her heart. She was so thin now I was distracted by the feel of hard bone just beneath the papery skin. I couldn't tell if her heart was beating or not, but I didn't want her to go without knowing it was okay.

I leaned in close and whispered in her ear, "It's okay, Mom. Don't worry about us. We'll be all right."

The lids of her eyes fluttered a tiny bit, just enough for me to see the pale blue irises and then they closed. She puffed out a bit of air not even strong enough to be called a whisper but I heard her. "Thank you."

That final breath left her, and she slowly slipped away. I sat on the edge of the divan, feeling numb. Babs Blumer who had shaped my life in so many ways good and bad, mostly bad, was gone. The crushing pain in my chest was almost unbearable, my throat was tight, and my eyes burned. I pushed it all back by sheer force of will.

"Hey," I whispered and nudged first Soph and then Em. Sophie lurched up, momentarily confused before blinking awake and registering the expression on my face, which I could only imagine was devastated.

"Mom—" Em jumped to her feet. "Is she better? Is she asking for me?"

My baby sister exuded optimism. It was then I realized that even though Em knew Babs was dying, she also clung to the hope that somehow Babs would recover, and everything would go back to normal. I felt horrible when I shook my head.

"I'm sorry, Em," I said as gently as I could. "She's gone."

"No!" Em cried. She reached for Bab's hand, clutching it in hers as she studied our mother, desperate for a response.

Soph leaned over and rested her cheek on Mom's hair. She closed her eyes probably saying her own private good-bye.

Feeling as if I'd had my time with our mother, I stepped away and let them have their moment with Babs. I found my cell phone and entered the hospice nurse's phone number. I let her know that Babs had passed. The words were harder to get out than I thought they would be, but Ashley was very kind and said a team would be there within an hour to take care of things for us.

The rest of the night became surreal. By dawn, we had a time of death certificate, the crematorium people had collected Babs's body, and our house, the house Babs had lived in for the last forty-two years, was suddenly without her.

The twins, Hannah and Harry, came to sit with us. They kept Em from swirling into a pit of despair, and Soph was also bolstered by her children's presence. Being the only one of us who had lived on her own for her adult life, I needed a few minutes by myself to process all that was happening.

I slipped out the sliding glass doors into the small backyard. It wasn't quite morning yet and the sky was gray. Babs had always taken great pride in her huge lemon tree. The Ponderosa lemon filled the corner of the yard and once a year it gifted us with lemons the size of footballs. It was so plentiful that most of our neighbors scattered when they saw Babs coming toward them with a bag of lemons. I crossed the yard and sat under the tree on the far side where I wasn't visible from the house.

This had been my favorite reading spot as a kid and hours had been spent weaving spells with Harry and the rest of Gryffindor. Just like then, I planted my feet on the ground and braced my back against the trunk of the tree.

The grief when it came was not pretty. It felt as if it was being wrenched out of me with a crowbar. Ugly crying big fat tears, snot pouring from my nose, guttural hiccups, and fish-out-of-water gasps echoed in the early morning air. It was chilly and wet grass soaked my butt through my jeans. I didn't care. I wanted it out, all of it, the pain, the sadness, the anger, the regret—I wanted it purged from my system.

There was serious irony here. I was gutted at Babs's death and couldn't reconcile the fact that I was so horribly sad about a woman who for most of my life had made me feel less than. And even at the end, she had singled me out as the unlovable one. God, that hurt so much.

Logically, I knew I should be relieved that the toxic presence in my life was gone, but I wasn't. Instead, I was destroyed by her passing, absolutely inconsolably wrecked.

I'd worked myself up with no end in sight when *his* arms came around me. I started, jerking away from him, not wanting anyone to witness me in this raw and vulnerable state. He gave me no choice. He swung me up into his arms as he took my seat under the tree and pulled me onto his lap, keeping his arms around me and gently pushing my head onto his shoulder.

My eyes were swollen and my vision blurred with tears, apparently tear ducts run deep, who knew, so I couldn't see his face but I recognized the feel of him, the scent of him that was uniquely Liam Mahony, a potent cocktail of citrus, sunshine, and the sea. Powerless to fight both him and my need for comfort, I twined my arms around his neck and held on while grief continued to beat me up with the relentless pull of a riptide.

Liam rested his head on mine and let me sob and wail and weep. He never said a word. He simply gave me his warmth while he held me close, with one hand curled around my hip as the other ran up and down my back in a gesture of comfort.

The memories that swirled around me were almost as thick as my grief. How many times had we been here exactly, with me crying and Liam comforting me when Babs and I had yet another argument, usually about my hair, my lack of femininity, or, more irony, him?

Babs never said it plainly but her disappointment in me came off her in waves of pinched disapproval and now, after all this time, I wasn't sure how I was going to define myself without the steady stream of criticism. I supposed it should have been liberating but instead, I was lost. Except with Liam's arms around me, everything shifted and repositioned itself and for the first time since I'd arrived in Gull's Harbor, I felt as if I was home.

I had no idea how long we sat there, but as I lifted my head from his shoulder the sun was rising, lighting the sky with a bright red ribbon along the horizon.

I pulled back from Liam. I let my crazy curls cover my face and I glanced at him from beneath them, hoping they hid my red nose and puffy eyes. He was having none of that. He leaned forward and planted a kiss on my hair.

When I tried to climb off of his lap, Liam simply scooped me up against him and rolled to his feet. He strode across the damp grass, with me in his arms, and up onto the patio where he gently set me down.

He brushed the hair away from my cheeks and our gazes met and held. My breath stalled in my lungs as I tried to figure out what I saw in his intense brown gaze. Tenderness, compassion, affection, but there was also an edge, a flash of anger and resentment that was being held in check. Or was I just imagining that?

He cupped my face in his hands, using his thumbs to wipe away the last of my tears. Then he leaned forward and kissed me on the lips. It was the sweet press of his mouth against mine, over before it began, and yet it changed everything.

Liam turned and left, striding across the small yard and vaulting over the fence that separated our homes, without ever saying a word. But now I knew, I knew where I belonged. It was as it had always been...with him. But I had absolutely no idea how to make that happen.

"Seriously, Aunt Jules, you need to tap that," Hannah, my sixteen-year-old niece, whispered in my ear as we acted as the greeters for the reception at our house after Babs's service.

I turned away from watching Liam across the room to look at her in alarm. "What do you know about "tapping" anything?"

"Nothing...yet," Hannah admitted with a grin. It reminded me so much of Soph at that age that I wrapped my arm around her and squeezed her close.

"What about you, Harry?" I asked my nephew, who was also working the door. My question drew his gaze away from one of our young neighbors who looked to be about twenty and had an impressive booty which she showed off to the best possible advantage in a bottom-clinging micro mini that made men, young or old, lose all brain function.

"What about me?" Harry never took his eyes off the rumpus. Poor bastard.

"You "tapping" anything yet?" I winked at Hannah, who laughed.

"Oh god, gross!" Harry cringed. "You're supposed to be the cool one, Aunt Jules. You can't ask a teenage guy stuff like that!"

"I thought being the "cool" one meant I get to ask these questions, no?"

"No, just no," he said.

Harry shook his head until his shaggy blond hair partially covered his face, which I figured was why he wore it that way.

Hannah, who had the same blond hair and blue eyes as her brother, as well as the same dimples, leaned close to her sibling and tipped her head in the direction of Liam. He was on the other side of the room, leaning against the wall and holding an untouched glass of wine.

"I'm trying to convince Aunt Jules to make a play for *him*," Hannah said.

Harry glanced at Liam and then at me. "Well, the guy has been staring at you for the past forty-five minutes so you should go talk to him or shoot him and put him out of his misery. I say this as a dude who has done his share of holding up walls and staring."

I hadn't seen Liam since the morning under the lemon tree. The days in between had been a flurry of activity as we were swept up in planning a service worthy of Babs's diva expectations. Thankfully, she'd left us an exacting list of instructions, telling us precisely what she wanted, so there was no debate or second guessing.

I'd ordered the flowers and food, notified the papers of her passing with an obituary she'd written herself, and created a PowerPoint slide show of the photographs Babs had picked out to be synced to the music she'd chosen which we'd played during the memorial service.

The few times I'd had a chance to peek during the week, Liam's workout room remained dark and I didn't see him moving about his house or his yard, not that I was stalking the guy or anything. Okay, maybe just a little. I assumed after our emotional clinch, he was steering clear of me, letting me know in no uncertain terms that he was not interested. Message received.

But then he arrived at Babs's service with his parents, the Professor and Mrs. Mahony, who had come from their retirement village to attend, and my heart had tried to punch right through my chest at the sight of him. I'd had to dredge up every bit of self-control I possessed to keep from running across the church and throwing myself into his arms, and I do mean every bit.

Yes, I was aware that I was grieving and not one-hundred-percent in my right mind. I knew I was vulnerable and likely running away from my emotions and probably seeking comfort from the familiar, which was Liam. Still, I had felt his eyes on me throughout the service and only resisted meeting his gaze because I wasn't brave enough to face the possibility of rejection, not today.

It didn't stop me, however, from checking him out on the few occasions he was speaking to someone else. And, hoo boy, if I thought Liam working out had been quite the eye popper, Liam in a suit, well, let's just say the urge to grab him by his tie and drag him upstairs to my room and have my way with him had crossed my mind every minute since he had stepped through the door of our house. I blamed the grief for making me think crazy inappropriate things.

In an effort to be more circumspect, I scouted the room for my sisters. Em was in the corner talking to several of Mom's closest friends, women who had moved into the neighborhood when Mom did, and like her had raised their children and buried or divorced their husbands here. They were a St. John-wearing, afternoon-card-playing, Friday-morning-hair salon tribe who drank Manhattans and met for mahjong once a week where they commiserated about the unfortunate choices their grown children were making. I was pretty sure I was one of their main topics of conversation and was more than happy to let Em be our emissary.

I shifted my gaze until I found Soph, who was standing by the front window with her husband. Stan and Soph had met in college, and Soph, still reeling from the death of our father, had fallen head over heels, crazy in love.

I don't know that Stan had ever felt the same way about her. They had only been together a few months when Soph turned up pregnant with the twins and the next thing we knew, she was married and a mom. To me, the loss of Sophie had been almost as big a blow as the loss of our dad. Watching her tight expression as she stood with Stan, I wondered, not for the first time, if my sister was happy in her marriage.

Stan was a big, lantern-jawed, Dudley Do-Right sort of guy with thinning blond hair, narrow blue eyes, and a bit of a paunch. He loved cross-fit, expensive wine, fast cars, season tickets, and exotic trips to exclusive places. Yeah, in short, he was a pretentious douche and I'd never really warmed up to him.

I never thought he was good enough for Soph, because I knew he saw her as nothing more than the mother of his children. She was the field he'd plowed to bear the fruit of his loins. If I could pick one word to describe how he treated her, it was dismissive. Even now, I saw her ask him something with a tight expression, putting her hand on his arm to get his full attention.

Stan shook her off and spun away from her, appearing irritated until he caught sight of the neighbor girl with the generous southern hemisphere strolling by. He perked up, giving the young lady what I'm sure he thought was a charming smile but was in fact a middle-aged creepy guy smirk. I squelched the urge to walk over to them and punch him in his big, stupid face.

"Julia, how pretty you look." A familiar voice pulled my attention away from my sister and her husband and I turned as Mrs. Giovanni approached the open front door.

"I was just devastated to hear about Barbara," the older woman said as she reached past me and handed Harry a casserole dish. The teen hurried to the kitchen.

Mrs. G was one of Babs's mahjong buddies and I knew that losing one of their own was a crushing blow not just because it left an empty space at the table, but it also forced them to acknowledge their own mortality. Never fun. I studied her face and could see that despite the carefully applied make-up, she'd been crying. I opened my arms and hugged her. She started to cry again.

"I just don't know how I'm going to get by without her," the woman said.

"I know," I agreed. "Mom was a force of nature."

Mrs. G stepped back. She smiled at me through her tears and then fished a tissue out of her purse, dabbing her eyes with it. People were moving around us, coming and going, while Hannah filled in as greeter until Harry returned and I focused on Mrs. G.

"Barbara loved her girls so much." The woman gently pressed the tissue to her lids. "She was so proud of how you went off to New York and made a new life for yourself. It was always "Julia this" and "Julia that." You made your mother so proud."

She patted my cheek as I stood there stunned. Babs had bragged about me? I couldn't reconcile it. I had to assume she'd done it to save face. The Babs I knew was pissed that I was in New York and therefore out of her control. Mrs. G stepped past me into the house to commiserate with her friends. I wondered what else Babs had said about me?

The thought fled as soon as I turned and saw *him* standing there. Liam was a mere foot away from me and I knew, I knew absolutely, that he had heard what Mrs. G said and judging by the way his jaw was clenching, he wasn't happy about it.

"I'm sorry for your loss," Liam said.

There it was, the low reverberating bass that was Liam Mahony's voice. It may have been nine years since I'd heard it, but like a tune that gets stuck in a loop in your head, I'd never forgotten it or how it made my insides bloom like flowers reaching for the sun.

"Thank you," I said.

We stared at one another. Up close in daylight, we had the opportunity to take in the changes time had wrought. Liam was harder, more chiseled, as if the softness of youth had fallen away to leave behind the more defined and resilient planes of a man.

I imagined he saw the same changes in me. I had borrowed one of Soph's dresses for the service rather than buy something new. The blue with the flared hem was slightly flirty yet reserved at the same time. I wore my hair up in deference to how much Babs had disliked my curls—I even wore mascara and lipstick, again, just for Babs. One stray curl had fallen free of my updo and curled around my neck. I saw him study it as if it was the key to unlocking the girl he'd once known.

"Well," I said for lack of anything better to say. This was not the time or place to try and make apologies or explanations, although they were his due.

"Well," he repeated.

Obviously, this conversation was going nowhere fast.

"It was a lovely service, Julia." Mrs. Mahony, Liam's mother, hugged me close before she moved to stand beside her son.

Mrs. Mahony was a handsome woman with a square jaw and arching eyebrows. She wore her gray hair long and didn't wear make-up, something that had always driven Babs crazy. Mrs. Mahony was the down-to-earth sort, and her husband the Professor, who had joined us, was very much her complement with his thick gray beard and dark-rimmed glasses. He, too, gave me a quick hug. My fondness for them had never diminished over the years and I was relieved to see their affection for me hadn't either, despite the circumstances of my abrupt departure.

"Your mother was an extraordinary woman," Mrs. Mahony said.

Given that my mother had never kept her disapproval of my relationship with Liam quiet, frequently complaining to the Mahonys that their son was a bad influence on me, I found her words very kind.

Professor Mahony removed his glasses and polished the lenses with a cloth he took from his pocket. He appeared thoughtful. "I can honestly say I never met anyone quite like her."

I smiled because I knew Babs would have approved the sentiment as it was spot on. There was no one like Babs Blumer and I doubted there ever would be again.

More people came in the door and the Mahonys took their leave as they needed to drive back up the coast to the retirement home they'd moved into when Liam bought their house. Liam let his parents walk ahead of him. He looked like he wanted to say something but then he shook his head.

We stared at one another for a few seconds and then with a curt nod, Liam turned and left. I could read in the stiff set of his shoulders beneath the fitted charcoal gray suit exactly what he was thinking. Ex-girlfriend confronted, feelings successfully held in check, neighborly duty done, game over.

Yeah, not even close, buddy. I hadn't booked my return trip to New York yet. I wanted to make sure my sisters were okay first but also, after the other morning, I was determined to try and explain to Liam why I'd left the way I did. After nine years, I owed him that much or maybe I owed it to myself. Either way, the overdue conversation was absolutely happening whether he wanted to participate or not.

Chapter Seven

"**W**hat is *she* still doing here?" Em asked. "Did you tell her she could stay?"

"Hell no," Soph said. "You know I can't stand her."

"Don't look at me," I replied as they both turned to do just that. "You know how I feel about her."

We were standing in the kitchen, glancing out at the living room where a few stragglers from the gathering lingered over the last of the wine. Soph had given the caterers the signal to clean up in the hope that the remaining guests would take the hint and leave us to our grief.

More accurately, it was time to meet with Babs's attorney, Mr. Howard Loren. He'd come for the service and asked our preference for the reading of the will. We'd decided to save us all a trip and have him tell us after the get together so that we knew what we were dealing with and could plan accordingly.

Unfortunately, Paisley Lawson, our obnoxious cousin on our mother's side of the family was one of the lingerers. What can I say about Paisley? She was Babs's older sister Jean's only child and smack between me and Soph in age. She was thirty-one, a serial marrier with three ex-husbands, gobs of money from the divorces, a bottle blond with a faux tan and fake tatas, platypus lips and, well, you get the picture.

Simply put, Paisley was a horror. She was spoiled, selfish, and mean. She had the same light blue eyes as Babs and Aunt Jean, but Paisley's were full of myopic malevolence.

My cousin had a way of studying you as if she knew all of your secrets. It was unsettling. Added to that she knew just what to say to make you feel badly about yourself all while couching the words in what sounded like a compliment but totally wasn't.

If we had to chuck her out, we'd need to draw straws to see who'd do it. Yes, this was just like who was going to catch and release the spider in the bathroom or answer the front door when a salesman knocked. Sisters or not, when it came to Paisley, bugs, or salesmen, it was every woman for herself.

"Let's get Mr. Loren to do it," I whispered to Soph. She looked at me as if I was a genius. Admittedly, I had my moments.

Soph approached Babs's attorney. Mr. Loren was a middle-aged man in a dark suit with a lavender tie. He seemed comfortable in his attire, as if most himself. His gray hair had receded to a neatly trimmed fringe around the bald dome of his head—not too pointy or too flat. It made me think he had a lot of brains tucked up in there, which was never a bad thing.

Soph murmured to the attorney as Em walked her boss at the insurance company, Mr. Drake, to the door. The man was tall, broad shouldered, and ridiculously good-looking in that Ivy league, clean-cut, speaks three languages and plays tennis every weekend, sort of way.

I didn't like him. I didn't like the way he looked at Em, his hand on her arm while he stared into her eyes with gentle concern. Mostly, I didn't like it because even from across the room I could see two things: One, Em peered up at him as if he was her entire world. Seriously, I expected heart emojis to explode from her eyeballs. Two, the hand he had on her arm was his left one and the gold glint of a wedding band shone on his ring finger for all the world to see. *Ay carumba*, Em was in love with her *married* boss!

I briefly wondered if it was too early in the day to break into the hard stuff. A shot or two of Cuervo might check all of these bad feelings or it could cause me to belt out *Guantanamera* in my loudest drunk voice...so, no tequila then. When Em finally shut the door, all of the guests were gone—except for Paisley, who was loitering in front of the windows, taking in the view of the neighborhood, the town below and the vast ocean. Or maybe not. I followed the line of her gaze and noticed she was fixated on the house next door, Liam's house. That's when I saw Liam, still in his suit, but with his tie loosened, taking a long pull off a Green Flash IPA while he watered some plants in the large pots on his front steps.

The look in Paisley's eye as she studied him was predatory, like she was sizing him up for a run at husband number four. *Hells to the no!* That's when I decided it was time for her to go, git, skedaddle, and move on.

"Paisley." I greeted her with all of my teeth showing. "So nice of you to come, really, great to see you, but I imagine you have a bit of drive to get back to Los Angeles, and we don't want to keep you."

I looped my arm through hers and dragged her to the door. She stumbled along beside me, as if she wasn't very good at walking on those crazy platform stilettos of hers or maybe the skintight, hoochie-mama orange dress—really, to a funeral? —she had on was impeding her progress. Hard to say.

As we passed Soph and Mr. Loren, Soph gave me a wide-eyed look and shook her head. Now I stumbled, pulling us to a halt. Soph gestured to Mr. Loren.

"Paisley, imagine my surprise when Mr. Loren told me you're here for the reading of the will as well," Soph said.

I dropped Paisley's arm without thinking to mask the shock on my face. What could Babs possibly have left Paisley? She loathed her as much as the rest of us, mostly because when Aunt Jean had passed, Paisley didn't even think to call my mother until two days later, after all of the arrangements had been made.

Babs had never forgiven Paisley for that slight so what the heck was she doing here now? Was it possible my mother had plotted some sort of revenge in her will? Did she leave Paisley something truly ghastly? I perked up at the thought. This might actually be fun.

Paisley tossed her head. It was a very expensive cut and color she had going, and the layered chop framed her pointy-chinned face becomingly to make her appear less witchy.

My cousin gave me a side-eye and said, "What? You didn't really think your mom was going to leave anything to you, her big disappointment, did you?"

I lunged for her, but Em captured me in a one-armed bear hug. Some might call it a headlock, if you ignored her forearm around my neck and her heels dug into the carpet, preventing me from reaching our cousin. Damn it!

I shook Em off with a look that said I was fine and we took our seats at the dining room table. Mr. Loren was at the head with Soph and Em on either side. I sat next to Em while Paisley was by Soph. I felt like we were in a situation room, trying to plan our next maneuver, except the person we were at war with had been invited into the planning session.

It might feel like I'm overstating the negativity of the relationship, but no. Paisley was one of those people who always got her way. When we were kids, she was the one who if she got tapped "it" in a game of tag, she suddenly had a horrible stomachache and couldn't play until some other poor shlub, usually Soph, volunteered to be "it" for her at which point Paisley would have a miraculous recovery and be able to play again.

Plus, having known her before the fake boobs, faux blond hair, nose job, and the plumped out lips, it was very difficult for me to feel affection for someone who clearly got all of her self-worth from her appearance. I like authenticity in my people and as far as I could tell the only thing authentic about Paisley was her meanness.

As if sensing the tension in the room, Mr. Loren cleared his throat and brought our attention to him. He had a sheaf of papers in front of him and a large box.

"If you're all ready," he said. "I'll get started."

We all nodded, and he began to read Babs's will. I knew I should have been listening intently, appreciating my mother's final wishes and all that but the finality of it made it hard for me to concentrate. My heart beat hard in my chest. My breathing was unsteady and I was starting to sweat. I couldn't seem to get passed the fact that this was the end. Babs was gone. We were reading her will. She would never complain about my hair, my clothes, or my personality again. I should have been relieved, but instead I felt empty.

I had come to define myself in opposition to Babs. It was a defiant stance that had formed when my father died and remained, propelling me across the country in an act of sheer fuck you, for lack of a better description. I had established a three-thousand-mile-wide boundary between me and Babs, even if it was all for show and deep down, I desperately just wanted her love and approval. Knowing I'd never get it, I became the human equivalent of a walking middle finger.

I lowered my head and closed my eyes. I forced myself to listen to Mr. Loren. I could do this, if not for me then for my sisters.

"And here is the proposed timeline," Mr. Loren was saying. He distributed a single sheet of paper to all four of us.

I glanced blankly at it. I had no idea what it was referring to because during my little existential meltdown I'd missed that portion.

"So, let me be sure I understand," Soph said. Bless her. "Mom wants the three of us to live together in this house for the entire summer."

"Correct," Mr. Loren said.

My eyes widened. Clearly, I had missed some pretty major shizzle.

"And if you don't, you lose everything," Paisley said with a grin. "The house and the money, all of it goes to me! Sorry, but that's my favorite part."

"Are you freaking kidding me?" The words were out of me before I had the brains to hold them in. I blamed the surprise of it all.

Paisley cackled as she read the piece of paper in front of her. She clapped her hands together with a sneer for me. "Looks like you don't get to go back to New York, doesn't it?"

I read the paper. Sure enough, the mean girl was right. For the months of June, July, and August, the Blumer sisters were to live together in this house unless we opted out and then everything went to Paisley.

I glanced at my sisters. Soph was reading over the document, clearly trying to parse out what Babs had been thinking. I knew what she'd been thinking. She'd come up with the perfect way for me to alienate both of my sisters when I refused to fall in with her deranged scheme.

I tapped the sheet and faced Mr. Loren. "This isn't going to work for me. I have a business in New York. I will lose my customer base if I'm gone for three months."

"I told her that," the attorney said with a sympathetic smile.

"And I have children," Soph argued. "I can't just move out of my house and leave my husband and two teenagers to fend for themselves."

"Actually, your mother took it upon herself to arrange for the twins to attend an exclusive camp in Switzerland for most of the summer." Mr. Loren cleared his throat. "She thought it would give them polish."

Soph slapped a hand over her forehead. "Hang on, I think I'm having a stroke."

Em looked between us. I could tell by the wobble in her lower lip that she was losing the battle to keep it together. "So, you're both out?"

"No," Soph and I answered together. Soph continued, "We'll figure it out. I'm sure there is a loophole or a way around this."

"Exactly." I scowled at the attorney. "There has to be some wiggle room."

Em's shoulders sank. "Right, because staying here with me in Gull Harbor is so horrible."

"Em, it's not that," I protested.

"Sure, it is," my youngest sister said. "Just leave then—after all that's what you do best."

With that, Em stormed out of the dining room, her feet pounding on the stairs as she dashed up to her bedroom. The slam of her door echoed through the house, and we all sat there as if waiting for someone else to erupt from the table.

"I think Em has had a very long day," Soph said.

"Understandable," Mr. Loren acknowledged. "I did try to persuade your mother not to do this or at the very least to talk to you all about it first but, well, you know your mother."

"And how," I said. Babs and her endless machinations had struck again.

"I'll go talk to Em," Soph said.

"All right," I said. "I'll hammer out the deets with Mr. Loren."

I ignored Paisley and Mr. Loren gave me a wary look while Soph left the room. I wondered if he thought I was going to pick a fight with my cousin. I would never, okay, that's another lie. I might one day but not today.

Mr. Loren stood and lifted the lid off the box on the table. Judging by his grunt it took some muscle to heft Babs's urn out of the box. He put it on the table with a solid *thunk*. I recognized it as the one the crematorium had listed in their paperwork. It was gold plated with mother of pearl and Swarovski crystals all over it. Very delicate and stylish as a final resting place.

"What is that?" Paisley asked. "Did Aunt Barbara leave her most prized possession to her favorite niece?"

"Not quite," Mr. Loren said. "This *is* Barbara."

"Oh." Paisley made a moue of distaste.

I reached out and ran one finger over the Swarovski crystals that encrusted the top of the urn.

I turned to Mr. Loren and asked, "Did she tell you what she wanted done with her urn? Are we to inter her in a cemetery or did she expect us to keep her with us for the next three months?"

"Yes, the latter," he said.

I blinked. "I was joking."

"She wasn't," the attorney replied.

"So, we'll keep the urn on the mantel or something?" Knowing Babs, she had a very specific placement in mind for her urn.

Mr. Loren checked his notes on the table. "She requested that you keep her on the sill of the main bay window—for the view." He gestured to the large window that overlooked the side yard, the neighbors' houses, the town below, and the sea. "She said this is non-negotiable and failure to keep her on the windowsill at all times would be considered breaking the terms of the will."

"Seriously?" I gestured at the urn. "What if there's an earthquake and she gets knocked off the window sill?"

"If I were you I'd put her back as soon as it's over," Mr. Loren answered. A cackle sounded from the other side of the table. I glanced at my cousin who looked positively giddy.

"What?" I snapped.

"This is just delicious. You have three months of babysitting Mommy Dearest's ashes and if you don't, all of this and the millions in the bank all become mine." Paisley held her arms out wide to encompass the house and all that was in it.

"That's not true, is it?" I asked Mr. Loren. "We can leave the house, can't we?"

He nodded. "Yes, but there are limits. Your mother was very specific. You can work, attend functions, live your lives, but every night you are to be here in this home, as are your sisters."

Like we were wayward teens or something. Talk about conditional love.

"I. Can't. Even." I raised my hands in surrender and leaned back in my seat, as if I could push away this bonkers final request from Babs.

Soph and Em reentered the room. Em was puffy eyed and red nosed as if she'd been crying while Soph looked exhausted. Well, this parting gift from Mom would likely perk them right up. Not.

I picked up the urn. It weighed about four pounds, sort of like hefting a sack of flour. I glanced at my sisters and said, "You're just in time. Babs and I were just going to see Paisley out."

Chapter Eight

Of course, Paisley refused to leave as easily as that, but I tried. She was very concerned with how she would know we were following the dictates of the will. Mr. Loren suggested that trust would be involved. Yeah, Paisley, didn't take that sitting down.

"I think there should be some way to check in," Paisley said. "Maybe we could put a tracking device on the urn and on all of you so that I know you are tucked in right and tight where you're supposed to be, you know, some sort of app or even better a body cam."

"Don't you mean ash cam," Em said. She delivered it without even a hint of sarcasm, and I had to turn away before I laughed out loud.

"This is utterly ridiculous," Soph said. Clearly, she was not in a joking mood. "Mom couldn't expect us to just give up our lives. I mean that's crazy, right? And there will be no tracking device or app. End of discussion."

Paisley planted a hand on her hip and tipped her chin up in full argument mode. "No, it isn't. There needs to be transparency as I intend to carry out my beloved aunt's wishes to the letter."

Em made a low growling noise in her throat. I looped my arm through hers just in case she made a diving tackle at Paisley. It seemed I wasn't the only one that Paisley brought out the best in.

"Whatever you decide to do to monitor the situation is up to you, Ms. Lawson." Mr. Loren scanned the room as if just realizing that he was outnumbered, four women to one man, and the women were getting agitated. "But I can assure you the two dictates of the will are simply that you sleep in your own beds at night and that her urn remains on the window sill for a period of three months." He sighed. "I tried to talk her out of this, but...the will is air tight. There is no wiggle room."

"But I live in New York and have pets," I cried at the same time Soph said, "What about my children?"

"I know and I'm sorry." Mr. Loren looked genuinely aggrieved. He turned to Paisley and in a voice that brooked no dissent, said, "Now if you'll excuse us, Ms. Lawson, there are some matters I need to discuss with Barbara's daughters in private."

Paisley looked like she'd argue so I made a preemptive strike. Circling the table, I caught her by the elbow and hauled her out of her seat. I pulled her toward the door, barely opening it before I shoved her outside. She tottered on her spike heels for a moment, but I didn't pause to see if she keeled over. I gave her a jaunty finger wave and slammed the door.

I returned to the dining room table to find Mr. Loren alone. I glanced around for my sisters, but they were gone. Interpreting my confusion, Mr. Loren said, "What I have to share next is just for you, so I took the liberty of asking Sophie and Emily to step out of the room for a moment. Would you mind closing the door?"

My inner alarm system was clanging really loud. I couldn't imagine why Mr. Loren would want to talk to me alone. All right, I could imagine why but none of it was good. Given our difficult relationship, perhaps Babs had cut me out of the will. Maybe he hadn't wanted to say so in front of the others. I supposed I should be relieved because then I could get back to my life, but instead I felt the hurt bubbling up inside of me, making me feel vulnerable and on the edge of tears.

I shook it off. I was not going to cry. I would accept whatever horrible thing my mother had done as just another twist of the knife in wounds that would likely never scar over. I closed the door and took my seat. I folded my hands on the table and waited.

"Go ahead," I said. "I'm ready for whatever Babs has cooked up next." Lies, but I hoped if I said it often enough, I'd start to believe it.

"This isn't from your mother," Mr. Loren said. "It's from your father."

I blinked and sat up. "Dad? But he's been gone for seventeen years. Why now?"

"When he gave me this twenty years ago, he instructed me that should he die before your mother, I was to wait until she passed before giving it to you," the attorney said. He took a large manila envelope out of his briefcase and handed it to me.

I studied it and then glanced at him. Howard Loren had been my parents' attorney since forever. He and Dad were golf buddies back in the day and he kept Babs's affairs in order after Dad passed. I had known him my whole life and never had I seen him appear ill at ease. Until now.

I ran my thumb under the sealed edge and peered inside. When I reached in, I removed an official-looking document, several photographs, and a letter written in my dad's distinctive spidery handwriting. A quick glance at the photos showed a much younger version of my dad in them with a woman I didn't recognize. My gaze strayed to the document. It was my birth certificate except where Babs name should have been there was a different name. It read Lisa Michaels. My hands started shaking and I tucked them under my arms as if I was a bird folding my wings, trying to stay warm.

"That's not my birth certificate," I said.

"It's your original," Mr. Loren said. "The one you've seen is your amended birth certificate, which is what the court issues when a child is adopted."

"I don't understand," I said, even though deep down I did.

Mr. Loren met my gaze. I saw sympathy and kindness in eyes, and with everything in me I wanted to flat out reject it, but I didn't.

"About twenty-eight years ago, your parents were in a rough patch in their marriage," Mr. Loren said. "Your father's work schedule left Barbara feeling neglected and unhappy which drove a wedge between them. Your father did what a lot of men do and sought solace elsewhere."

"Is that lawyer speak for he played hide the salami with someone else?" I tapped the papers. "Might her name be Lisa?"

Mr. Loren looked pained. I wasn't sure if it was my false bravado or the fact that I'd forced him to spell out for me what all of this meant. He started to explain but I couldn't hear him over the loud rushing noise in my ears. I watched his lips move but there was no sound. It didn't matter. I was just stalling. I knew what I was looking at. I knew what all of it meant. And for the first time in my life, I even knew why Babs had hated me all these years. She wasn't my mother.

The words clicked in my brain like the opening of a lock. My entire life story smashed like a mirror under a heavy fist. The shards tried to reorder themselves into making sense, but I couldn't put the pieces together. They simply didn't fit anymore. As if an escape hatch opened, I glanced to my right to see the floor rushing up to meet me. For the first time ever, I blacked out.

"You have her hair," Soph said. My older sis was sitting in a chair beside the couch where I was lying with a bag of frozen peas on my noggin. I had clipped the table on my way down and now had a nice lump the size of a robin's egg on my hairline. Apparently, Mr. Loren had managed to catch me before I crashed to the floor otherwise the damage likely would have been worse.

At the sound of his yelp, my sisters had come running. Neither Mr. Loren nor I thought to hide the papers from them and after they hauled me to the couch, Em jogged back to the dining room to retrieve my glass of water and saw the birth certificate. Freak out is a woefully inadequate way to describe her reaction, but it's all I've got. It took us another twenty minutes to calm *her* down.

I gave Mr. Loren permission to tell them everything and when he left, he looked like a man who had climbed Mount Everest without a Sherpa. I sort of felt bad for him but thought it might be an excellent life lesson for him to screen his clients more carefully in the future. Clearly, my parents were the worst.

"I always thought you had Dad's hair." Soph had not set down the pictures since Mr. Loren had given them to her.

"Me, too," I said. Suddenly, the image of Babs coming at me with a straightening iron made much more sense.

"I can't believe they did this," Soph said. "I was so sick with the measles right before you were born that I didn't remember much about it. I never remembered Mom being pregnant with you. I always thought it was because I was sick, but it was because she wasn't. I remember they even told me she had to go away because my illness might harm her or the baby. She must have been hiding out, pretending to be pregnant while just waiting for you to be born."

"It's mental," I said. "Who does that sort of thing?"

"Mom," Soph said. She stared off at nothing. "I remember Nana came to stay with us and she made me peanut butter and chocolate chip sandwiches every day for lunch." I just stared at her and then she said, "Sorry. I'm just trying to put it all together."

No one spoke for a while and then Em, sounding stressed, said, "You have a letter from Dad."

"Yes."

"Are you going to read it?" she asked. I thought I heard a note of jealousy in her voice.

"When I'm ready," I said. Another lie. I would have read it right then and there except I didn't want to share it. It was mine. All mine.

"Oh." Em was sitting in the chair beside Soph's. Even though we were not as close as we'd once been, I knew the look on her face. It was the one she got when she wanted something but didn't know how to ask. I wasn't going to help her out. Not this time.

"Are you going to search for her?" Soph's voice was soft as if the question would have less impact if she spoke quietly.

No such luck. The thought of having a mother I'd never known shook me to the core, as if the very foundation upon which I'd built my life had suddenly fallen into a sink hole, or more accurately, a bottomless pit. I felt like I was free falling, with no idea where I would land.

"I don't know," I said.

Soph stared at me for a moment. She put the pictures on the coffee table and said, "I'm going to make some coffee."

Em and I were quiet for a while, each lost in our own thoughts. Babs's urn still sat on the table in the other room. In my mind, I had flashes of such anger that I pictured taking the stupid thing and throwing it through the picture window she had asked to be placed beside. I wouldn't do it, but I imagined it.

"Why?" Em asked.

I glanced at her from under the bag of peas and saw the confusion in her eyes.

"You're going to have to give me more if you want an answer," I said. "Why didn't they tell me? Why hide my original birth certificate? Why didn't Babs just tell me why she hated me all these years? Give me a direction, Emily."

"That." Em waved her hand, making a circle in the air. "All of that."

"I have no idea. Honestly, I don't know who I am more furious with right now, Babs or Dad. All I know is my entire life was a lie."

"Not all of it, we're still sisters," Soph said as she came into the room bearing a tray with a coffee press, three matching mugs, milk, and sugar.

"Sisters, yes," I said. "But apparently only half sisters, at least *I'm* only a half."

We were silent while Soph fussed with the coffee. It was weird to feel as if I was suddenly less a part of the three siblings we had always been. I didn't know how to feel about it.

"Bullshit," Soph said. The word boomed in the quiet room and both Em and I started. "You survived growing up here with *her*, there's nothing half about you."

That helped. The three of us nodded in understanding as only siblings who have shared their life journey with each other and know what a long, strange trip it's been can. Growing up with Babs made for an unbreakable bond. There was a survivorship in navigating a relationship with a volatile woman who viewed her children as reflections of herself instead of people in their own right and we had each developed our own coping skills.

Soph went to college and got involved with Stan Timmons, a medical student at the same university, and by the end of freshman year, she was pregnant and getting married. It was a rather dramatic way to put some distance between herself and Babs, and ironically, since Babs bought Soph and Stan their first house, not coincidentally in Gull's Harbor, they had settled nearby, meaning Soph never managed to go too far.

I had bailed by going to school as far away as humanly possible without leaving the country, and Em, well, she had done the opposite of Soph and me. She had stayed with Babs and become her primary companion, her best friend, her caretaker.

I'd never understood why Em didn't fly the coop when she was eighteen and ready for college, but she didn't. She commuted to school in San Diego, got a degree in communications, and now worked for an insurance company. Despite the bombshell sitting in my lap, of the three of us, I was most worried about Em and how she would deal with the loss of our...her...mother.

Soph pushed down on the top of the press filling the carafe with hot coffee while moving the grounds to the bottom. She then poured three cups and passed one to each of us before she sat down.

"I imagine Mr. Loren will be in touch and tell us what Mom meant exactly about us living together," Soph said. "Probably, she just meant we needed to stay together until the estate is settled."

I sipped my coffee and arched my brow in her direction. "This is Babs we're talking about. That will sounded pretty tight to me."

"Please stop calling her that," Em said.

Both Soph and I glanced at our baby sister. Em's long hair was loose, a beautiful wave of honey that cascaded over her shoulders to ripple halfway down her back. She had two bright spots of pink on her cheeks and her brown eyes looked sad.

"I'm sorry, what?" I asked.

Em didn't meet my gaze but stared resolutely down at her coffee.

"Stop calling her 'Babs,'" Em said. Her voice held a note of panic. "Even if she wasn't your birth mother, she still raised you and you should call her 'Mom.'"

"Other than when talking directly to her, I haven't referred to her as 'Mom' since I left home," I snapped. "And I'm not going to start now—especially now."

I tried to keep the emotion that was boiling just below the surface from showing. I could see that Em was upset and I didn't want to make her more so but I was the one who'd just found out that I wasn't who I thought I was and that my parents had hidden it from me for twenty-seven years.

"I just think if you tried to see things from Mom's perspective—" Em stammered.

"It wouldn't matter. My relationship with *Babs* was always doomed," I said. "Don't you get it? She hated me. Hated. Me. Because of course she did. I was walking talking proof that her husband had strayed. It must have eaten at her every single day."

"We don't know that—" Em took a deep breath and tried again. "I mean just because it looks that way—"

I didn't want to shatter Em's fuzzy ideal about our family, but the reality was that while Babs and I shared a few quasi-tender moments at the end I wasn't going to remember her in soft focus for the rest of my life. We weren't even blood. Too much damage had been done for me to remember Babs as anything less than the vindictive angry woman who'd never forgiven a baby for where she came from.

"I'm sorry, but no," I said. "I can't forgive her or Dad for keeping this from me. They had no right."

"Fine. Cling to your righteous anger. I hope it makes you feel better." Em pushed back her chair and stomped from the room, leaving her coffee behind.

I pulled the partially melted peas off my head and dropped them onto the coffee tray. I glanced at Soph and said, "If she didn't want coffee, she could have just said no."

Soph's gaze was full of sympathy as if she understood that I was suddenly in the unfortunate spot of being the one Em was going to direct her anger about Babs's death upon. Oh, lucky me.

"She didn't mean it," Soph said.

"Yeah, she did." Then I met her gaze. "But I'm okay with it. Em had a different relationship with Babs than I did. I imagine it's hard for her to understand why I am so angry and I am. God, Soph, I am so pissed."

"I know." She nodded and her blonde bob swept across her cheeks. "You have every right to be. I can't believe they did this to you."

We sipped our coffee. The bitterness of the brew curled my tongue. Soph had always like her coffee strong enough to sprout chest hair. I resisted the urge to glance down the front of my dress just in case tweezers were going to be required later.

"I saw Liam today," Soph said after a few minutes. "He said he was sorry for my loss."

"He said the same to me. I wonder how long he had to practice to get the words out."

"He never took his eyes off of you." Soph sipped her coffee, watching me over the rim.

I snorted, ignoring the relieved flutter inside my chest that at least the man wasn't immune to me despite our past. "You sound like your daughter. Hannah told me I should "tap that.'"

"What? My Hannah?" Sophie lowered her cup.

"The only Hannah Banana I know," I said.

"Do you think I need to talk to her?"

"No, she admitted she hasn't "tapped" anything yet," I said.

Soph's spine relaxed, and she sagged against the seat back. "Oh, thank god. I am not up for that. I barely got through the discussion on how tab A goes into slot B and makes baby C and why you don't want to do that until you are at least thirty."

I briefly closed my eyes. "Please tell me the sex discussion between you and your kids did not go down like an IKEA furniture manual."

"It might have," Soph said. "I even used visual aids, which I really think upped my birds and bees game."

"Do we have any vodka for this coffee?" I lifted my mug.

Soph laughed. "You should have seen the twins' faces when we got to the STD portion of my PowerPoint presentation on why they should keep a lid on it. Nothing screams "abstinence" quite like the image of a cankered wanker with a full-blown case of syphilis."

"Sweet baby Jesus!" I shook my head. "And how is their therapy fund?"

"Plentiful," Soph said. "They've grown up so fast. I feel as if I'm losing them and if they go away this summer...I don't know if I can let them go, Jules."

"I know," I said. I didn't. I mean I only had two cats, which was not even close to the same thing, but I hated the idea of not being with them for three months, so poor Soph had to be reeling. "Maybe Mr. Loren can find a loophole. I mean, we can't really give up our lives for three months. Babs can't reasonably expect that. Maybe we could contest the will."

"Maybe." Soph glanced over her shoulder at the stairs. "But I think I know why Babs asked this of us."

"Why?"

"For Em. She's never lived alone. I think Mom wanted us to watch over her for awhile."

I nodded. That, at least, made sense. It was still impossible but at least there was some rationale behind it.

We finished our coffee. Em's cup sat untouched. I knew my younger sister was upset with me, but I still felt like I was the one taken out at the knees and I just didn't have it in me to coddle her right now.

"So, what are you going to do?" Soph asked.

"About?"

"Everything," Soph said. "Your birth mother, New York, Liam, all of it."

"New York isn't going anywhere," I said. "I can work just easily from here as there, although I do miss my cats."

"How are Spaghetti and Meatball?"

"In good hands," I said without elaborating. I was going to have to cry, beg, and plead to get Jessie to continue watching them for me, but desperate times and all that.

"As for my birth mother, I don't know," I said. "It's been twenty-seven years. Who knows where she is or if she'd even want to see me." The mere thought of looking for her made me queasy.

"We can ask Mr. Loren, I guess." Soph looked at me as if this whole situation was surreal, which it totally was and then shook her head. "So, what about Liam? Any idea what you're going to do about that?"

I knew I could have put her off. I could have denied my feelings but to what purpose? To protect myself? As if that had ever done me any good.

"It might just be on my end," I began, wanting her to know that I wasn't being stupid, "but I think there is still something there, something worth investigating. At the very least, I need to tell him I'm sorry."

Soph opened her mouth to speak but then closed it, tilting her head to study me. The affection in her gaze was as warm as the sun.

"If he doesn't give you another chance, he's an idiot," my older sister said, ever my protector.

Soph rose from her seat and took the coffee tray back to the kitchen. She'd sent Hannah and Harry home with enough leftovers to keep the family of four eating for a week. She picked up her purse and glanced through the dining room doorway at Babs in her pretty urn on the table. "I guess I'll go get my toothbrush and prepare to sleep in my old room."

"Is Stan going to be okay with this?" I asked.

"Until we can figure out an alternative, he'll have to be, won't he?" Soph shrugged. "Back in a flash." She ran her hand over the knot on my head and nodded. It was weird to have her doing the mom thing with me. Weird but also kind of nice.

I hugged her before she left just because we both seemed to need it. Soph was much thinner than I remembered, the bones of her shoulders evident beneath my touch. When my older sis was stressed, she didn't eat. I blamed whatever was going on between her and Stan. Would she tell me if I asked her flat out?

I rolled up from the couch, planning to make it an early night. I paused by Babs's urn. I put my hand on the top and a rage so intense it made my fingers shake filled me. I wanted to knock her to the floor. But I didn't.

Instead, I dropped my hand and gazed out the window at Liam's house. His workout room was dark. Not a big surprise, but I was disappointed not to have at least a glimpse of my favorite distraction. Given that I had memorialized the life of my mother, rather my adoptive mother—okay that was weird—today, the fact that I was hoping to ogle the boy next door made me a complete reprobate. Yeah, I was pretty sure I was going to hell.

But honestly, in that moment if I could have looked my fill at Liam, hell would have been totally worth it.

Chapter Nine

It had been three days since the service, three days since I had learned that my origin story was a sham, a charade, a big fat whopper. That I was likely the product of my dad not pulling out in time rather than a miracle achieved by two loving parents. It took me twenty-four hours to find the courage to read my father's letter. As if the emotional beat down of the past few weeks hadn't been enough, I felt myself completely unravel when I read his words.

My dearest Peanut,

If you are reading this, then your mother and I have passed. I know it is selfish, but I hope our departure causes you to grieve at least a little, knowing full well that after you receive this, you'll likely curse us both – justifiably so.

Obviously, Howard has given you the envelope with your original birth certificate, the few photos I had of your mother, Lisa, and this letter. I wish I could hug you as I know this must be a bit of a shock, and I'm sure you're wondering why we didn't tell you sooner. In the simplest terms, I made a vow.

Your mother, Lisa, was a free spirit, a lover of butterflies, ramen noodles, the spicier the better, the sun on her face, and the wind in her hair. She was unlike anyone I had ever known and she cartwheeled into my life just when I needed her most. You were conceived out of that love.

Those were some of the happiest days of my life, anticipating your arrival with the woman who filled my life with everything good. But then your sister Sophie got sick with measles which caused encephalitis and we were sure she was going to die. Being a man of faith, I prayed to God for her to be spared and she was. I knew afterwards that I had to make things right, so I told Barbara about

Lisa and you. She seemed to take it well. She wanted to meet your mother. Looking back, I should have said no, but Barbara had been unhappy in our marriage, too, and I thought we were in agreement to end it. I assumed we'd find a way to raise Sophie and you separately but together. It was not to be.

After one meeting with Barbara, a new plan was suddenly in place. Lisa would give us full custody of you and she would go away for good. My world fell apart after that and the only thing that kept me going was you. When you laughed I heard your mother's laugh. When you smiled, I saw the kindness she had shown me and countless others. She was a good woman, selfless and kind. Do not judge her harshly for walking away. It was not easy for her, but she knew once she met Barbara that your life would be impossible if she tried to stay with me. She felt no child should suffer through that.

When she held you in the hospital that one and only time, she wept and said you were the most beautiful baby she had ever seen. She was right. Then she asked me to make sure that I loved you enough for both of us. As I write this, you are sleeping in the bassinet beside my desk. I hope that when you read this, you will feel that I did love you enough for both of us. You are and always will be my greatest joy.

I have no right to ask, but if you decide to find your mother, please tell her that I never stopped loving her just as I will always love you.

Forever yours,

Dad

I read the letter, cried over it, read it again and again and cried some more. I was in a whirlwind of emotions, running the gamut from sad to angry and back to sad. Frankly, it was exhausting.

After hours of chewing on it, I came to some conclusions. My mother had been bought off by Babs. That was my first thought because I wasn't stupid enough to believe that my birth mother ditched me without some seriously green incentive. My second was what a spineless frail thing Lisa must have been to give up her baby to a shrew like Babs. In my scorching disappointment, I thought maybe I was better off not having been raised by someone so weak. But then, I remembered this was Babs. She always got what she wanted no matter the cost to the other person. I knew this because she had cost me plenty.

Rage filled the vacuum left by my disappointment. I wanted to hurt someone, flay them bloody with caustic words and, if possible, back over them with a car. And not just someone but Babs. I desperately wanted to torture her the way she had tortured me over the years with her scrutiny and nitpicking and withholding of affection. Me, whose only fault was that I was conceived out of love by a woman who wasn't her.

But Babs, that wily bitch, had outmaneuvered me once again. Tying me to my half-sisters—

yep, still weird—with this house and our substantial inheritance. The only way I could hurt Babs would be to pack a bag and walk away, letting her two precious darlings lose everything. That would teach her. That would show her. Yeah, except Babs was dead. There would be no showdown where I got to watch the pain of my betrayal crush her spirit.

And if I did walk away, it would destroy my sisters. Em, who didn't even know who she was without Babs, and Soph, whose marriage in my opinion was rocky at best. If I let the house and the inheritance go to Paisley, what would happen to them? Did I care? Yes. I loved my sisters. Damn it!

I studied the best picture of my birth mother out of the three my father had left me. It was a profile shot of her sitting on the beach watching the waves. She had a determined chin and a slightly upturned nose that I recognized in the mirror as my own. I couldn't tell what color her eyes were but I was betting they were a dark blue, like mine. Her smile looked generous and her hair, oh, her glorious hair. Just the sight of the wild dark curls being tossed on the breeze made my eyes burn and my throat get tight. What would it have been like to be loved by someone like her? By someone who gloried in my rebellious nature? By someone who resembled me, who understood me?

It hurt so damn much. I stuffed the pictures and the original birth certificate, honestly, what was I supposed to even do with that, and the letter from my father into its envelope and then slid the whole thing into a T-shirt. I loved Em, but she was a world class snoop and this, all of it, I wanted to be just mine for a while until I could think about being given up by my mother and raised by Babs and not feel like throwing up. I suspected it was going to take a while.

Thankfully, there was enough that needed to be done around here to keep me occupied, especially since the boy next door had made himself scarce and I didn't even have random sightings of Liam to distract me. If that wasn't enough of a pisser, any time I tried to get Em to confront the reality that was our mother's bedroom, she freaked out. She didn't want anything touched, moved, or donated to charity.

Soph and I were at a loss. Despite the will's dictate that I stay through the summer, I wasn't going to be in Gull's Harbor forever and since Babs had been a shopper right up until the bitter end, her walk-in closet was crammed top to bottom with clothes, jewelry, cosmetics, you name it, if the shopping channel carried it, Babs bought it.

When I looked at her array of stuff, most of it still unused, I couldn't help but think there were a lot of women's shelters who could really use these goods. It killed me that Em was unwilling to part with any of it.

"This is going to take weeks, possibly months, to sort," I said. We were standing in the main bedroom that had been our parents' and then Babs's on the first floor of the house.

"So?" Em asked.

"So, unless you want to be stuck with the burden of doing it by yourself, you need to let me at least start the process," I said.

"No!" Em shouted. She sounded panicked. "Nothing is being given away. Nothing!"

Em was red in the face with her fists clenched at her sides like a three-year-old in the throes of a tantrum. Just like when we were little, this irritated me more than it made me want to jolly her out of her mood.

"Listen, Em," I said. "I know this is hard—"

"Don't!" Em cried. "You've been away for years. You don't get to pretend that this," she paused to gesture wildly around the room, "is the same for you as it is for me."

I sighed. It shouldn't have hurt because she spoke the truth and yet, it did. Now I understood why everything had been so toxic for me here, so not only did I feel like a neglectful sister, I also felt like an interloper, too. Good times.

"Listen, I get that you were closest to Ba...er...her." There, I was trying to make an effort. "And I know you're hurting, we all are, but we still need to deal with this stuff."

I'm a pretty simple gal at heart and clutter of any sort makes me hyperventilate. Frankly, just looking at the closet made me woozy.

"I'm not ready," Em said.

"Okay, how about we talk about it again in a week or two, maybe we could start with just the new items where there's no sentiments attached." I didn't know what else to say. There was no getting around the fact that we had to start sometime and since I was here, now seemed the best option.

"We had a routine," Em said. "I miss it."

Uncertain of where this was going, I listened.

"We had breakfast together every day, then I went to work and Mom spent the day with her friends but in the evening, it was just the two of us." Em brushed a tear from her cheek. "We'd fix dinner together, talk about our days, discuss my outfit for the next day and how I should wear my hair. I don't know how to do these things without her to guide me."

Alarm bells clanged in my head. Em looked like she was on the verge of another meltdown, and I was too stunned by the level of co-dependency that had developed between my baby sister and Babs to ward it off.

"So, you were like, what, a live dress up doll?" I asked.

Yes, I spoke without thinking, clearly, and the expression of frustrated hurt Em turned on me was almost scary in its intensity. It would have been more so if she wasn't hugging one of Babs's wide-brimmed sunhats to her chest at the time.

"No!" she snapped. "Yes. Maybe. Oh, god, I don't know. I just...it was all so much easier when Mom was here. I don't know what to do, how to dress, what to eat, where to go..."

The flow of words stopped as she dropped the hat and sobbed into her hands. My heart ripped right in two for her. It hit me then that she had lost so much more than just a mother, she'd lost her best friend.

"Oh, Em." I pulled her into my arms and held her while she cried.

Soph entered the room and stopped when she saw us. I was more than willing to share the task of comforting the sobbing baby sister. Maybe Soph would know what to say because I sure didn't.

"Hey, you okay, Em?" Soph joined our hug, making it a group thing.

"No," Em said.

"What's wrong?" Soph asked.

I slid out of the hug and let my big sis take over. Through her tears, Em sobbed the same story to Soph that she had to me. Soph glanced at me over Em's head and I shrugged. I'd had no idea that Em was so reliant upon our mother for everything and judging by the look on Soph's face, she hadn't either.

"I'm sorry, Em." Soph's voice was soft, a mom's voice, as if she was talking to one of the twins when they were younger and had just skinned a knee. "I understand how lost you must feel, but you're going to be all right. It's just going to take some time for you to adjust to doing things on your own, but I know you can do it. You can find the new normal. Hey, maybe you'll discover you even like being in charge of your life."

Em's back went rigid. She looked at Soph and then at me as if we had completely let her down. I realized she thought we should step in and take over where Babs had left off. She wanted us to tell her what to do, what to wear, how to style her hair, all of it. Well, I didn't even own a comb, so that was never going to happen.

"You don't understand!" she cried. "You're both so self-involved. You have no idea what I'm going through. None. You just don't get it!"

Em strode out of the room. Soph and I looked at each other. When the front door slammed, we both jumped.

"On the scale of dramatic exits, that was a solid seven," I said.

"Well, she did live with Mom the longest; stands to reason she would have picked up that trait." Soph walked over to the closet and sighed. "This is too much. How are we going to deal with all of this stuff?"

"A match?" I offered.

She laughed.

"We can't do anything without Em," I said. "If that existential crisis is any indicator, she'll flip out."

"Agreed," Soph said. "Should we go after her?"

"No," I said. "Let's give her a little more time."

Soph nodded. We left Babs's room, and I felt my shoulders drop a bit in relief. Maybe I hadn't been as ready to start sorting as I thought.

"How are the twins holding up?" I asked.

"They loved their grandmother, but they're also sixteen," Soph said. "Since they're taking off to do a glam summer of service abroad, their sadness is tempered by the adventure that awaits."

I remembered how Liam had been the center of my teenage world; every thought and emotion was filtered through my relationship with him. I glanced through the living room window over at his house. There was no sign of him, per usual.

"And how about Stan?" I asked. "I barely got a chance to speak to him at Babs's service. Is he doing all right? The doctoring business is good?"

"Yeah, it's good," Soph said. "Really good."

Her smile didn't reach her eyes, and I remembered how tense Soph had been in conversation with Stan. She took her role as older sister very seriously and I knew she wouldn't share personal information readily.

"Is everything between you two okay?"

"Yes, Jules." Soph sounded exasperated, or maybe defensive, either way my radar was flashing that the bridge was out on this convo and I should shush. Naturally, I disregarded it.

"It's just that things seemed off between you," I persisted. I wanted her to know that I was here for her as well as Em.

Soph met my gaze and tossed her mom bob. "Stan is Stan. Have you read Dad's letter yet?"

"Maybe," I said.

"Uh huh," she said. Stalemate.

Neither of us were ready to talk, fine. Except, I wanted to push. "Stan is Stan." What the hell was that supposed to mean? I didn't like Stan and never had. I gave him a pass mostly because he helped to spawn the twins, who were becoming two of my most favorite people in the world, but otherwise, yeah, he was a pretentious jerk with his three-hundred-dollar bottles of wine, golf weekends with his doctor buddies, and his need to buy himself a new luxury car every year. We had nothing in common except our mutual affection for Sophie and the kids.

"Listen, if we're not sorting today, I have a million things to do for the PTO. Call me if you talk to Em first and let me know how she's doing and I'll do the same."

"Roger that," I said. Soph gave me a quick squeeze and then she was gone.

I took a deep breath and absorbed the silence around me. It was lovely. I hadn't been alone, truly alone, since I'd arrived and I found that I missed it. I enjoyed rummaging around in my own head. In New York, I worked at home and spent days with just me, myself, and I, my cats and no one else, and I really, really liked it.

I made a mental note to ask Jessie to text me a picture of my kids. Maybe I could do a quick round trip to New York to pick them up. I really didn't think I could go three months without them.

My friends had warned me for years that I would slowly turn into a crazy cat lady, but so far I had just the two finicky felines and only because I'd found them abandoned. I still traveled, brunched with friends, and maintained a solid rapport with my neighborhood shop owners. The librarian at my branch library adored me and we had weekly chats about books that usually tripled my to-be-read pile, so it wasn't like I was agoraphobic. I was just at peace by myself and navigated the world quite well as a solo unit.

That said, since I'd come home, I was aware that something was missing in my life. It had been a really, really long time, meaning well over a year, since my last relationship and I missed sex. There, I said it. I missed it. I wanted it. And not surprisingly I knew exactly with whom I wanted it.

Babs had spent the time after my father's death alone—seventeen long years with no dates, boyfriends, or significant others to squire her around. She had chosen instead to hunker down and find her companionship in her daughters, mostly Em.

There was nothing wrong with that, I supposed, except I wanted more out of life and it hit me like a slap upside the head that if I didn't get my butt back out there, I stood a very real chance of becoming the bossy older sister Em was searching for to guide her life. No, thank you.

My pulse raced and I needed to get out of this house. I needed the sun on my face, the wind in my hair, and the smell of the sea in my nose. Fifteen minutes later, I had my laptop in its bag in the front basket of my old beach cruiser bicycle, and I was on my way to Liam's Coffee Shop. He could avoid me next door, sure, but he couldn't ignore me as a paying customer. At least, I hoped he couldn't. If the man tossed me out on my keister there wasn't much I could do about it, but I was betting that he wouldn't...although given our past the odds were not in my favor.

I wound my way down the hill, the Pacific's strong breeze wreaking havoc with my crazy brown curls, toward our quaint little town below. It was hard to believe that this was the first time I'd ventured out since I'd arrived. There had been so much happening, I hadn't really had a chance before now. All of the old shops still circled the small green which was anchored by a Methodist church on one end and a Jewish synagogue on the other.

I pedaled past the card shop, the bakery, where I almost stopped, the florist, the bookstore, almost stopped again, the shoe repair place—really, how did old man Mancusi stay in business—

the pizza joint, and finally I turned at the corner and found myself in front of Liam's Coffee Shop.

My heart was pounding so hard that I was pretty sure it was determined to slam right out of my chest, and suddenly the term "ribcage" had a whole new meaning for me. It felt as if my ribs were the only thing keeping my unruly heart from staging a prison break.

"Keep it cool," I muttered to myself as I locked up my bike. "Keep your freak in check. You're just here to get coffee, no big deal."

At that moment, I almost climbed right back onto my bike and headed for home, but the road back was all uphill and I really wanted a cup of coffee, okay, that was a lie. I desperately wanted to see Liam again. Like a worm in my head the idea just kept burrowing deeper and deeper into my gray matter until it was entrenched. There would be no leaving the center of town until I got my fix.

I slung my laptop case over my shoulder and entered the shop in what I hoped was a casual way. Bells hanging on the door handle chimed, announcing my arrival. No one noticed.

The place was bigger on the inside than it appeared from outside. Two baristas were behind the counter in front of me, but the shop then opened into a large L shape. Most of the tables were full and there were shelves of tchotchkes for sale strategically placed to relieve customers of their hard-earned money.

At the far end of the L was a small stage and a chalkboard over it announced that a band called Yuma Beach would be performing that night. Cool. The surf theme was prevalent throughout the shop with surfboards hanging from the ceiling and fastened to the walls. The decor reminded me of the endless hours spent surfing with Liam which were some of the best memories of my life.

I ordered the largest latte they had while scanning the joint for a glimpse of said boy. There was no sign of Liam. I tried to squash my disappointment. According to my sisters, the man owned three of these places. It had been a long shot at best that he would be here instead of one of his other locations.

There was a small table in the corner and I headed toward it, thinking I could at least get some work done while I was here. While my laptop booted up, I took the opportunity to people watch. Typical So Cal crowd: an older, sun-weathered hippie couple that smelled faintly of patchouli, two wannabe celebutantes dressed in micro-minis and chunky boots with their boob jobs fully on display in their mid-drift baring halter tops, a pasty pale balding businessman in a snappy suit talking on his cell phone—seriously, get some sun, dude—and a middle-aged Black guy in baggy shorts, a polo shirt, and a golf visor.

Then there was the guy in aviator glasses who took a seat at a table two over from me with thick blond hair revealed by a partially lowered navy hoodie, reading a newspaper. Well, more accurately, he was skimming the sports page while watching me over the top of his shades.

I studied his face. Maybe thirty, with a firm jawline. He was too young to be an acquaintance of Babs but might be a friend of Soph, although I didn't recognize him. Hmm. Could be he wasn't staring at me but looking past me to see outside. Then again, it was totally possible that my hair had reached all new levels of poof and now resembled a big brown cloud that he couldn't tear his gaze from. I couldn't fault him for that.

I checked my reflection in the black mirror that was my cell phone. Yeah, the hair was decidedly bushy but not enough so that it would encourage staring. I thought about calling him out on his rudesby behavior, but that would mean I had to engage, and I didn't care enough for that sort of scene.

Instead, I opened my email and began to triage my client's requests. Some were urgent, some were not, and some were the whining of high maintenance clients who thought "miracle worker" was part of my job description as their webpage designer. Lucky me.

I started stomping out fires and as always once the issues were crushed into piles of smoking ash, I had lost all sense of where I was and how much time had passed. A prickle of awareness brought my attention from my laptop. Figuring it was the hoodie guy, I glanced over at his table only to find it occupied by an elderly couple playing Scrabble.

Huh. Still, I felt someone's eyes on me. I turned my head and scanned the coffee shop more thoroughly and there he was. Standing just inside the door, with his wetsuit unzipped and riding his hips, his surfboard held by one arm, his hair slicked back with sea water, and his exposed skin a deep sun-kissed bronze. Oh, my Liam.

His baristas greeted him by name, and he gave them a tight nod. Without looking at anyone but me, Liam propped his board against the wall and then he was striding forward right to my table with barely contained fury. Uh oh.

Chapter Ten

Saltwater dripped off the ends of his shaggy dark hair. Normally, I would have jumped up to protect my laptop, but I sat rooted to the spot, unable to speak under the intensity of Liam's gaze. His jaw was clenched, his nostrils flared, and his fingers flexed. I briefly wondered if he was trying to keep from wrapping them around my throat and strangling me.

Without saying a word, he picked up my laptop, tucked it under his arm, and turned away from the table. What? Huh? Crap! Nothing like taking a girl's livelihood to make her snap out of her stupor.

"Hey! Wait," I protested to his back.

He didn't slow down but continued across the coffee shop toward a narrow wooden door tucked into the wall. Given no choice, I snatched up my empty laptop bag and hurried after him.

I pushed through the small door into an office—his, I assumed. It had a large desk with a bookcase behind it, surf art on the walls, and a window with a view of the narrow alley between his building and the one next door.

He stood by his desk with his hands on his hips.

"Liam, please, don't—"

That was all I got out before he grabbed my laptop case from my hands and dumped it on his desk where my laptop sat. He herded me toward the wall until it was at my back, and he was at my front. Then, Liam's mouth was on mine, and I completely lost any sense of myself.

Aggressive and hungry, his lips were slightly parted encouraging me to do the same. As his tongue slid across mine, coaxing my acquiescence, I tasted the salty tang of the sea on him and the memory of all the saltwater kisses we had shared in our youth hit me with a deluge of homecoming and nostalgia that almost took me out at the knees. I grabbed his shoulders and pressed closer, reveling in the feel of his bare skin beneath my hands. I couldn't get close enough.

As if he felt the same longing, he placed one hand on my lower back, anchoring me to him while the other fisted in my hair, angling my head to receive the world's most perfect kiss. He held my body still as he used his lips, teeth, and tongue to plunder my mouth until I was left shaking in his arms, unable to stand on my own and willing to give him anything...just like I'd given him my virginity all those years ago.

Forced to come up for air, Liam wrenched his mouth from mine. He was winded as if he'd just been rolled by an ocean wave. His chest was heaving and I noticed mine was, too. How could nine years have passed, and we still had this combustible reaction to each other?

"At least I didn't have to play dead to get you to notice me this time," Liam said.

I laughed, the sound a breathy growl that heated the air between us.

"You're driving me crazy." Liam pressed his forehead to mine while plunging both of his hands into my hair, holding me in place. His gaze smoldered.

"Same," I gasped.

Then he was kissing me again. His lips moved over my mouth, my jaw, the sensitive spot just beneath my ear that made my insides liquefy. I caressed his sides and felt him shudder. I was pleased to feel his reaction and I smiled against his lips.

"Good," Liam murmured throatily. "It's just so damn good."

His next searing kiss seemed to be without end. Still, it wasn't enough and he lifted me up by the waist, pressing my back to the wall. He reached down and grabbed my leg by the knee and lifted until I got the idea and I wrapped both legs about his waist, pulling him in close and tight.

Liam groaned as he ran his hands down my sides until he found the hem of my shirt. He tugged it up until my skin was exposed and then we were skin to skin. I pressed into him, trying to ease the clawing need I felt for his touch.

As if he understood, Liam moved his hands between us to flick his thumbs over the hardened peaks of my breasts. A gasp and a moan left my lips. I arched my back, pushing my pelvis into his crotch, cupping his hard boy parts with my soft girl ones.

"Sweet Jesus!" He inhaled deeply and yanked my bra aside to suck one of my nipples between his teeth. Instinct took over and I ground against him unleashing a frenzy of need between us as he turned his attention to my other nipple. I grabbed him by the hair, holding him in place.

With a grunt, Liam lurched upright taking me with him. He turned and strode toward the desk. He plopped me down on the edge and then bent over me, tugging at my clothes as I pushed at the wetsuit at his hips.

Bang. Bang. Bang. A fist rapped on his office door, startling us both.

"Liam, the coffee distributor is here and she's got some paperwork for you," a girl's voice, I recognized it as one of the baristas, called through the door. "She says it's important."

"I'll be right out." He gritted the words out. His jaw tight.

Liam pressed his forehead to mine, cupped my face, and kissed me once firmly on the mouth. "I'm coming to see you tonight," he said. He held my gaze and added, "Not for a conversation."

He tugged my clothes into place and stepped back from me. The scorching look in his eyes made it perfectly clear what he meant. Us. Sex. Tonight. Yes, please!

"Okay." I nodded with an enthusiasm that might have been embarrassing if I wasn't so hard up. He gave me a wicked grin and then left me alone in his office to get my act together. What an optimist that boy was. I was a hot mess and likely to remain so.

The ride uphill was not nearly as arduous as I'd expected, mostly because knowing Liam was coming over later was a great motivator. I pedaled right into the open garage and parked my bike against the wall. Em's car wasn't there so I assumed she was still out. That gave me pause.

I'd assumed she'd be home by now. I hoped she'd met up with some friends, mostly to take her mind off of Babs but also, selfishly, because it would be great if she wasn't here when Liam dropped by. Even though we weren't going to be talking, I suspected we were going to be loud.

My insides started to hum in anticipation. I couldn't believe we were going to do this, more accurately, do *it*, but then I supposed I should have seen where my voyeuristic tendencies were leading. Obviously, I had given Liam the signal that I was his for the taking. The thought made my heart pound even while my brain paused and asked if this was what I really wanted. I told my brain to shut the hell up.

Before jumping into the shower, I decided to call my friend and cat sitter, Jessie Lopez, and check in. Yes, the same Jessie Lopez I had left Gull's Harbor with all those years ago.

Jessie answered on the third ring.

"Jules, sweetie, how are you?" Jessie asked. "And how is our seaside little hamlet nestled in the heartland of fruits and nuts?"

"It hasn't changed a bit," I said. "Even Mr. Mancusi is still here fixing shoes."

"How does that guy stay in business?"

"I know," I said. "It boggles. How are my kitties?"

"They miss their mama," Jessie said. "No, that's a lie. They love having me dote on them, they hardly even remember your name."

"You're funny, but really, I can't thank you enough," I said.

"Don't mention it. And I mean that. Don't mention it. I don't want anyone else taking advantage of me like this."

I laughed and was hit with a pang of longing to see Jessie. Having moved to New York City together, we were bonded by that adventure which started with us being two surfboard-riding, beach-bum-So-Cal kids three thousand miles away from home transplanted in a fast-paced frenetic city that never slept and had ended in serious best friends forevership.

"How are you doing really?" Jessie asked. "I know you and Babs had a complicated relationship but it's still got to be tough, especially now that you know—"

"Understatement," I interrupted. I had told Jessie about the bombshell of my birth mother, but I wasn't up for talking it over right now.

"Yeah." Jessie got it. Having a similar complicated sort of thing in the parental department, Jessie understood more than anyone the mix of emotions I'd been churning through since I'd arrived in Gull's Harbor. "So, have you seen *him* again?"

Jessie sounded casual, too casual, and I knew Jess, too, had a million unresolved feelings for Liam who was a former best friend. They had been the best of the best, right up until the night Jessie fled town with said best friend's girlfriend—i.e., me.

I wasn't going to lie to Jessie. Lies, I had discovered over the years, forced a new identity onto the liar, like wearing one of those hideous latex Halloween masks that makes it hard to breathe, only you can never take the lie off and it slowly suffocates the person you once were. Yeah, sure, wearing the mask seems like a good idea at the time but after a few hours in it, you realize it's killing you and there's nothing you can do about it. So, no lies.

"Actually, he's coming over tonight," I said.

Silence greeted this news.

In my mind, I could see Jessie mulling this over, probably pacing in a bathrobe with an espresso or a martini, or an espresso martini in hand.

"How did that come about?" Jessie asked. "I thought you were just enjoying the view of the man candy from your bedroom window."

I had already confessed my voyeuristic tendencies a few days ago when I'd called to tell Jessie about Babs's passing.

"Yeah, well, I was in his coffee shop earlier." I winced at Jessie's loud shout of disbelief and lowered the volume on my headset.

"You were in his shop?" Jessie sounded stunned. "Exactly when did you level up to out-and-out stalking?"

"I wasn't looking for him," I fibbed. Technically, a fib is not a lie. "I can't help it if this tiny town only has one coffee shop."

"Puleeze, you can buy coffee at the gas station or, you know, make your own."

"Whatever," I said, feeling defensive. Tension filled the airwaves.

"What are you going to tell him about me?" I detected a tiny hint of worry in Jessie's tone.

"Nothing," I said. "He very specifically said he wasn't coming over to talk."

"Oh...oh! Well, that escalated quickly." Jessie's voice had a bit of bite to it. "Good old, Liam, always gets the *girl*, doesn't he?"

"Jessie, don't..." I said.

"It's all right. I'm in a better place now, a great place, really. I'm so over it."

"Are you sure?" I asked. "You're my best friend. I don't want to do anything that would hurt you, but I...I need this. I need *him*."

"No, it's cool." There was a pause and then Jessie's voice was filled with mischief. "I forgive you so long as you call me tomorrow with all the juicy details."

"You're a pervert," I said with a laugh.

"This is news?"

And just like that, things were okay between us. The relief I felt was huge.

"So, what are you wearing?"

"And now we're done." I opened the refrigerator and debated pouring myself a glass of white wine to help my nerves.

"No, no, you can't leave me hanging. Just give me a hint! Are you going for casual or slutty? I vote for slutty by the way."

Panic surged through me. I hadn't even thought that far ahead. I glanced down at my jean capris and bohemian blouse. Liam had already had his way in this outfit, probably, I should mix it up, but in what? I really was a blue jeans and T-shirt sort of gal, raising my game was going to require, oh, damn, I probably needed to shave my legs.

"I have to go," I said.

Jessie laughed. "You're freaking out now."

"No, I'm not," I fibbed, again. "Do you think a dress is too much?"

Jessie's voice was soft. "No, I think that's perfect."

"Thanks, Jessie," I said. "Love you."

"Love you more."

I ended the call. My palms grew sweaty, my heart raced, and for a minute I couldn't remember my name. It took three laps of pacing around the house, a half glass of wine, and a long hot shower to get my nerves if not steady at least marginally under control. Since I didn't own a dress, I borrowed Soph's blue one, again, along with a pair of strappy silver sandals that would put me eye-to-nose level with Liam. I felt it might balance the power in the room.

Ha! Who was I kidding? He had all of the power. I had none. I was weak-willed and pathetic when it came to Liam Mahony, as this afternoon at his coffee shop had proven. The only thing that allowed me any dignity at all was that Liam seemed just as powerless against the pull between us.

Since Liam hadn't given me a specific time to expect him, I assumed he'd arrive sometime around six o'clock which, according to my hyper focus on all things Liam, was when he usually arrived home to work out.

Soph wouldn't arrive until late, as she planned on staying with her family until they went to bed to get all her time in with the twins before their epic adventure. There was still no sign of Em, however. I texted her to let her know Liam was coming over but didn't really expect a reply since she was most likely still angry with me and Soph, and the news that Liam was dropping by wasn't going to win her over; if anything, she'd probably be even more peeved with me.

I was in my room, checking my reflection for the fiftieth time, not an exaggeration, when the doorbell chimed. With a quick glance around for anything out of place I spied a sock under the bed and tossed it in the closet, which was a total time warp. Seriously, it was exactly like when we'd stolen moments together in high school when Babs was out of the house.

I raced down the stairs with my dress billowing around my knees. I felt very feminine and for a second, I considered wearing more dresses and then I was at the door. I yanked it open without checking to see who was on the other side. I didn't need to—even through three inches of solid oak I could feel the tension, the awareness, the longing inside of me that only Liam could conjure. It spiked to a fever that flared as I took in the sight of Liam Mahony standing on my front stoop.

His dark brown hair was in its usual disarray, as if he hadn't combed it since I'd had my fingers burrowed in it that afternoon. He wore a fitted short-sleeve, pale-blue button-up shirt that made him seem even more muscled than when he was shirtless, dark jeans, and brown leather Vans. He smelled like aftershave. I wasn't the only one who'd put in some effort for this evening.

His arms were crossed over his chest and his sexy gaze took in my loose curls, pausing for several heartbeats at my lips, then slowly slid down my curves, all the way to my delicate sandals and then back up until his eyes met and held mine.

"I like the dress," Liam said. "Take it off."

Chapter Eleven

Heat flared inside of me and I grabbed Liam by the shirtfront and pulled him into the house, slamming the door shut behind him.

That was the last move I got to make. Liam had me pressed up against the wall with his mouth on mine, his fists in my hair, his hips locking me in place before I even had a chance to take a breath.

"You look the same, you feel the same, you even smell the same," he growled in my ear. "After all this time, how is that possible?"

I would have said the same about him, but he didn't give me a chance as his mouth came back to mine. His lips were fierce as if staking a claim, making my heart thump hard in my chest while I kissed him back. I wanted him to know how much I had missed him, this, us.

"Liam," I said his name on an exhale that sounded an awful lot like surrender. It was. In those moments, I would have given him anything and judging by the look in his eyes, he knew it.

"Tell me that you want this," he demanded. He ran his lips down my throat to nuzzle at the neckline of my dress.

I arched up against his mouth, desperately wanting more. I whispered, "I do."

I felt him smile against my skin as he tugged down the neckline of my dress. His fingers dipped inside and he pinched the already hardened peak of one breast. My head fell back against the wall and I groaned. As if this encouraged him even further, he hooked my bra cup with one finger and yanked it down. He put his mouth on me and it felt as if my nipple was hot-wired to the pulsing throb directly between my legs.

"So good," I murmured.

He purred against my skin and then he tugged my clothes back into place. I blinked at him, registering the loss of his wet mouth right before he pulled me away from the wall and guided me toward the stairs.

"If we stay here much longer I'm going to take you right here against the wall," he said. "And that's not how I pictured this going."

Oh, my!

On shaky legs, I turned and led the way upstairs. When his hand ran from the small of my back down over the curve of my ass, I stumbled. Liam didn't let me fall but rather caught me close, putting his arm around my back, pressing his body into my side as his warm palm cupped my hip, keeping me close, as if my hipbone had been shaped specifically for him to hold.

Every cell in my body was hyperaware of him. The hard roped muscles barely restrained by the form-fitting shirt, the scent of sunshine and sea that swirled around him, the feel of his hot gaze on the side of my face as he studied me. I was torn between stripping myself bare in front of him to offer him everything I had, and pushing out of his arms to run as far as fast as I could.

Stripping won.

We reached my room and I pushed the door open, leading the way inside. I supposed if I'd been in my rational mind or even marginally polite, I would have started a conversation or offered him a beverage, but I wasn't rational or polite. In fact, I was barely in control of the crazy, lust-infused desire I felt for this man, who I had never, not once, stopped loving over the past nine years.

It was a truth I knew I couldn't share with him or anyone.

Liam followed me inside and then kicked the door shut. He didn't glance around the room or pause to assess whether I was a good housekeeper or not. No, his focus was solely on me. I didn't turn on the light, preferring to stay in the shadows. Liam had no such reservations. He snapped on the bedside lamp, casting the room in a soft glow.

He started to walk toward me. I stood my ground right in front of the bed, refusing to back up or look away. I didn't want him to know how overwhelmed I was by him, by us, by our dramatic past that slithered around us in the shadows just waiting for the first sign of weakness to raise havoc and mayhem between us. I refused to let it.

When he stopped in front of me, I reached for him. Without saying a word, I grabbed him by the shoulders and pulled him in. He didn't fight me. When I twined my arms about his neck and put my mouth on his, he stood completely still as if committing my every move to memory.

I pressed myself into his chest while my arms moved over his shoulders and down, holding him close while I parted my lips and let my tongue trace the seam of his lips. I was gentle, teasing, tasting, drawing his lower lip into my mouth and then nipping it with my teeth. He groaned a low rumble in his throat and opened for me, letting me slowly make love to his mouth, mimicking with my tongue what I was hoping his body would do to mine.

He stood perfectly still while I drank him, wooing him until I felt the telltale hard press of his erection against my pelvis. Yes! I wanted to pump my fist, but I was too busy running my hands across his muscled back and then spreading my hands to cup his butt and bring him in closer.

I thought I was in control of this seduction. I thought I was the one making love to my ex-boyfriend. I thought wrong, so very wrong. He wrenched his mouth away from mine.

"Tell me what you want," he demanded.

His fingers were at the hem of my dress. He lifted the skirt and put a hand on each of my thighs. His thumbs ran up along the inside. I couldn't breathe. I couldn't think.

"Tell me," Liam ordered. His hands stilled and I got the feeling that if I didn't tell him what I wanted he was going to stop, which was not even comprehensible to me at this moment.

"This," I said. "I want this."

"Be specific, surfer girl," he said. His voice was stern. The teenage boy I'd been so in love with had never spoken to me like that. I was alarmed that I found the command in his voice to be incredibly hot. What was wrong with me?

He started to move his hands away. I panicked. I wanted those hands to stay right on course.

"You," I gasped. "I want you."

He raised one eyebrow at me and I knew I'd said what he wanted to hear. His hands began to move again, slowly, tracing circles on my skin, back toward the ache that throbbed between my legs. He was so close, so deliciously close, I was sure if he didn't put his hands on me soon I would die.

I pressed closer to him and dug my hands into his hair to angle his head just the way I liked it so I could fully claim his mouth with mine. And, oh, his fingers were close so close. Given the chance, I would beg, I would absolutely plead, to feel him press his thumb on my clit.

Finally, his fingers were within reach. One thumb slid over the hot, wet part of me that was positively throbbing but as I moaned in sweet relief, he yanked his hand away.

No! I wanted to cry out in protest but I couldn't even form the word.

"Jesus, Jules, you...you're not wearing...Christ, you're bare assed," he said.

At any other time, I would have taken great pleasure in his surprise but right now I had other needs, specifically, getting us both naked down under.

"Sorry, laundry issues," I said, my voice breathy and bewildered. "I keep forgetting to run a load so..."

"Do. Not. Apologize." He punctuated every word with a kiss and the heat in his gaze let me know just how much my inability to maintain my laundry turned him on. "I think you should always forget."

His hands dove back under my dress and a slow smile curved his lips as his hands moved back up my legs to cup my bare backside. I barely had a chance to register the feel of his callused hands on my skin when he was lifting me and tossing me back onto the bed. He wasted no time but flipped the fabric up so that I was completely bare to him from the waist down.

He hissed a breath and when I would have sat up to pull him down with me, he put a large warm hand right below my breasts and held me still.

"No, don't move," he said.

I flopped back against the mattress. I stared up at him and the man before me merged in my mind with the young man who had stood over me just like this. Back then we'd been so young and totally inexperienced but we'd fumbled through it together with laughter and wonder as we'd unlocked the mysteries of each other's body. Did he remember it like I did?

As if in answer to my unspoken question, he shifted so that he was lying on his stomach in between my thighs. When I glanced down, I could see his sun-browned hand pinning me to the bed while his thick thatch of dark hair tickled the soft skin on the inside of my thighs as he moved closer to my sweet spot.

"This," he said. His lips parted and his breath puffed against the hot flesh that was pulsing with need. "This is all I have been able to think about."

"Please," I begged. "Please, I need..."

I lifted my hips, trying to get closer to him. He held me still with a *tsk* and then with his other hand he swiped his thumb right over my clit making me lurch up at the jolt of pure sensation that rocketed through me.

"What is it that you want, Jules?" Liam kissed my inner thigh. "My mouth?"

"Yes," I growled.

"My fingers?" He swiped his thumb over the sensitive flesh again.

"Ah, y...yes." I panted.

"Or my cock?" His voice was a low growl that made me shiver and sweat at the same time. "Is that what you want, Jules, my cock inside your pussy?"

"God, yes," I cried. His dirty talk was making me dizzy and for a second I thought I might pass out.

"I'm going to make you come with my mouth," he said. He opened his mouth and put it right on my girl parts, sliding his tongue across the aching, throbbing folds. I ground my head into the mattress feeling like this was going to be the fastest orgasm I had ever achieved. But he pulled away before I got there and I almost wept with frustration.

"Then I am going to make you come with my fingers," he said. When he said it, he slid a finger inside of me and my muscles convulsed around him as if they could keep him prisoner. They couldn't. He withdrew his hand and this time I actually felt the pinprick of tears behind my eyelids.

"And then I am going to fuck you and make you come again and again and again," he said.

He took his hand off of my middle and put one hand on each thigh, spreading me wide open. I was beyond any shyness or second guesses. All I knew was that I needed him, needed this, and I would give him anything just to make the aching throb go away.

He put his mouth on me and began to work his magic. He sucked, licked, nuzzled and then when I didn't think I could stand it another second, he used his tongue to go deep while he used his thumb on my clit like it was a trigger. Before I could even register it, I was arching my back and crying out as a wave of bliss burst from beneath his lips and shot out to the edges of my skin in waves of pleasure that had me gasping and panting and swearing.

I collapsed against the bed but Liam wasn't having any of that. He pulled me up to a seated position, tugged my dress over my head and tossed it into the corner of the room. Clad in only my high-heeled sandals and my bra, I was too blissed out to be self-conscious. In one deft maneuver, Liam had the bra unhooked and it went the way of the dress.

I reached for him, cupping him through his jeans and giving him a gentle squeeze. I wanted to return the favor of one of the best orgasms of my entire life, seriously, I was game to swallow and everything, but he gently moved his hand away.

"Not yet," he said.

"But I want..."

"Shh," he said. "It's still my turn."

Oh, wow.

He kissed me and I could taste myself on his lips. It made my pulse thrum and I wrapped my arms around his neck and clung to him, kissing him with everything I had, trying to get him to understand that I had never stopped loving him.

He pulled my arms from around his neck and pushed me back onto the bed. Now that he had full access to my body, he took full advantage. His mouth nipped my more sensitive places, sometimes leaving marks. I didn't care. I welcomed the evidence that I had him back in my life, in my bed, and in my heart.

The naughty feel of his jean-clad thighs between my bare ones made my insides writhe and twist in the most delicious way. The slow burn of desire churned inside of me, bubbling up to the surface, looking for release. Only Liam could fill me with such longing. In all the years we'd been apart, I'd had only a few relationships—all of which were doomed before the start because nothing and no one had ever compared to Liam Mahony.

Sensing I was close, he slid first one finger inside of me, teasing me by pumping it in and out before adding a second and swirling them together. Again, I was bucking my hips, trying to get him closer, get him deeper, feel him all the way down deep inside my core.

"What do you need, Jules?" He moved his fingers in and out and then leaned down to nip the hardened point of my nipple.

Unable to form a coherent sentence, I moaned. I tried to show him what I needed by grabbing his hand and encouraging it to go faster and deeper. He used his other hand to capture both my wrists, dragging them over my head and holding them down while he kept moving his fingers in and out in a slow leisurely slide that did nothing but make me crazy.

"What do you need, Jules?" he asked again.

"Faster," I panted. "Deeper."

His dark eyes met mine and he looked like he wanted to devour me but was holding himself back.

"And who do you need it from?" He lowered his head and put his lips on the sensitive spot right below my ear. His voice was a gruff whisper, making me tremble. "Who, surfer girl, who do you need?"

"You," I cried out. The sound of his old nickname for me in his gravelly voice made my insides spasm.

"Say my name," he said. His voice was firm with the demand. "Say my name, Jules."

He pulled his fingers almost all the way out of me and paused, not moving his hand, and I was desperate to feel his touch. Desperate to feel him fill up the huge emotional void inside of me.

"Liam," I said.

"Say it again," he ordered.

"Liam, please," I cried. "Liam."

Satisfied, he shoved his fingers in deep again and again and the relief was so great that my body began to shudder and convulse from some sort of epicenter that his touch had tapped. I arched my back and pushed up against his touch as I cried out, "Liam. Liam. Liam."

I felt as if I'd been blown apart and my pieces had to float down from the ether and fall back into place. Aftershocks hit me, rippling through me as I blinked into awareness. I found Liam standing beside the bed. He had his arms crossed, his jaw clenched and his nostrils flared.

Without saying a word, he grabbed one of my legs and flipped me over onto my stomach. I heard the zipper on his jeans slide down and I went to rise up, but he put his hand on my back and held me in place.

"No, don't move," he said.

I stilled. I wasn't sure what he wanted from me, and I was so undone, I was willing to do whatever he required. I heard the rip of a wrapper and knew he was putting on a condom. Liam was going to do exactly what he said. I should have been sated. I should have been happy to curl into a ball of contentment and sleep for a week, but the thought of him pressing inside me made my insides liquefy and the desire inside of me lifted its big blocky head and roared.

He pushed my thighs apart and without saying a word, he slammed inside of me in one fierce thrust. My body wrapped around him like a tight fist and he leaned over my back, pressing his lips into the nape of my neck.

"So good," he whispered. "So fucking good."

The heat inside of me unfurled and when he grabbed my shoulders in his callused palms and held me still while he pounded into me, I fisted the comforter in my hands and arched my back meeting him thrust for thrust. He grunted and swore, and I felt my body tighten around his, clenching him as it climbed back toward orgasm.

"Damn it, not yet," he said.

He pulled out of me and flipped me over. Without taking off his shirt or his pants, he spread my legs wide and thrust back up inside of me but this time he didn't move. He held still. There was a dangerous look in his eyes and I knew it didn't bode well for me. He had said he was going to fuck me for hours, oh my god, and as much as I loved the idea of that I realized he was working awfully hard to maintain control of what was happening between us. Yeah, that didn't really work for me. In the orgasm department it was great but I wanted him to feel as mindlessly out of control as I did.

I ran a hand through his hair and he shuddered. Then I traced the curve of his lips with my finger before moving my hands to his shirt, which I unbuttoned while he stayed motionless, staring at me as if trying not to be distracted by the feel of my hands on his skin as they slid down his sides to reach into his jeans and gently cup his balls.

"Don't," he growled.

He shook his head as if he was trying to shake me off. His hands were locked into fists on either side of my head. It was clear he was keeping himself immobile to try and regain his control. Not if I had anything to say about it.

I arched, pushing myself up against him. His breath hissed out between clenched teeth.

"Jules." His voice was full of warning.

I ignored him and lifted one leg, sliding it up over his shoulder and then the other. I grabbed the belt loops on the side of his jeans and pulled him in tight.

"Damn it, Jules, stop," he said.

"Make me," I said.

I met his gaze and was surprised I didn't see flames leap up in his irises the look he gave me was that hot. I smiled at him and then I started to clench my inner muscles around his cock, squeezing him tight the same way I had when we were just young teens figuring it out.

"Oh, fuck me," he said.

He grabbed my hips and began to slide in and out of me, picking up speed, creating the sort of friction that started fires. It sparked inside of me, igniting the embers of my need.

Together, we became a frenzy of heat and desire. I met him thrust for thrust, raising my hips and bringing him deeper inside. Sweat poured off of him, dripping onto my chest and making our skin slick. He let go of one hip and fisted a hand in my hair. He pulled me up to meet his kiss and his tongue dove into my mouth mimicking the possession below until I felt wholly consumed by him.

The orgasm when it started made me catch my breath. Slicing me wide open on the razor edge of pleasure and pain, I cried out into his mouth as I was torn apart by the euphoria that ripped me asunder. My body convulsed around his, causing him to thrust deep inside again and again until his own body went tight, locked with mine, as he came with a shout and a groan and collapsed on top of me in the spent embrace of a lover.

It was the same sound he used to make when he came inside of me and the feel of him holding onto to me as if I was all that grounded him to this place and time, that, too, was poignantly familiar. Again, I was filled with the sense of coming home.

I was half afraid that I was blacking out so intense was my release and I held onto him, trying to get my bearings. Liam was having none of it, however. He pulled my arms from around his neck and pushed away from me. He staggered to his feet, removed the condom and tied it off before tossing it in the trash. He tucked himself back into his jeans and zipped them up.

His shirt was still undone but he didn't seem to care. Liam stared down at me but instead of the soft gaze of a man becoming reacquainted with the lover of his youth, he looked cold and hard and emotionally removed.

"Well, that's that then," he said.

"Excuse me?" I blinked at him not understanding.

"This," he said. He gestured in between the two of us. "We're done now. I just needed to get you out of my system."

"Out of your system?" I repeated. Horror chilled the blood pumping through my veins, making my entire body grow cold. He wasn't searching to reconnect. He was looking to fuck and forget. The bottom dropped from my stomach.

"You heard me." Liam didn't meet my gaze but instead attempted to fasten his shirt buttons. Irritated with his own shaky fingers, he gave up and glared at me. "What did you think this was, Blumer? A reunion? You left me. You left me without saying a word, no goodbye, no note, no nothing, and you took off with my best friend. Surely, you didn't think there was ever any coming back from that, did you?"

"But there's so much I—"

"No, there isn't." Liam tipped his head to the side and then ran the back of his hand over his mouth. "There is nothing between us. I wanted to fuck you to make sure that what Jessie took away from me all those years ago wasn't worth having anyway. And guess what? I was right."

Chapter Twelve

Liam went back to fastening his shirt as I remained stretched out on the bed, naked, vulnerable, and more devastated than I ever could have imagined. It felt as if Liam had reached right into my chest and ripped my heart out. As if that weren't enough, he threw the still beating muscle to the ground like so much trash. It occurred to me that it was a small miracle I was still alive; honestly, it hurt so bad I was stunned to find I hadn't keeled over dead.

I grabbed a pillow and hugged it my chest, hiding myself from him and comforting myself all at the same time. I pushed the curls out of my face and willed myself not to cry. What had I been thinking, plunging headlong into sex with him when I knew he had to despise me for leaving town with Jessie all those years ago? If the situation were reversed...yeah, I would still love him...just like I knew, I *knew*, he still loved me.

He finished the last button and I sprang from the bed, moving to stand between him and the door. He'd had his say and now it was my turn.

"Move aside, Jules, we're done here."

"Liar!" I pointed a finger right at his chest to emphasize my argument.

He blinked. Obviously, I'd surprised him. Maybe he thought or even hoped that I'd curl up into a ball of sobbing heartbreak, but he hadn't counted on one thing. I knew him better than anyone save myself. I knew when he was happy, sad, angry, frustrated, and being a big fat liar.

We'd spent much of our youth lying to our parents so that we could be together. We fibbed about going to the library, really, we were surfing. We prevaricated about going on a school field trip, when actually we were skipping school to hang out in San Diego for the day. And I'd stood silently beside him while he'd looked his parents right in the eye and told them we were just studying together; yeah, only if human sexuality was the subject at hand, by which I mean our hands on each other all the time.

Liam's tell had always been to tip his head to the side and run the back of his hand over his lips, which he had just done when he told me there was nothing between us. Ha! Busted!

He raised his hands in a calm down gesture. So patronizing. Did he really think that was going to work with me?

"Listen, I get that you're upset—" he began.

"Oh, I'm not upset," I said, cutting him off. "No, I think a better word for what I'm feeling would be determined."

He narrowed his eyes at me. "I'm not following."

I laughed. "No, but you will be."

Now he looked wary. Smart boy.

"What are you up to?"

"Me?" I tossed the pillow aside and placed my hands on my hips. He tried not to look at me standing in front of him butt naked with my chest thrust out and one knee bent in a red-carpet pose. He tried and failed.

"You." He made it sound like a curse.

"Nothing." I shrugged. "I am however calling you on your bullshit."

His eyebrows shot up and he reared back as if I'd slapped him. Caught off guard, it was the perfect time for me to wrap my arms about his neck and pull him close. He hissed out a breath and I felt his crotch instinctively press closer to me.

"Jules, this doesn't mean anything," he said. "I'm a dude. If there's a strong wind blowing my dick gets hard."

"More bullshit." I leaned up on my toes and pressed my mouth to his. I half expected him to push me away. He didn't, so I made the kiss count. It was long and lingering, and he shuddered as if it was taking everything he had not to drag me back to bed.

Good.

"Here's the thing," I paused to run my lips up the side of his neck to the pulse point beneath his jaw that was beating pretty fast for a guy who said this meant nothing. "I get that you're angry with me. You have every right to be, but there are reasons, things I can't explain, well, it doesn't matter. The truth is I know how I feel about you and I know you feel the same way about me, too."

"You're wrong," he said. It might have helped his argument had he not said it through gritted teeth.

"I don't think so." I released him and stepped back, letting my eyes linger on his obvious reaction to my nearness. "I'm going to win you back."

Liam looked equal parts aroused and affronted at my declaration. He closed his eyes and stretched his neck as if he could shrug off whatever he was feeling by cracking the tension in his shoulders. Yeah, no.

When he opened his eyes, it was clear that anger had won. He lowered his brows, looking foreboding, and took a step toward me. I refused to cover myself or back up and instead I tipped my chin up as if daring him to come closer. He did. He invaded my personal space and loomed over me. Despite wanting to touch him, I kept my hands to myself and made my face as bored as possible.

"Let me be very clear. There is no chance, none, that we are getting back together—ever," Liam said.

I continued to stare at him like a mom patiently waiting out her child's tantrum. Yeah, it was condescending and probably not my best strategy, but I was operating on reduced brain capacity since the man had just banged me senseless.

"I mean it, Jules," he said. I continued to stare. "Damn it, I'm serious."

"I'm sure you are." I tried to sound sincere and not like I was humoring him, but I don't think it came out that way, at least, not judging by his flared nostrils or jaw muscles bunched into hard knots.

"Years of my life were spent getting over you," he said. "I am not going back there again. Not when I have finally moved on with my life."

We had just slept with each other. How did he figure he'd moved on? My thoughts must have shown on my face because he stomped over to the bed and yanked off the comforter, shoving it at me.

"I'm seeing someone," he said. "And before you ask, yes, it's very serious."

It was a punch to the chest that I hadn't seen coming. I sucked in a breath as my cheeks flamed hot with mortification. He was seeing someone else? What? Who? And he'd just slept with me! Who did that?

He stared at me. "Do you get it now? I am over you."

Well, that hurt. Oh, god, it was true what he'd said then. He really *was* over me. He'd just wanted to fuck me as he so nicely put it "to get me out of his system." I felt a tiny bit queasy, okay, not a tiny bit. I was pretty sure I was going to gack on his shoes, the shoes he hadn't even bothered to take off while we doing the horizontal mambo. Then again, I hadn't taken off my shoes either...for some reason that leveled the playing field.

Wait a second. How could he be seeing someone and I didn't know? Why hadn't I seen this woman at his house, working out with him, in his yard, or at his coffee shop? If it was so serious, wouldn't she have been around at some point since I'd been here?

"Serious, huh?" I shook out the blanket and wrapped it around myself.

"Very," he said.

I don't think I imagined his relief at my body being covered up. Interesting. I let the blanket drop, exposing one boob. His pupils dilated. Hmm. I let the blanket stay dropped.

"Are you going to tell her about this, about us?" I asked.

His gaze met mine. He ran a hand through his hair, making it even more mussed than it had been.

"Yeah, sure, of course," he said. "There is nothing but honesty between us. I really value that in a woman."

It was his way of slamming me. I got it.

"I don't imagine she's going to forgive you for giving your ex-girlfriend three orgasms in one evening," I said. Yeah, because I can be bitchy like that.

He dragged his eyes up from my exposed nipple to my face, meeting my gaze with an angsty look of his own. He closed his eyes for a moment, probably trying to get his head together.

"I'm sure we'll work it out. She's very understanding," he said.

"She'd have to be," I said. Nope, not letting it go.

Liam straightened, irritation stiffening his spine before he walked around me to the bedroom door. He put his hand on the knob and turned back, saying oh so casually, "It'll be fine, especially since I'm asking her to marry me and all."

Boom.

He opened the door and walked through it, closing it softly behind him. I snatched up the pillow from the floor and hurled it after him. It bounced off the door and fell to the floor much like my heart. I stood staring at the closed door for a moment and then I picked up the pillow, tossing it on the bed. No. This was not over. Not even close.

Two hours later, I was sitting in a chair beside Babs's divan—funny how no one ever sat there anymore—sipping tea and brooding when the door banged open. A ridiculous part of me hoped it was Liam, which was stupid since he didn't exactly have a key, now did he?

I heard the click of heels on the tile foyer and then a handbag sailed into the great room, landing with a thump against the wall before it slid to the floor. Next a pair of legs came into view wearing boots that I was quite sure I had never seen before. They were black patent leather platform stilettos that went all the way up to mid-thigh, specifically Em's thighs. She strode into the room, pairing the boots with a micro-mini skirt that outlined her butt. Huh. Little sis had booty, who knew?

Over the skirt, Em wore a cropped white halter top that showed off her toned mid-drift and her small but perky cleavage. The only thing she had on for warmth, aside from the boots, was a long black crocheted sweater with lacy accents. I squinted at her. I had never seen Em in anything other than Babs's chosen outfits which were an homage to 1980s preppy housewife chic. While I admired Em for breaking away from headbands and Bermuda bags, she looked like she should be working a corner.

"Who are you and what have you done with my baby sister Em?" I asked.

"The name is Emily," she said.

Em slid herself onto the divan and crossed her boots at the ankles. Well, so much for the sacred space. She closed her eyes and I noted the dark circles beneath her lashes. She was either utterly drained or possibly sauced.

"I'm guessing you didn't wear this outfit to work," I said. She ignored me. "Been doing some shopping?"

"Something like that." Em didn't open her eyes or elaborate.

Irritation battled with empathy inside of me. Of all of us, Em was taking Babs's death the hardest. I knew I needed to be patient and yet the desire to shake her was really strong. I opted to try some humor and see if that sparked a little life in her.

"So what's with the new duds, exactly?" I asked. "Planning a new profession, one that involves swiveling around a pole in a G-string by chance?"

"Shut up, Jules." Em rolled away from me, pressing her face into the fabric of the couch.

I stared at the back of her head. Em was twenty-five years old. She'd just lost her mother, her best friend. I needed to be here for her and not beat her up about her current fashion choices. Clearly, she was going through stuff.

When I heard her emit a soft sigh, I rose from my seat and went into the kitchen where I texted Soph to let her know Em was home and seemingly still pissed at us. I did not mention the outfit.

When I returned to the living room, Em was snoring. Not super loud, just the exhausted deep breathing of a person who'd spent the entire day running away from herself. I got that, too.

I pulled a thick aqua afghan off an armchair and tucked it around Em so that she was completely covered. We could talk about this, whatever this was, tomorrow.

Back upstairs in my room, I was hit with the lingering scent of Liam. How had he managed to fill my bedroom with his particular scent of sea and sunshine? I glanced at the rumpled covers on my bed and actually debated going back downstairs and crashing in the chair beside Em.

He was seeing someone, but he'd made love to me. How could he do that? Had he lied just to put distance between us? That seemed highly likely, especially as I had never seen this supposed girlfriend.

It didn't matter. I had things to tell him, important things, things that I probably should have told him nine years ago, and definitely before we got naked but, hey, it had been a really long time, and I'd been watching him for days. A girl could only take so much hotness before she got a little mental and, honestly, impulse control had always been one of my bigger issues.

I crossed the bedroom to look out across the yard. His window was dark. Not a big surprise given that his nightly workout had happened over here instead. Just the thought of it made me a little dizzy. How could he be so dismissive of what had happened between us?

I was no expert but there was a connection there that seemed to span years, miles, hurt, and betrayal. But maybe I saw it that way because I was the betrayer and not the betrayed. I so desperately wanted to tell him why I had left and explain that it hadn't been what it seemed, that I was given no choice, but I had no idea how to get his attention and keep it, you know, while fully clothed, long enough for him to listen to me.

When designing websites, I knew the single most important feature was navigation. If a site was too hard for a user to page through, then it needed to be simplified with an intelligent use of space and a clear layout.

I stared at Liam's window. Surely, chasing a man could not be that much different than designing a slick website, right? Nervous flutters erupted in my belly as I contemplated my crazy idea. I would use the tools at hand, Em's boots sprang to mind, and manipulate the space between Liam and me so that he became accustomed to seeing me in his world. My invasion would be constant, relentless, and yet, with enough pull back to make him miss me when I wasn't there. Either that, or I'd have him nervously looking over his shoulder, waiting for me to spring out at him. That mental picture made me laugh.

Yeah, I supposed I could do as Liam wished and let him have the last word, breaking things off between us forever. But I was a bit too contrary to be that accommodating, especially because if this woman he was seeing really did exist, it was as obvious to me as the nose on my face that she could not possibly be the love of his life. Firstly, because that was me, and secondly, because there was no way he could have been with me the way he had if he was head over heels for someone else. No freaking way.

There were years of hurt in between us, yes, but the Liam I had known would never, could never, be with me like that if he didn't still have feelings for me. Even if they were really angry feelings right now, they were still feelings, and that was as good a starting place as any.

Chapter Thirteen

"So, what you're saying is that you're totally chasing Liam, but it needs to appear like you're not," Soph said.

"Exactly," I said.

Soph blew out a breath. "Huh, I don't think I can help you. I was knocked up at nineteen from my very first time at bat. I've never chased anyone in my life. I've never been chased either for that matter. It sounds like it could be fun, though."

She let out a wistful sigh and took a sip from her steaming mug. She and Em were in the kitchen with me, sharing morning coffee while I told them both about my evening with Liam. I left out the three orgasms, keeping it vague, but told them pretty much everything else. Soph was the only one of us who was showered, dressed, and ready to face her day.

Em and I were in pajamas, mine being Wonder Woman and hers being those buttoned down stripey things she wore. I preferred mine, but I was relieved that at least she had dragged her butt off the couch at some point during the night to actually put on her jammies and sleep in her own bed. Presently, she was chomping down the biggest bowl of sugary, crunchy cereal I had ever seen. Given that Babs had never let anything with that much sugar and artificial everything into the house, it was quite shocking.

"Don't look at me," Em said. She didn't bother looking up from her phone. "I don't know how to do any of that stuff, although you're welcome to borrow my boots any time you want. They were a huge hit at the farmer's market last night."

"You went to a farmer's market dressed like that?" I asked.

"They were having a happy hour." Em shrugged. "Free wine samples."

"But you don't drink," I said.

"Maybe I do now," Em retorted. This time she did look up, tipping her chin in a defiant manner, the impact of which was diminished by the messy ball of hair on top of her head. I glanced at Soph, fearing Em might have an epic tantrum at any moment.

"Okay, let's table that." Soph waved a hand in Em's general direction as if to say it was too much to deal with so early in the morning. "And focus on one Blumer sister issue at a time."

"That's fine with me," I said. "So long as you're not going to try and talk me out of pursuing Liam."

"You mean stalking," Em said.

"Whatever." I shrugged.

"I have to ask," Soph said. "Why can't you just tell him the truth about why you left with Jessie?"

"I've been thinking the same thing." Em gestured with her spoon, splashing milk on the table, which Sophie dabbed with a napkin. "I mean I know it must be hard revisiting the past, but do you really think Liam can forgive you if you never tell him what actually happened and why?"

My sisters had a solid point but given that they only knew half of the story, and I wasn't at liberty to share the rest of it, it was a tricky question to answer.

"I want to tell him," I said. "I do. I wish I had before. It took me a long time to get over what Babs did, and now that I know she wasn't even my moth—"

I glanced at Em, worried that my harshing on Babs would set her off again. Amazingly, it didn't. Instead, she nodded as if she understood.

"She wasn't your mother," Em said. "It's okay, you can say it. I'm getting used to it just like you are."

She looked at me with an understanding I hadn't expected, and I felt my shoulders drop in relief from their high alert position up around my ears.

"Yeah, I am." I nodded. "As for Jessie, well, those secrets aren't really mine to tell, are they? I mean the stuff between Jessie and Liam isn't any of my business, right?"

"I don't know." Soph sounded miffed. "Since you've never told us the details of you and Jessie. I can't really say, can I?"

"I promise someday I will, but Liam deserves to hear it first," I said. They seemed marginally accepting of that.

We were quiet for a moment, and then I looked at the clock. It was after eight. I turned to Em and said, "Not to panic you or anything but aren't you late for work?"

She didn't glance up from her cereal. "Nah, I told Mr. Drake I needed more time."

"And he's okay with that?" Soph asked.

"How long are you planning on taking?" I asked.

"Yes, he is, and I don't know." Em shoveled more cereal into her mouth while still studying her phone. She must have felt us staring at her because she finally looked up and swallowed. "What? It's the world's most boring job, sitting at a desk all day dealing with people complaining about their claims, their coverage, their shitty marriages, and their lousy kids. I need to get away for a while."

"Okay," I said.

"Yeah, sweetie, we get it," Soph said. "It's just that you've been there for a few years, and you don't want to lose your benefits."

"It'll be fine," Em said.

I hadn't told Soph my suspicions about Em being in love with her boss. Probably it was for the best that she was taking extra time to herself. Maybe the distance would help her gain some perspective on him as well as losing Babs.

Em pushed out of her seat, scraping her chair against the tile floor, and then brought her bowl to the sink. She was still studying her phone but paused in the doorway to face us.

"Jules, if I were you, I'd find out who this woman is that Liam is dating," she said. "Then you can figure out if the relationship is as serious as he said or if he was just trying to throw you off; either way you'll have a better idea of how to proceed with your stalking."

I blinked as I took in her rather savvy advice.

"That makes sense," I said. "Thanks."

"No prob." Em turned and left the kitchen, leaving Soph and I puzzling after her.

"Okay, what are we doing about that?" I pointed with my thumb in the direction of the doorway.

"Nothing," Soph said. "At least, nothing yet. She's grieving and we all do that in different ways."

There was something in her tone. I looked at her and saw her frowning at me.

"What?" I gave her a side eye.

"Jules, do you think maybe you're using Liam to run away from the bombshell Mr. Loren dropped on you? I mean shouldn't you be dealing with the fact that our parents hid the truth of your parentage from you? That you have a birth mother out there who may very much want to meet you?" Soph asked.

"Well, that was blunt."

"Sorry, but it's been several days and you're not talking about any of it. Instead, you're off chasing your old high school flame." Soph shrugged. "It just seems so frantic, as if you're trying to distance yourself with something else, something all consuming, like the boyfriend you never got closure with."

I stared at her. Did I like what I was hearing? No. Was it something I'd already thought of myself? Yes. Did I care enough to change my behavior? No.

"You're probably right," I said. "I know I'm not dealing with my new reality very well." I was quiet for a moment. "You know what I keep thinking?"

Soph shook her head. She cradled her coffee in her hands as if she knew a cold wind was coming and she'd need the warmth.

"Babs took everything from me—my real mother and Liam, too. I hate her for that."

"I know," Soph said. "You have every right. What she did the night you left. I can't..." She shook her head as she placed her hand on mine. "I hope you know you have us, me and Em. She could never take us from you. Ever."

My stubborn streak pushed the tears back. I was so over crying. "Thanks," I said. "As for the Liam thing? Maybe getting him back is so important to me because then it's one less thing Babs stole. I didn't expect to still feel this much for him, not after all these years. We only get one shot at this thing called life, and I've already made a mess of it, Soph. I really don't want to walk away from something this good, not again, not when I know for sure that he's the one for me."

The look in her eyes was full of sympathy tinged with sadness, and her voice when she spoke was so soft I had to strain to hear her. "But are you the one for him?"

Ouch! I had thought of that, too, and rejected it. Leave it to big sister to toss it out there in the open. The only answer was an honest one.

"I don't know," I said. "But if I don't try, I'll always wonder."

She stared at me for a long moment. "You really are the bravest woman I know."

I laughed. Maybe. But I suspected it had more to do with an overabundance of bullheadedness in my DNA. I wondered if I got that from my real mom. It seemed unlikely, otherwise, why would she have given me away? I shook off the thought.

"Whatever happens, I'll be fine." Big fib. "The bigger concern is Em. What are we going to do about her?"

"We need to give her time. We all need time."

"Time or a slap upside the head?" I asked. Soph gave me an unamused look and I sighed, "Fine. We'll give her time."

I decided the boots were too obvious to begin my campaign with and that it was better to ease Liam into the reality that I wasn't going away. I figured my best move was to go back to where it all began. I dug out my old surfboard from the shed behind the house and cleaned it up. I mounted it on the side holder on my old beach cruiser

Judging by the day I'd seen Liam in his coffee shop, his preferred time to surf was when the waves were in abundance. Clearly, one of the perks of owning your own coffee shop empire was the ability to take a break whenever you wanted one. I had checked the surf report and knew that right now was going to be the best time of the day.

I'd spent two days lying low and licking my wounds, prepping my gear. It was a relief to finally head for the nearby beach which was locals only. Because of its rocky coastline, Gull's Harbor was a turfy stretch of beach where tourists and visitors were actively discouraged. By this, I mean with really harsh language and occasionally fists were involved.

When I arrived, nostalgia swelled inside me, churning just like the surf in front of me. The very few times I had come back to visit my family over the years, I hadn't taken my board out of storage, mostly because I hadn't wanted to run into Liam, but also because it was something I had loved so much that I didn't want it to call me back to this place. I had needed to break away from Babs and her toxic hold and if I reconnected with the things I loved, like surfing and Liam, I might get sucked in, and I couldn't let that happen. I was back now, and I wasn't leaving, at least not for a while.

I locked my bike on the rack loaded with other cruisers, grabbing my bag and board. I started the steep walk down the trail that snaked the face of the cliffs to the narrow beach below. This particular surf spot was one of the few in the area that wasn't peppered with big rocks. Since it had been a while, I thought it best to wait before taking on anything like Devil's Backbone. Besides this was where I'd seen Liam go yesterday. Yeah, in a town this small, it's pretty easy to track a person's movements.

The weight of the board was familiar, but I was out of practice and it was a bit unwieldy. I slid on some loose gravel and had to catch myself before plowing into the back of another surfer headed down the trail. I managed to kick some rocks at his heels and he whipped around, probably to see if I was about to fall on him.

I gave him a small smile and a finger wave. He glowered.

"This is locals only, girl," he said. He wore his hair in long dreadlocks that touched his waist. His black wet suit, which covered him from neck to ankle, accentuated his thin long limbs, giving him the look of a spider.

"I know, Ten," I said. "I am a local or at least I used to be."

He planted his vintage long board in the loose dirt and studied me like a lost person might study a map.

"Well, I'll be damned," he said. He smiled and his gold incisor winked at me in the sunlight. "Little surfer girl is back."

"Not so little anymore," I said. My face heated under his scrutiny.

Ten, so nicknamed because he could hang ten, meaning have all ten toes curled over the front edge of his board longer than anyone else in Gull's Harbor or likely San Diego County, had seen me grow up on these beaches. He was a local legend, like Mission Beach had their SloMo, we had our Ten, and I was ridiculously pleased that he remembered me after so many years away.

"You and coffee boy used to spend hours down here on the water." Ten smacked his lips together as if considering why I was alone. "He still comes down here."

"So, I've heard," I said. I glanced out at the surf as if studying the waves.

Ten was the watcher of our local beach and our downtown for that matter, given that he never had a permanent residence and yet never left town. No one knew exactly where he crashed but I suspected he moved from place to place and knew exactly who was who and what was what. If I was looking to see if Liam was serious about this girl he said he was going to marry, Ten might be the guy to ask.

"So, does coffee boy bring any girls down to the beach to surf?" I asked.

Ten blinked at me. His old eyes were full of information, unfortunately not the kind that answered my questions. "He almost got himself killed on Devil's Backbone when you left."

There was no judgment in his voice just facts, but it made my breath catch and my heart hurt all the same. I hung my head. What was I doing here? I had no right to try and win Liam back after what I'd done to him.

"But he didn't," Ten said. His voice was suddenly upbeat as if he'd just announced great news. "And now surfer girl, the only woman I've ever seen him surf with, is here. So that's an interesting development, don't you think?"

My head snapped up and I met his considering gaze. I wondered if my relief showed. Probably. I decided I didn't care. Liam's whatever she was, I refused to call her his girlfriend, didn't surf. That was a check for me in the cool chick column. Booyah.

"Did you wax your board?" Ten asked.

"Duh," I said.

"Don't drop in on anyone."

"As if."

"And don't be a kook," he said.

"Really?" I asked. "You're calling me a kook, like I'm a noob who's never surfed."

"I didn't call you one," he argued. "I said 'don't be one.' There's a difference."

"I think I can handle it," I said. "It hasn't been that long."

He studied me for a moment and then his brown wrinkled face burst into a huge smile.

"Yes, but can you handle him? Hee hee." Ten hooted and turned back to the path. He was humming and it took me a minute to recognize the theme to the old TV show *The Love Boat*.

Kill me now. Maybe showing my hand to Ten had been a bad bet.

Once on the beach, I found a place off to the side to practice, away from the other surfers. I pulled off my T-shirt and shorts and dug my wetsuit out of my bag. It still fit, yay, and I felt as if I was slipping on an old familiar skin. I wore a thick wet suit in winter months. Since summer was coming, I had lighter gear that kept my core warm but didn't cover my arms and legs. The Pacific was cold, but it was a lot of work to surf, which kept a girl warm.

Ten stopped on the beach to do his usual sun salutations. He always did a series of them before he entered the water. For some reason, the continuity of this, the feeling that the more things changed the more they stayed the same, gave me great comfort.

I glanced up at the cliffs, hoping to see Liam's familiar head of dark hair. Instead, I saw a shock of blond hair, a pair of aviators, and a navy hoodie. It took me a second, but I remembered the man who'd been staring at me in Liam's coffee shop. I couldn't be positive, given the shades, but I got the distinct feeling he was watching me, and my creeper meter went into the red zone.

Well, he could watch me all he wanted, but if he couldn't surf, he couldn't catch me. With that, I jogged out into the ocean with my board tucked under my arm and the water churning around my knees as if eager to play.

My dignity was the first thing to go. It had been a long time since I'd surfed and as much as some of it was like riding a bicycle, I was nine years older and not nearly as strong as I was back in the day. It was a battle to get past the surf and out to where the waves were breaking. There were about thirty surfers out today and the lineup was well established. Ten, who had done his warmup and still managed to beat me out to the break, waved me in and introduced me to a few of the locals, including a woman named Ruby. Like her name, she had deep red, not natural, hair and a sleeve of tattoos most of which depicted mermaids.

"Ten says you used to be good," she said.

I shrugged. I knew it was best to keep it humble until I got my cred back. I straddled my board riding over the top of a set of waves. I needed to catch my breath and get my head together before I dropped in. Also, I was preoccupied with watching the cliff looking for Liam. I didn't want to be cruising a wave and miss him.

The blond man had left his perch and was walking down the trail to the beach. In addition to the hoodie, he was wearing jeans and sneakers, not exactly beach attire in May.

A big roller came our way and I watched as Ruby and another surfer got ahead of it and started paddling. Ruby caught it but the other surfer didn't. It washed right over him, but she rode it almost all the way to the shore, whipping her board around and diving into the surf at the last second. I felt a surge of adrenaline hit me. I hadn't surfed in so long and I'd missed it so much.

"It's yours, surfer girl!" Ten called to me and I glanced behind me to see a perfect wave rolling my way. In the lineup it was clearly my turn and I decided to take it. Belly down on my board, I started to paddle, trying to build momentum. I knew the minute my board merged with the wave, and I popped up into a crouched position. It took me longer than I would have thought to get to my full height but when I did, I felt the same sense of glory sweep through me that I always had when the wave and I became one. Best feeling in the world.

As I neared the shore, I saw the blond man, bent over my stuff. I stared until I noticed he was rifling through my bag! What the hell?

"Hey!" I shouted. He couldn't hear me over the roar of the surf, so I waved a fist at him and yelled again. "Hey, that's my stuff!"

Of course, that's when Liam appeared, walking down the beach, carrying his board, staring at me as if seeing a ghost. I tried to gesture for him to grab the man, but at that moment, the wave dropped out from beneath me. I went one way and my board went another and the next thing I knew I was sucking in saltwater and getting a sand facial. Damn it!

Chapter Fourteen

I was yanked out of the water by the collar of my wetsuit and dragged up onto the beach.

"Jesus, Blumer, what the hell were you thinking?" Liam snapped. "You can't just jump on a board and think you're going to be as good as you were as a kid."

I was too busy hacking to put up an argument so I was left to wheeze and shake my head violently, which he completely ignored while he continued his rant.

"Don't you realize what could have happened? You could have drowned, given yourself a concussion, or worse, hit another surfer with your board," he said. "How would you feel then, if you caused someone else an injury?"

I squinted at him and tried to crawl up the beach toward my stuff. The blond man was gone but I could see my bag was open. My arms and legs felt weighted as if I'd eaten enough beach that I was now just one big useless sandbag. I sank onto the ground on my belly not even caring that the waves continued to wash over my feet.

"Aw, shit," Liam cursed. He knelt beside me and pushed me until I flopped over like a dead fish, looking up at him. "Are you hurt? Can you breathe?"

His brow was furrowed in concern. He cared! I almost let him think I needed mouth to mouth but felt like that might be overplaying my hand; besides he'd already used that move on me and we really needed to make a fresh start. Also, I really wanted to check my bag.

"Fine, I'm fine," I choked. I craned my head to look at my bag and then I pushed up to a sitting position, forcing him to give me a little space.

"You are *not* fine," he said.

"I need to get to my bag," I said.

"Easy," he said. "Don't rush, you'll only make it worse."

129

Liam reached down and released my ankle tether. He dragged my board up onto the beach, dropping it next to his. He crouched beside me and put my arm over his shoulders. With little to no effort, he helped me to my feet and I hobbled toward my bag. I let go of him and sank to my knees. I moved aside the beach towel and there was my stuff. I dug through it—wallet, house keys, clothes. Nothing was missing. Phew!

Perhaps I was crazy and didn't understand what I'd seen. I mean, who the heck would steal stuff off a beach in front of everyone? But why had I run into this guy twice? And why was he going through my stuff? I checked and my cell phone was still in the zippered pocket on the side. WTF?

Maybe I had lost more oxygen than I'd thought when I was rolled by the wave. Maybe I had seen it wrong and the guy hadn't been digging through my stuff. I pulled my fluffy striped beach towel out of the bag and dried my face off.

"What are you doing here, Blumer?" Liam asked.

He sounded uncomfortable, as if my presence on the beach made him feel weird. He hadn't seen me since he'd told me he'd moved on, but I'd seen him. I wondered if he suspected that I'd been watching him and was surfing here today specifically because I knew he'd be here.

Well, even if it was true I planned to disabuse him of that accurate notion right now. My stalking him was on a need-to-know basis and he did not need to know just yet.

"Let's see... wetsuit, surfboard, hmm, I'd think it's perfectly obvious that I'm golfing," I said.

His mouth twitched but he didn't give me an actual smile, and then he opted for stern.

"Blumer, you haven't surfed in years," he said.

"So what?" I asked. "It's like riding a bike or sex." He swallowed hard. Yes, I was trying to work sex into every conversation, because I'm helpful like that. "Learn to do it right the first time and you never forget how."

His brown eyes crackled with intensity. "You can't—"

"Watch me." With that I dropped my towel and grabbed my board, pausing to reattach the tether.

"Jules, wait, you're not ready."

He was right behind me, but I ignored him and dove into the waves. The ocean was cold and even in a wetsuit, my breath hitched the first time I went under, feeling the water tug on my long curls, soaking them and flattening them to my head when I surfaced.

I climbed onto my board and paddled out to join the others. I forced myself not to turn to see if Liam was following me. When I reached the group, Ten was straddling his board while he looked in my direction and then just beyond me. I glanced over my shoulder. Yep, Liam paddled right behind me. Ten gave me a small smile, his gold tooth glinting in the sunlight. My smile deepened to a grin. I felt like I had an ally in my mission to win my ex-boyfriend back.

Ten caught the next wave and I watched spellbound as his dreadlocks danced in the air as he rode the board, perched on the front like a mermaid on the prow of a ship, until he chose to end the ride by diving into the surf.

"No one is as Zen as Ten," Liam said from beside me.

I met his gaze. So many memories were formed right here with the two of us straddling our boards, waiting for our next wave. Back in the day we'd been so in sync, we'd been able to catch waves together and ride them in side by side. I wondered if we still had the surfer mind meld and if we did, would it bother Liam to ride side by side with me now?

"Listen, Jules, I think you should let me spot you for your first few runs," Liam said. I opened my mouth to thank him, but he never let me speak. He held up his hand and spoke over me. "Yeah, I know you're fine and you don't need any help, but I think you should err on the side of safety, all right? It's not just you out here you know, you really need to consider everyone else."

"That would be fine," I said. "Thanks."

One of his eyebrows quirked up.

"You weren't going to argue with me, were you?" Liam sounded rueful as he reached down and squeezed water through his fingers, making it shoot up into the air.

"No," I admitted. "I know I'm out of practice."

He nodded at me as if surprised that I was being so level-headed. We rode out the next set of waves, letting the others surf them in. And then off in the distance, I saw the swell build. It was an indicator of a new set of waves coming. I felt the eager anticipation that meant the surf was prime.

"This is it," Liam said. He moved into position on his board.

"Ready." I moved onto my belly and began paddling. We were just feet apart and the wave lifted us up together.

"Now!" Liam yelled.

We both paddled hard and then popped to our feet and as if no time or distance had separated us from the last time we'd surfed together, we rode in perfect sync. We were both goofy footed, meaning we rode our boards with our right foot forward, and we fell right back into our old pattern. Balancing on our boards side by side, becoming one with the sea, was magical.

I glanced at Liam and caught him grinning the same smile I'd seen a million times when we surfed. Full lips parted over white teeth in a grin that turned up in the corners and made the harsher lines of his face soften with affection and the pure joy of catching a wave. My heart lurched with how much I had missed that grin on this man. My board bobbled, and I flailed before plunging headfirst into the icy water.

When I broke the surface, Liam was there, having whipped his board around to check on me.

"Woo hoo!" he cried. He pushed my board toward me while straddling his own. "That was one hell of ride, surfer girl!"

A grin burst across my face as I climbed back on my board. Liam leaned over and pulled my board up alongside his. Just like the old days, he leaned close to me and I braced myself for his lips to meet mine in a salty cold kiss. I felt my heart surge right up into my throat. Was it going to be this simple to find ourselves again?

Yeah, no—instead he tugged a long piece of kelp out of my hair.

"Nice catch," he said. "It blends in with your crazy hair."

My heart shriveled. He had always loved my hair. When Babs had railed at me to just cut it short instead of letting it run wild, he'd been the one to tell me that he loved it, that it suited me, that it was one of the things that made me beautiful. Now, he was comparing it to seaweed.

"Thanks," I murmured.

A large wave was about to break over us and I took the opportunity to slide off my board and duck my whole body under the water to hide my hurt as if I could wash away my feelings with a cold splash of water. A small part of me wanted to stay under and just let the ocean push me back to the shore so I could crawl up the beach, defeated, grab my bag and disappear. But I wasn't a quitter.

What had I expected? I had skipped town with his best friend and made Liam look like a jilted idiot. Did I really think a morning spent surfing would turn all of that around? Baby steps, I reminded myself. Newly resolved, I surged back up into the air.

He was waiting for me. That was something.

"Come on, Blumer, the waves await."

I nodded and followed him out. I knew if I was going to win him back, I was going to have to play the long game. First, he had to get used to having me in his day-to-day life, as a neighbor and a friend, then I could bring out the heavy artillery and push him to see me as a woman. I knew my sisters were right and the best thing I could do was tell Liam the truth about Babs and Jessie, but I just couldn't. Not yet.

I supposed it was stupid but I wanted him to care about me in spite of the past. Plus, there was the very real possibility that he would be furious about the decisions I'd made without telling him. I knew if the situation were reversed, I would be.

I'd been so hurt and angry and stupid when I left. I had thought I was being self-sacrificing and noble but looking back, I had taken the first opportunity to get away from Babs and to heck with anyone else. Liam and, yes, even my sisters, were abandoned in the process. At the time I didn't care because I was so sure I was never coming back.

But now I was here, and I knew that the love I'd found in Gull's Harbor all those years ago was something so unique and rare that I needed to see if I, we, could find it again. Was it worth humiliating myself for? Yep. A large swell was coming, and Liam glanced back to make sure I saw it. I nodded and together we dove through the wave, knowing as all surfers do that the best way out of something is through it.

The afternoon passed quickly, and I left the beach before Liam...I didn't want to clue him in to the fact that I was pursuing him.

As I toweled off and shimmied out of my wetsuit, I was tempted to sneak a look at Liam, but I played it cool. I had an objective in mind, the two of us back together, which meant I couldn't be too in his face until I started breaking him into the idea of "us" first. Then Em's boots were coming out and anything else I could think of to throw his way, for that matter.

As I trudged back up the hill with my board under my arm, I allowed myself one last glance at the water. If my gaze tracked a certain bright green board, well, that couldn't be helped. When I did spot him, I knew from the way my insides shivered that he was looking at me, too.

And so began my campaign to wear Liam down. In an ideal world, he'd see me enough to realize he wanted me back and would dump this girlfriend of his and we'd get back together. Easy peasy, right? Yeah, no, after all he was a man, and they can be a thick bunch. When confronted with what is best for them, like asking for directions when lost, they seemed to always get defiant and dig their heels in.

With this in mind, I made sure to tread that fine line between just being around living my life and shadowing his every move. Some ideas worked better than others.

Knowing that Liam swam every morning, I began to drag myself up out of bed at the crack of dawn not only to watch him swim laps in his pool but also to change into my clothes for the day in front of my window with the lights on. Yep, I was a peeping Tom's wet dream.

This went on for three days. I never looked to see if Liam saw me from his pool. I tried to time it so that I changed when he was done with his swim, but I never verified that he saw me, wanting to pretend that this was sheer happenstance and not a ploy on my part to get him to notice me.

When a fist pounded on the front door just moments after I had finished changing into my yoga pants and halter top, my heart soared thinking maybe it was Liam and he just couldn't resist me anymore. Yay, me.

I opened the door with a wide smile which promptly fell when I took in Mrs. Rodriguez in her flannel cat pajamas, looking peeved.

"I don't know what your life in New York was like, Julia Blumer, but here in the suburbs, we do not flaunt our bodies in front of the window," Mrs. Rodriguez chided. "We close our curtains or move away from the window. Honestly, what would your mother say?"

"Uh." I was pre-coffee so this was the best I could do.

"My twelve-year-old son's entire boy scout troop has been meeting in his tree house every morning to watch you get dressed."

"What?" My jaw dropped and I crossed my arms over my chest.

Over Mrs. Rodriguez's shoulder, I saw a pack of boys standing at the curb, looking mortified. I could only assume this was the perv troop. None of them met my eye, except for Danny Rodriguez. When he caught my eye, he puckered his lips and gave me a slow wink. *OMG!*

"Did you ever think the problem is the boys not respecting my privacy and not me changing in my own home?" I asked.

"No."

I would have argued further, but I saw movement out of the corner of my eye and turned to see Liam was standing on his front porch, enjoying his morning coffee and watching the show. Oh, horror!

"It is not the boys' fault you have no sense of common decency. They have been diligently trying for their bird watcher's badge," Mrs. Rodriguez said. "Until you distracted them."

"Tweet tweet," I said.

She stared at me, her nostrils flaring in fury. I stared right back.

"Draw your shades, Julia, or I will call the police and have you charged with indecent exposure."

She turned on a fluffy pink slipper and strode down the walkway where the boys were waiting. They fell in line behind her with Danny bringing up the rear. Before he disappeared, he held his hand up to his ear with his thumb and pinky out, miming a phone, and mouthed the words, "Call me."

I turned to go back into my house, ignoring the guffaw that I heard coming from next door. Once inside I glanced out the side window to see Liam doubled up with laughter at my expense. Jerk! It did not help that his morning attire of jeans and a dress shirt looked *fiiiine* on his muscle-sculpted body. Damn it!

"Who was that?" Soph asked as she came down the stairs. She had a raging case of bedhead and it looked as if she hadn't washed off her makeup from last night. This was not the Soph I knew.

"Mrs. Rodriguez from down the street," I said.

"This early in the morning?" Soph frowned at the door. "Why?"

"I don't know," I said. "Something about bird watching."

"Huh." Sophie continued to the kitchen.

I uncrossed the fingers behind my back and started to follow when Em appeared in the doorway to Bab's bedroom. Was she sleeping in there now? Judging by the dark circles that were even darker than they'd been the other day, that would be a no, there was no sleeping happening. She shook her head until her long blond hair covered her face.

"You are such a liar," she hissed. Her voice was filled with scathing contempt and I winced mostly because what she said was true in this instance. Still I wasn't one to get kicked and not kick back.

"Oh, *I'm* the liar?" I snapped. Soph and I had been giving her space, but it didn't mean I wasn't keeping an eye on her. "I heard you call your boss, Mr. Drake, yesterday. You cried and said you were so overwrought about sorting your mother's things that you couldn't bear to come into work. You haven't sorted jack. So, why the lies?"

"That's none of your business."

"It is so my business," I argued. "I saw you with him at Babs's service, Em. You're in love with him."

"Ah!" Em gasped. Her face went bright red and then pasty pale.

"What's going on in here?" Soph appeared in the kitchen doorway.

"Em's in love with her boss," I said.

"Shut up, Jules!" Em's face went red again.

"That's why she's been calling out of work," I continued. I looked at Em. "What did you think was going to happen? He'd miss you so much he was going to show up at the door and beg you to come back to work? Or did you think he'd leave his wife for you?"

"What?" Soph cried.

"Oh, yeah," I said. "He's married."

Chapter Fifteen

Soph's head swiveled between us, her mouth agape.

"At least I'm waiting for him to come to me and not stalking him like you are Liam," Em fired back.

"Liam is not married," I said. "But your boss is."

"So what?" Em's teeth were gritted, and I really thought she might take a swing at me. "What I do is none of your business. You're not even my sister!"

Well, that checked me. I blinked, feeling as if she had clobbered me after all.

"Emily. Grace. Blumer." Soph spat out each name like a string of cusswords. She sounded ferocious as if it took every bit of her mom mojo not to turn Em over her knee. That made me feel a little better. "That was completely uncalled for and you will apologize right now. All nine words."

Em tossed her hair. She seemed defiant for about a half second and then she looked at me. The hurt must have shown on my face, because she mumbled, "I am sorry. I love you. Please forgive me."

I met her anguished, brown-eyed gaze and couldn't be a bitch about it. I nodded. "Sure, I forgive you."

Em stomped back into Babs's room, slamming the door behind her. The coffeemaker beeped in the kitchen and Soph and I headed for it like it was the source of all that was good in the world.

Em did not reappear and join us. Soph and I agreed it was probably for the best. As much as I wanted to pretend her words hadn't hurt, they had. Every time I heard her voice in my head, it was like pressing on a bruise. I suppose it smarted so much because she'd said exactly what I'd been thinking. Did I belong here in Babs's house anymore? I mean, if I wasn't Babs's rebellious daughter, who the hell was I? I didn't know.

Southern California weather in May is fairly consistent, much like the rest of the year, and the temps are usually in the high seventies with the occasional spike into the low eighties. When we had a solid eighty-two-degree day, I upped my game, sauntering out into the front yard in the tiniest bikini I could find at the surf shop in town.

School was still in session, so I assumed I was safe from the "birdwatchers" but even better Liam was doing yard work in his front lawn. Shirtless. I figured it was only fair that I read my book, a romance novel set in Maine with a really cute dog in it, while taking in some rays and slyly ogling the boy next door, who was doing his best to ignore me.

Liam ran the mower back and forth across the grass, then he edged the walkway, the garden beds, and along the driveway, all the while never looking at me. Fine. I'd do all the watching. I appreciated that his board shorts hung low on his hips and a fine sheen of sweat coated his upper body.

I fanned myself with my book. I was pretty sure the weatherman had lied. It certainly felt a heck of a lot warmer than eighty-two degrees. I put my book away and grabbed my iced tea. I fished an ice cube out. It dripped on my chest and I smoothed the water over my skin in an effort to keep from overheating. I popped the ice cube in my mouth, hoping to cool myself off from the inside out.

As if it wasn't hot enough, I was abruptly aware of the heat of Liam's stare. I glanced out of the corner of my eye to see him standing there with his hose in hand—the gardening one to be clear—watering the shrubs that ran along the short wall between our yards.

This was my moment. I turned my head in his direction with every intention of lowering my sunglasses and giving him my best *"come here, big boy"* look, but in that moment a car backfired on the street, causing Liam to jump and jerk the hose, which sent an arch of icy cold water splashing down on me.

I yelped and leapt from my chair. Yes, I wanted to be cooled off, but that shit was freezing! I clutched my middle with my arms as the water dripped off of me.

"Oh, sorry!" Liam called.

Then he got a wicked, wicked glint in his eye and he sent another steam of water in my direction, soaking me from top to bottom.

"Oops!" he shouted. "My bad!"

"You did that on purpose!" I cried.

"What?" He cupped a hand to his ear as if he couldn't hear me over the sound of the running water.

Argh! He blasted me again, leaving me no choice but to snatch up my things and make a run for it. When I was out of range, I glanced back to find him, once again, doubled up with laughter at my expense.

I slammed into the house, furious. Then I glanced out the window and watched him laugh. Despite the puddle that I was dripping onto the floor, I loved the sight of him cracking up with genuine humor even if I was the cause.

Maybe the sultry siren was the wrong tack to take; one of the best parts of our youthful relationship was the amount of laughter we shared. When the world was dark or scary or just too much, we could always make each other laugh. God, I missed that.

Right now, the only place Liam and I seemed able to communicate was on our boards while surfing. For me, the mid-day jaunts had become so much more than an opportunity to stalk him. I felt as if I was getting a part of myself back, the best part.

Ten and I got reacquainted, and I began a friendship with Ruby. Now that she'd seen me surf a few times, her cool reserve was more a steady chill and I realized that was just how she rolled.

But curiosity about Liam's girlfriend began to eat at me. I really wanted to know who she was, especially since I never ever saw her around his house. Weird, right?

Figuring the coffee shop was my best shot at a chance to see her, I started to pop into Liam's for a java-boosted hour or two while doing my web design work every few days. I figured even if I didn't see the girlfriend, maybe I would hear something about her.

Now why did the "g" word taste as bitter as a dark roast espresso on my tongue? Oh, yeah, because I was jealous as hell, that's why.

Several days passed but there was no sign of her, and I wondered if maybe Liam really had invented her to keep me away. As I warmed to my theory, it occurred to me that I should probably verify it. Who better to know Liam's actual status than his counter help?

"Hi, Jules," Rachel greeted me as I arrived late in the afternoon. She tossed her blue braid over her shoulder, which was the same shade as her eyes, and turned to face me so I could fully admire her nose ring.

Yes, most of the staff knew me by name now, possibly from the day I had chased Liam into his office when he grabbed my laptop, but also because I am a very pleasant person, very low maintenance, and an excellent tipper.

"Same as this morning?" she asked.

Okay, so sometimes I stopped in twice a day. Sue me.

"Yes, please," I said.

Lately, I'd been hooked on the flat white and I waited eagerly while she called it out to be prepped. I glanced around the shop and noticed that I had hit the afternoon lull. I figured now was as good a time as any to do some prying.

"So, Rachel," I said. "Have you been working here long?"

"A year and a half," she said.

"And you like it?"

"Oh, yeah, Liam's great about letting me work around my school schedule."

"So, he's a pretty good boss?" I asked.

"The best," she said. "We get Christmas bonuses and everything. My dad says no one does that anymore."

"Yeah, that is pretty cool," I said.

Having never gotten a Christmas bonus from any of my clients, I had to agree. But now I wasn't sure how to segue into talking about her boss's personal life. I didn't want to make it weird but I had no idea how else to find out if his girlfriend really existed.

"He even lets us study on the job during finals," Rachel said. "How many bosses let you do that?"

"None that I know of." Then I had an idea. It wasn't nice of me to cause her a panic but I considered it collateral damage. "Do you think that will change after he gets married?"

"What? Married! Liam?" The barista gaped at me. "How do you know this?"

"Oh, you didn't hear?" I asked. Truly, I can play dumb like nobody's business. "Huh. Liam is my neighbor and when I bumped into him a few days ago, we got to talking." Yes, this was the G-rated version of our encounter. "He was pretty stoked about this chick he's seeing and how they're getting married and all. He made it sound like she's the love of his life."

"What? No!" Rachel looked horrified.

I had a horrible moment of doubt where I thought maybe she had a crush on him, and I had just squashed her hopes and dreams. That would have made me feel awful but thankfully, no, that wasn't it.

"Simone!" Rachel turned and yelled at the tall, thin girl with dark eyes and deep brown skin, who was half hidden behind the coffee machine, making my flat white. "Did you hear that?"

"Hear what?" Simone asked. I leaned over the counter to see her frowning at the machine which was making a loud hum.

"Liam is going to marry *her*!" Rachel's eyes were huge and the look of repulsion on her face was one usually reserved for zombie movies.

Uh oh. My stomach clenched. The girlfriend was real and judging by Rachel's reaction not well liked. My heart thumped like a deflated basketball in my chest. Somehow, I had convinced myself that the girlfriend wasn't real. The realization that there really was someone else made me feel a bit hurly.

"No, way!" Simone glanced up from the machine and saw me. "Oh, hi, Julia. I'm almost done."

"Take your time," I said.

Simone turned back to Rachel. "Where did you hear this?"

"From Julia," Rachel said.

I raised my hand. "Me."

Simone gave me a stunned look and finished making the flat white and then joined us at the counter.

"When did he say that?" Simone pushed the coffee toward me.

"A few days ago, maybe last week? We're neighbors and we got to talking and he said he had a serious girlfriend, and was going to propose soon."

The two girls exchanged grim looks.

"Ugh, that explains so much," Simone said. "He's been so weird lately."

"Weird?" I prompted. I took my coffee and handed my debit card to Rachel.

"Way weird," Rachel confirmed as she totaled my order then swiped my card. "He's constantly late, he's always moody, he's been forgetting stuff, totally not himself. I mean, I used to be able to set my watch by him and he was always smiling, now he's just a hot mess and all kinds of cranky."

"Totally," Simone agreed. "He even got all aggro with Todd the other day. Liam is never aggro and how can you even with Todd? It'd be like kicking a puppy."

"I can't believe it," Rachel said. "She's so...and he's...and...oh, man, this could ruin everything, like, what if she's here all the time or tries to have input on the shop?"

"I will quit, obvi," Simone said. "Oh, god, I wonder if I should go apply at Starbucks?"

"Oh, don't do that." I pried the lid off my coffee and blew on the froth of white as I studied them over the lip of the cup. "He hasn't asked her yet. How bad is she really?" Yes, I was fishing.

"Are you kidding?" Rachel looked at me as if I was as thick as the foam in my cup. "Have you met her?"

"No, I've never even seen her." I glanced at them under my lashes. "Is she pretty?"

"Only if you like the super high maintenance, hair extensions, boob job, and weekly mani-pedi type." Rachel straightened the napkin holder by her register.

"Yeah. Believe me, if you'd seen her, you'd remember her," Simone said. "She is the most attention-seeking, needy, whiny diva I have ever met."

"Totes," Rachel agreed.

The two girls rolled their eyes in perfect sync and then Rachel said in a grating, high-pitched voice, "'Rachel, get me an espresso and this time make it right. I'd hate to tell Liam that you can't handle this job.'"

"'Simone, bring me a glass of ice water, and don't forget the lemon wedge and make sure you get all the seeds out.'" Simone's full mouth twisted in a sneer. "'I'd hate to have to tell Liam that his staff can't even handle ice water.'"

"If he marries her, I swear it'll destroy his business," Rachel said. "She's a horror!"

Simone nodded.

"Who is she?" I tried to make it sound like a perfectly plausible question and added, "I mean, is she from town? Do I know her?"

"No," Rachel said. "Her name is Courtney Jonas, and she lives up in Los Angeles."

And now I had a name. Yes! And L.A. How perfect, since my current nemesis, Paisley, currently resided there as well. A twofer.

"Then she's not around very often," I said. "Maybe it won't be so bad."

"Unless she moves here," Simone said. She and Rachel exchanged a worried glance.

"Don't panic," I said. "It's a long journey from a proposal to an actual wedding."

I intended to interrupt the process completely. I left a big tip and hunkered down in my corner seat of the café with my flat white and laptop. I wasn't sure where to begin the search for information about Liam and Courtney, but figured I'd start with all the standard social media sites.

It was not as illuminating as I'd hoped. While Liam's Coffee Shop had several prominent business accounts, I couldn't find any personal pages for *my* Liam Mahony. There were other Liam Mahonys, just not mine. So, he either didn't have them or he had pretty high security.

The search for Courtney Jonas was not much better. I could verify her on social media, but she had all of her privacy blocks on, meaning I could see she was there in her teeny tiny profile picture but not much else. Very annoying.

I tapped my finger to my lower lip. The coffee shop in Los Angeles was his most recent enterprise, where Courtney lived. If he got any press coverage for the opening, it stood to reason that she might have been there. I found the location of the Los Angeles shop and looked at their website. It was a bit cumbersome and not navigationally friendly, but I did finally find some pictures of the grand opening.

Liam popped right out of the pictures at me. There were tons of them, and he was smiling as was his beaming staff. He was clearly enjoying the success of his endeavors and for a moment I just marveled at all he'd accomplished. I was so very proud and happy for him.

Since he had spent our high school years working as a barista, owning a chain of coffee shops had always been Liam's ultimate goal. He'd gone to San Diego State and gotten a business degree, then returned to Gull's Harbor and opened his first shop after college with loans from his parents and the bank.

Babs had kept me up to date on his goings on. I used to think she was just being cruel but now I wondered if she'd done it to prove that she'd been right. I never would have had the big adventurous life I'd dreamed of if I stayed with Liam, because the reality was that I never would have left Gull's Harbor, I would have stayed with him.

I tried to picture what my life would have looked like had I stayed but I couldn't get it to crystallize in my mind.

I scrolled through the grand opening pictures on the coffee shop's website and stopped when I saw one of him with his arm around a woman the size of a pencil with long, sleek, black hair, unnaturally white teeth, and ginormous cleavage. She was tucked against his side and staring up at him with her bright smile and big, brown doe eyes, and I felt like I'd just swallowed a fistful of tacks. This had to be Courtney. I was sure of it.

I scanned the photo to see if it listed her name anywhere. It did not. I studied the picture hard. They were clearly a thing. It was obvious in the way she gazed at him. My stomach rolled a bit. My Liam was dating her; he was going to marry this busty being.

For a second, I thought I should take it as a sign from the Universe to back off and leave the poor man alone. But if the Universe was really sending me signs, then the fact that Liam and I still had some crazy chemistry going, a truckload of unfinished business, and I'd learned that his staff clearly hated Courtney, well, it seemed like the signals were actually urging me forward with my plan to win him back, right? Right.

There was no doubt I'd need to up my game. I pondered what I should do next and it seemed I had no choice. I was going to have to bust out Em's boots but where and when? Hmm. I considered my options then I noticed that a band was playing at the coffee shop that evening. Seemed like an excellent time to strut my stuff, especially if I could get my niece and nephew to act as human shields. They were leaving soon for their Swiss summer camp, so I figured this was an opportunity to bond. Yes, with an agenda, but still.

I sent the twins a text telling them to meet me at Grandma's house. The best way to win their sixteen-year-old devotion was to pay them, and I added that if Hannah could bring any clothes that her parents refused to let her wear out in public because they were too sexy that would be hugely helpful.

Harry texted his horror with a bug-eyed emoji, but Hannah replied with a thumbs-up, so I was good to go. Yes, I was putting my entire future into the hands of two sixteen-year- olds. Heaven help me!

Chapter Sixteen

"Hey, Aunt Jules," Harry greeted me as he and Hannah entered the house. "What's the plan? Are you trying to give the guy a heart attack or a perpetual stiffy?"

"The second one," I said.

"Well, Hannah brought outfits for both," Harry said. "Personally, I'd go for the miniskirt with the cropped top, but she likes the minidress."

"It's just a bit subtler. I also like the leggings and red sweater combo—casual but hot." Hannah had several hangers draped over her shoulder.

I was relieved that they'd both dressed for the occasion, knowing my plan to see the band and bag the guy. Harry was in jeans and a dress shirt and Hannah wore a cute pink minidress paired with cowboy boots. Adorable! I felt sort of bad using them as decoys, but then again, it was quality family time together and they were getting paid.

"This is the same guy who was staring at you at Gram's funeral, right?" Harry asked. "The poor bastard whose heart you ripped out when you were teenagers?"

"Yes," I said. "Thanks for the phrasing there, by the way—you make me sound like a total beyotch."

Harry shrugged as if to say he called it like he saw it. Men!

"Well, *I* think trying to win back your high school sweetheart is very romantic," Hannah gushed.

She dropped the clothes on the couch and clasped her hands in front of her in a total Disney princess pose that made me smile.

"Maybe I should just have a chat with him." Harry cracked his knuckles ominously.

I realized my nephew was several inches taller than me and on his way to being a real live adult male. I glanced over at Hannah in her dress and saw that she was more woman than girl. When the heck had this happened?

It had been our tradition that every year they came to me for their spring vacations. We did it all: Central Park Zoo to the Empire State Building to tickets to the Late Show, but now they were like mini adults and pretty soon they would be leaving home for reals.

"You two are really growing up," I said.

They both looked at me, and then at each other, saying together, "She sounds just like Mom."

No wonder Sophie was struggling with her babies becoming adults and off for a summer in Switzerland, and the year after that, college. What would life be like for her and Stan with the twins gone?

"How is your mom handling your upcoming departure?" I asked.

The wore matching wary expressions.

"Tell me the truth." I placed my hand to my heart.

"She cries a lot," Hannah said.

"Yeah," Harry nodded. "And staying here with you and Aunt Emily isn't helping."

"Because she's missing you?" I asked.

"That and..." Harry's voice trailed off and they exchanged another look.

"What?" I asked. They were quiet, so I pushed. "I can't help if I don't know."

"She and Dad fight a lot." Hannah said the words quickly as if speed would make it less damning.

"It's not good, and it's not Mom. It's not her at all. To be frank, Dad is being a real prick," Harry said. He donned a look of someone wiser than his years who expected better than what he was seeing in his father. In his young face, I saw the man he would become. It filled my heart because I knew he was going to be a good one.

"Tell you what," I said. "While she's here with me, I'll see what I can find out and I'll make sure she's okay."

"Thanks, Aunt Jules," Hannah said.

They relaxed in relief, and I realized they'd hoped to talk to me tonight about this. It made me feel good to know that I could do this for them. Despite the miles between us, I had always adored these kids.

Harry glanced at his phone. "Okay, I have a hot date at nine, so if we're doing this, we need to get going."

"Nine?" I asked. "Who has a date that starts at nine?"

"Me," Harry said. "Since that's when she gets off of her shift at Deluca's."

"You're dating a waitress at Deluca's?" This was news. I wondered if Sophie knew.

"Hostess," Hannah clarified.

"Still," I said. Deluca's had been Gulf Harbor's family-owned Italian restaurant for generations. It was well known that they only employed family members. "She's a Deluca? Have you met the folks yet?"

"Not yet," Harry said.

He sounded as if he was trying to be confident but since everyone knew that if Johnny Deluca took a dislike to you, you were never setting foot in Deluca's again. Harry was wise to be nervous; they had the best linguine and clam sauce for fifty miles. No one wanted to be banned from that.

"Just mind your manners and respect her curfew and you'll be fine," I said.

"No worries, I got this." Harry winked at me and pointed at me with both index fingers.

"Yeah, that," I said, twirling my finger at him. "Don't do that."

He laughed and Hannah, at the end of her patience, grabbed my hand and dragged me toward the stairs.

"Come on, let's get you dressed. I am dying to see these boots of Aunt Emily's. Do you think she'd let me borrow them?"

"Sorry," I said. "I'm pretty sure you have to be over twenty-one." Not even kidding.

Hannah and I rejected several outfits until we found the right combo of "knock him to his knees" and "don't get arrested."

When we arrived downstairs after an inordinate amount of time on make-up and hair, honestly, being a girl is a lot of work, Harry glanced up from his phone and gave us a wolf whistle.

"Wow!" he said. "Liam is definitely going to have "the second one" at the sight of you. Now I'm glad I'm going to be chaperoning this outing. I might have to throw a few punches to keep the men from getting grabby."

"You think?" I glanced down at the thigh high boots we'd managed to pull up over a pair of black leggings paired with a red off-the-shoulder cropped sweater that hugged my curves in all the right places.

"No need, we're not going to be there that long," Hannah said.

"Huh?" Harry looked bewildered.

"Liam needs to see Aunt Jules," my niece explained. "Just long enough so that she's seared onto his brain when he goes home tonight, and then she needs to poof!"

"Poof?" Harry asked.

"Poof," Hannah repeated.

"Do all girls work this hard to get guys?" Harry shook his head in disbelief.

"Yes," Hannah confirmed at the same time I said, "I have no idea."

"Trust me, bro." Hannah spoke as if she had a direct line to the experts. "If a girl likes you, she puts in effort. If she doesn't, well, that's your answer and you should probably just move along—nothing to see there."

Harry glanced between us, and I shrugged. "It's my first run at man chasing. Frankly, it hasn't been going well."

He looked thoughtful and I had a feeling his hostess had better put in a token effort, or the boy would be completely flummoxed.

A friend of Em's had picked her up earlier, so I helped myself to her keys. I was mostly confident she wouldn't mind and led the way out the door.

"Aunt Jules, I have a question," Harry said.

"If it's birds and bees stuff, ask your mom," I said.

The twins blanched. I almost laughed, knowing that Soph hadn't been exaggerating about her sex talk PowerPoint. I unlocked the car and we all piled in, Hannah and me in front and Harry in the back.

"No," Harry said. "This is family stuff."

"Okay, shoot," I said. I started the car and backed out onto the road. I saw Babs's urn sitting on the window ledge per her request. I felt a surge of resentment that she could still manipulate all of us from behind the veil but I shook it off. I was on a mission tonight and could not afford to get distracted.

"If Gram wasn't your mom, are we still, like, as related as we used to be?"

I flinched. I hadn't seen that one coming. My voice when I spoke was fierce. "Yes! Of course! Your grandfather was my dad and your mom's and Aunt Em's, too, so yes, absolutely we're still blood. Why do you ask?"

"Cousin Paisley came by the house," Harry said. Hannah swiveled around from the front passenger seat to glare at him in the back, but he squared his shoulders and kept going. "She was trying to get Mom and Dad to cut you out of the will since you've been gone for so long and 'cause you're not really Gram's daughter."

I felt all of the blood drain out of my head into the pinched toes of my boots. My temples contracted with rage, but I took a deep breath through my nose and cleared my throat.

"What did your mom say?" I asked.

Hannah burst out laughing and said, "She told her to fuck off."

"Hannah!" I cried.

"She did." Harry grinned. "That's a direct quote. It was pretty epic."

I tucked my smile into my cheek. If Soph was here, I'd have squeezed the stuffing out of her. "Then what happened?"

"Paisley was butt hurt and stormed off," Harry said. "And then Dad lit into Mom for her language and for not being polite to Paisley. It got rough."

"I'm sorry," I said. "Long marriages go through growing pains. It could be that's what's happening with your parents."

"Yeah, maybe." Harry sounded doubtful.

I reached back and patted his knee. "Don't worry. Like I said, I'll keep an eye on your mom."

"Cool." He nodded and his shaggy blond hair covered his face.

I couldn't believe Soph hadn't told me about Paisley. I supposed she figured I had enough on my plate given that I was dealing with the big reveal about my origins, but she didn't need to protect me. Not from Paisley. If there was one good thing about this whole melodrama, it was discovering that I wasn't blood related to that royal pain in the ass. See? There's always a silver lining. Sometimes you just had to look for it.

We arrived at Liam's Coffee Shop to find the band was already playing. They were a guitar-heavy jam band, and the crowd was grooving. It was standing room only so I planted myself at the back, but Hannah grabbed my arm and shook her head. She forcibly dragged me—and I do mean dragged since I was afraid to lift my feet and was doing this weird loping slide-walk so as not to trip and break my neck in these ridiculous boots—until Liam's office door was in our line of sight. My hands started to sweat and I almost bolted. I wasn't sure I was up for this, especially if rejection was looming.

"Hang tough, Aunt Jules," Hannah said. "We just need to know that he's seen you and then you're free to run."

"Okay," I said. "But how will I know?"

"Oh, you'll know," my niece said with confidence.

Harry arrived with cappuccinos for the three of us and the two of them started to groove to the band. I did not move for fear that I would fall over. As it was, I had to mince my steps because the pencil thin stilettos were making it impossible to keep my balance. Seriously, how had Em walked in these?

The band was really good and as my balance improved, I bobbed a bit to the music. Okay, mostly I was just nodding my head, but still I was in motion. I took that as a victory.

We'd only been there a few minutes when I got the feeling someone was watching me. I turned, all aflutter, expecting to find Liam staring at me. It was not Liam, rather, but some other guy whose gaze was locked on my boots like they were the answer to his every fantasy. Ew.

This dude was short, stocky, with a sweaty upper lip, a bad comb-over, and thick fingers, one of which he used to dig wax from his ear while he stood there. He stared at my boots with an intensity that made me think he wanted to try them on. Oh, *ish*!

I gave him a withering look and turned away. The crowd had gotten thicker, and a few people had wedged themselves between me and the twins. I wondered if I should push my way forward, but didn't want to risk falling on my face.

Someone approached my side and when I glanced down, I discovered short guy staring at my boots, licking his fleshy lips.

"You can't have the boots," I said.

"Can I just touch one?" His hazel eyes were wide and glassy. "I just want to feel how the leather hugs your calves."

"No," I said. "Absolutely not."

"Just one finger," the man said. "Aw, come on, I promise I won't do any more than that."

"No!" I used my cat scolding voice. It worked as well on him as it did on my cats. In other words, he ignored me.

"Please," he whined, beginning to pant. "I'm begging you."

No one around us was paying any attention to the shoe perv beside me. Hannah and Harry were too far away to hear my shout over the band. And the troll next to me looked so excited I just wanted him to go away. Feeling trapped, I figured if I let him touch one boot with one finger maybe he'd be satisfied and git.

"All right, fine," I snapped. "One finger on the toe of the right boot for three seconds and that's it."

Excitement flared in his eyes like a banked fire getting hit with a blast of oxygen.

"My lovelies!" he cried.

The next thing I knew I had some strange guy's head wedged between my knees as he hugged my boots with both arms. His momentum made me teeter on my already shaky pins and I flailed my arm as I tried to catch my balance and not spill my cappuccino.

"Hey! I said one finger, you little pervert," I shouted over the din of music. "Get off me!"

The strange little man had quite the grip, however, and I couldn't move never mind shake him loose.

Desperate for help, I glanced up and, of course, this was how Liam found me in the middle of his coffee shop with a strange man smooching the instep of my right foot.

"Argh!" I tried to jostle the stubby guy off. "Stop that! Oh, god, no tongue! That is disgusting!"

"Problem?" Liam asked as he moved through the crowd to join us.

I blew out a breath and studied the balding head between my feet. This was so not how I had expected this evening to go. Instead of Liam giving me scalding-hot looks and having the image of me burned onto his brain, yeah, no, my ex had his lips pressed together as he tried not to erupt with laughter.

"Rodney," he said as he bent over so the guy could hear him. "We've talked about this behavior before. You need to rein in the shoe fetish and let go of her boots."

"But they're black patent leather and go to mid-thigh," Rodney mumbled with his face pressed against the inside of my knee as he smelled the leather. "You know that's my weakness."

Enough was enough. I didn't think Liam was going to be able to talk the guy off the leather, so I figured it was time to bring in some back up I'd learned during a self-defense class.

I lifted one foot, bent my knee and shouted, "Incoming!"

I clocked the short man in the temple and Rodney dropped like a stone, letting go of my boots. I took several wobbly steps away from the boot-licker and sipped my cappuccino.

"Whoa," Liam said. "Nice move."

"Thanks." I shrugged.

"Rodney, you okay?" Liam reached down and slapped Rodney's cheek with three quick pats. Rodney blinked, and Liam helped him up to his feet. "What do you say, Rodney?"

Rodney peered at me with dazed eyes. "Sorry."

"It's fine," I lied.

"I really, really love your boots." Rodney braced like he was going to lunge again but Liam held him by the back of his shirt.

"I got that," I said. "Go away now."

"Rodney, you broke your promise and now you can't come in here anymore," Liam said as he hauled him toward the door. "Next time I see you, I'll call the police. Got it?"

Rodney gave him a dejected nod. I watched the two of them walk away and felt decidedly grossed out. I grimaced at my boots. There was some saliva on them. *Gag!* Em was going to kill me.

Realizing there was absolutely no way to salvage the night, I leaned over the people in front of me to tap Hannah and Harry on the shoulders. I figured it was safe to call the time of death on this outing.

They both looked back at me, and I jerked my head in the direction of the door. Hannah's eyes went wide while Harry looked around, wondering if he had missed something. Boy howdy, had he and I was so glad that I didn't have to explain to his mother how her son got to see a shoe fetishist up close and personal because of me.

"So, did he see you?" Hannah asked as we reached the outskirts of the crowd.

"Oh, yeah," I said.

"Was "the second one" involved?" Harry asked.

"In a manner of speaking." I was pretty sure that good old Rodney had been sporting wood at the sight of my boots. Harry and Hannah gave me an identical inquisitive look and I said, "I'll explain on the way home."

When we reached the door of the coffee shop, I scanned outside to make sure that Rodney was gone. The coast was clear, but as I walked out, Liam walked in. We blocked each other's paths, and I noticed he took a moment to let his gaze wander down my body from my wild curls to my toes.

"Nice boots." Liam chuckled and walked around me into the coffee shop, leaving me feeling as sexy as Sunday dinner leftovers.

Hannah and Harry stopped behind me as I stepped into the night air and paused to draw a cleansing breath.

"Call me crazy," Harry said. "But that doesn't seem to have gone as planned."

"Boots!" A high voice squeaked from my right.

"Ack!" I cried. "It's Rodney! Run, kids, run!"

Thankfully, their survival skills kicked in and both Hannah and Harry dove for the car. I managed to shove the key into the ignition and jet out of the parking lot before Rodney could reach us. I had a feeling he would have happily jumped onto the front like a hood ornament if it meant he got one more lick of my boots. *Bleck!*

As we high-tailed it home, I explained to Harry and Hannah about Rodney's infatuation with the boots. Harry laughed so hard he was sure he strained some muscles he'd been planning to use on his date. Hannah seemed a bit sick. I was with her there. There was no way I wanted to tell Em what had been done to her boots and I hoped to heck that we had some industrial leather cleaner back at the house.

"I have to declare Operation Boots on the Ground a complete bust," Hannah said.

I parked in the driveway, and we all climbed out of the car.

"I don't know," Harry said. "They sure worked on Rodney."

"I can never unsee that," I said. "I might need therapy, or shock treatment, or something. What a waste! These bad boys sure didn't work on Liam."

"Maybe you just need to be straight with the guy," Harry said. "I saw how he looked at you before. If you tell him how you feel, I bet he's all in."

"Or he'll inform me that he hates me and get a restraining order," I said.

"Then he's a moron and you're better off without him," my nephew said.

I hugged Harry tight and ruffled his hair. "I love you."

"Love you, too, Aunt Jules," he said.

"This is just a minor setback." Hannah hugged me too. "I'll keep thinking. There has to be a way to crack this guy. Love you."

"Love you, too, pumpkin," I said.

I watched them walk to their car, feeling the slightest bit envious of their youth and optimism. At the moment, I felt neither, so I went into the house and decided to eat my feelings with a bowl of Tillamook horchata ice cream while I debated the funk I was in.

"Em?" I called my sister's name. There was no answer. I yelled louder. "Em, I'm home and I need ice cream therapy. Join me?"

I stood listening. Nothing. Having lived alone for the past five years, I was surprised by a sudden blast of loneliness. I tried to shake it off. It wasn't like me to feel that way; honestly, I preferred being alone most of the time and living with my sisters had been an adjustment.

Mr. Loren had been very clear that there was no wiggle room in the will and we were all reporting home every night to sleep in our own beds as dictated.

I assumed it was my spectacular defeat in the man-catching arts that had me bummed. I debated calling Soph to see what she was doing but remembered she and Stan had some event at the country club and she would be home late. My sister was probably busy charming all of the other doctors' wives. She was brilliant at making other people feel at ease. It was like her superpower. Except when she told Paisley to fuck off. That made me cackle.

While I plowed through my bowl of ice cream over the kitchen sink, I wondered how Soph felt about the role of doctor's wife. She had always been the creative one of the three of us and her passion had been art, painting specifically. While I'd spent my days riding the waves, Soph had painted the waves and Em had curled up with a book under a nearby tree ignoring the waves. A feeling of nostalgia hit me and I missed the peaceful simplicity of our youth even if I now knew a large portion of it had been a lie.

I thought about my birth mother, Lisa, and what my life would have been like if she hadn't walked away. I couldn't imagine. And wasn't that saying something? I had no idea what it would be like to have a mother who loved me just for me. I had been sharpened on the rough stones of Babs's disappointment and disapproval. Who would I be without it? I had no clue. I felt a snuffle shoot down my nose. I refused to give in to it. I was so very tired of crying for what could have been. I put the bowl in the sink and rinsed it out.

The house was quiet, too quiet. Where was Em? I hadn't seen her all day and I missed her. Come to think of it, I had no idea how she was keeping busy these days during her leave of absence from work. I hoped it was fun or at the very least distracting. Em was so serious for a woman her age, I paused to glance down at her boots. Okay, she had been serious—maybe she was overdue for this rebellion.

I opened the cupboard under the kitchen sink looking for something to clean the leather with as I could not in good conscience return the boots with Rodney's saliva on them. *Ew.*

I found a tub of leather furniture wipes and figured that was good enough. I used the window seat in the kitchen to prop my leg up as I ran a couple of leather wipes from the thigh all the way down to the toes and back, repeatedly. It was easier to clean them while still wearing them. Also, I dreaded taking them off because I was afraid my feet were going to spasm.

I dumped the first set of wipes and reached for more when I got that old familiar feeling of being watched. At first, I thought Rodney had tracked me down for the boots, *gross*, but as if my body was in tune with his, I knew immediately that it was Liam.

Out of the corner of my eye, I could see the light coming from the second story of his house. I didn't look at him and instead checked the reflection of his window in the glass vase that sat on our kitchen table. It was distorted but it was easy to see that a large male was standing with his arms crossed over his chest, staring at me while I scrubbed down the boots.

Well, well, well! It seemed I was going to be putting on a show after all.

Chapter Seventeen

"**B**ow chicka wow wow," I hummed to myself as I swiped the leather wipes over the boot. I started at the toes and slowly worked my way up to the thighs. Conscious of Liam's gaze upon me, my heart beat triple time and as smooth as I was trying to be, my movements felt clumsy and awkward.

Okay, so stripper moves are not as intuitive as one would think. I tried to wiggle my hips but the tiny toothpick heels holding me up didn't accommodate the shift in weight as easily as one would expect. I bobbled, I wobbled, and I hoped he was too far away to see me grab the back of a chair to keep from face planting.

No, no, no, not again. Seriously, I could not make an ass of myself again twice in one night.

With my confidence squashed, I went back to just casually cleaning the boots. I could still see his reflection in the mirror, and I figured maybe now was the time to lose the boots. I reclined on the window seat and lifted one leg. I worked the zipper down all the way to the sole and then toed off the boot. A glance at the vase showed that he was still there. His arms were no longer crossed over his chest but had dropped to his sides. I envisioned his fists clenching and unclenching. The thought of making him crazy made me all kinds of naughty girl giddy.

I slowly lifted my other leg and hummed my stripper music again. I pulled the zipper down, slowly, painfully slowly, seriously, my fingers started to cramp, until I was able to wriggle my foot out of the boot, which I dropped on the ground. His reflection was still visible, and I wondered if I should go for broke and lose my sweater or the leggings. I was just reaching for my waistband when Em blew into the kitchen.

"Oh, my god, do not tell me you are about to strip in our kitchen for that man!" my little sister cried.

Em pointed right at Liam's window, and I shifted his direction as if I'd been unaware he'd been there. Our gazes locked and one of his eyebrows rose ever so slightly as if daring me. Without hesitation I reached for the hem of my sweater.

"Oh, hell no!" Em snapped off the light, plunging us into darkness.

"But—" I protested.

"No," she said. "Come here."

Emily headed out of the kitchen and into the dimly lit hallway where Liam wouldn't be able to see us. I picked up the boots and followed.

"You are out of control," baby sis lectured. "You need to get a grip. Where's your self-respect?"

"I still have it, some of it anyway," I said. "I mean I'm not over there groveling for him to come back to me. I'm just trying to stay on his radar, so he'll realize that we belong to—hold up! Wait one mother-fluffing minute, *what* did you do to your hair?"

"What?" Em's eyes were wide with innocence. "Nothing. It must be the lighting."

"That is not lighting," I said.

I grabbed her hand and dragged her into the living room. Under better light, I could see dark blue and teal streaks running through her hair from the crown to the tips. It looked awesome. It looked badass. Except it was on Em, and Em didn't do awesome or badass. Em did cute and nice and sweet.

"Your hair is blue," I said.

"Really?" she asked as if mildly surprised. "Huh."

"What...why...ugh," I paused and tried to get my thoughts together. "Em, are you okay?"

"I'm fine," my sister said. "Shaking things up a bit, you know, trying to get my feet back under me."

"With blue hair?" I asked.

"No, this was just something fun to do." The joy of a new hairstyle didn't exude from Em's demeanor. Did she hate it? Love it? Regret it?

"Soph is going to freak." I noticed that her skin was pale, and she was thinner too.

"Why? It's not her hair."

"Good point."

Em took the boots out of my arms and headed toward the stairs. She was dressed casually in jeans and slip on sneakers with a thermal shirt. Maybe that's what a person wore to the salon when they dyed their hair blue. I had no idea. I just wasn't buying what she was peddling. She could pretend she was fine all she wanted, but the shdows beneath her eyes were getting darker every day, which the blue hair did not help. This was not a person who was dealing with her stuff.

"Em, grief can be really difficult to navigate," I said. "I hope you know you can talk to me about anything anytime. You *do* know that, right?"

"Yeah, I know." Em shrugged, jostling her armful of boot. "But I don't need to. I'm fine."

"Fine is usually code for not fine," I pressed.

"Well, this time it isn't. Fine is fine," she said. "And now I'm going to bed. Good night."

"Good night," I called after her.

"And *do not* go back and finish your striptease in the kitchen," Em called over her shoulder.

"I wasn't going to," I lied.

She snorted and I knew she didn't believe me because she was smart like that. With a last regretful glance toward Liam's house, I checked the locks and secured the first floor before climbing the stairs to my bedroom.

The light across the way had gone dark and I didn't bother putting on mine while I changed, sensing that he would not be looking for me again tonight. Maybe Em was right. I might be sacrificing my self-respect for a lost cause. Was Liam worth it? Yes, definitely yes. If I could have a second chance at what we'd once had, I would give up the above and throw in my pride and dignity, too.

It occurred to me as I slipped between the sheets that maybe Soph was also right, and that chasing Liam was my own thigh-high-boots-and-blue-hair way of dealing with my grief and shock.

Perhaps pursuing him was more about having a distraction than a mission. Maybe I didn't want Liam as much as I wanted to not think about the fact that I wasn't who I thought I was. That all the years of criticism and scrutiny weren't about me so much as they were about Babs's rage at my father's betrayal. I wished she had told me. I wished we'd gotten therapy or something, but mostly, I wished she'd given me a chance to love her and mourn her the way Em and Soph were. I never had and never would. The hurt ambushed me and before I knew it, I was rolling onto my pillow and sobbing until the pain ebbed and I could breathe again.

Ambush grief. One minute you were fine and the next you were a mess. It had hit me several times over the past few days, but usually, I redirected my thoughts to Liam and pushed it away. This time I didn't. I let myself grieve for the woman I had thought was my mother and for the relationship we could have had that was now lost to me for good.

I let the sadness, the bitterness, the wish that it could have been different, fill me up inside. It spilled over my rim and splashed down my sides. It seemed unending, and I thought about distracting myself from the anguish with thoughts of Liam, but I didn't. Instead, I concentrated on Babs. I thought about how she'd said she wished she could have loved me. Then I thought about Mrs. G and how she'd said Babs was so proud of me. The pain in my chest eased. It would have to be enough.

I realized it was time for some self-truth. I didn't want to believe that I was using Liam to manage my grief, but I couldn't deny that my interest in him had become much more focused after Babs's death and after learning the truth of my own origins.

Oh, sure, I'd thought he was a hottie before she died and we clearly had unfinished business, but in the days leading up to her death and after, it became a mission to get him to notice me, to give us another chance.

Why was I suddenly so desperate to revisit a relationship I had left years before without a backward glance? It wasn't coincidental. I was running away from my grief or trying to, anyway. With my new awareness, I knew I needed to step back, to reevaluate, and reassess.

If I was chasing Liam for the wrong reasons, things weren't going to work out for us. I refused to be responsible for ruining his current relationship if I was uncertain that us being together was the outcome that I truly wanted. It wasn't fair to any of us, and I knew what I had to do.

Em had split before I got up the next day. Since she still wasn't working, I had no idea where she could be, and I was more worried about her than ever. Given how close they had been, losing Babs had to be an emotionally crushing weight that she couldn't lift alone. I wished I knew how to get her to talk to me.

Soph wasn't home either, as she was volunteering at the twins' school, so I left her a message about Em's blue hair but didn't hear back from her all morning. I drank my coffee in the kitchen, feeling more than a little mortified to think of how far I would have gone if Em hadn't crashed my little striptease the night before.

In an effort to step back and do some thinking, I didn't go surfing or to the coffee shop. The shade over my bedroom window remained down and I worked all day, not breaking to loiter in the front yard to sunbathe, or anything else for that matter.

Instead, I chugged endless cups of coffee until I was so wired, I was certain I could smell sounds. It was late afternoon with my heart hammering and my fingers shaking, I finally backed away from my laptop and pulled on some jogging gear. I gulped a big bottle of water and then stretched. I would run my demons out of my head or at the very least speed walk them into silence.

Shoving earbuds into my ears, I cranked Guns N' Roses's *Appetite for Destruction* from the phone in my arm holster and began to jog. In my sports bra and yoga pants, I started down the street and through Gull's Harbor to the narrow strip of pavement that had been created specifically for people who wanted to run or walk along the tops of the cliffs with an ocean view.

The ripping crunch and grind of the guitar along with the singer's raw vocals blanketed my senses to any other sounds. I kept my head forward and ran, clocking the miles as if they were no big deal. I knew I needed to save enough strength to turn around and go back so at a small park on the rise of a grassy hill, I paused.

Sweat was pouring off me. My lungs heaved as I sucked in gulps of the damp salt air. I lifted my face to the strong, cool breeze blowing in from the ocean and let it chill my skin. I shut off the music and closed my eyes. I did some yoga breathing and tried to feel my feet sink into the earth as I became one with my surroundings. A seagull flew by, cawing at me as if trying to pull me out of my Zen moment, but I refused to budge.

The sound of a motorcycle roared by, still, I maintained my calm. I was standing just off the path so as not to be in the way of any other joggers. The motorcycle's engine revved again. I huffed a breath and concentrated on my breathing. In with the good air and out with the bad, yada, yada, yada. The engine growled one more time and this time, I lost my patience.

I whipped my head around prepared to give the motorcyclist a blast of stink eye that would overheat his engine, but when my gaze met the motorcyclist's, it was my engine that boiled over. Liam, in a leather jacket astride a big behemoth of a ride, was staring at me as if he couldn't decide whether to push me off the cliff or kidnap me.

Liam switched off the engine and rolled the bike onto its stand—he swung his leg over the seat and strode toward me. His intense brown gaze made me want to run. I just couldn't decide if it should be to him or away. So, like a moron I stood frozen, watching him approach with a titillated horrified fascination that I was certain made me look as if I had the shallowest brain pan in existence.

I expected him to stop a few feet away or at the very least on the edge of my personal space. He didn't. He cruised right up until he was flush against me with one hand clutching my hip while the other gripped the back of my head. His lips landed on mine with the same force of a rolling wave crashing on the beach. His mouth fit perfectly against mine and he made love to my lips just like he had to my body the other night. Oh, wow.

Every bit of me wanted to wrap myself around him and return his kiss measure for measure, but I stood frozen, uncertain what to do. I had promised myself I would step back and figure it out but the only thing I had figured out was that despite my best intentions, I had spent all day missing him, thinking about him, and wanting him. Was it because he was the love of my life or because I was channeling my grief into the beautiful chemistry between us that simply would not fade?

As quickly as Liam grabbed me, he released me except that he kept his hand on my hip, as if to reassure himself that he could stop me if I ran.

I wasn't running anywhere. Instead, in a perfect moment of clarity, I realized that my feelings for Liam had nothing to do with Babs passing or the revelation that she wasn't my mother. I didn't want him more because I was trying to escape my grief but rather, I wanted him because now that Babs was gone so was one of the biggest obstacles to our being together. Maybe when Babs had said she'd wished she had more time to make it right, she had meant this, Liam and me together, finally.

His gaze moved over my face as if he was trying to figure out what I was thinking. I couldn't find the words, so instead I rose on my toes, looped my arms around his neck, and pulled him in for another kiss. I wasn't tentative or gentle, rather it was my turn to claim and possess and to let him know quite plainly that I considered him mine.

He pulled me in tight and kissed me back, making it clear that he felt the same way. He tipped my head and kissed my jaw just below my ear, working his way down my neck as I clung to him.

"Surfer girl, you are driving me crazy," he said. "I can't fight this anymore. Come home with me."

"Okay," I said.

Chapter Eighteen

Liam blinked at me. I don't think he expected my acquiescence to be so swift. Maybe after all of my embarrassing stunts, I should have played hard to get and made him work for it, because truly, he had been a real prick the other night. But I was running on empty, and I wanted to be with him, naked with him, as swiftly as possible. And not for nothing, but the run back home was mostly uphill and riding with my arms and legs wrapped around the back of him sure seemed like the better option to me.

He grabbed my hand and yanked me across the park almost as fast as I'd been when I was running. When we arrived at the bike, he took off his leather jacket and held it out to me. I was just reaching for it when my phone rang. I glanced at the display. It was Soph. I desperately did not want to interrupt what was happening here, but my sisters came first. I'd just answer quick and call her back later.

"It's Soph," I said.

Liam nodded. He'd always understood the Blumer sister bond.

"Hi, Soph," I said. "It's not the best time right now, can I call—"

"Em is missing," Soph interrupted. She sounded upset and my stomach clenched.

"What?" I asked. "That's not possible. I just saw her last night."

"She never showed up for our lunch date today," Soph said.

"Maybe she didn't want you to see her hair," I suggested. "She's been acting really weird."

Liam watched me with eyebrows raised, and I made a sorry face and held up a finger to indicate I just needed a moment. He unstrapped the helmet off the back while he waited. As he stood there with the Pacific breeze tousling his dark brown hair, I almost forgot I was on the phone.

"Jules, it gets worse." The tight note of anxiety in Soph's voice brought my attention back to her.

"What do you mean?" I asked.

"I've been calling and texting her cell phone all day and there's been no answer until just a few minutes ago," Soph said.

"So, you got in touch with her?" I tried hard to track why my usually calm older sister was worried.

"No! A man answered," Soph said. "A strange man."

I gasped. Our innocent Emily?

"I know," Soph said. "Jules, I'm scared. He sounded like a very bad man, and when I demanded to speak to Emily, he hung up on me and when I called back it went right to voice mail. Jules, I think she's been abducted."

My insides went cold, and it occurred to me that terror had its own temperature—like ice, freezing my lungs and making it hard to breathe.

"Don't panic," I said. Ironic given the note of fear in my voice. "I'm on my way home. Meet me there. We'll figure this out. We'll find Em, I promise."

I ended the call and glanced at Liam. He was frowning and I wasn't sure how much he'd heard. I squeezed his forearm. "I'm so sorry," I said. "There's an emergency. I have to go."

With that I bolted. Panic had me running far faster than introspection. The green park and blue ocean were watercolor blurs as tears filled my eyes and I sprinted to get back to the house.

Em! Where was she? Who had her phone? What had happened in the twenty hours since we'd seen each other? Oh, god, if anything had happened to her I don't know what I'd do. Why hadn't I forced her talk with me? I ran faster, cursing myself with every step.

How could I have just let her be when I knew she'd been struggling? I let her go to bed with her blue hair and shadowed eyes, allowing her to keep all her pain and sorrow to herself. So self-involved in my own ridiculous junk that I hadn't reached out to her when she so obviously needed it.

Self-loathing choked me, and it was harder and harder to make it up the hill when the panic whispered in my ear that she'd likely been abducted and was even now lying in some cockroach-infested drug den with sweaty men doing horrible things to her. What if we never found her? What if she was murdered? It would be all my fault.

"Jules! Damn it, Jules, wait!"

It took a second for the sound of the motorcycle and a man yelling to cut through the paranoid monologue in my head. I glanced to the left and saw Liam on his motorcycle roaring up beside me.

"Em is missing! I have to go home!" I cried.

He jumped the curb and pulled up in front of me—I had to stop or run right into him.

"I got that," Liam said. "Get on. I'll get you there a hell of lot faster."

"Oh. Thank you," I panted.

I climbed onto the seat behind him, and he plopped the helmet onto my head. "Hang on."

The bike roared to life, and we were off, skimming over the earth like we were flying. I wrapped my arms tight around his middle in a death grip. At any other time, I would have enjoyed the feel of my front pressed to his back, but right now all I could think about was my baby sister and where she was and how I was going to find her. Tears leaked and I let them, pressing my head into Liam's strong back as we jetted home.

Sophie was standing in the front yard when we pulled up. I let go of Liam and yanked off the helmet, thrusting it at him as I swung my leg over the seat and jumped off before he'd even gotten to a full stop. I rushed Soph and when she saw me coming her arms opened and we hugged, clutching each other for support in our mutual terror.

"This is all my fault," we said at the same time and then again, "No, it isn't."

"Have you tried her phone again?" I asked.

"There's no answer," Sophie said.

"I'll try it." I pulled my phone off my arm holster and tried to call Em. It rolled right to voice mail. Damn it!

Liam approached. He looked wary as if uncertain of his role here but still he asked, "How can I help?"

Soph stepped toward him. "You haven't seen Em at all today, have you?"

"No, sorry," he said.

"Em didn't meet me for lunch and when I tried to track her down through friends, no one has heard from her and then when I called her cell phone a strange man answered." Soph brought her knuckles to her lower lip. "And now all I'm getting is her voice mail."

Soph started to cry. Liam gave her a quick, bracing hug, which I knew was one of his specialties.

"I'll call Ryan, my buddy at the Gulf Harbor police department, and see what he says. Even if we can't declare her missing officially yet, I know he'll get the word out to the patrol units to keep an eye out. Then we need to go search for her," Liam said. "I'm sure she's fine. She's lived in this town her entire life. Everyone knows her. People will look out for her if she's gotten herself into a jam. I'm sure of it."

"You're right." Soph exhaled with force as if she'd been holding it in for hours.

I didn't know if Liam was trying to convince us or himself, but his words made me feel better nonetheless.

"I'll call my staff at the coffee shop, too," he said. "The more people looking, the better."

"I'll call Hannah and Harry," I said. "They can get all of their friends to be on the lookout as well."

"I'll call Stan." Soph reached for her phone. "Maybe he can help us search."

My call was easy. Hannah and Harry were actually at Liam's Coffee Shop but promised to spread the word to their friends and then rendezvous with us at the house. Liam was on his phone considerably longer.

"Do you have a recent picture of Em?" he asked. "It'd help the patrol officers to know who they're looking for."

"Hang on," I said. I was not a big picture taker, but I checked the photos on my phone. Shots from my life in New York popped up, including some of Jessie and me when we went ice skating at Rockefeller Center this past winter. I quickly scrolled through, hoping Liam didn't see. It was a bust. I had no photos of Em. "I've got nothing."

"What about social media?" Liam had his phone to his ear.

"Em's not online," I said. "Babs forbid it."

"Are you sure?" he asked. His brow rose.

I shrugged. I supposed it was worth checking although I couldn't imagine my introverted baby sister had any desire to have her life played out on social media, especially if it was met with maternal disapproval.

I opened up a search engine on my phone and did a cursory search. I got nothing on Emily Blumer. I tried a variety of name and initial searches and even some of the nicknames I called her. Nothing. Lastly, I did an images search for Emily and Gull's Harbor and my phone blew the fuck up.

Picture after picture filled the small screen. Huh. Who knew there were so many Emilys in Gull's Harbor? As I scrolled through the pictures, I realized there weren't. There was just one; my baby sister who apparently had a whole other life happening online.

"Holy crap!" I cried.

"What is it?" Soph raced over to me, looking at my phone as I held it out for her to see. There had to be more than fifty pictures, memes, and short videos of Em. I glanced up at the top of the page. The girl already had thousands and thousands of followers, and it looked like she'd only recently gotten online. In fact, she'd joined the day after Babs passed away.

"Is that *our* Em?" Soph asked.

I played one of the videos. It was footage of Em getting her belly button pierced. We both cringed as the guy put the clamp on and we watched in shock as Em in her shorty shorts and knotted T-shirt flirted with him while he did it.

"I'm speechless," I said. "I am without speech."

And I was. Soph's phone rang, and we both jumped. She glanced at the display. It was Stan. She turned away from my phone and took the call while I continued to scroll through all of Em's posts.

Liam joined me and peered over my shoulder. He frowned. "Is that Em?"

"Yeah," I said. "I'm assuming this is how she's decided to manage her grief. See? She's using the hashtag grief and another hashtag Emily for every post."

"Processing bereavement by becoming a social media star?" Liam gave a low whistle. "She's got a ton of followers. I don't even have that many for the coffee shop and I've been in business for years."

"Looks like a celebrity shared her posts and now she's trending." I frowned. "Except now she's missing, and a stranger has her phone. Oh, god, what if it's one of those woman-hating-incel-troll types and he's abducted her?"

My voice was shaking, and Liam put his hand on my back to steady me. "It's going to be okay. We'll find her."

I knew he was bullshitting me, but I was ever so grateful for how assured he sounded. He messaged the link to her social media account to all of his employees and his friend Ryan.

"My sister is missing!" Soph was pacing and her voice was raised. "I know and I'm sorry. I don't mean to interrupt. Isn't there any way you can cancel your dinner with your colleagues for a family emergency?"

I couldn't make out his words, but I heard Stan's deep drone on the line, and it was all I could do not to snatch the phone out of Soph's hands and tell him to get his ass over here and help us. Perhaps it was my panic kicking in or maybe I just didn't like a man who couldn't be there for his wife when she needed him. Then again, I couldn't remember a time when Stan had ever put anyone ahead of himself.

Liam squeezed my shoulder and I realized I'd taken one step forward as if I would actually grab Soph's phone and curb-stomp it like I wanted to Stan's head. I glanced at my sister's face. She looked upset enough. She didn't need me brawling with her husband to make it any worse.

"Aunt Jules, has there been any word?" Hannah and Harry asked as they parked in front of the house and jumped from the car.

"No," I said. "But we have discovered that your Aunt Emily has a lot going on in her life that we didn't know about, but I'm guessing you two did."

I turned my phone around so that they could see it. Hannah and Harry were in a couple of the pictures and they both looked duly alarmed that I had found Em's page.

"We can explain," they said together.

"I'm listening," I said.

Soph shoved her phone in her pocket and joined the group. One look at their mother's face and both Hannah and Harry hugged her close.

"We'll find her, Mom." Harry sounded as absolute as Liam had. "Don't worry."

Soph nodded but her eyes were watery, and it looked as if it was taking all she had not to cry. I had the urge to kick Stan's ass for the second time in ten minutes. It must have shown on my face because I felt Liam squeeze my shoulder again, reminding me to stand down.

"Hannah and Harry were just going to tell me what they know about Emily's posts," I said.

I showed Soph one of the pictures on Em's page with the twins in it. The three of them were each wearing some kind of faux animal skin hat with the pointy ears and the sides trailing down to make a scarf with mittens sort of thing.

Soph looked from the phone to the teens. "When did you three do that?"

"Farmer's market," Hannah said. "Some guy was selling those spirit hoods."

"Spirit hood?" Liam asked.

"Yeah, like it's your spirit animal," Harry said. "I'm the lion."

"Uh huh," Soph said. "And you didn't mention to me that Em has this social media site thing happening?"

"Everyone has one," Hannah said. "NBD."

"Em never had one before," Soph said. "That makes it a very BD."

"The farmers market? Wasn't that the night Em was wearing her boots?" I asked.

Harry nodded. "She had a trail of dudes following her. That's why we stayed with her until she went home. She kinda needed a bodyguard."

"Those are Em's boots?" Liam asked. "Interesting."

My cheeks heated as Soph shot me a questioning glance. I made my face blank as I shut out the memory of the night before and tried to ignore him. Must focus on missing sister, I told myself.

"Have you two tried calling her?" I asked Harry and Hannah.

"Yeah," Harry said. "And texted her, too."

"No answer," Hannah added.

"Why don't we all split up and search town?" I suggested. "We can cover more ground. Soph, maybe you should stay here in case she comes home and then you can call us and let us know."

"Hell no," she said. "We'll leave her a note telling her to call us if she comes home. I am not just going to sit here and go slowly crazy when she's out there possibly hurt or harmed."

"Is Dad coming to help?" Hannah asked.

There was a beat of awkward silence and then Soph said, "No, honey, he can't. He has a work thing."

I saw the twins exchange a glance. Soph might have been trying to protect their opinion of their father, but something told me it was already too late.

"Okay, then, we'd better get going." I turned to Liam. "Thanks so much for the ride."

"Oh, no," he said. "You're not getting rid of me that easily. This is Em. I'm not going to be able to function until I know she's okay."

"Huh," Harry grunted. "I wish Dad felt that way."

There was another awkward silence and I desperately wanted to ask Soph what was going on in her house, but I resisted—it was definitely not the time.

"Thank you, Liam." Soph gave him a smile of gratitude. "Hannah and Harry, take your car and try down by the water, I'll take my SUV and search the center of town, Liam and Jules, you have the motorcycle so you can zip around the perimeter of town faster than any of us can. Keep your phones on and call the second you see her."

I looked at my sister in surprise. She hadn't done the bossy older sister thing in a while, and I'd forgotten how good she was at it.

"Got it," Harry and Hannah said and took off for their car.

Soph squeezed my hand as she passed me to go to her own vehicle. I grabbed her fingers and stopped her. "Are you sure you don't want me to go with you?"

She glanced past me toward Liam. "I'd love it if you were with me, but Liam's going to need you to show him all of Em's favorite places like the jogging trail up in the hills, the winery on the edge of town, and the old, abandoned church. She loves that creepy place. We can cover more ground if we split up."

"All right," I said. "But stay in contact and be careful."

"I will," Soph said. "You, too."

Soph hugged me hard and then hurried to her SUV. With a wave, she zipped out of the drive and headed toward town. Watching her brush away a tear from her cheek, I felt impotent fury with my brother-in-law for making her do this by herself. What an asshole.

"Hey, you ready?" Liam asked.

I nodded and followed him to his bike. He held out his leather jacket and I pulled it on. It was getting dark, and the temperature was dropping. The sweat from my earlier run had already dried and I was feeling the chill on my skin. I zipped up the jacket and Liam's scent, the sea and sunshine, filled my nose. The jacket was baggy, and the sleeves hung halfway down my fingers. I didn't care. I was warm.

He plopped the helmet on my head, and I fastened it while he climbed onto the bike. I followed, wrapping my arms around him just as I had before. He put on his own helmet and glanced back once with a small smile and then we took off.

We jetted all the way to the outskirts of town, trying the most popular places as we went. Em wasn't at the creepy church, thank god, and there were no cars parked nearby.

Liam drove to the popular hillside jogging path, positioning the bike in the small lot at the trail head which was illuminated by two tall streetlights. There were several cars but none belonged to Em. If she'd come here with a friend, I had no way of knowing whose vehicle they'd taken. We walked onto the trail. We didn't go far but I couldn't help but notice how quiet the area was after the noise of the motorcycle.

"How are you holding up?" he asked.

"Okay." I was so far from okay I was sure we weren't even on the same planet. In a panicked voice, I called out into the darkness, "Em!"

We both stood still, listening. There was no rustle in the darkness, no muffled cry for help, nothing.

"Em!" Liam yelled. Unlike me, he had no problem bellowing. If someone was out there hiking to enjoy the quiet, they were not going to be happy with him.

We stood still again, listening. There was no response. I started to tremble. I couldn't help it. Maybe it was the stress of the past couple of weeks coupled with all the emotional stuff that came with it, but my eyes welled and my throat closed. If something had happened to Em, well, I just didn't think I'd survive it.

Liam must have sensed my impending crash because he folded me into his arms, pressing my face against his shoulder while his arms locked around me, holding me close while I pretty much lost my shizzle in a torrential downpour of tears.

"Shh," he said. He ran his hand up and down my back. "We're going to find her."

I nodded. We had to press on. I needed to get it together so that we could. Time was a critical factor here and there was no time for a breakdown.

"Sorry." I stepped back from him and wiped my face with my hands. "It's just, yeah, there's been a lot going on."

"*I'm* sorry," he said. "The other night, what I said, what I did, I was such a son of a bitch. You're already dealing with so much; I never should have—"

"No, it's fine," I interrupted. "Totally fine. We really should get going."

I began to walk away. While I was grateful for his apology, I didn't want to hear him say that he shouldn't have slept with me. Maybe he was in love with someone else and maybe he was moving on, but that night with him had meant so much to me, you know, before he crushed my poor heart, that I couldn't bear to let him dismiss it as just a fallout from our past.

Liam grabbed my hand before I made it more than a yard. He tugged me around to face him. Oh, man, he was going to tell me how the other night had been a mistake and my heart was going to shatter right here at his feet.

Instead, he kissed me. He cupped the back of my head and kissed me until I was clinging to him, and he had one hand fisted in my hair and one hand at my lower back, locking me up against him.

"Where were you today?" His voice was a low rasp that made me shiver.

"I thought you might appreciate some space from me," I said.

He moved his lips to that trigger spot right under my ear and I promptly forgot my name, my purpose, where I was, or what I was supposed to be doing.

"I can't eat, I can't sleep, I can't think about anything but you," Liam said. He returned his mouth to mine and kissed me deeply. "I missed you all damn day, surfer girl."

My heart melted into a puddle. He had missed me. I hugged him hard.

"I missed you, too, new boy," I said.

He kissed the top of my head and hugged me tight one more time. "Okay, we're talking later. Finding Em now."

He clasped my hand and we hurried to the motorcycle. Something had shifted between us. I didn't know what, and I wasn't sure I wanted to look too closely at what was happening on the chance I was wrong, and he was going to kick me to the curb again. Instead, I followed where he led and hoped that once we found Em, the talk we were going to have wasn't going to decimate my poor heart...again.

We hit three other places that Em was known to enjoy. There was no sign of her, her car, or any of her friends. I checked in with Harry and Hannah and Soph and none of them had spotted her either. I hated that panic was beginning to be my default setting, but I couldn't seem to switch off the feeling that my sister was in pain and needed me.

We were headed toward the center of town when Liam pulled over the motorcycle. While the engine idled, he took out his phone and checked the display. His eyebrows went up and he looked at me.

"There's been a sighting by one of my employees." Liam glanced at his phone. "She's in Duff's bar."

"Duff's?" I asked. "The most diviest of dive bars where the surf crowd and the bikers hang out?"

"Yup," he said. We gave each other a wide-eyed look and then he gunned the motorcycle while I clutched him close and prayed we weren't too late.

Chapter Nineteen

"Could you hold my hair out of the toilet, please?" Em, ever polite, asked as she wretched into the dingy porcelain bowl in Duff's pint-sized ladies' room.

"You bet, sugar." The biker chick standing beside her, with the bandana around her forehead and the Willie Nelson braids, had a kindly way about her despite the leather vest, faded tattoos, and missing front tooth. I got the feeling she had done this a million times before as she lifted Em's blue streaked hair away from the puke-filled toilet.

My nose wrinkled at the smell at the same time relief pumped through me in a huge rush, making me dizzy and a teeny bit nauseous. Sensory overload.

I poked my head out of the swinging door where Liam stood waiting. "I found her."

He sagged against the wall with relief, the first time he'd betrayed any hint that he'd been worried. And didn't that just make my heart squeeze up tight? He'd been putting up a brave front for me all along.

"Can you text Soph?" I asked. "We're going to need her car to take Em home."

"Got it." Liam glanced over my shoulder and saw the biker chick. He leaned close and asked, "Are you okay in there?"

"Yeah, I got this," I said.

I don't think I imagined the pride in his eyes, which made my heart do a little toe tap of joy right up until I had to go back into the vomitory. Ugh.

I forced my mouth to curve up in a smile as I entered the bathroom and introduced myself to the formidable woman holding my sister's hair. So, this would be fun, right?

"I'm dying, aren't I?" Em asked as Liam carried her to Soph's car.

"Not yet," Sophie said. "But pull another stunt like this and I'll kill you myself. What the hell were you thinking?"

"I was having fun," Em said. Then she turned a sickly shade of green and her eyes widened. She cried, "Down! Put me down!"

Liam let her feet hit the ground but braced her under the arms so she didn't fall. Em bent over and projectile-vomited right behind the dumpster. Liam and I watched while Soph turned away, looking a bit green herself.

"She's got some good range," Liam said.

"Yeah, not bad for a rank amateur," I agreed.

Being rebellious sorts in our youth, Liam and I had done our share of underage drinking at Duff's with the other surfers. On more than one occasion one or both of us had "enjoyed" a night just like Em's.

"You are so lucky that Hannah and Harry aren't here to see this," Soph chastised. "You are twenty-five years old. You're supposed to behave like a grown-up not some stupid frat boy."

Em wiped her mouth off with the back of her hand and spun around to face Sophie. She overshot and staggered three paces to the right. Liam went to grab her, but I caught her before she fell off the curb. She stomped on my foot with her biker boots, and I opened my mouth to yelp but no sound came out. Yes, it hurt that bad.

"What do you know about frat boys?" Em weaved toward Soph with one finger pointed. "You were knocked up by a med student in your freshman year. You probably never even got felt up by a frat boy."

Soph's eyebrows went up. She glanced at Liam and then at me with a mortified look on her face.

I waved a hand at her. "Don't be embarrassed—he knows all about it."

Soph closed her eyes as if praying for patience. It must have worked because Em swiveled her vibrant blue head in my direction and frowned.

"Jules is the only one who's had a frat guy, right Jules?" she asked. "While I missed it all because I was living at home with Babs and Soph missed it because she was pushing out the twins, you got all four years at an Ivy League school with some of the best and the brightest. I bet you humped your way through Suckma Cum Lauda—"

Liam stiffened beside me as my past was dragged forth and dropped in between us like steaming pile of dog poop.

"And we're done, Em-C Hammer!" I grabbed Em's arm and marched her to the parking lot.

Soph jogged up beside me and used her fob to unlock her car. She opened the door and I put my hand on Em's head to protect it as I pushed her into the nearest seat. I felt like a cop making a bust. Then I closed the door.

"I'll meet you back at the house," I said to Soph. "I have to do some damage control."

"Gotcha," she said with a side-eye at Liam.

"Oh, and you'd better give Em a bag in case she hurls again," I said. Soph yanked her door open and dove into her car, undoubtedly hoping to spare her leather interior if she put the pedal to the metal.

Liam was walking toward his motorcycle. When we'd arrived, I had ditched my phone arm band in one of the bike's side compartments. Now it was my excuse to see if Em's words had riled him or not. Oh, joy.

"Hey!" I called out.

He spun around, looking surprised to see me headed his way. Surprised but not mad. That was promising.

"I just wanted to say thanks for your help and for giving me a lift and all," I said.

"No prob," he said.

"Can I ask one more tiny favor?" I put my finger and thumb together as if to show that it was miniscule, really.

"What?" He looked wary. Smart boy.

"Well, I don't really want to be in the upchuck bus," I said. "And I didn't really get to enjoy the motorcycle before because I was too busy freaking out about Em, so I was wondering if you were headed home, could I possibly hitch a ride with you?"

We stared at each other for a moment and then he nodded as if he knew resistance was futile. He plopped the helmet on my head, and I slid onto the bike behind him. This time when I wrapped my arms about him, I wasn't freaking out about my sister and I could savor every sight, every sound, every touch.

Liam put on his helmet, fired up the engine and we shot out of the parking lot. It took everything I had not to whoop and yell as I wrapped my arms tight around my man as we blasted through town. Yes, he was my man—even if he didn't know it yet. With the cold, dark ocean on our right, the rolling hills on our left, and the sweet scent of spring blossoms thickening the air until it tasted like spun sugar, it felt as if there was magic all around me.

The lights of the towns along the California coastline shimmered. As much as I loved my sisters, there was a part of me that wanted desperately to ride all night long, not stopping, just flying down the road, and feeling free with *him*.

We arrived at the house all too soon. Liam parked the motorcycle in his driveway. I glanced next door and saw Soph's car at the curb and a light on inside. I removed the helmet and turned to thank Liam, but he took my elbow in his hand and led me across his yard and over the short wall that separated our properties.

"I'll just make sure you get in okay.," He sounded almost shy and again I got the feeling that something had shifted between us.

"Thanks." I walked slower, trying to make the sweet moment last.

This was a kinder, gentler Liam than the man who had wanted to fuck and forget me. I wondered what had changed. Had I worn him down with my constant presence in his life? Did he just feel badly that my family was obviously imploding in the aftermath of our matriarch's death? I had no idea. I just knew that I really, really liked this version of Liam. This guy was very much like the boy I'd given my heart to so long ago and, damn, I had missed him.

The door was unlocked so we strode right in. Em was lying face down on Babs's divan while Soph was in the kitchen, whipping up a cure for stupid drunkenness. We paused in the doorway and Liam glanced first at Em and then at me.

"Remember when she used to follow us around on her bicycle?" Liam's voice was low, and I had to lean in close to hear him. "She was the pesky little sister I never wanted, particularly as I was trying to make time with you."

I laughed. Em had followed us, exhaustingly, but Liam had never been anything but kind to her.

"You were so great about it," I said. "You never lost your patience. She worshipped you."

"I just treated Em the way you did," he said. "She was a good kid, so it wasn't hard, but it was clear that you adored her, so I did, too. She's lucky to have you and Soph."

My throat got tight. Was she? I'd been so self-involved; I'd barely noticed the pain she was in. If Liam hadn't helped us find her tonight...I couldn't even think about what might have happened to her.

"Thank you for everything," I said. "You went above and beyond the call and were...well... you were really great tonight."

"No problem," he said. "Give Em my best, okay?"

"Sure."

Liam turned and headed back to the door. I followed. There were a million things I wanted to say to him, like, 'Hey, hot stuff, spend the night?' but I suspected it would be inappropriate, so I said nothing.

"Lock up after me," he said.

He stepped outside but before he could close the door behind him, I grabbed it and stepped through. Rocking up on my toes, I kissed him on the cheek, really quick, so he didn't have a chance to react. Then I stepped back and closed the door, collapsing against it. Seriously, it took every ounce of self-control I had not to open it again and tackle him to the ground.

I peeked through the window and watched him cross our yard back to his, noticing how his jeans and T-shirt molded to his muscled surfer's body. I glanced down and realized I was still wearing his leather jacket. Oh, darn, I guessed I was going to have to return it. Maybe.

Soph came out of the kitchen as I stepped into the great room to check on Em. I thought it spoke very well of me that upon discovering the jacket I didn't race right back to Liam. Much as I wanted to, Em was more important.

My gaze met Soph's and hers looked heavy with concern. Em was lying with one arm over her eyes and tiny sobs hiccupped out of her.

"Hey, you all right?" I sat down beside her. "Can I get you anything?"

"I brought you some tea," Soph said.

"Urgh." Em made a gurgling noise. Soph wisely moved the teacup away.

"You're going to be all right," I said. "Although you may not want to drink alcohol again for a very long time, which would probably be wise."

"I didn't mean to drink so much." Em's voice was soft from behind her arm. "I just...I liked feeling out of control."

Soph and I exchanged worried glances.

"What were you drinking?" Soph asked.

"Tequila, mostly," Em said.

"Yeah, that'll take you to another plane of existence all right." I patted her shoulder. "The crash landing sucks pretty hard though."

"I think I threw up everything but my socks." Em lowered her arm, looking pasty and pale and smelling a bit of vomit. She was the picture of misery. "I miss her."

Both Soph and I reached for her hands to give them a squeeze. I kicked myself again for the state she was in. I had known she was taking Babs's death hard. Why didn't I pay closer attention? Demand that she talk to me? Drag her to a counselor?

"And then I don't," Em said.

Both Soph and I sat up straight to stare at her in a *Whaaaat?* sort of way.

"I'm going to hell for admitting this, but I can't keep it in any longer." Two bright spots of color lit Em's cheeks and her eyes flashed with rebellion. "I finally feel *free*!"

Em pulled her hands from ours and clapped them over her mouth as if she couldn't believe she'd said it. Then she dropped her head to her chest.

"See? I'm a horrible person!" Em cried. "My mother is dead and while I am sad, desperately sad, I also feel like a bird whose cage was left open. I can do whatever I want, wear whatever I want, eat whatever I want, I feel like I can fly for the very first time in my life and it makes me feel so guilty, I can't breathe."

Soph and I just stared at her, blinking and open-mouthed. I couldn't believe what we were hearing. I had always thought that Em loved living at home with Babs. If she didn't, why hadn't she left? My thoughts must have registered on my face because Em looked at me and nodded.

"Mom made me feel so selfish," Em said. "If ever I brought up getting an apartment with friends, she'd say it was a lovely idea and how I was not to worry about her in the slightest, that she would manage to live on her own with no one to help her."

"And you didn't say okay and go?" I asked.

Babs had tried that crap on me when I graduated from university. I knew she wanted, no expected, for me to come home but I had been burned before and was never going to let her control my life again. It was one more reason why I left without a backward glance.

"I'm not you, Jules," Em said. "I'm a pleaser."

"What's the point of being a pleaser if you're the only one who is never pleased?" I raised my hands in exasperation.

Em stared at me and blinked repeatedly. "I've never thought of it that way before."

"Most pleasers don't," I said.

"Why didn't you tell us this?" Soph appeared hurt by this revelation. "We would have helped you stand up to Mom. We would have gotten you out of here."

Em heaved a sigh. "Because a part of me wanted to remain her little girl. It was so easy to never have to make any hard decisions, well, any decisions at all, really. Plus, there was John, Mr. Drake, I didn't want to leave him." Her cheeks flared with color.

"I knew it." I pointed at her. "You are in love with him."

"Desperately." Em sniffed. Her face crumbled and she began to cry. We all did at that bombshell. There was no happy ending for our sister in this scenario.

Soph made more tea and we settled in to discuss our complicated feelings about Babs. Soph was just as conflicted as the two of us with the added burden of being older, having screwed up bigger by getting pregnant in college, and having Babs feel as if she could weigh in on Sophie's life whenever she wanted because it was her money Soph and Stan had begun their lives with. The money Babs would have spent on Soph's college went to their first house instead.

"I feel as if I have been apologizing for seventeen years," Soph said. "I'm sorry I got pregnant. I'm sorry I didn't finish college. I'm sorry I wasn't the perfect daughter you envisioned." Her eyes exuded sadness and she tucked her mom bob behind her ears. "I am so sick and tired of apologizing. And honestly, I'm not sorry. Mothering Harry and Hannah has been the happiest experience of my life and I'll never regret them. Not ever."

"You never have to apologize to us," I said. "We love those stinkers."

"Completely," Em agreed. "And the twins are so lucky to have such an amazing mom."

A sob burst out of Soph. "Thank you. They are the only reason," she paused, and I knew she was rethinking what she was going to say. "They are my greatest joy."

She didn't fool me. I didn't call her on it, because I suspected she wasn't ready to talk about it, but I was certain she was going to say they were the only reason she stayed in that craptastic marriage to Stan.

"What about you, Jules?" Em asked. "How are you doing?"

"Processing," I said. "I think I'm still trying to grasp it all."

"Are you..." Em hesitated and then as if the tequila was still in charge, she met my gaze and asked directly, "Are you going to search for your birth mother?"

My sisters both looked at me. I didn't admit that I had already done an online search. I'd found several matches for Lisa Michaels, but I hadn't been able to force myself to go any deeper with it. I figured I should probably hire a professional. Not knowing what one would cost, it occurred to me I might want to wait until I received my inheritance.

"Not now," I said. "I feel like I need to come to terms with all of it first."

"Does it help, knowing about her?" Soph asked.

"You mean, is it easier knowing that Babs didn't hate me so much as she hated Dad's cheating on her?" I asked. Soph nodded. "Yeah, it helps." A tear slid from my eye and down my cheek. I brushed it away. "I just wish she had told me, you know, then maybe we could have had something different."

Soph didn't say anything. She simply put her arm around me. Em reached over from the couch and grabbed my hand, giving my fingers a squeeze. "I'm glad Dad did it."

I swung my gaze to her. "Why?"

"You wouldn't be here if he hadn't cheated, and I can't bear the thought of my life without you in it, so I'm sorry for Mom, but I'm glad Dad had you."

I didn't know what to make of that, except it made the gaping hole in my chest close just a bit. She was right. I was here because of my father's affair, and I wouldn't change me either.

"Em's right." Soph ran a hand over my crazy curls. "You are perfect exactly as you are, and I can't believe I'm saying this as a married woman, but I'm glad he did it, too."

More healing. Was this what healed emotional scars? Not *I'm sorry's* or *it's not your faults*, instead what healed was *I see you and I love you exactly as you are*. Acceptance. My god, I loved my sisters, not half-sisters, never half. Just sisters.

"Do you know what my favorite childhood memories are?" Em asked after a bit.

"No," Soph and I answered together.

"When Mom would get a migraine and have to stay in bed all day," Em said. "That was the only time we were allowed to order pizza and we'd watch movies and paint our nails and play dress up all night long. I loved it."

"Me, too." I could see nine-year-old Em, wearing eighteen-year-old Soph's high heels and tripping around the room, dancing to Avril Lavigne's *My Happy Ending* while trying to look sophisticated, while I painted my toe nails an unrepentant black that would make Babs gnash her teeth when she saw them.

"Me three," Soph said. "I missed you two so much when I left."

"Remember the time we snuck out to go to the concert on the green?" I asked. "I thought Babs was going to lock us up and throw away the key."

Soph laughed. "Well, she did take my license away for a week. Totally worth it."

We laughed and cried some more, and we kept talking and remembering our shared past until Em let out a soft snore. Soph used the aqua afghan to tuck around her and the two of us watched our baby sister sleep, stunned by her tequila-induced revelations.

"Think she's going to remember this tomorrow?" Soph asked.

"Yeah, I do," I said. "And if she doesn't, we'll remind her."

Soph glanced out the window to the house next door, several lights were still on, and then back at me.

"I'm going to bed." Soph reached out and poked me in the chest right through the leather jacket. "Looks like you have something to return to the boy next door."

"Maybe I should stay with her," I said. "I feel as if I've failed her by not noticing how she was struggling."

Soph reached down and pushed a long hank of blue hair out of Em's face. "I feel guilty, too, but I think she's done for tonight. We can talk more tomorrow."

I hesitated. It was so tempting. Still, I hesitated.

"Go." She pushed me toward the door. "There's clearly unfinished business between you two."

She had no idea.

"If you're sure," I said. Decision made, I was already striding to the door. "I'll be back before morning, because...you know."

"Yeah, the will," Soph said. "Why did Mom have to have such a good attorney? I mean this staying here every night could seriously impede a love life, you know, if you have one." She stifled a yawn.

"Right?" I wanted to ask her about our cousin Paisley and if what the twins had said was accurate, but I figured it would keep until morning. "Night!" I hurried outside before I changed my mind.

The door shut behind me and I took a deep breath. Now. Now I would find out if things had really changed between Liam and me. A nervous flutter started low in my belly with the soft beat of butterfly wings. By the time I got to his front door, the flutter had morphed into terror and was beating like a pterodactyl trying to fly off with me for dinner.

I raised my fist to knock, but the door opened before my hand connected with the wood. Standing there in just a pair of plaid pajama bottoms was Liam. I tried to speak but nothing came out. No matter, with one hand he grabbed the lapel of his own jacket and tugged me inside.

Chapter Twenty

"You forgot your jack—"

That was all I got out before his mouth landed on mine and I was pushed against the wall as he kicked the door shut.

I clutched his shoulders, delighted with the warm skin and firm muscles beneath my fingertips. He peeled the leather jacket off me and threw it on the floor like it offended him. His mouth was running up and down the side of my neck and I arched to make it easier for him.

"Probably, we should talk," he said, his words muted as he spoke against my skin. He pressed into me, and I felt his erection beneath his pajamas and had to suck in a gulp of air to make sure my brain didn't short circuit from lack of oxygen.

"Later." I panted. "Plenty of time later."

I felt him grin against my skin when he kissed my shoulder. He grabbed my hips and hoisted me up. I instinctively wrapped my legs around his waist, and he cupped my bottom as he turned and carried me upstairs. When we reached the landing, he wasn't even breathing hard, nor did he slow down.

An enormous bed filled the sparsely decorated room, and this was where we landed, sitting in a tangle of arms and legs. I kicked off my running shoes while he pulled my top over my head and dragged my yoga pants down, tossing them onto the floor.

"Still no time for laundry?" he asked, noting my lack of underwear with a grin.

I shrugged. "I've had other things on my mind."

"Such as?" he asked.

"You," I said. It came out on an exhale, making it all breathy. His grin deepened.

With one hand on his chest, I pushed him down until he reclined on the bed. I pulled off the plaid pajama bottoms and sent them to the floor with the rest of our clothes. With a long lingering look at his seriously hard cock, I pulled the hair tie out of my hair and let my long curls run wild. I swear the man got even harder. A glance at Liam's face and I saw him swallow as if nervous or excited or both.

"About the other ni—"

"Shh." I straddled him and grabbed his hands, pushing them back against the bedspread by his head. Then, I kissed him. It was a long, slow, exploratory sort of kiss, where my mouth molded to his while my tongue played peekaboo, darting back and forth, getting the taste and the feel of him. It was the sort of kiss shared by new lovers who are learning everything they can about their partner through taste and touch.

Although I remembered most of our misspent youth, it was nice to get a refresher course. I cataloged what made him groan, what made him half rise up and try to take over, and what made him buck his hips beneath me. This enthusiastic response happened when I plunged my tongue into his mouth in the most blatantly sexual way I could manage. I had to try it three or four times to be sure. Yeah, it never failed.

This was an exquisite way to learn things about this man. I could feel my own desire spike with each new revelation of what made this guy hot. Liam and I were hardly new to one another, yet I felt like this was a new time for us. We were different than the teenagers we'd once been. Different than the estranged lovers who had come together in a frenzy just recently. Life had hardened us, given us new and different experiences, but still, the one true thing was the combustible chemistry that never seemed to fade between us.

One more plunge with my tongue, and Liam broke my hold and rolled me over onto my back. Then he took over the kiss until I was arching up against him, trying to nudge him into action.

He didn't take the hint, but instead ran his hands down my sides pausing at my breasts to let his fingers tease and taunt my nipples into stiffened peaks that yearned for his mouth. When he finally sucked one in between his lips and gently bit down, I was pretty sure I was done for and any semblance of dignity was gone, baby, gone. I proceeded to beg.

"Liam, please," I moaned.

"Please what?" he asked. He licked me like an ice cream cone until I was just as wet and melty. He pulled back a bit. A furrow appeared in his brow. "Maybe we should talk, clear the air before we keep going."

Yeah, that would be the smart thing to do; mature, logical, responsible, yada, yada, yada. The problem was when it came to this man I was as dumb as a bag of hammers.

"Can't talk. Need you," I said.

"Need me for what?" He tried to sound innocent, the big faker. I knew exactly what he was trying to do, get me to talk dirty to him. Well, all righty then.

I ran my fingers into his thick dark hair and forced his warm brown gaze to meet mine. In a lust filled voice I barely recognized as mine, I said, "I need you to fuck me. Hard. Like you mean it."

The man went perfectly still for the space of a heartbeat and then he was delightfully, deliciously, deliriously crazed. Well, okay then. His mouth moved over my skin as if he fully intended to kiss every bare inch of it. Oh, my!

I ran my hands over his shoulders, his chest, his abs. I felt him clench wherever my fingers touched, and his response kicked my own desire up a notch. I arched and kissed him while his fingers blazed a trail down between my legs, finding my sweet spot and moving in relentless gentle circles until I started to push against him, longing for more. He ignored me.

His fingers kept moving in the tenderly insistent caress that didn't stop but didn't go further and it was slowly driving me mad. When I glanced up at him from beneath my lashes, his lips were turned up in a look that could only be described as wicked. The boy knew exactly what he was doing to me, and was utterly unrepentant. So, he wanted to play. Fine.

I circled his erection with my fist and gave a gentle tug. He let out a huff of breath and I laughed. Then I moved my other hand so that it cupped the boys below. This time he growled. I worked him over firmly but gently using both hands until I saw a sheen of sweat bead up on his skin. If this was a game, I was playing to win, and I was, right up until he put his lips back on my breast. He gently bit down and the rhythm I'd maintained stuttered as I arched my back and gasped. This time, he laughed.

He pushed my hands away and settled himself between my legs. Now I was trapped with him right there, so close to where I wanted him to be, and yet, he didn't commit, he didn't slide into me, and I was left with an aching, throbbing need that was making me thrash in a decidedly unfeminine way against him.

"Liam," I panted his name.

"Yes, Jules," he said.

He sounded so calm and reasonable I wanted to hit him. His devious grin was firmly in place as he lowered his mouth to my other breast, taking the tip between his lips and sucking hard until I felt the corresponding zap of desire between my legs.

"Why are you torturing me?" My voice came out needy and whiny. I could tell how far gone I was that I didn't even care.

"Because we need to get some things straight," he said.

My heart plummeted. Oh, man, we were going to talk *now*? I didn't want to, talking only made things tricky and weird and there were too many secrets and so much pain. My desire began to flat line at the imagined fall out.

He must have sensed my lust dissipating because he let his full weight come down on me with his thighs in between mine and his firm boy parts pressing insistently into my soft girl parts. I was pretty sure I saw stars as my desire ratcheted right back up to the level of *why aren't we doing it right now*?

He wagged his eyebrows at me, and I clamped my lips together to keep from begging for more. We were at an impasse, but then he kissed me. He dug his hands into my hair to angle my head so he could plant a lip lock on me that stole my breath, hell, I was pretty sure it stole my soul. When he pulled back, his gaze met mine and the intensity made me shiver.

"I need to be clear that if we do this right now then we're a thing," he said.

My eyes went wide. "A *thing*? Please define "thing." Do you mean as in a romantic couple or a freak show at a circus?"

His stare intensified even as his mouth twitched. "As in a couple, a pair, a twosome, although if you want to get freaky..."

My heart started to hammer in my chest, as if trying to get my attention to let me know how it was voting. It was an ay. Shocker, I know.

"But what about—"

"Done. Over. History," he said.

"Oh." I had a million questions but sensed, as he shifted against me and I got distracted, that this was not the time. Still, shouldn't I find out what happened? What if, oh horror, she broke up with him and he was on the rebound and I was just his transition woman?

He stared at me and then nudged me, again, with a not-so-subtle thrust of his hips which got my attention back where it belonged. Transition smansition. It was details, who needed details? I blinked and nodded my head.

"A thing then, definitely, a thing," I said. I grinned at him, and he blinked in return.

"Thank fuck!" he muttered right before he pulled me up tight against him and kissed me.

The kiss was tender and fierce, and we clung to each other which made his attempt to put on a condom a bit tricky, but once he was ready, I grabbed him by the hips and pulled him in. No hesitation. No waiting. I wanted him to belong to me completely.

We both gasped as he entered. He was hard and I was wet, but the fit was tight and the friction intense. As my body relaxed around his to let him in and then clenched to pull him in even deeper, I glanced up at his face and saw such tenderness that my throat burned and tears stung my eyes.

How had I walked away from this man all those years ago? How much time had we lost that could have been ours? Regret made me hug him close. He was mine right now and I had no plan to let him go ever again.

"Hey, new boy." My voice was just a whisper, but I had to tell him. I had to say it.

"What is it, surfer girl?" He leaned in close and kissed me quick and then put his ear near my lips as if he knew I could barely get the words out.

My lips brushed his ear, causing him to shiver, as I said, "I am so sorry that I left you, so very sorry."

The tears that had been threatening spilled now. He pulled back and followed their trails with his lips, catching them on the tip of my chin before putting his mouth back to mine in a kiss that tasted of tears.

"It's okay," he whispered. "You're here now. That's all that matters."

Our gazes met in perfect understanding. We had a choice to let the past destroy the present or to move on from it. There was much more to be said, we both knew it, but for now, right in this moment, we understood each other, and we were okay.

He began to move, slow at first as if he was determined to savor every second of our coming together. I matched him, moving with him, wanting the same but it wasn't long before my desire to feel wholly consumed by him overrode the savoring.

I twisted up in his arms, forcing him back until I was on top, and Liam was reclined across the bed. I loved having him laid out before me; I straddled him and splayed my hands on his chest like a kitten kneading a blanket. The muscles in his arms bunched, his thick brown hair was mussed, and the look on his face was one of awe mixed with scorching desire—for me! He was simply glorious.

I started to control the rhythm, going faster and deeper. He gripped my hips in his hands and slowed me down when I would have sent us both, okay, mostly me, right over the finish line. I was no match for his upper body strength so when he caught me and held me up, not allowing me to move, I realized any control I thought I had was just an illusion.

This was clearly Liam's show, and I was merely a player. His eyes were half closed as he glanced up at me and slowly moved his hips up, not allowing me to grind down. I could feel my nostrils flare and his wicked grin returned. I was beginning to think the man was a sadist.

He watched me as he moved, no doubt noticing how I tried to break his hold. It occurred to me that much like the waves we liked to play in, I would do better to go with the tide than against it, which was why when he went to slide back in, I moved in the same direction which took me away from him, thwarting him. When he moved, I moved. Two more times until he got it. Heat flashed in his eyes as he caught on pretty quick to my sexual shenanigans.

"You're in trouble now!" With a laugh, he grabbed me around the middle and rolled until I was underneath him.

He lifted my legs up around his waist and this time there was no teasing. He pushed all the way in, deeper than I thought was possible, until I actually felt impaled by him. It was almost enough. Then he did it again, and it was enough.

The orgasm when it hit was one for the scrapbooks, you know, if one was to take pictures of this sort of life moment. Much like getting rolled by a wave, I felt completely disoriented; I didn't know which way was up as my entire body convulsed in spasms of pleasure that made me cry his name even as he held me tight and rode out his own orgasm.

Spent, we stayed entwined waiting out the slowing of our heartbeats and allowing the sweat to dry on our bodies. It was the sweet surrender I had longed for the last time we were together, but I'd take it now. It had so been worth the wait.

Chapter Twenty-one

I dozed hard but my internal alarm clock woke me up on the darker side of dawn. The bedroom window was open, letting in the cold ocean air. It made me burrow down under the fluffy comforter and press up against the warmth that was at my back.

Judging by the hard length of the dude pressing between the backs of my thighs, I was not the only one awake. Ever accommodating, I lifted one thigh, giving the man better access. He moved my hair to kiss the nape of my neck, making it tricky for him to wrap his rascal before sliding into my wet heat.

We both gasped at the contact. He didn't move, instead letting his fingers roam all over my curves as if enjoying having something to play with in the wee hours of the morning.

"Hey," he whispered in my ear.

His voice was low and gritty, and it made me push my ass back against him. He caught my hips as if knowing that if I were given the chance, I would bang him right into unconsciousness. Here's the great thing about a guy with early wood, they have like no control. I let him think he was steering the ship and then as soon as he relaxed against me, I started to move.

"Jules." His voice had that delicious note of warning that I so loved to disregard.

"What?" I asked.

Somehow, I managed to sound like a complete innocent, even as I was guiding his hand over my hip and putting it right on that spot that loved his callused fingertips rubbing against it. My head fell back against his shoulder, and he took complete advantage of it, letting his lips trail across my skin until every pleasure point in me, seriously, exploded.

"Oh, god," he grunted. "I can feel you coming."

My vagina was clenching so hard around his cock it felt as if it was trying to choke it out. There was a tense moment where the pleasure was so close to pain that I gasped. It was terrifying how good we felt coming together and a part of me almost shoved away from him, as if I was giving away too much by being together like this. I chose to be brave and ride it out, and just like catching a perfect wave, it was worth every bit of fear to find the bliss.

I reached back and clung to him as he began to move inside me, drawing out my orgasm and following it with his own. Once the tremors subsided and our breathing slowed, he pulled me in tight. His body was pressed against mine and I was sure I had never felt this close to anyone in my life.

We were never going to be more in sync than we were right now, so I figured this was as good a time as any to get to the heart of it.

"What happened between you and Courtney?" I asked.

He stilled. I rolled in his arms so I could look up at him. He rubbed a hand over his face and I could see each whisker of stubble that I'd felt gently abrading my skin. I reached my hand up to run over his chin. I liked the way it tickled my palm. Our eyes met and he leaned down, kissing me quick.

"You found out her name, huh?"

I shrugged. Couldn't deny that.

"I broke up with her."

"When?" It shouldn't have mattered but, yeah, it totally did. I needed to know if the breakup happened because of our previous night together, my not-so-subtle stalking, or because of something completely unrelated to me. Call it ego, but I really hoped the last one wasn't the case.

He blew out a breath and eyed the space between our bodies. I pressed closer, getting his attention most definitely downstairs. He glanced up at me and his expression was rueful.

"If I tell you, do you promise not to be mad?" he asked.

I narrowed my eyes...I could think of only one reason why I would be mad.

"You haven't broken up with her yet, have you?" I braced both hands against his chest to shove him off me.

The blanket dropped down around his waist, and I was confronted by half naked Liam with his muscly arms and sculpted torso on full display. For a second, I forgot why I was supposed to be irritated. A second was all he needed to grab me and flatten me beneath him with my hands trapped in his.

"Yes, I have," he said. "I wouldn't have slept with you otherwise."

"But we slept together the other night—" My voice trailed off and he looked at me, one eyebrow raised, as if he was waiting for me to do the math. "You had already broken up with her by then? Seriously? When?"

"The night I found you under the lemon tree and held you in my arms while you cried about your mom," he admitted. "While I was holding you, I felt as if you were giving me back a piece of myself that had been missing for a very long time. I didn't know what would happen between us, but I knew I was never going to feel about anyone the way I felt about you, and it wasn't fair to her, so I ended it that day."

I stared at him for a moment going over the timeline in my head. That meant that when he was so mean after our first night together, which would also be when he said he was getting married, he had lied to me.

"You lied to me," I said. "And you were really, really mean."

I thrashed beneath him. No idea why. It wasn't as if I really wanted to get away or push him off, but it felt like I was supposed to take some sort of moral stand on this lying thing. Yeah, me, the one with secrets up the wazoo was being all high and mighty. He relaxed his weight on top of me, making it even harder to buck up against him.

"Aw, come on, surfer girl," he cajoled, which was nearly impossible to resist. "Don't be mad. Honestly, what happened that first night scared the hell out of me and I panicked. I know it was a dick move to treat you the way I did, and I have no excuse. I guess I was just trying not to fall too hard too fast, and potentially I was getting even with you for leaving me for Jessie nine years ago." He sighed. "I am really sorry."

And just like that the fight went out of me. This was the thing about Liam. Not counting the fibs we'd told our parents so we could be together when we were young, Liam was the most honest and self-aware man I'd ever known. Back in the day, I'd had no idea how incredibly rare that was. Now I knew. Just like I knew I had hurt him so badly when I left that I couldn't blame him for exacting some payback.

I wrapped my arms around him and pulled him close. I had so much to make amends for,

but given that the truth wasn't just mine to tell, I didn't know how to start or where to begin.

"There's so much I need to explain to you," I said. "I want to tell you some stuff to make things right between us, but—"

"No," he interrupted.

Something flickered in his eyes, a flash of pain or jealousy. It was gone before I could get a bead on it, but it put me on notice that he might not be ready to have that conversation just yet.

"You already said you were sorry for leaving me," he said. "Why don't we just leave it at that for now and start over?"

"Do you really think that's possible, new boy?" I desperately did not want to lose this man again.

He stared into my eyes, looking for something. He must have found it because a slow smile turned up the corners of his full lips. He leaned in and whispered, "I think we've already started."

After more sexy time, heaven help me, I rose from the bed and began to get dressed.

"You don't have to go," Liam protested.

"Yeah, I do," I said. "Babs, being Babs, put it in her will that Soph, Em and I have to live together in her house for the next three months, and by that she meant sleeping there every night, or our entire inheritance goes to our cousin Paisley."

"What? That's mental."

"That's Babs."

He studied me while I slid back into my yoga pants and sports bra. A slow grin spread across his face.

"What?" I asked.

"Three months," he said. "I have three months to convince you to stay."

My heart swelled until I thought it might explode. He wanted me to stay. There was still so much I needed to tell him, but the fact that he wanted me here made me giddy. Still, I tried to play it cool.

"I suppose it's always good to have a project, new boy," I teased.

He tugged me back onto the bed by the waistband of my pants and kissed me stupid. Then he walked me downstairs to the door, watching as I floated my way over the short wall that separated our front yards until I got back home.

Em was in the same place that I'd left her. I didn't wake her up but took the recliner next to her and fell into an exhausted slumber.

It was three hours later when I awoke to the sound of Soph in the kitchen, using Babs's smoothie maker to whip up some foul concoction to cure the hangover that was looming over Em like a fog of hurt.

I stretched and glanced at her slouched body. In my loudest conversational voice, I asked, "Em-bryo, how are you this morning?"

"Not funny." Em groaned, opening her eyes to mere slits, and then quickly closing them with a hiss. "How were things with the boy next door?"

"Amazing!" It felt like my smile might split my face wide open.

Em held up a hand as if to ward off a light. "Stop that. Sheesh, your post-coital glow is practically nuclear."

"She's right." Soph joined us carrying a large glass with a very green beverage in it. *Ew.* "I'm surprised you don't have sparklers shooting out your fingertips, or anywhere else for that matter."

"Sorry," I said. "I'll try and turn it down for you all."

They looked at me expectantly while I tried to wrestle the smile from my face. "Yeah, sorry, I think I have an advanced case of perma-grin."

"Did the two of you at least talk?" Soph asked.

"Yes, well, a little bit." I told them about Liam breaking up with Courtney right after he consoled me about Babs's death. Soph made an "aw" face while Em shrugged.

"That doesn't excuse his mantrum on the first night you two got together," Em said. "He was straight-up mean."

"No, it doesn't," I agreed. "But he owned it and he apologized. Besides, you have to remember how much I hurt him when I left town with Jessie."

"Which you still haven't explained to him or us." Em reached for the green beverage Soph held out to her and took a long chug. "Oh, ergh, ugh."

While she gagged, I looked questioningly at Soph, who shrugged. "It'll either make her feel better or wish for death, hard to say."

"I hate you both, go away." Em flopped back onto the divan, which was an invitation for Soph and I to snuggle into her. "Stop. Go away!"

"No can do, little sister," Soph said. "Because we *lurve* you."

"If I promise to never ever drink tequila again, will you go away?" Em asked.

"Oh, I don't think you'll be drinking tequila again, whether we leave you right now or not," I said. "After a night like yours, you won't even be able to smell tequila without gagging for, like, five years."

"Five years would be fine with me," Em said. "Especially since I'm going to join a convent today. Clearly, I should not be allowed to run loose."

"Our Catholic Dad would be very proud, but that's a tad extreme. Maybe you could dial it back, just a little." Soph's voice was serious as she wrapped an arm around Em. "I know you're hurting but we'll get through it together."

A couple of tears spilled from under Em's closed eyes and she nodded. "It's just so hard. I don't know who I am anymore."

I pulled out my phone and opened her social media page. "Really? Because the rest of the world knows who you are. I swear with this many followers, you're trending, even with hurl shots of you and the biker chick. Oh, my god, was her name really Daisy?"

Em cracked one eye open. "Ugh."

"Come on," Soph said. "Your public awaits your latest post. Let's get you showered so you don't offend them."

"Nope." Em dug her own phone out of her hip pocket. "I'm trying to be one-hundred-percent authentic with everything I'm doing. So, here goes: hungover selfie with sisters." She held up the camera, which was not kind to her ratted blue hair and smudged mascara. After my sexual gymnastics of the night before, I didn't look much better. Only Soph managed to appear pretty and serene as Em ordered, "Say 'tequila' girls."

Em snapped a pic and uploaded it to her account with the hashtags Emily, grief, and sisters. In moments, the responses were lighting up her phone. She sighed and tucked her phone away without reading the comments. I couldn't help but wonder if this was her way of holding herself accountable while taking charge of her life for the very first time. With every decision she made, she allowed strangers to weigh in and support or shun her. Little sis was braver than me, that was for damn sure.

I knew I was channeling my grief into fixing my relationship with Liam. It occurred to me that Babs's death had forced me to complete the unfinished business in my life, which had always been my relationship with him.

As Em conked out on the divan, Soph smoothed her wild hair back and tucked the blanket more snuggly about her. Soph seemed to be the only one of the three of us who was steady as she goes. Even though her husband was a big jerk, and her children were almost grown and gone, or maybe because of all that, she seemed centered and right on course. Then again, maybe it was just that her denial ran deeper than ours. Hard to say.

"I failed Em by not noticing what she was going through," I said. "I don't want to do the same with you. What's going on in your life, Soph, because while you seem very together, I feel like something is wrong and it's not just the twins going away. What is it?"

She looked at me in surprise as if no one ever really asked her how she was feeling about things. Two emotions slammed into me pretty hard. One was that her husband was an asshole if he wasn't helping her through the grief of losing her mother and from what I'd seen of Stan since I'd arrived, it was a safe assumption that he was doing jack shit. Jerk. And two, was a blast of shame that I was the worst sister ever, because not only had I not clued in to Em's struggle with her emotions, I hadn't really been there for Soph either.

Yes, I'd been away for a long time, and I was out of practice with the day-to-day sister stuff but still, I was better than this or at least I should have been after weeks of living together.

"I'm okay," Soph said. "I'm taking it day by day, trying not to dump too much of it on my family. Mostly, it still seems surreal, like I can't believe that she's actually gone."

I glanced at Babs's urn on the windowsill, where she'd spent the night watching over her baby with the hangover. Her snazzy urn sparkled in the morning light.

"Maybe it's because she's got us all living here for the next few months," I said. "But I don't really feel like she's gone, every move I make feels like she's right there with me, judging me."

Soph followed my gaze to the windowsill. "Yeah, I know what you mean. Babs's hold is strong, even from the grave. Honestly, I don't really mind. It makes me feel less alone."

She said it plainly without too much thought and no heavy emotion. It was just a fact, and it occurred to me then that despite the husband and the twins, Soph was lonely. Well, that was easily fixable and unlike Em's frantic emotional swings, this I could manage.

"Liam and I are going to the art show this afternoon," I said. "Wear something pretty because you're coming with us."

"On your date?" Soph asked in horror. "No, thank you."

"Oh, I'm sorry, did it sound optional?" I asked. "It isn't. We're all going. You, Em, the twins, and Stan if he can manage to tear himself away from the golf course."

"I'm sorry, I don't think—"

"Again, not optional," I said. "We're a family and we're going to spend some time together and have fun, damn it."

"Well, when you put it like that, how can a girl refuse?" Soph's voice was grumbly, but I couldn't help notice that a small smile played on her lips.

Chapter Twenty-two

"What are these supposed to be?" Liam leaned close and whispered in my ear.

"No idea," I said.

We were at the annual Gull's Harbor art show, standing in front of an artist's booth. This particular artist, Sadie Gentle-Wing according to the sign, worked in ceramics and seemed pretty obsessed with big, we're talking huge, ovals in vibrant shades of pink, red and purple, which she displayed upright on enormous wooden stands.

Personally, I was not really focused on the art, because my man was holding my hand. Liam was holding my hand, yo! We were in public in our hometown at an art show and I was with him. We were together, a couple, the real deal. I was so giddy I was bouncing on my toes.

"It looks like a big sphincter to me," Harry chimed in from behind us.

"Shh," Soph hushed him, frantically searching for the artist, who was, yeah, standing right there.

Sadie was all decked out in flowing purple scarves and a bohemian blouse over a red broomstick skirt. She smelled faintly of sage and lavender and her long gray curls had streaks of purple and red in them.

"So close, young man." Sadie clasped her hands together. "Actually, it's a physical representation of the core of the female form, you know, the cradle of all human life, the vagina."

I felt Liam's fingers tighten around mine and when I glanced at him, his lips were pressed together as if he was trying very hard not to laugh. A snort came out of his nose, which he tried to turn into a sneeze. Yeah, he fooled no one.

"Come here, young man, and you can stroke it," Sadie said.

The artist grabbed Harry's hand and pulled him forward. He gave his mother a horrified look but was too polite to put up any resistance. Soph opened her mouth to speak, probably to try and stop the humiliation of her teenage son, but Hannah and Em were not about to let that happen.

"Oh, yes, just like that," Hannah purred. "Stroke it."

"Better yet, use some tongue," Em said.

Soph gave her a shocked look and Em shrugged. Our baby sis took a selfie of herself inside one of the va-jay-jays, with her tongue out. Very risqué. Which I was certain would be on her social media account in five, four—my phone chimed. Yep, there it was, and I had no doubt it was about to break the internet.

Now that we knew Em was working through her grief in such a public fashion, we had all signed on as followers to her account, figuring we could track her and hopefully jump in to help her should it be required.

"Save me." Harry mouthed the words at me. His eyes were wide, and he tried to hide behind his choppy blond hair to no avail. He was the picture of discomfort as Sadie guided his hand up and down inside the large ceramic oval.

"On it," I mouthed back. I stepped close to get the artist's attention. "Sadie, tell me, is your work limited to the female form or do you also render the male sexual organ as well?"

Liam was standing behind me and when I said, male sexual organ, I heard him snort-sneeze again. Harry gave me a *you're my hero* look and disengaged his hand from Sadie's and knees-to-chested it from the booth where he hid behind Soph. I couldn't blame him.

Sadie was talking about the plethora of examples of the male form in our society which was why she focused on the female. Liam remained behind me, looking as if he was listening. He was not. Instead, he was pressed up against me, whispering wicked things in my ear whenever Sadie turned to gesture at one of her sculptures.

My heart was hammering hard in my chest and my eyes were becoming unfocused as desire began to heat up my insides when I felt Liam's lips so close to my ear.

"This is fascinating," I interrupted Sadie. So rude! Meanwhile I started to back into Liam, forcing him to walk backwards or risk being trampled by me. "But we have to go."

"We do?" Liam asked. I could hear the laugh tucked into his voice and was determined to make him pay for that.

"Yeah, I think I left the stove on." I gave him a wide-eyed stare to get him to go along with me.

"Oh, the stove," he said. "Right."

With that, I spun around and pushed Liam away from Sadie's booth. I didn't bother to look at my family but yelled over my shoulder, "Don't wait, we'll catch up."

I dragged him past several more artist booths until I found a footpath that led into a small community garden. Lots of trees, shrubs, benches, and trellises. Perfect!

As soon as we found a secluded corner, I jumped him. Anticipating my move, Liam caught me close and in moments we were making out with all the enthusiasm of two high school kids before the late bell.

I dug my fingers into his thick, soft hair while he pulled me up against him with his hands on my lower back locking me into place while his mouth met mine. The sounds of people chatting and laughing blended in with the scent of flowers in bloom on this warm sunny day, creating a happy background for the groping that was happening in this secluded little park.

"Having a good time?" Liam asked as he broke the kiss and pressed his forehead to mine.

"The best," I said.

I couldn't remember when I'd been this purely, simply happy. My feelings when I was with Liam buffered the sadness and confusion that had seemed to fill me to bursting in the aftermath of Babs's death. I knew my grief was a combination of losing my mother and losing my sense of identity all in one blow but having Liam in my arms, well, it made up for a lot.

"We should probably get back before I take advantage of you right here," he said.

"Discreet sex in public?" I asked. "That's on my bucket list."

He groaned. "You are killing me."

"In a good way?"

"In the best way." His voice was gruff and gravelly as he glanced around us. "Far be it from me to deny your list maybe we should check that off right now."

"You have to catch me first," I teased.

I laughed and danced back a few steps from him. The sun shone on his hair, and I saw strands of copper mixed in the dark brown. His eyes crinkled in the corners when he smiled at me and his big, callused hands reached out to grab me, making me feel small and delicate, which was a rare and beautiful thing given that I wasn't exactly petite.

"Surfer girl, do you have any idea of what I'm going to do to you when I catch you, and you know I will," he said.

Oh, I had a pretty good idea, and I was one-hundred-percent all for it. I skirted around a fountain and peeked at him from behind it. He was striding forward, his T-shirt hugging his ripped torso, very intent in his purpose. I almost pretended to trip just so he could catch me, but I didn't. I couldn't make it too easy for him, could I?

"I have no idea, new boy," I lied. "Do tell me and in great detail."

I feinted one way and he dodged to catch me, then I doubled back the other way, but he anticipated my move and with a spin and a lunge, I was good and truly caught against him and the look in his eyes promised delicious retribution.

He carried me out of the small park with his arms around my waist and mine around his neck. Our faces were just inches apart while my feet dangled a good six inches off the ground.

"I think I'll start kissing you here," he said as he nuzzled my neck, which was like pulling a rip cord to get my motor running. Oh, my!

"And then, I'll move my hands here." Liam moved his hands to cup my rear and I instinctively thrust my hips against him. Uh oh, my engine was beginning to seriously overheat.

"Now you're killing me," I panted.

We were leaving the small park behind and mingling into the crowd. It was time to take this PG-13 and change its rating to a G. A few more hours with my family, okay, maybe just an hour, and we'd be able to excuse ourselves and hide back at his place. I loosened my arms and he let me slide down his front. Okay, a little bit of an R rating there.

"Should we say good-bye to the others and go home?" Liam asked.

"Yes," I said. So much for an hour.

I grabbed his hand and turned to lead him in the direction of my family. I spotted them several booths away and began to wind my way through the crowd.

As we passed a booth, I caught sight of a navy hoodie out of the corner of my eye. Maybe I was paranoid, but my head whipped in that direction and I froze, causing Liam to plow into my back and knock us both forward a couple of steps.

The man in the sweatshirt glanced up and I recognized the aviators he always wore. It was him, the blond man who had been at the coffee shop, the same one who had looked in my bag while I was surfing, and now he was standing in an artist's booth full of still life paintings of flowers. Coincidence?

My heart pounded in my chest. Gull's Harbor was a small town, sure, and it was likely that I would run into a person a few times while going about my life, but this felt different. I got the feeling this guy wasn't local. I also sensed that our meetings hadn't been by chance, especially the one where he'd searched my bag on the beach.

Behind the aviators his gaze felt speculative. Why would he follow me? With Liam beside me, I knew this was my opportunity to get some answers. I moved toward the booth where the man in the sweatshirt stood.

"Are you okay?" Liam asked.

He must have felt me enter mission mode because he glanced between me and the hoodie guy and asked, "Do you know him?"

"No," I said. "But I think he's been following me."

"What?" Liam's back went straight and his muscles bunched. He looked like he was gearing up to do some damage.

"Easy." I squeezed his hand in mine. "Let's be sure before we start cracking skulls."

He gave me a quick nod but the tension in his posture didn't lessen one little bit. As we neared the booth, the man in the sweatshirt began to back up, looking for an exit that wouldn't take him by us. This only added to my suspicions.

We were almost there, and he was trapped between three walls of floral paintings, the artist, two other tourists, and us, and we were closing in.

"Liam!"

A shrill voice to the left interrupted our pace as we both glanced in that direction. Standing there looking shocked was a woman with long straight black hair, wearing a body-hugging yellow dress and sky-high heels. In her hand was a tall frosty pink beverage with an umbrella in it. Her brown eyes went wide as she noticed Liam holding my hand.

"You bastard!" she cried. With a flick of her wrist, she tossed the beverage at Liam, a strawberry concoction judging by the smell, hitting him square in the chest.

In a flash of recognition, I knew this was Courtney. The beverage-tossing-anger helped me put her into context and I recognized her from the pictures I'd seen on the internet.

"Yow!" Liam sucked in a breath as the frozen drink soaked his shirt in a frosty deluge.

"Hey!" I shouted. I got that she was upset but seriously do not throw things at my man. "That was totally uncalled for!"

"It's okay," Liam said as he swiped chunks of strawberry off his shirt.

"It is not okay." I stepped forward, ready to rumble, but Liam held me back.

"Jules," he said. "I love that you want to kick ass on my behalf, but I got this. Just give us a minute."

"Fine, but if she does anything else..."

I let the threat linger there and Liam's lips twitched. He pulled me close and kissed me quick. I glanced over his shoulder to see the other woman wince. Okay, I felt a little bad about that.

"Don't worry, I'll be right back." He turned to her and said, "Courtney, can we talk about this?"

Courtney dropped the empty plastic cup and covered her face with her hands, starting to sob. And, yeah, now I really felt bad. I knew from personal experience how hard it was to get over Liam. How could I blame her for being upset?

"I'll just wait over there." I gestured in the direction of my family and Liam nodded.

As I turned to walk away, I noticed that the hoodie guy wasn't in the booth anymore. Damn it. I had been so close to confronting him and finding out what he wanted and with Liam at my back, too. Had we gotten to chat with him, he would have left with a clearer understanding about boundaries and personal space.

I scanned the area. No sign of hoodie, but I found my family at a food truck. Shocker. This one had churros. Yes, please! While we loaded up on deep-fried cinnamon sugary goodness, Soph plucked a chunk of strawberry out of my hair.

"Saving it for later?" she asked.

Em snorted and I said, "No, that little gift came from Liam's ex-girlfriend."

"What?" Em glanced around. "Where is he? I assumed he just went to the bathroom."

"No, they're talking," I said. "We bumped into her, and she threw her daiquiri at him. I suspect she has some things to get off her chest."

"And you left him alone?" Soph looked stunned at both revelations.

"Sure, why not?"

"Because she's probably trying to win him back right now," Soph said. "And you left the gate wide open."

"I'm not worried about Liam." I waved her concern away.

Soph smacked her forehead with her palm as if she could not believe that I could be this stupid.

Em took a bite of her churro and through a mouthful said, "Jules is right. I've never seen a man look at a woman the way Liam looks at her." She patted my arm. "It'll be fine. They'll talk and he'll come running back to you."

"Sorry but in my experience, men can have their heads turned in a blink." Soph bit her churro as if it had done something to piss her off.

I frowned. I hated that Soph's doubts were making me edgy. I knew she was just looking out for me but still I couldn't stand to think that after all we'd been through, Liam would dump me to go back to Courtney. But really, what did he have with me? A fresh start? Great. But he'd never let me explain why I'd left to begin with, and I really felt that he needed to know.

I bit my churro. It tasted like deep fried paste. I scanned the throng to see if he was coming back. There was no sign of him. I tried not to worry and failed spectacularly.

Harry and Hannah had found friends of theirs and zipped by to shake Soph down for money before they disappeared into the crowd. Em, Soph, and I wandered through the rest of the art show. Still, there was no sign of Liam and my phone remained ominously silent. I was just beginning to think I was going to ditch the sisters and head back to his house to do boyfriend recon when my phone chimed. Yes!

Had to take Courtney home. She's in no state to drive. Text you when I get back.

Now mature me wanted to text back that this was fine but immature me, who seemed to be in control of my fingers, wanted to shut my phone off and ignore the text that was making my internal organs shrivel up like grapes in the sun.

"Good news?" Soph asked.

"Yeah, sure, it's cool," I said.

My older sis leveled me with a gaze. "Do not tell me he is taking her home."

"Okay," I said. "I won't tell you he's taking her home, but yeah, he's taking her home."

"Oh, for Pete's sake," Soph said. "What is it with men who cave to a woman's tears when she's not even his woman? There should be a repellent spray for that sort of thing."

"Like bug spray?" Em clarified.

"Exactly," Soph said with a snap of her fingers. "Then you could spray your guy before he went out and you wouldn't have to worry about some crazy beyotch manipulating him with her boo hoo hoo."

"Jules does not have to worry." Em shook her head. "Liam has finally gotten her back. He's not going to do anything to screw this up."

"I have never loved you more." I hugged Em close. "You're right. We just got our second chance. We're not going to mess that up. Right?"

They both looked at me with hope shining in their eyes aaaaand a smidgeon of doubt. Ugh.

"Jules, sweetie, I have been looking for you everywhere!"

I turned to see an off-the-charts gorgeous woman headed my way. A tall and curvy Latina, with thick wavy black hair that hung down to her waist, she strutted through the craft fair booths in a form-fitting red sundress and strappy sandals as if she owned the place. I felt my heart clutch in my chest. Worlds colliding!

"Jess!" I cried. My mouth dried and I instinctively scanned the area for Liam, but he was long gone. Thank god!

"Hey, girl," Jessie scooped me close and hugged me hard. "Surprise!"

When she let me go, I glanced at Em and Soph. Both of their mouths were hanging open, in fact, a bite of churro fell out of Em's, and their eyes were huge, like, anime huge. Yep, because the boy they had known, hot guy Jessie Lopez, who I'd left Gull's Harbor with nine years ago was now hella hot gal Jessica Lopez.

Chapter Twenty-three

"What are you doing here, Jess?" I asked.

"You weren't at the house, so I figured you'd be at the art show, since it's literally the only thing going on around here this weekend," she said.

"I didn't mean here." I gestured to the art show. "I meant here as in Gull's Harbor, California, the west coast."

"Long story," she said.

She waved a perfectly manicured hand as if it was nothing, but I knew Jessie better than I knew myself. Truly, I had been there for all of the changes, the hormone replacement therapy, the vaginoplasty, the breast implants, even the speech therapy to get her falsetto where she wanted it. I knew this chick inside and out. Out of the corner of my eye I noticed my sisters hadn't moved. Seriously, they resembled garden statuary.

"Jess, you remember my sisters, Emily and Sophie," I said. "Em, Soph, this is Jessie, you remember, my friend who I left Gull's Harbor with."

Jessie threw her long hair over her shoulder and struck a pose. "I imagine I look a bit different." Then she winked. She looked Em over in her thigh-high boots and miniskirt. "Look at you, Em. Baby girl is all grown up! Rawr!"

A giggle burst out of Em and she clapped a hand over her mouth but it did no good as she kept laughing.

Jessie turned to Soph next. She took in the capri pants and sleeveless blouse with a frown then reached up and tousled Soph's bobbed haircut. "Who buttoned you down like this? We have got to liven up this cut and color. You look like you're fifty instead of thirty-five."

"Jess works in the theater in costume design," I said. "She's won a Tony."

"No way," Em said.

"Way," Jessie said. She blew on her nails and polished them on the front of her top. "Not bad for a surfer boy from Cali, eh? I know my shit." She looked back at Soph. "So, you can trust me when I say with a hotsie figure like yours, you could totally work the milf thing if you put in a smidge of effort."

Soph went beet red, but the twinkle in her gaze showed she was pleased by the sentiment. She asked, ever polite, "So, is this your first trip back to Gull's Harbor?"

"Yes." Jessie gazed around the art fair. "I can't say I've missed it." Then she threw her arm around my shoulders. "I need to borrow Jules for a sec if that's okay? We have some stuff to talk about."

As one, my sisters looked at me and I nodded. I had no idea what Jessie was doing here but I was dying to find out.

"All right, we'll meet up back at the house." Soph's tone made it clear I would explain everything later or else.

"Sounds like a plan," I said.

Jess and I walked through the festival, while I kept one eye open for Liam on the off chance he was still around. Per Jessie's request, I hadn't talked to Liam about her and if he saw her here without warning, well, I didn't see a happy reunion coming out of it that was for sure.

"Jessie, I'm thrilled to see you, obviously, but what are you doing here?" I asked.

"I'll explain all when we get back to your house. In the meantime, I have a surprise for you," she said.

"You do?"

"Yeah, come on." Jess cut through some booths and led us to a parking lot on the far side of the town green, tucked behind the town hall and the fire station.

She hit the button on a key fob and the doors unlocked on the rented SUV which had its windows half rolled down. Then she hit another button and the back hatch automatically lifted. Inside was a suitcase, a carry on, and two cat carriers. A yowl sounded and my eyes widened. I knew that sound!

"Ah! Spaghetti? Meatball? Is that you?" I rushed forward. Sure enough my furry babies were glaring at me from inside the two plush carriers. I turned back to Jessie and asked, "But how? Why?"

"Well, since I was coming here, I couldn't watch them for you, and I didn't want to have a stranger do it, plus, since you can work anywhere and you clearly have a lot going on here, I figured I'd better fly them out with me."

I rubbed my kitties' heads through the opening in their carriers. Spag purred and Meat growled. I took that as a good sign that their personalities remained intact.

"Let's get them home so I can hold them," I said. "Oh, I've missed them and you so much."

Jessie closed the back hatch and we climbed into the front. It was a short drive up the hill to the house. Once there, we got the kitties inside and gave them lots of attention and some food and water before letting them roam or, in Meatball's case, sit on the ottoman like a pissed-off blob.

I started a pot of coffee for us, and we sat in the kitchen while it brewed. I took out milk and sugar, knowing how Jessie liked her coffee, and when the pot was done, I brought it to the table.

I poured us each a cup and said, "Okay, I have been more than patient. What's going on?"

"Dante is going on." She sounded glum.

"What's wrong with Dante?" I asked. "You two didn't break up, did you?"

"Not yet," she said. "But he told me I either have to woman up and tell my parents about me and us or he will leave me."

"Oh." My mouth stayed in the shape of an O for a solid minute before relaxing.

Jessie's parents had no idea their son was now their daughter. Because they were very conservative and traditional, Jessie had never told them. When she moved to New York, the many miles between them had made it easy for her to hide her gender reassignment so she had.

"Why now?" I asked.

"Because he's asked me to marry him," Jessie said. Then she squealed and held out her left hand, which sported a chunky Tiffany Soleste diamond engagement ring.

"*Squee!*" I cried. For the record, I am not one to make that noise. I grabbed her hand to take in the ring and gently turned it to let the diamond sparkle in the sunlight. I let go and then clapped my hands, bouncing in my chair. I was so excited for her. "Congratulations, this is the best news ever."

"Except for the minor detail of telling my parents." Jessie sighed. "He said he won't marry me until I tell my parents the truth and introduce him to them. He's flying out here in two days. Jules, I have two days to tell my parents everything or I lose the love of my life."

"Oh, wow," I said.

We both stared into our coffee cups. This was big time. Jessie had spent the past nine years carefully cultivating the bogus image of a New York ladies' man to build up the cred with her very macho father. Her mother was forever begging her to find a nice girl to settle down with so she could have grandchildren. To say they had no clue about Jessie's transition was putting it mildly.

Her mother had long hoped that Jessie and I would marry, but despite what everyone believed, Jessie and I had never been a couple. Obvi. I alone knew the real reasons she had fled Gull's Harbor with me all those years ago and even now I was afraid to ask if her situation had changed.

The truth was that Jessie had left Gull's Harbor because, one, she knew she was really a woman inside a man's body and that her parents could never accept that and, two, she was desperately in love with her best friend, Liam, my boyfriend! Being near Liam every day and not being with him was killing Jessie so she decided to leave.

On that fateful night, when Babs and I had the mother of all blowouts, Jessie had found me walking on the side of the road. Her car had been packed to bursting as she was leaving town. When she heard about my situation, she asked me if I wanted to come with her. I didn't even hesitate. I jumped in the car, and we took off. Halfway to New York in the middle of Oklahoma—Oklahoma OK, my ass—Jessie confessed to me that she was really woman and, oopsie, she had been in love with Liam for years.

The crazy thing was that Jessie had never resented my relationship with Liam. She had loved us both. Although she was in love with Liam, she had frequently wished that she'd been in love with me instead because she thought she'd get over me more easily than Liam. I understood this completely. Liam was the sort of person who inspired deep and abiding love, which was probably why I had never gotten over him either.

The thought of what Liam would make of Jessie's arrival made my stomach cramp. Maybe Jessie coming out to everyone was for the best. I hoped I wasn't being selfish for acknowledging how much easier it would make things for me and Liam, but it totally would. I wouldn't have to keep the secret anymore, which was such a relief.

"Since you're here and about to have a tell-all, would it be all right if I told Liam?" I asked.

"Yes." Her answer was decisive but then she added, "Just let me tell my parents first. I can't risk them finding out secondhand. It would kill them. You understand?"

"Absolutely, of course," I said.

Jessie looked so bleak that I reached across the table and squeezed her hand.

"It'll be okay," I said. "Do you want me to go with you to talk to them?"

"No, every time my mother sees you, she gets fixated on the two of us giving her bambinos." Jessie shook her head. "It would just confuse her."

"Gotcha," I agreed.

We spent the next hour role playing different ways for her to tell her parents while the cats scampered around the house, mostly Spaghetti, which was a vast playground for them compared to my tiny Brooklyn apartment. We debated what she should wear, super girly dress and heels or more like a long-haired guy and pretend to be a gay man. Jessie rejected that because she knew Dante would never go for it. He wanted full transparency. Oh, boy.

In the end, we decided it would be best if she just came right out and told them, while wearing her best Tadashi Shoji and carrying her favorite Kate Spade bag. Much like Babs, Jessie firmly believed that fashion makes the woman.

Em and Soph hadn't returned by the time I walked her to the door. Jess was staying at a nearby resort, believing a full spa treatment might help her get through the next couple of days. I wondered whether I should call my sisters or deal with the as yet unanswered text from Liam on my phone. Probably, I should deal with the text. I glanced at his house wondering how his conversation with Courtney had gone. I was trying very hard not to worry, not to be jealous, and not to fret. I was failing exponentially at all three.

"Hey," Jessie paused on the doorstep. "I've been all about me and you look worried. Is everything okay?"

And that, right there, was why Jessie and I had remained besties all these years. We knew each other's tells and genuinely cared about one another.

"Yeah, I'm fine," I lied. She had enough on her plate. She did not need to add worrying about me to it.

I studied the woman who had been my friend when I had none, who had let me cry all over her shoulder when my heart had been shredded over leaving Liam. Together, we had carved out new lives for ourselves three thousand miles away and for the most part we had succeeded, and yet, here we were back in the place it had all started. It just proved that you could never outrun your past, no matter how fast or how far you ran.

"Come here," Jess said. "Come in for the real thing."

She held her arms open, and I stepped into them, comforted by the familiar feel of my gal pal, her warmth, her own particular scent, a delicate perfume that always reminded me of nights out in the city. Despite the pain of our mutual heartbreak, we'd had a lot of good times, too.

"It's going to be okay, girlfriend." Jess pushed some of my curls back from my face and kissed my forehead like a mother comforting a child.

"Am I interrupting something?" At the sound of Liam's voice, Jess and I jumped apart.

Jessie's eyes were wide with shock. She hadn't seen Liam since we'd left nine years ago. This had to be excruciating. I clutched her hand in mine. I had no idea if Liam would recognize her or not, but if I lied to him now, I knew with a certainty I'd only felt about one other thing in life—white chocolate is not really chocolate—that there would be no coming back from it. Still, it wasn't my secret to tell. I left it to Jessie.

"Not at all." Jessie squeezed my hand once before letting go. Then she did the bravest thing I'd ever seen anyone do. She turned and looked Liam right in the eye and said, "It's good to see again, Liam."

Liam frowned. He studied Jessie's face. There was no light of recognition. "I'm sorry. Have we met?"

Jessie's expression was bittersweet. "A long time ago." She looked at me and I nodded. Jess turned back to Liam and said, "It's me, Jessie, well, Jessica now. Jessica Lopez."

Liam's eyes narrowed and then went wide. He turned to me, two spots of color burning on his cheeks. "Is this a joke?"

"No," I said, my throat tight. "No joke."

His head whipped back to Jessie. I saw the second the recognition hit. Jessie had always had fine features, a real pretty boy, with wide brown eyes, a thin nose, and full lips. And her smile, her smile was a killer, with full lips over straight white teeth, I'd seen her dazzle lesser men with that smile. She gave him a shy version of it now.

"Surprise," she said.

Liam shook his head. He staggered back a step. He looked at me. "How long?"

We didn't need him to spell it out.

"I started transitioning the minute we got to New York," Jessie said.

"So, you're a..." Liam gestured wildly at her.

"A woman?" Jess asked helpfully. "Yes."

"But I thought—" He glanced between us. The hurt in his eyes made me wince.

"Liam, I'm sorry," I said. "Jessie and I were never that. We're friends."

"Best friends," Jessie said.

It was the wrong thing to say. Fury rose up in Liam like I had never seen before. A vein throbbed in his temple and he looked like he wanted to hit something or someone.

"You were *my* friends," he snapped. Liam looked at us with such anguish, I thought I might get sick. "You were my *best* friends. Do you have any idea how I felt when you two disappeared? My best friend and my girl. It fucking destroyed me."

"I'm sorry," Jessie said. "We never wanted to hurt you."

Liam laughed but there was no amusement in the sound. "Never wanted to hurt me? I wanted to die that summer. I even tried to kill myself on Devil's Backbone a time or two."

Jessie blanched. It was as bad as Ten had said, but I knew it would have been worse if I had stayed. Babs had made sure of that. It was time to tell Liam the whole truth.

"Liam—" I began but he cut me off.

"No," he said. "I don't want to hear it. There's nothing you can say to me to make this okay. Do you know how many nights I spent picturing you two together, feeling like a tool, hating you both but still loving you, too?" He looked at Jessie. "You were my best friend! Did you really think this would have changed anything between us?"

A tear streaked down Jessie's cheek. She reached for him but drew her hand back. "I couldn't do it anymore. Don't you understand, Liam? It was killing me."

Liam sucked in a breath and stared at her. He shook his head and buried his fingers in his hair. "You should have told me."

Jessie nodded. Liam was right. We all knew it, but we'd been young adults navigating stuff that was bigger than us when this went down. Then he turned on me. He dropped his hands from his hair and took a step toward me. Frustration poured off him in waves of heat. "And you, you left me without a word. No note. No explanation. Nothing."

There it was. The hurt he'd been pushing down, down, down, until Jessie's appearance ripped the lid off his pain and anger.

"You broke my god damn heart," he said.

"Liam—" Now I was crying, too. There was so much I needed to tell him.

"Save it," he growled. "You know what? I can't do this. I thought I could, but I can't. Keep your secrets and your bullshit and stay out of my life, both of you."

He turned and stormed away, leaving wreckage in his wake, which was only fair as I'm sure that's what we'd done to him all those years ago.

Jessie and I went back into the house. I took a tissue and handed her the box.

"This is a mess, isn't it?" she asked.

"A bit," I said. "Can I ask you something?"

"Sure." She shrugged as she dabbed her eyes.

"Are you still in love with him?" I could feel my shoulders rise up to my ears. I didn't want Jessie to be in love with Liam in that way. I knew it was selfish, but I wanted Liam all to myself, and I wanted Jessie to be okay with it, so I didn't lose her friendship, too.

"Nah." She waved her tissue in the direction of the door. "He was a crush. An intense first love crush, but I think he's a bit too manly man for me. I mean, he's totally hot, but I'm much more into the suave and debonair type these days."

"A metrosexual like Dante?" I clarified.

"Yeah, I'm so in love with him, Jules," Jess said. "Otherwise, I'd be happy to lie to my parents until my dying day."

"Well, I for one am glad you're going to tell them the truth," I said. "As we surfers know, the only way out of something is through it."

"I know. I'm sorry I caused a problem for you, Jules," she said. "I knew he'd be angry, but I figured since you two were doing the horizontal mambo again, he'd mellow out about us leaving town together."

"Well, he's likely still feeling betrayed. He doesn't know about Babs and our huge fight, her ultimatum, or that she's not my mom," I said.

"You haven't told him about Babs?" Jessie asked. "Why not?"

"We've been a little preoccupied," I said. "And I just didn't want to talk about it. I didn't want the past to taint the present and I'm struggling to figure out how *I* feel about everything never mind explain it to someone else."

"Jules, I say this with great love, but you need to get your shit together," Jess said. "I know it was one hell of a complicated mother-daughter thing you two had going, and I can only imagine how much more complicated it became when you found out she wasn't your mother, but this is stuff you tell your boyfriend, like, right away. I hate to say it, but you need to figure out whether you want Liam in your life or not and if you do, you have to let him all the way in...and not just in your womanly portal so to speak."

"Oh, god, I'm such an idiot," I said. "What am I going to do, Jessie? He's the love of my life and I've probably lost him...again."

Jessie wrapped her arm around me and pulled me in for a hug. We were standing in the kitchen in front of the window, which looked out across the yard into Liam's house. I saw his silhouette in the room opposite just before the window shades slammed down. The thought of losing him permanently twisted in my chest like an unsharpened knife blade. I really didn't think I would survive it this time.

Chapter Twenty-four

I did not sleep. I could not eat. Every minute that passed I knew Liam was thinking the worst of us, that we had just cut him out of what was happening with Jessie and left town without a backward glance. I wanted to run next door and demand that he listen to me, but being impulsive hadn't worked for me before so I forced myself to wait until Liam cooled off. I knew he wouldn't be in a place to hear me until he had settled down.

Oh, man, we sure were going to laugh about this big ol' misunderstanding in the future, right? Yeah, right.

Em came home in the early evening, saying something about Soph and one of the artists at the festival hitting it off and that Soph would be home later. I wasn't really paying attention, but I hoped it wasn't Sadie of the ceramic va-jay-jays. Then Em headed back out, leaving me to my brooding.

Spaghetti and Meatballs had made themselves right at home on Babs's divan. I was surprised her ghost didn't appear to shriek about cat hair on the furniture. I checked the urn on its spot on the windowsill. It didn't glow or rattle or anything. Amazing.

I kept one eye on Liam's place while I worked at the kitchen table. I thought I heard a car pull up outside, but by the time I got to the window, the car was gone, and no lights were on in his house. Must've been another neighbor. Too bad. I would have used any excuse to go see him in the middle of the night even if it was to yell at him to keep the noise down.

Jessie had texted that she was going to talk to her parents in the morning, so I tabled my worry about Liam to focus on Jessie. I spent the next day with my phone right beside me. Jessie's ring tone was *Shoop*, and I had never wanted to hear Salt-N-Pepa coming out of my phone as badly as I did that day. The morning dragged on.

Finally, at half past ten, my phone lit up. I snatched it into my hand without even waiting for the tune to start.

"What happened? How did it go? How'd they take it? Were they mad? Are they coping? Are you okay?" I fired questions like I was using an automatic weapon.

"Whoa, slow down, sweetie," Jessie said.

Then she started to laugh. It was the confused laugh of a person feeling unexpected emotions. Maybe everything was going to be all right.

"They disowned me," she said. So *not* all right then.

"No!" My heart did a free fall from my chest to my feet, and I felt woozy. All these years, the one thing Jessie had been terrified of was that her parents would cut her loose if they discovered the truth; that she would lose their love simply for being herself and now she had.

"It's okay," she said, but her voice was thick, and I knew it wasn't.

"Oh, Jessie." Tears coursed down my face and my chest ached.

"No, really, it's cool." Jessie cleared her throat and took a deep breath. "Because you know what, Jules? I'm free. I don't have to hide or pretend or bullshit them anymore. If they want me back in their lives, they can find me. I told them I'd leave the door open."

"I just can't believe it." And I really couldn't. I had known Jessie's parents since we were kids. They loved their child so much. How could they disown her now just because her path wasn't one they understood? I was a bit sick and a lot angry. "I'm going to go talk to them."

"Ah, no, I don't think that's a good idea," Jessie said.

"Why not?" I protested. "Maybe they'll listen to me. They like me."

"Yeah, there was some discussion, and by that, I mean yelling at optimum volume, that maybe your tomboy ways led me astray." Jessie sounded like she was trying not to laugh.

"Come again?" I shook my head, truly at a loss.

"It was one of many theories being batted around, you know, after pearls were clutched and a fist went into the wall."

"Holy crap!"

"Yeah, I'm thinking we all want to steer clear of Casa de Lopez for a while," Jessie said.

"That sucks!"

"Eh, what can you do?"

"Kick some parental ass?" I offered. She laughed, which had been my intent.

"Hey, I'm fine," Jessie said. "After all, I've still got you."

"Always," I said.

"So, you can be my family now," she said.

"You are going to make such a lovely Blumer sister, really, you'll put us all to shame," I said. This time she belly laughed.

"Shut up, brat," she said. "Listen, Dante is flying later today. He changed his flight and got on the first plane out of New York when I told him what happened. I'm going to have my hands full with him as he, too, would like to have a chat with my parents."

"Oh boy." If Jessie's parents were rejecting her, I didn't see them embracing her lover.

"Have you talked to Liam yet?" she asked.

"No."

"Why not?"

"I was waiting to hear from you."

"No, you weren't. You can *not* bullshit a bullshitter, Jules," Jessie said. "You were chickening out. Get your butt over there and tell him what's what. He was right last night. We should have told him the truth before we left. You owe him the truth now."

"I know, but it was nine years ago," I said. "And it's hard to explain how terrified I was of Babs's threats back then. She would have made good on them."

"No doubt, but she can't do it now. Go. I'm going to bounce while you go clean up your mess. We'll talk later and you can tell me what happened with you and Liam and whether you need backup or not."

"All right," I said. "Hey, I love you."

"Love you, too, sweetie."

I ended the call and jumped up from my desk, where absolutely no work was getting done anyway. I dashed toward the door, thinking only of making things right with Liam, but then stopped. Did I want him to see me like this? Hair mussed, no make-up, and wearing my pajamas. Yeah, no.

I ransacked my closet. There was nothing that felt right. I ran down the hall and burst into Em's room.

"Sorry, Em," I cried. "I just need to borrow an outfit."

Her bed was neatly made, almost as if it hadn't even been slept in. Huh. Then again, it was almost eleven, maybe she'd gone out for donuts or a run or whatever.

I charged her closet. Miniskirt, the boots, and a slinky top that would frame the girls just so. No, no, no. I needed to channel my inner ingénue and present myself as good and innocent and sweet, you know, as Em before she'd gone viral. I needed to make Liam want to listen to me about that night nine years ago, the epic blowout with Babs.

I used a light touch on the make-up and styled my long curls. I didn't go too crazy since my hair was a feature he loved. I shimmied into the delicate, off-the-shoulder white ruffled sundress I'd chosen and slipped my feet into a pair of girly pumps with daisies on the toes. I looked practically virginal.

Babs's urn was sitting on the windowsill where we always kept it per her directive. I ran my finger over the sparkly top as if I were trying to call forth a genie. I had so many questions for Babs that would never get answered, not the least of which was why she'd forced me to give up Liam. At the time, I'd thought she didn't want me knocked up at nineteen like Sophie but now I wondered if she just couldn't stand that I was happy, that I'd found true love when she never had.

I remember how that night she'd arrived home unexpectedly early from Mahjong due to a headache and found Liam and me in my bed, buck naked, and recuperating from doing the wild thing while we talked about our dream wedding. Babs had flipped her shit. And believe me when I say that's a gross understatement.

Babs threw Liam out and forbade him from ever seeing me again. When I argued with her, we went toe-to-toe and she leveled me with an ultimatum. I could give up Liam or I could give up going to my first pick college, which was my father's alma mater, Columbia University in New York City.

My entire academic career I had busted my butt to get accepted there—I'd loved my dad so much and wanted to be just like him. I had scholarships but not a full ride. I was, frankly, dependent upon my mother's generosity to make up the difference. I screamed and yelled and called her hateful names. She gave as good as she got, calling me an ungrateful whore. We fought for hours and finally, she told me I had to choose.

I told her I chose Liam. It was a major mistake. Made with the brash impetuousness of youth. My mother upped the ante. She looked at her hand and noted that her diamond ring was missing. She then tapped her index finger to her lips and said that she bet Liam stole it and it was a shame she was going to have to call the police on him.

In that moment, staring into the light blue eyes that I had thought were so like my own, I realized she had me. She'd shoved Liam's backpack at him when she'd tossed him out, and I knew without a doubt that she'd taken the opportunity to plant her ring in his bag. I was stunned. She was willing to sacrifice her most prized possession, a ring with three individually cut one carat flawless diamonds, each one given to her by my dad on the day she birthed each of their daughters, or in my case bought a daughter, to send an innocent boy to jail all to beat me at this power game we were locked in.

"Tell me again what you choose," she demanded. "A life full of opportunity in New York, or a crap existence being married to a boy with a criminal record, who you will grow to hate by the time you're twenty-five after you have pushed out his three, four, or five brats."

I screamed that I hated her and that she wouldn't get away with it, but she already had. I would never let her go after Liam like that, because she would, I knew that. Just like she knew I would do anything to protect him.

I had refused to answer her and slammed out the front door and into the night. Striding past Liam's house, I passed Jessie sitting there parked in his Jeep. He told me he was leaving, and I began to cry. He was one of my oldest friends and suddenly it felt as if everything I had ever held dear was being ripped from my grasp.

We drove to the nearby park, and I told Jessie the whole story about Babs and me and the choice she was forcing me to make. Jessie had been my friend since grade school and knew how hard I'd worked to get into Columbia. He was also aware that my mother was not one to be fucked with; if she said she was going to have Liam arrested, she was not bluffing. He then told me he was headed to New York, and if I wanted to catch a ride, he'd be grateful for the company. I said yes.

It had been the decision of a hotheaded eighteen-year-old and I had wished a million times over the years that I had made a different one. I wished I had told Liam the truth about my mother, what she'd done, and about Jessie, and how I had never cheated on him. In fact, I didn't date another man until my senior year at Columbia when I knew I was never moving home and any lingering feelings I had for Liam Mahony needed to be buried so deep inside of me that they suffocated. I thought I could plant them deep enough. I was wrong.

"Did you know that, Babs?" I scowled at the urn. "Did you know that Liam was the love of my life? That I would never get over him? I would never stop missing him? That I would never be complete until I was with him again? Did you?"

Not surprisingly, no answer was forthcoming. I refused to dwell on the fact that I was now having full conversations with Babs's ashes. It had been a stressful couple of weeks culminating in this drama between Liam and Jessie. No wonder I was on edge. It was time. I had to tell Liam everything and hope that he could understand and forgive me.

"I used to believe that you were doing what you thought was best," I said. "I really did, but the damage you caused, it's marked my whole life, and I don't know if I can ever forgive you for that."

A couple tears streaked down my cheeks. I wiped them away with my hands. This was accomplishing nothing. I had to go confront Liam. I had to explain and hope that he had enough love and understanding in his heart to listen and give me one more chance. My kittens were sprawled on the divan and I paused to scratch their chins before I left.

"Wish me luck," I told them as I shut the door behind me. I was only going next door, so I didn't bother bringing my phone. I did not want to be disturbed by anyone or anything when I talked to Liam.

Because of the dress, I chose the long way—the sidewalk. It took a few more seconds to get to his house but I figured I needed the time to shore up my courage. He had been so angry last night. How could I blame him? If the situation was reversed, I'd have been furious, too.

"Hi, Liam, I need to talk to you," I practiced as I walked. No, that sounded too serious. I needed to really get his attention right away. Maybe I should just whip off my dress. We seemed to communicate best on the physical plane. Would that work? Maybe. Ugh. This was when I really wished I had an advanced degree in the male brain.

I blew out a breath and walked the three short steps to the front patio and then crossed to his front door. I pressed on the bell, hearing it ring faintly inside.

No sound came from within. I checked to see that his motorcycle was in the drive. It was. Still, he didn't answer. I stood in my dress and heels, feeling a bit like a church missionary making the rounds. Had I dressed too innocently? Would he think I was trying to play him? I debated dashing home to change before he saw me? *Gah*, I was a nervous wreck.

I heard footsteps coming from inside. Okay, escape was not an option. I stiffened my spine. All I had to do was explain and everything would be okay. Liam had said before he didn't want to discuss the past—that he wanted a fresh start but that had been before Jessie showed up. We weren't going to be able to move forward together until he listened to me. I just hoped I wasn't too late.

The door was pulled open, and my breath caught in my throat. Liam stood there, bare-chested in just his pajama bottoms. This sight was absolutely never going to get old for me. Except for the expression on his face, the glare he leveled at me was so fierce I was surprised little fires didn't break out all over my body. Yes, he looked that mad.

"Hi," I said. My voice sounded weak, and I cleared my throat. "I was wondering if we could talk."

He said nothing. His gaze raked over me, taking in the loose hair, the flowing dress, and cute shoes. Somehow, he made the look insulting. Okay, that stung.

"It doesn't seem like you came to talk." Liam did not sound even remotely interested in talking or anything else for that matter.

"I was hoping to remind you of better times," I said.

"What do you want, Blumer?" Ah, so we were back to the last names. Fine.

"There are some things you don't know," I said. "Things that I should have told you years ago, but I was so angry and confused—"

"Who's here, darling?" a voice, a woman's voice, spoke from behind Liam.

I felt myself go rigid. He had a woman here? *Now?* My gaze darted to his. His eyes narrowed, taking in my alarm as if assessing it to see if it was genuine.

And then Courtney appeared behind him. She was wearing a silky pink robe over a matching nightie. She pressed her big busty self up against Liam's bare back and hugged her arms around his middle, propping her chin on his shoulder as she stared at me.

What the holy hell was going on? Had they...? Had he...? I thought my head might explode or I might throw up or both.

Liam didn't embrace her, but he didn't push her away either. He just stood there, staring at me with the coldest eyes I had ever seen. I shivered.

"Never mind," I said. I wasn't sure how I choked the words out, but I did. "I can see you're busy."

"Very busy," Courtney cooed with a throaty laugh.

The urge to punch *her* was swift and fierce. I even balled up my fist, but I thought better of it. I raised my hands in surrender and backed away.

I was halfway down the steps when Liam called after me, "Hey, I think we've said all we need to say, Blumer." He huffed out a breath and added, "Don't come around here anymore."

I gave a curt nod to let him know I got it and then with my dignity trailing behind me like toilet paper stuck on my shoe, I walked home.

I spent the rest of the afternoon face down on my bed, crying. The only time I got up was when I heard Liam's motorcycle fire up. I watched as he and Courtney drove off into the beautiful evening together with her sitting on the back of his bike and her arms wrapped around him, her head pressed to the middle of his back. This time when my heart shattered into a thousand pieces, I knew there would be no putting it back together.

Crash!

I woke up to the sound of something breaking. It took me a moment to realize it was completely dark outside and I had been asleep for several hours. Night had fallen and I was still in Em's dress and my lips and tongue were pasty dry, probably from mouth breathing since my crying jag had clogged my nose. I pushed into a seated position, noting that Spag and Meat were curled up on my pillows just like they did at home.

Crash!

Again? What the hell was happening downstairs? I was up and moving, shoving my feet into my slippers, before I was fully operational. Accompanying the sound of something breaking was the muted tirade of a person muttering, swearing, and *crash!*

I ran the rest of the way down the steps to the kitchen. Em was already there, peering around the doorjamb as if afraid to enter. I slipped in beside her and she turned her head toward me. Her brown eyes were huge.

"What's going on?" I whispered.

She pointed to the kitchen and shifted so I could see.

Crash!

"Oh, I'm sooooo sorry," Soph said to no one.

She was standing in the center of the kitchen, holding a stack of plates that I recognized as Babs's wedding china. White plates with platinum edges that Babs had used for every corporate dinner party when Dad was alive and every holiday dinner as a family. It was the same set she had coerced Soph to register for when she got married so they could be matchy-matchy. Soph hated them.

"Wait, no I'm not!" *Crash!* Soph hurled another plate toward the floor. "I hate these fucking plates!"

My eyes went wide. Soph seldom if ever swore.

Crash! Crash! Crash!

My older sis hurled the plates at the floor and then reached onto the counter for a gravy boat and pitched that, too. Her bob was mussed, her mascara smudged, and her dress wrinkled. She looked like she'd been caught in a street fight and lost.

"Sixteen years of marriage," Soph yelled. *Crash!* "Sixteen! And what do I find when I stop by your office? You with your pants down around your ankles while you plow your office manager on her desk from behind! Argh!"

Crash! Crash! Crash!

"Oh, Stantastic, you miserable prick," I muttered.

Crash!

"You weren't attached to those dishes, were you?" I asked.

"No, they're awful," Em said.

Crash!

"And as if that wasn't enough, you son of a bitch, you actually wanted me to apologize for interrupting you by not calling or knocking first. Argh!" Soph let out a feral cry, reached for a stack of dessert plates, and hurled the whole lot of them at the ground. Em and I covered our ears.

"Apologize? Apologize? Do you know how many times I apologize in a single day? Seventy- eight! How do I know? Because I've counted. Seventy-eight times! Who does that?" Soph cried.

Her chest was heaving and her brown eyes were snapping with rage. I had never seen Soph this angry. It was as if her fury had cracked open the *everything is awesome* façade that she wore every single day like a Mardi Gras mask on Fat Tuesday.

"I'm getting scared. What do we do?" Em asked.

"Wait until she's out of plates," I said.

"I'm sorry it rained on your golf game." *Crash!* "I'm sorry I can't volunteer for the blood drive on top of the food drive while planting seedlings at the dog park which we're having a five K run to raise money for while I drive twelve children in a carpool, only one of which is mine, for music lessons." *Crash!* "I'm sorry you can't find the ketchup in the refrigerator. I'm sorry I've gained five pounds. I'm sorry the house is a mess. I'm sorry I'm not enough!" *Crash! Crash! Crash!*

Em and I stood at the door waiting to be sure there were no more dishes anywhere. When Soph started to sink toward the floor, which was ankle deep in china shrapnel, we rushed forward with our arms open and bookended Soph, keeping her upright while we hauled her out of the kitchen. We sat her in the middle of the couch and took positions on each side of her.

"Soph, breathe." I was worried about her pallor and feared she might faint.

She took a shaky, shuddering, breath and said, "I'm sorry."

Then she laughed a bit hysterically as it was mixed with sobs. Em rubbed her back while I held her hands. There was so much I wanted to say, like how much I had always disliked Stan and how I always suspected he was a no-good piece of garbage. I forced myself to be quiet, to listen, to support her. It was so freaking hard when I really wanted to get in the car, find Stan, and run over him two or three times.

"Do you want to talk about it?" Em asked.

"No." Soph shook her head. "It's the oldest story in the book. Middle-aged husband loses interest in old, boring wife and cheats." She glanced at the ceiling and sighed. "I guess Mom and I have something in common now, huh?"

I studied my sister's ravaged face and slowly exhaled. I wondered if Babs had felt this betrayed by our dad. It made me uncomfortable but knowing how much Babs valued her status of "wife," I had a feeling she had felt exactly like this if not even worse, because, of course Dad had stuck her with me, a living breathing testament to his infidelity. My stomach cramped. Since discovering the truth of my birth, I had made Babs the villain, but the truth was, she'd been the victim and didn't that just make things even more complicated.

"What are you going to do?" Em asked.

"I don't know." Soph sounded forlorn and that hurt more than anything. My sister who always had it together seemed completely lost.

"He's a selfish prick, Soph, and he always has been," I said, my temper getting in the way of my common sense.

"Don't!" she snapped. "He is my husband and the father of my children. We have been together for over sixteen years so, yes, maybe things are a bit strained, but that's life. Not all of us just runaway when the going gets tough."

The very air between us stilled. If I thought she meant it, I would have been crushed but since I knew she was lashing out, I just paused, waiting.

"I am so sorry," Soph said. "I didn't mean that the way it sounded. God, I'm such a bitch."

That made me laugh. If there was ever anyone who wasn't a bitch, it was Soph.

"You are not, and you're forgiven," I said. "I'm the one who pushed. I owe you an apology. I am sorry. I love you. Please forgive me. Your situation with Stan is none of my business. I just care."

"You're my sister," Soph said. "Of course, it's your business. Please don't say anything to the twins. They leave in a few days, and I want them to have a fabulous trip and not worry about their parents' marriage. It's good that I'm staying here for the summer. It'll give me some time to figure things out."

Soph twisted her fingers in her lap and then rose to stand. "I should go cleanup my mess."

"Stop," I said. "We've got this. Why don't you go get some rest? I'll order us some dinner. Thai food, okay?"

"I'm not hungry." Soph's narrow shoulders bowed. Em and I exchanged a look of utter helplessness. This sucked.

"You know, I met a Voodoo priestess down by the pier the other day," Em said. "Want me to ask her to make a doll of Stan? We could stick pins in his wanker."

"Yeah, a case of permanent limp dick," I cheered.

Soph blinked and then busted out a laugh. She hugged Em and then me. "I love you guys."

"We love you, too," we said together.

We watched as she slowly climbed the stairs. My bright bubbly older sister looked gutted. Oh, I wanted to punch Stan until my arm gave out.

It took us an hour to clean the kitchen. Tiny shards of china managed to get into every crack and crevice, and we took turns sweeping, vacuuming, and hauling bags out to the trash. The Thai food arrived, and Em brought some up to Soph, but she insisted she wasn't hungry. We put it in the fridge for her if she changed her mind.

We decided to eat outside by the fire pit. Halfway through our meal, Em's phone buzzed, and she glanced at the screen. Her eyebrows lifted a little, and I knew she was about to disappear to wherever it was that Em had been disappearing to. I swear she was worse than the cats and I was beginning to suspect the three of them had access to a magical portal that took them to another dimension, because honestly one minute they were there and the next minute – *poof!*

"I have to go," she said. "There's a thing."

I stared at her over my cardboard carton of pad thai. There had been a lot of "things" lately and every time we asked her about them, she was vague, like CIA-operative vague, and then later we'd see the "thing" posted on her social media account.

"Just promise me you're not jumping naked out of a plane or anything," I said.

"I'm not...not tonight anyway," Em said. Then she smiled.

I snorted. My kid sister, the rebel, I gotta say I never saw that coming.

"Are you going to be okay?" Em asked. I had told her about the Liam debacle while we cleaned.

"Yeah," I said. "I'm good."

Em studied me as if she knew I was lying and wished she knew what to say to make it better. There was nothing anyone could say. I had lost the love of my life twice and both times it was my own stupid fault for not telling him what was going on before it was too late. I really was too stupid to live.

"I'm sorry," Em said. "I wish I could fix this for you."

"Me, too, Em-ergency." I grabbed her hand and gave it a squeeze as she walked by.

Em paused and then leaned over my seat to give me a hug. I hugged her back. Coming home had been brutal in so many ways, but the one thing I held dear was that the bond with my sisters was growing stronger every day. Oh, how I had missed them. Em planted a kiss on my head and then disappeared into the house. I couldn't help but wonder what that girl was up to now.

Chapter Twenty-five

I sat outside by the fire pit, mulling over Soph, Em, and me. I tipped my head back and studied the sky. There wasn't as much light pollution in Gull's Harbor as New York City, so the stars were bright and twinkled down at me in eternal optimism. I had always loved stargazing. They reminded me that I was really just a teeny tiny bit of cosmic dust in a vast universe and from that perspective, my problems became miniscule, too. I found comfort in that.

I heard a noise. It was a soft thump, like the sound of a footstep of a person trying to sneak up on someone. I whipped my head in the direction of the house. I didn't see any movement. Still, my skin prickled with unease.

"Who's there?" I called out. No one answered, which, if I'm being honest, was much less scary than if an unfamiliar voice had said, *I am.*

For a second, I wondered if the presence I felt was the guy in the hoodie and the aviators. No, I had no proof that he'd been following me, just a gut instinct that something with that dude was not right and that his interest in me wasn't normal.

Mercifully, I did not see a shock of blond hair, a blue hoodie, or aviators. In fact, I saw no one. The hair on the back of my still prickled, however, and that had me moving toward the house at a pretty fast clip for a girl who had just been stargazing.

Habit had me glancing over my shoulder at Liam's house. It was dark, presumably no one was home. My heart sank at this observation. The reality was that even if Liam did come back right now, I wasn't sure I was up for taking on Courtney's sloppy seconds not when I'd had so much to tell him, and he just refused to listen and then left—with her.

For the first time in days, my sadness was replaced with something else. It took me a second to identify it, but yeah. I was kind of pissed. Sure, I had left town with Liam's best friend, Jessie, *years* ago, and, yes, it was all hush hush, mostly, to keep Liam's butt out of jail because my mother was a crazy vicious shrew, or she had been. Now she was dead, and not actually my mother, which I was still processing.

But that wasn't the point. The point, and I really did have one, was that after the past few weeks of finding our way together again, instead of giving me even a nanosecond to explain, Liam had stormed off with some other woman wrapped around him like a dollar-store necktie. Well, I was done!

I snatched up the dinner cartons and slammed into the house, locking the sliding glass door behind me. If Liam wanted to call it quits, fine. I didn't need him. I didn't need anyone. I never had and I never would.

And as for Babs, well, the heck with feeling guilty about that relationship, too. If she'd wanted me to remember her nicely, then she should have treated me better when she was alive and not just in the final hours before she kicked the bucket.

The woman had never admitted that she was wrong and had never apologized when she'd put me through some serious shit in my life. Saying she wished she could make it right hours before she died did not make it okay, and I was tired of feeling like I was supposed to be all forgiving and loving about her. And the same thing held true for my birth mother. She gave me up for money, so fuck her, too.

Granted, I should have told Liam what Babs threatened to do that night so many years ago. I should have told him that I was sorry for the choice I made at the time, but I was eighteen. Give me a break for not being mature and all-knowing at that age. I did what I thought was best for him, for me, for our futures, and frankly, I had to get the hell away from that woman for a while.

I blew out a huge breath. Babs was dead but the things she had done hadn't changed and I was no longer going to pretend that they had. I could still grieve for what could have been without pretending she was more to me than she was.

I tossed the remainder of the Thai food into the garbage and went upstairs. I paused to check on Soph and was relieved to see her asleep in her bed. Feeling as if I bore a passing resemblance to myself for the first time since I arrived, I climbed into my bed and slept the peaceful, exhausted slumber of a person who has shrugged off all her burdens, at least temporarily. It was a lovely sleep right up until Meatball landed on my chest with a thump and a yowl, demanding his breakfast.

"Get off," I said. He flattened himself more fully on my chest. "Can't breathe." He did not care.

I turned my head and found myself forehead to forehead with Spaghetti, who showed his affection with head butts. He bumped his nose into mine about three times before he finally gave up and patted my face with his paw. This was the signal that I needed to be upright and filling their bowls pronto before they got really annoying.

"Fine, fine," I mumbled. I rolled, dislodging Meatball. He hopped off the bed as if this had been his intention all along and Spaghetti followed him, tails in the air as they marched and waddled, accordingly, out of the room. I listened to them scamper down the stairs, okay, it was more galumphing on Meatball's part but still down they went.

I didn't bother to look in the mirror and instead shrugged on a comfy sweatshirt against the morning chill and made my way to the kitchen. I was mentally high fiving myself for not going to the window to see if Liam was home. What the hell did I care? I didn't. Boom. Yay, me!

When my feet reached the first floor, I heard whistling. Happy, off-key, annoying whistling. Em did not whistle. Neither did Soph. I followed the noise.

I entered the great room and stumbled to a halt. I squinted at the faux blonde standing by the window with a measuring tape in hand. My cousin Paisley. What the hell was she doing here?

"Paisley, is that you?" I asked, stupidly, as if she could possibly be anyone else.

She turned to look at me and gave a little start. I imagined I had the Medusa of bedhead going.

"Good morning, Julia," Paisley said. "I hope I didn't wake you."

"No." I watched her jot something down on a pad. "The cats took care of that."

"You have cats?" Paisley's tone was disapproving. "Since when? Aunt Babs was allergic."

"Yeah, well, she's gone now." I wondered briefly if Babs was going to haunt me for sounding so callous. "So, we have cats."

"They had better not spray anything," my cousin said.

"Um, what do you care if they do? And not to be rude, but why are you in my house?"

"I'm measuring the windows for my new curtains," Paisley said.

"Your what?" I snapped.

"Cur-tains," Paisley spoke slowly as if I was too stupid to grasp the English language.

My temper began to heat, but I forced myself to keep it cool. In a voice much calmer than I felt, I asked, "Again, why are you doing that?"

"Well, because the house is about to become mine." Paisley tossed her hair and gave me a victorious look. "Since Em never came home last night, that violates the terms of the will, thus the house and the money are all mine."

We stared at each other. She embodied the beauty queen in the pageant, all false humility and fake boobs, while I appeared like the help, the unshowered help.

Em didn't come home last night? A cold feeling started at the crown of my head and worked its way down my skin until I was chilled from the outside in. Mr. Loren, our attorney, had said that there were two terms to the will that were unbreakable. One was that the three of us came home very night and two was that Babs's urn stayed in the picture window so long as we owned the house. I got the feeling from Paisley's smug smile that she had somehow been tracking us. If so, Em not being here meant Paisley could swoop in and take everything. Oh, crap! Oh, crap! Oh, crap!

I tossed my hair back and licked my lips. I was striving for casual when really my heart had stopped, my hands were sweating, and my mouth was completely dry.

"I don't know what you're talking about," I said. "Em is upstairs."

"Really?" Paisley asked. "Go get her for me. I'd love to see her."

I scoffed. "I'm not waking her up for you."

Paisley stared at me and then took out her phone. She tapped the display before holding it to her ear. "Yes, Mr. Loren—Howard—it's Paisley. Could you swing by the Blumer house at your earliest convenience? Yes, it's important. Yes, right now. And bring a pen. I think you're going to have to make some changes to the ownership of the estate."

My cousin hung up without waiting for him to reply. My heart was beating so hard in my chest I thought I might pass out. I decided to bluff.

I shook my head. "You are going to look so ridiculous when Em comes down those stairs. Make yourself at home. I'll be right back."

I turned and walked up the stairs, forcing myself not to run. As soon as I hit the hallway, I sprinted and ran into Em's room. Sure enough, it was as neat as always and she wasn't there. Damn it!

Panic set in and I was pretty sure I was going to hyperventilate. Paisley wanted to see Em, and I couldn't produce her. Paisley had already speed-dialed Mr. Loren and if he got here before I could find Em, we were so screwed. The terms of the will were very clear that Babs's wishes were to be met or Paisley would inherit everything. Oh, hell no!

I grabbed my phone and thumbed through my apps. I opened the one I had installed on both of my sisters' phones after Em's drunken debacle at Duff's. So long as their phones were on, I could track them. I opened the app and watched the bubble that was Em pop up on my phone. Yes! She was five minutes away, in fact, it looked like she was on the beach. This sitch might be fixable after all.

I called her. She didn't answer. I texted. Still, nothing. Short of installing something on her phone that emitted electric shocks when she didn't answer, I didn't know how to get her to notice that I was frantically trying to reach her. Ugh. The warm fuzzies I'd been feeling for my sisters evaporated like the morning marine layer mist under a hot sun. How could she be this irresponsible? Paisley was just looking for us to screw up.

Since Em wasn't there, I took a moment to toss her room, making it look like she'd slept in her bed but hadn't made it. Then I dashed to the bathroom, opened the window, and cranked on the shower, locking the door behind me. Next, I dashed down the hall and shook Soph awake.

"We have a situation," I said.

"Huh?" Soph's eyes were puffy, and she looked hollow as if someone had scooped out her insides, or more accurately, as if her prick of husband had cut out her still beating heart.

"Em never came home last night," I said. "Somehow Paisley knows this and she's here demanding to see her while she measures our windows for her new curtains."

"Ah!" Soph leapt out of bed. "Should we call the police? Oh, my god, what could have happened to Em?"

"She's fine," I said.

"How do you know?"

"Well, I sort of put an app on her phone that tells me where she is." I peeked at her from under my lashes. "Yours, too."

Soph blinked. "Genius."

"Yes, I am, now you go stall Paisley, while I drag Em back here," I said.

Soph nodded, so I raced to my room to get dressed. Quickly, I pulled my hair back into a tie, changed into the first things I could grab, baggy skateboard shorts, slip on Vans, an orange tank top, and my favorite oversized hoodie. Surveying my options, I knew there was no way I could go downstairs without Paisley seeing me. It was going to have to be the window.

Sliding open the pane, I glanced down. On the upside, if I broke my neck, I would not have to deal with the fallout from Em being gone. On the downside, I'd be dead and even worse, it would probably hurt really bad. Okay, then, no falling.

I sat on the sill and sent another quick SOS text to Em, letting her know we had an uninvited guest in the house and that I was coming to get her right now. Then I put one leg outside and leaned out, trying to determine if I could reach the roof or not. Just glancing up made my hands sweat and my heart race.

"Blumer, what the hell are you doing?"

My head snapped in the direction of Liam's house. He was leaning out the window of his workout room, shirtless, of course, and glaring at me.

"Shh!" I put my finger to my lips.

If Paisley heard him and caught me, I was doomed. I gestured with my hand up to my ear for him to use his phone. He growled in response and disappeared from the window. I took my phone out of my bag just as it buzzed. It was him.

I wondered what it meant that I was still in his contacts. Probably nothing but my foolish heart clung to it anyway.

"What the fuck are you doing?" he asked.

"Language," I snapped, just because.

"Blumer." Liam's voice held a warning note. Whatever.

"Mahony," I returned. "If you must know I'm on a search and rescue mission."

"Through the window?"

He'd moved back to his own window so I could see him. He was still glaring and shirtless. Damn, that did not help my concentration, not even a little.

"It's complicated," I said.

He said nothing as he waited, looking at me with one eyebrow raised higher than the other. He was not going to let me jump or climb or anything until I explained myself. Fine.

"I told you Babs put in her will that my sisters and I had to live here for three months and if we don't, she cuts us out of the will and our horrible cousin Paisley inherits everything. Well, Em never came home last night, and Paisley is here, looking for her. I think she's been spying on us and that's why she's making her move. I have to get Em back and upstairs before Paisley gets our attorney here."

"You're joking."

"I'm about to jump out of a window to avoid admitting to my cousin that Em didn't come home last night—does that seem like joking to you?"

"It's official," Liam said. "You Blumer women are bat shit crazy!"

"That's not fair. I'm not really in a position to argue that point right now."

"Do. Not. Move."

He disappeared from the window. Oh, man, what was he going to do? Storm the house? Threaten Paisley? None of that would help me. Yes, it was incredibly macho in a Neanderthal-helping-the-little-female sort of way but, yeah, the feminist inside of me was gagging on her Wheaties. Still, it was kind of hot that he wanted to help.

I couldn't risk it, however. If he made a scene and Paisley figured out Em was gone, we were boned and not in a good way. I shoved my phone back into my pocket and heaved myself up until I was standing on the windowsill. With one hand I clung to the window while I stretched and tried to reach the roof above with the other. I was ten inches too short. I couldn't even jump up or I'd surely fall.

Bang. Bang. Bang.

"Julia, what are you doing in there?" Paisley called through the door.

I glanced at the handle. It was locked. Phew!

"I'm coming, Paisley." I crouched on the sill so it sounded as if I was more in the room than out. "I just need to get dressed, since Em is in the shower. We'll be down in a few minutes. Have Soph make you some eggs—hers are the best."

Paisley had seen me at my worst earlier. There was no way she could be suspicious or argue with my need for a change of clothes.

"We'll see about that," Paisley said. "And you'd better hurry up. I don't have all day."

I sucked in a breath. Given that I was pretty sure she was up to something, I figured she had all the time in the world whereas I did not.

"Psst."

I glanced down. Liam stood there with an extendable ladder. My eyes went wide as I gaped at him. A ladder? I could have kissed him!

"Come on," he said, casting a worried glance at the house.

He didn't have to say it twice. He gently propped the ladder on the side of the house, and I shimmied down it like I climbed up and down ladders every day.

Shouldering the ladder, he grabbed my hand and pulled me into the backyard behind the cover of the enormous lemon tree. Then he leaned the ladder against the wall between our yards and gestured for me to go. He was right behind me, and I tried not to be distracted by the fact that he was eye level with my butt. Focus, Jules, focus!

I jumped from the top of the wall, and he followed. He tipped the ladder toward us and pulled it over, dropping it to the ground. We both jumped when it rattled, and he stood on tiptoe to peer into our yard and see if Paisley was about to come flying out of the house.

Weak from nerves, I sank onto the thick grass and put my hands over my eyes. I could not believe I'd just had to climb out the window to escape my greedy cousin.

"One quick question," Liam said.

I moved my hands and opened one eye. "What?"

"Where is Em?" he said.

"The app I have tracking her says she's on the beach," I said.

"You're tracking her?"

"Do not be judgy. My sisters are a handful."

"Come on," he said. "I'll drive you down to the beach."

"Thanks," I said.

"I'm not doing it for you." Liam looked cranky again. "I'm doing it for Em and Soph."

I sighed. "Whatever."

We crept around the side of his house, where he kept his pickup parked. He grabbed his keys and we climbed in. I scooted down in the seat on the off-chance Paisley was still measuring for curtains and might see me.

Once we cleared the street, I popped up, scanning the road in case Em suddenly appeared. I checked the app on my phone and saw that she was still on the beach. Good grief, had she slept there? Was she toying with becoming an unemployed transient? Was an intervention required?

Liam reached across the console and took my hand in his. He gave my fingers a quick reassuring squeeze. "Relax. Em is okay and we'll get her home with Paisley none the wiser."

He sounded so sure that I took a deep breath and blew it out. In my mind I saw him again with Courtney wrapped around him like a poisonous vine. I removed my hand from his and stared out the window. There was so much I wanted to say, so much I wanted to explain but I couldn't seem to get the words out around the big bubble of hurt in my chest. So, I said nothing.

When we arrived at the beach, Liam double parked and we jumped out of the truck. A crowd had gathered at the water's edge. Had something happened? Had there been a shark attack? Is that why Em hadn't answered me?

I broke into a run, stomping down the rocky path, skidding a few times in my race to get to my sister. Liam was right behind me. We jumped onto the sandy beach and sprinted toward the mass of people. I elbowed my way through the bodies not caring that I was being rude.

"Excuse me, sorry, my sister," I said as I pushed my way to the center where I stumbled to a stop. There was Em, sitting in the sand in the same clothes she'd had on the night before. In one hand she held a lethal-looking knife while cradling an enormous sea turtle on her lap with the other.

"Em, what...?" Words escaped me.

"Jules," Em cried in sheer joy. "Can you believe it? I found this poor guy all wadded up in a fishing line. I saved him."

A man sat with Em cutting away the last of what looked like a net that had been wrapped around the little guy's neck.

"Oh, Em." I was torn between wanting to hug my turtle-saving sister and wanting to strangle her for scaring me to death. "This is why you were out all night?"

"Yup," she said. "We were having a bonfire on the beach and then when it was breaking up for the night, I saw this turtle in the water. It kept flailing and I just knew it needed my help. Pretty cool, right?"

"Yeah." I simply did not have it in me to scold her when, I swear, the big brown-shelled turtle in her lap peered at her from beneath heavy eyelids with something in his round face that looked like worship.

"Okay, this dude is ready," the man sitting beside Em said. He was a neo-hippie, skinny, with a head of long dreadlocks, a fair amount of chin stumble, and wearing a Grateful Dead T-shirt. "Back to the sea, shell man."

"Swim safely, buddy," Em said. She leaned forward and kissed the turtle on the head before pushing him off her lap into an incoming wave. The turtle struggled and Em and her new friend each took a side of his shell and helped him to get deeper into the surf. The people around were all filming the rescue and Em with her long blue and gold hair, her tank top and broomstick skirt now plastered to her legs resembled an actual mermaid as waves broke around her and she pushed her turtle pal out to sea. Finally, the big guy achieved lift off and rode the next wave out like a pro and then with a flap of a flipper, he was gone.

Em and her friend waved him off while the crowd cheered, taking pictures and video until the turtle disappeared.

"That was righteous," neo-hippie guy said.

"Totally," Em said. She turned toward him and they exchanged a high five and a half hug.

"How about an acai bowl and protein shake?" the guy asked. "My treat."

"She'd love to," I said. "But we have a thing."

"We do?" Em asked. She yawned. "I don't think I can do a thing. It took us three hours to cut that turtle loose. I am exhausted."

"Paisley is at our house," I said. "Looking for you. Because you didn't come home last night, she thinks we've broken the terms of the will and she's called Mr. Loren to come and verify the situation."

"What?" Em asked. "But that's mental."

"Yes, and now we have to go," I said. "Liam will give us a ride."

"Oh, hi, Liam," she said.

"Hi," he responded. "Nice rescue."

"Thanks," she said.

I took Em's arm and dragged her through the crowd. Lots of people were patting her on the back, and she absently smiled at them as we headed toward the path to the truck above.

"This should be a great piece for your social media followers," I said. "But you might want to post it later so that Paisley doesn't use it to prove you weren't home."

"Doubtful," she said. "I dropped my phone somewhere on the beach while we were trying to haul the turtle in."

"Does this mean your celebrity days are over?" I asked.

She shrugged.

"Not to rush you girls," Liam said. "But we've been gone exactly twenty minutes. We'd better hustle if you're going to convince Paisley that Em was in the shower all this time."

I texted Soph that I'd spotted a beehive on my side of the house and that she should keep everyone away. I hoped she understood the code. The thumbs-up emoji in return assured me that she did.

In minutes, we were back at Liam's, and he was sneaking across our yard with the ladder. He gestured for us to hurry, and we ran behind him. Em disappeared through the bathroom window—all she had to do was slip into the house without Paisley seeing her.

"No one takes showers that are this long," a voice said from the glass doors that led to the yard.

Liam and I exchanged a look. He snatched the ladder and dropped it behind the thick hedge of rosemary bushes, then grabbed my hand and hauled me around the side of the house just before Paisley pushed open the door and stepped outside.

"Come on." Liam pulled me around to my front yard and we dashed down the sidewalk then around to the far side of his house, where we stood in the shadows, gasping as we caught our breath.

"I need to know what's happening," I said once my head had stopped spinning.

He nodded. Together we slipped into his backyard and peeked over the wall that separated our yards just in time to see Em come out the sliding glass door of our house and greet our cousin.

Chapter Twenty-six

"Paisley, I'm sorry, I didn't know you were here, or I wouldn't have taken such a long shower." Em was wearing a fluffy bathrobe and had a towel wrapped around her hair. "Soph said you wanted to see me?"

"You." Paisley pointed at her. "Were here?"

"Of course," Em said. "I live here. Where else would I be?"

"You're lying," Paisley snapped. "You and your miserable sisters are liars and cheats, and I am going to prove it." With that she stalked back into the house, slamming the door behind her.

Em shrugged and fell into a lounge chair, laughing in relief. I waved at her from the wall and then dropped down to Liam's lawn. We exchanged smiles. "We did it." I put my hand on my forehead. My adrenaline rush was abating, and I thought I might pass out.

"Need some coffee?" Liam asked.

"Oh god, yes, please," I said.

I followed him into his house and sat at the counter while he fussed with the coffee pot. The kitchen was sparse, with the departure of his parents he'd clearly made it a guy's kitchen with steel appliances and black dish towels. Who had black dish towels? He fussed with the coffee maker. Of course, it was some high-tech gadgetry that made super octane lattes and frothed the milk. I wasn't complaining. I knew the man could make a cup of joe that would make the angels sing.

He looked so handsome in his unshaven, sloppily dressed, man-in-no-hurry attire that I felt the usual longing rise inside of me, and because it's me, I couldn't resist poking the bear.

"Isn't your girlfriend going to be upset that you helped me out?" I rested my chin in my hand while I watched him steam the milk.

"She's not my girlfriend." Liam gave me one piercing glance over his shoulder and then went back to work.

"Please," I said. "You've been shagging the squash tart for the past two days, how is she not your girlfriend?"

"There was no shagging," he said.

251

I raised my hand in a stop gesture and stood up. Coffee or no, I did not want him to deny what my own eyes had seen. He was better than that and even if he was mad at me, I deserved the truth.

"I'm serious, Jules," he said. "Nothing happened between me and Courtney. I took her home after the art festival but then she had an Uber bring her back that night, trying to win me over. It didn't work. I was too upset about...things. She slept in the guest bedroom."

I crossed my arms over my chest. I wanted to believe him so badly, but I just couldn't get the sight of her hugging him out of my mind.

"Nice try," I said. "But I saw her crawl all over you in her cute little robe."

"Yeah, I let her do that," Liam said. "It was dumb, and it caused more problems than it was worth. I only did it because I was still so pissed about you and Jessie."

He sounded sincere. I wanted to believe him. I wanted to believe him so bad.

"All right, if you weren't with her, where have you been the past few days?" I held my breath. Please do not say her place because I could not make myself believe that nothing had happened there.

"I went to down to San Diego to check on my coffee shop there and do some surf therapy in Pacific Beach."

"Alone?"

"Yes, pitifully tragically alone."

I opened my mouth to pepper him with more questions when his doorbell chimed. We looked at each other in alarm. Had Paisley heard us? Had she figured out I was here? Was she going to try and cause more trouble?

"Stay here." Liam left me in the kitchen and went to answer the bell.

I crouched in the kitchen, peering around the wall to see the front door. If it was Paisley, I hoped Liam would be able to chase her away before she caused another ruckus.

But when Liam swung the door open, it wasn't Paisley standing there. It was Jessie. Uh oh!

I hurried out of the kitchen, thinking I should have grabbed the fire extinguisher in case things got heated.

"What the hell are you doing here?" Liam asked. Yeah, like that. Although truthfully, I wasn't completely sure that was what he'd said because his teeth were clenched.

"*We* are looking for Jules," Dante answered.

Dante stepped around Jessie, who looked nervous, although really outstanding in a bright pink wrap dress and low heels with her hair up in a twist and her make-up light but still accentuating her best features. I had spent years sitting at cosmetics counters with Jess while she learned the fine art of makeup application. Liam didn't move aside but that did not deter Dante as he pushed past Liam into the house. Liam lifted his fist like he was going to take a swing at him.

"Who the hell are you?" Liam asked Dante before glaring in my direction. "Boyfriend of yours?"

"No, Dante's spoken for. Pity," I said.

All three of them turned toward me and I can only assume I must have been quite a sight, because both Jessie and Dante looked horrified while Liam seethed.

"Jules, what is *this*?" Dante waved his hands in the air as if to encompass my entire ensemble. He clutched his chest as if pleading for mercy. "You're killing me here. You know that, right?"

Dante was a tall, lithe black man whose style was legendary among our set in New York. His suits were all bespoke, his shoes maintained an optimum gloss, his head was shaved to perfection, his eyebrows threaded into matching arcs of irreverence, his hygiene was scrupulously maintained, and there was never an ounce of extra fat on his perfectly sculpted physique. Ever. I was pretty sure he wasn't human.

"Sorry," I said. "Things have been a bit hectic and by that, I mean completely insane."

Dante reached out to hug me tight and then pushed me back to study my outfit, which made him frown, and then he used both hands to grab fistfuls of my wayward curls as if he had no idea what to do with them. Join the club. I heard a noise behind him and glanced over his shoulder to see Liam's eyes narrow into slits, and a low growl emitted from his throat.

"This is the moment," Dante hissed at me. "It's the big love scene at the end of the movie, the one we've all been waiting for, and you look like this. Could you not have put in a token effort, like with a comb or some lipstick?"

The laughter welled up inside of me before I could stop it. I hugged Dante close and said, "Babs would have so preferred having you for a child in place of me."

"Don't be a dumbass," Dante said.

"I'm not," I said. "You're suave and debonair—everything she ever wanted."

"But she cared about you," Dante said. "It's so obvious."

"How do you figure?" I asked. "She did everything she could to ruin my life."

"Did she really?" Dante tapped his chin. "Or was she so desperate to keep you from throwing away your life on a relationship you weren't ready for that she chased you away instead? Do you really think that was easy for her? Losing you, even if you were her whipping girl, that sort of loss takes more heart than most mothers have."

I sucked in a breath and ducked my head. Was he right? Had Babs forced me out for my own benefit? The thought boggled.

"Think about it," Dante said. "You were about to give up the college of your dreams for an eighteen-year-old boy. Right or wrong, she did what she thought was best at the time. Can you really say that isn't some sort of love? If she really hated you, she would have squashed your Ivy League dreams instead."

I blinked at him. Oh, my god, all this time I thought she'd driven me away because I was the daughter she couldn't stand with my wild curls and rebellious ways and then when I found out she wasn't actually my mother, I'd thought it was because she hated me. But maybe, just maybe, Dante was right, and Babs had driven me away so that I could have choices, more choices than an eighteen-year-old marrying her boyfriend would ever have.

"I don't know why you're here, Jessie, and I don't really care, but Jules stays with me. Now take your friend and get out of my house." Liam's tone was harsh. I glanced at Jessie who seemed on the verge of tears.

Okay, no time to dwell on Dante's revelation. I patted his arm and moved to stand in between Jessie and Liam.

"Liam, don't," I said.

"Don't what?" he asked. "Kick him...sorry...her out? It's no more than she deserves."

Dante moved to stand beside me in front of Jessie.

"I'm sorry. We haven't been introduced. I'm Dante Williams." He extended his hand. Liam just glared. Dante brushed his hands together and continued, "Listen, I know there is some history here, but if you touch my girlfriend Jessica in an aggressive manner, I'll have to kick your ass. And I will. There won't be enough left of you for Jules to scoop up with a spoon."

Liam's head tipped to the side like a dog hearing a very high-pitched whistle. He looked at me. I nodded. He looked at Dante. He nodded. He looked past both of us at Jessie, who stepped between us and faced Liam with her hands spread wide as if to say sorry.

"Girlfriend?" Liam asked.

"Actually, I've recently been upgraded to fiancé," Jessie said. She held up her left hand so we could all admire her sparkler.

"Excellent choice," I whispered to Dante.

He, the king of cool, actually blushed. "She's worth it."

"So, this." Liam gestured to the pretty pink dress Jess was wearing. "This is really you. You're a chick for real. You're not fucking with me."

"No, I'm not," Jessie said. She shook her head at him. "I went all in on the gender reassignment, and I have to say I turned out fabulous."

"That's my girl," Dante cheered.

"Holy shit," Liam said. He clapped a hand to his forehead as if he was trying to hold the idea in his head. "How did you know? When did you know?"

Jessie stared up at the ceiling. "Well, I had my first wet dream, in which you had a featured role by the way, when I was fourteen. At first I thought I was gay but I soon realized I didn't feel the way a man feels about another man, I felt the way a woman feels about her man. That was when I began to realize that my exterior didn't match my interior, if you get my drift."

"Oh." Liam said. A red blush crept up his face that was pretty freaking cute now that he'd stopped yelling and all. No one moved. No one spoke. The ticking of the clock on the wall seemed inordinately loud as we all stood there, watching him process.

"Wait for it," Dante muttered to me.

"So, you had feelings for me?" Liam asked. He looked like he was trying to get comfortable with the thought.

"Not just feelings," Jessie said. "I was deeply, desperately, in love with you."

I didn't think it was possible, but Liam's face got even redder. His gaze shot to me before he turned back to Jess. "So, it's true, you and Jules never..."

"No, urgh, gross," Jessie gagged.

"Um, thanks?" I said.

Dante snickered.

"Wait!" Liam threw his hands up in a stop gesture. He stared at me wanting to understand. "Did you know about this? Did you know when you left with him...er...her?"

"No, not until we reached Oklahoma," I said. Jessie and I exchanged a look. That had been the defining moment in our friendship.

"But you two left town together. You were a couple," Liam insisted.

"No, we were just two young people escaping some very tough situations," Jessie said.

Liam looked at Jessie then at me. His brow furrowed and he opened his mouth to say something but closed it. He turned away from us. He turned back. He was so clearly a man wrestling with the knowledge that everything he had ever believed to be true was wrong that I longed to close the distance between us and hug him. I resisted. He had to come to grips with this on his own. Finally, he stopped spinning and glared at Jessie.

"But you were my best friend!" Liam shouted.

"And now we're there," Dante muttered again just to me.

"And you were mine," Jessie said. "You can imagine how difficult it was for me to realize I was as in love with you as you were with Jules. When you told me you were going to ask her to marry you, I broke. I just couldn't face the fact that you and I would never be together in the way I'd hoped even though I knew it was impossible. I mean, I loved you and I loved Jules, and I loved you two together, but I..."

The pain on Jessie's face was as raw as it had been the first time she'd told me all of this somewhere in the middle of Oklahoma. I didn't fault him then and I couldn't fault her now.

"If it makes any difference, when we arrived in New York I tried to look out for Jules for you," Jessie said.

My throat grew thick. I had always suspected Jessie was keeping watch over me, now I knew it to be true, and why.

"It doesn't," Liam gritted out between clenched teeth. He turned away while flexing his fist, looking like he wanted to plant it in the wall. He took a deep breath and tossed over his shoulder, "Okay, maybe it helps a little."

When he turned back and glanced at his friend, the hurt in his brown eyes was like a bruise. "You could have told me, Jessie. I would have stood by you. I loved you like a brother. You could have told me anything."

Jessie barked out a humorless laugh. "Dude, I was nineteen. I could barely admit my feelings to myself, and you know what my father's like. I was terrified I'd be disowned, which I have been, by the way.

"I had to leave. It just happened that Jules and her mother had a big blowout over your proposal, and she was running away, too. I didn't know where to go and she was headed to New York, so I told her I'd drive her there and then I stayed. I never wanted to lie to you, but the truth hurt too much. I honestly felt like I would die."

I heard a sob as Dante pressed his knuckles to his mouth and swiveled on his heel, facing away from us. My eyes were damp, and my chest hurt as if my heart was being squeezed by a giant fist. I couldn't look away from the two people who meant so much to me.

They stood staring at each other and then Jessie drew a ragged breath and said, "I am so so sorry, Liam. I never wanted to hurt you. I never wanted to lose you. I just didn't know what else to do."

Liam nodded. It was a jerky sort of nod as if he was still trying to process all that he had learned but he was getting there. In one swift motion, he grabbed Jessie by the hand and pulled her into a bear hug. It was the same sort of hug I'd seen him give Em a million times.

"I get it," Liam said. His voice was gravel rough. "I wish I could have been there for you, but it's okay. We're good."

Now Dante was openly weeping, and tears coursed down my cheeks as well. Jessie glanced at me over Liam's shoulder. She gave me a watery smile and reached for me, pulling me into the hug. I half expected Liam to push me out of it, but he didn't. Instead, they both hugged me into the circle.

"So, am I forgiven?" Jessie asked. "You know, like that time I dropped your new motorcycle and scratched the chrome?"

Liam chuckled and the sound was hoarse. "Or that time I took a sucker punch from that bully Kyle Markus because he swung at you and you ducked, forgetting to tell me to do the same when I was standing right behind you?"

Jessie let out a strangled laugh. "Yeah, like that."

Liam stepped back and looked at Jessie with a slow smile lifting the corner of his lips. "Of course, I forgive you. You're my best friend."

Heart explosion! That would explain the swelling feeling in my chest as I was so happy and relieved that these two were burying the hatchet and not in each other.

"Listen, Liam," Jessie said, abruptly serious. She stepped out of the hug and put her hands on her hips. "If you're forgiving me, you have to forgive Jules, too. I made her swear not to tell anyone, especially you, about me. I put her in a really tough spot."

Liam turned to look at me with a grim expression. I didn't suppose there was forgiveness in his heart for me. Too much had happened. Too much hurt had accumulated.

"We do have some unfinished business." Liam pointed between the two of us and I nodded. He glanced at Jessie and Dante. "Make yourselves at home. We'll be back in a bit."

He took me by the elbow and led me into the master bedroom on the far side of the house. I saw Jessie take a step forward as if to follow, but Dante hooked her elbow and held her back.

Liam let go of me as soon as we stepped into the room. He also shut the door and put his back to it, crossing his arms over his chest as he glared at me.

"Why were you running away that day?" he asked. "I understand why Jessie did what she did but why you? Why did you leave me? Was it because of what I asked you that night?"

So, here it was. The moment of truth. It took everything I had not to look away to avoid the ragged edge of hurt I could see in his eyes. Instead, I squared my shoulders and said, "No, when you asked me to marry you and I said yes, I meant that with all my heart. I left Gull's Harbor for you. I did it to save you."

"From what? From loving you?" Liam uncrossed his arms and ran a hand through his hair. "Because I can tell you right now that didn't work."

A sob burbled up and I pressed my fingers to my lips. Tears coursed down my cheeks and my throat was clenched so tight with emotion that I could barely get the words out.

"Oh, Liam," I said.

"Just tell me why, why did you leave me?" Liam's voice was raw.

I fidgeted with the zipper on my hoodie. *Zip Zip.* Until he stared at my hand, and I stopped.

"Babs heard you ask me to marry you, and she heard me say yes," I said. "That's why she freaked out on us. Not so much about the sex, although that didn't help, but definitely the proposal pushed her right over the edge."

"Why?"

"I don't know," I said. "But I think it has to do with the fact that she," I paused to swallow before pushing out the words I was still coming to grips with. "She isn't really my mom."

"What?"

"Yeah, at the reading of the will, I was given a letter from my dad. In short, he fell in love with a woman named Lisa Michaels and she got pregnant with me. When Soph was sick with meningitis, Dad prayed for her to live and offered to give up Lisa in return for sparing his daughter. When Soph got better, Dad told Babs everything about Lisa and me. Babs paid my birth mother to give me up and go away and she did."

"Whoa," he said. "You've been dealing with that on top of everything else?"

"Dealing is a more active verb than what I've been doing," I said. "I should have told you all this before but I just...I just wanted to be with you."

A small smile tipped his lips. "Oh, surfer girl, what am I going to do with you?"

"Accept my apology for that night and for all the misery I caused you," I suggested. "I really am so sorry."

"First tell me what she did to make you run away?" He kept his arms clenched over his chest.

"Do you remember when she slammed into the room and start screaming 'Get out!'?" I asked.

"Oh, yeah," he said. "That moment has been seared into my brain since it happened."

"When she was handing you your backpack, she slipped her diamond ring into it," I said. "Babs told me after you left that if I chose marriage to you over college, she was going to call the police and have you arrested for the theft of her ring. She would have done it, too."

Liam went pale and staggered on his feet. I knew exactly what he was feeling as I'd felt the same the night Babs had hit me with the ultimatum.

"I found the ring in my bag," Liam said. "I brought it back to her the next day. I thought she'd lost it when she tossed me out on my ass. I was hoping to see you, but she said you were gone and then she shut the door in my face."

This did not surprise me at all. Babs never pulled her punches.

"Why would she do such a hateful thing?" he asked.

"Dante says she did it for my own good, because she didn't want me to end up married and trapped like Soph, but I don't know. I've long suspected she did it to get rid of me once and for all," I said. "And despite wanting to believe she did it for commendable reasons, I still believe it's more likely that she wanted me gone because I was a constant reminder of my father's infidelity. It must have eaten her alive."

"You know I never would have let you give up your dream of going to Columbia," Liam said. "Yes, I wanted to be engaged to you, to know that we were going to stay together no matter what, but I never would have stopped you from going to New York or finishing college. I was planning to wait for you, for as long as it took."

"I know that," I said. "But maybe I was the one who couldn't wait."

"What do you mean?"

"I chose you," I said. "When Babs forced me to choose between college or you, I told her that I chose you."

"Oh, Jules." His voice was so soft I could barely hear him.

"I would have chucked away all those years of study to get into my dad's alma mater, my scholarships, my dreams of living in the Big Apple for a few years, all of it, to be with you. Babs knew it, which is why she gave me no choice, whether it was for my own good or hers, I don't know."

Liam stared at me. "Did you really mean it?"

"Mean what?" I asked.

He began walking toward me, his gaze intent on my face, purpose in his every stride. My heart rate kicked up a notch when he stopped right in front of me.

"Would you have thrown it all away for me?" he asked.

Chapter Twenty-seven

"Yes," I said. No hesitation. No doubt. To spend my life with him, I would have given up everything.

"Oh, surfer girl." Liam cupped my face. His thumbs wiped away my tears and then he kissed me.

I had never been much of the polished princess type, you know, the sort who believes in true love and happily ever after. I was too wild and untamed and, I suppose, volatile. But if ever there was a moment where I believed in true love's kiss, this was it.

His mouth fit mine perfectly, just as it always had. He was gentle, even tentative at first as if the honesty between us begged a new beginning. But the heat that always simmered just below the surface bubbled up and as I wrapped my arms around his neck and pulled him in close, our kiss became fierce.

He lifted me up off my feet and strode toward the bed. I wrapped my legs around his waist, perfectly okay with the direction this kiss was taking. I dug my fingers into his hair, holding his head at the perfect angle so I could kiss him as deeply as I'd wanted to for days, weeks, or a few years at the very least.

"Liam," I gasped his name. "I need—"

Whatever I'd been about to beg for was interrupted by the bedroom door slamming open against the wall.

"Jules, we have a problem."

Liam and I turned to find Soph standing in the doorway, with Dante and Jessie right behind her, looking like they were trying to see what was happening. Judging by the smile on Jessie's face, she was a-okay with finding me clinging to Liam like a sloth hugging a tree.

"What's going on?" I asked.

"Much as I love talking to you when you're hanging off your boyfriend, do you think you could put your feet on the ground for a sec? We have a crisis happening," Soph said with exasperation.

"Someone's salty," I said. "I thought the crisis was averted."

Liam relaxed his hands, and I slid down his front with deep regret; make-up sex was going to have to wait.

"Paisley is now looking for Babs," Soph said.

"Huh?"

"Mom's urn is missing," she explained. "It's not in the windowsill where it's supposed to be. You don't have it, do you?"

"No," I said. "She specified in the will that it was to stay in the window."

"Yes, and it's not there. I told Paisley you had probably taken it out to be cleaned," Soph said.

I gave her a look. "That doesn't even make sense."

"Don't criticize, I was panicking." Soph flapped her hands at her sides. "You have to help me find it!"

Soph turned and led the way back to the main room. She pointed out the window toward our house and I saw Paisley in the yard, looking up at my bedroom window. As Paisley swung around in our direction, Soph grabbed my hand and yanked me down beneath the window ledge. My knees hit the wood floor hard, and I grunted.

"Who is that?" Dante asked.

"Our evil cousin," I said.

"Oh, my god, she's looking our way," Jessie said. "What do we do?"

"Just act natural," Soph hissed at the three of them. They all stood still like they'd been hit with a Superhero's freeze ray. "I said act natural. Move, throw a football around, do something!"

"No ball in the house." Liam gestured for Dante and Jessie to follow him into the kitchen. "Let's get some coffee." He glanced at me. "I'll tell you when the coast is clear."

Soph and I stayed huddled on the floor. Minutes passed. I heard the three of them talking and, be still my aching heart, actually laughing. More minutes ticked by. Good grief, how long was Paisley going to search the yard for Babs like she was an Easter egg?

I glanced up to see Liam, standing in the doorway drinking a hot cup of coffee. At that moment, I would have given my first born for a cup of coffee. The java lust must have shone in my eyes because he strolled into the room and lowered the hand with the coffee mug, all casual like, until it was right in front of me and hidden by the wall below the windowsill. I took the mug, feeling the warmth seep into my fingers just before I took a big restorative gulp. It was safe to say I had never loved this man more.

"Is she still out there?" Soph asked.

"Yep," Liam said out of the corner of his mouth. Then he raised his hand and waved.

"Oh, my god, is she flirting with you?" I asked.

"Well, she just unbuttoned the top three buttons on her dress, and now she's bending over," Liam said.

"That's it. I'm going to curb stomp her," I said, rising to my knees. Soph grabbed my arm, holding me down.

"Later," Soph said. "First we have to figure out where Mom is."

"Okay, now she's hiking up her skirt and showing me some thigh." Liam frowned down at me. "I'm kind of scared. And for the record, she does not have your hot bod, your finesse, or your boots."

Mollified, I drank my coffee. I turned to Soph and said, "I thought I heard someone in the house last night. You were in bed and Em was out. I was alone and I could have sworn I heard someone but when I looked no one was there."

"My god, do you think we were robbed?"

"And the only thing they took was an urn?" I asked.

"Weird." Soph slumped against the wall.

Jessie and Dante came in with their own mugs of coffee and Jessie handed hers to Soph. She looked as grateful as I'd felt. After Sophie took a sip, she seemed calmer.

"All right, we need to think about who might have taken Mom," Sophie said.

"Paisley, obvi," I said.

"Wait a minute." Liam stared out the window and then glanced down at me. "I know her."

"Oh, no, please tell me you didn't sleep with her," I said.

"No...urgh." Liam made a gagging sound. "But she's come into the coffee shop in LA with Courtney." His expression turned suspicious. "She's friends with Courtney."

I narrowed my eyes. "The same Courtney who was here last night?"

"Yup." Liam crossed his arms as he studied my cousin. "She might have helped Paisley."

"Wait. I'm confused," Soph said. "Who is Courtney?"

"Yeah." Jessie tossed her hair and echoed Soph. "Who is Courtney?"

"Liam's ex-girlfriend," I said. "And quite possibly the person who took the urn given that she is friends with our cousin."

"Liam, then you know where she's stashed the urn. Let's go get her," Soph said.

"It might be complicated," Liam said. He turned away from the window. "Okay, your cousin went inside but I'd stay down just to be on the safe side."

"Wait, is Courtney the one from the art festival with the fake bazooms?" Soph put her hand in front of her chest as if to demonstrate the enormity of Courtney's rack.

"Yes," I said.

"Oh, yeah, she was furious," Soph said. "This could get ugly."

Jessie gave Liam a look. "I didn't think you were a boob guy."

"I'm not," Liam said. "I much prefer a smaller package."

I tipped my head and frowned at him. His face went pink. "There's no saving me is there?"

"Nope," I said.

Liam hung his head and I laughed. Soph gave me a look and I said, "What? He's cute."

She rolled her eyes but there was a small smile on her lips, and I knew my older sis was happy for whatever was happening between Liam and me.

"People." Dante clapped his hands. "Jessie and I are booked on a flight out of here this evening, so if you want our help, and I'm thinking you do, then we need to make a plan."

Just then Liam's front door burst open, and Em stood there. She was still in her bathrobe and stared at all of us with a crazed look in her eye.

"OMG, my FOMO was literally spot on," Em declared. "Why didn't you come get me?"

"FOMO?" Soph asked. "It's like she's a foreign exchange student and I only get about half of what she's saying."

"It means fear of missing out," Jessie said. She rose from her seat, crossed the room, and pulled Em into a hug. "Em, sweetie, come in, sit on the floor with your sisters. We're making a plan."

"Oh, yay, I'm right on time then." Em wedged herself between me and Soph and in her best Joey from *Friends* voice, said, "So, how you doin'?"

This is why it is impossible to be mad at Em. Soph grinned and I threw my arm around her and hugged her.

"Here's the thing, Em-bolism," I said.

"That's just mean," my baby sis said.

"We have another situation," I continued, ignoring her frown.

I went on to explain everything that had happened and what we suspected about Courtney and Paisley and Bab's missing urn.

"Wow," Em said. "Okay, first we need to distract Paisley. She called Mr. Loren three times while he was in a meeting and now he's finally on his way over."

"Oh, shit," Soph said.

"Exactly." Em glanced at Dante and Jessie. "Do you two think you could help me with that?"

"Absolutely," Jessie said.

"I'm in," Dante agreed.

"Liam, you're going to have to confront your girlfriend," Soph said.

"Ex-girlfriend." I felt compelled to correct her.

"Ex-girlfriend, just so." Soph nodded. "If she's friends with Paisley and she took the urn, she is either out for revenge against Jules for ending your relationship or Paisley is paying her."

Liam's expression became determined. "We'll get the urn back. No worries."

"We?" I asked.

"Yes, we." Liam closed the shades on the window and reached down for my hand. "Come on, let's go get Babs."

"Wait!" Soph opened her purse and took out her keys. "Take my SUV. Your girl—ex-girlfriend might recognize your truck and there isn't room for the urn on the motorcycle."

"Good thinking," Liam said. "Soph, if you are staying here, that makes you ground control for the operation. We'll call when we have the urn."

I could hear the others discussing their surprise visit to Paisley. Dante was arguing that he could pose as an architect or an interior designer while Jessie was thinking they should be town employees there to inspect the property lines. Meanwhile, Em was busily tapping on Soph's phone, muttering something about a much better idea. I didn't get to hear what they decided as Liam hustled me out of the room to the back door.

He paused to grab a Padres baseball hat from a peg on the wall and shoved my hair into it. Next, he slid a pair of sunglasses on my face and kissed my nose.

"Let's do this!" He opened the back door and we sprinted around the side of the house to Soph's car, which was parked on the street.

We slammed into the SUV, Liam fired it up, and we shot out onto the road and away. I didn't realize I'd been holding my breath until I sucked in a big gulp of air.

"Okay, let's devise a plan," I said. "First, we need to figure out where Courtney is. You know where she lives, obviously."

"She won't be there...she's at work," Liam said.

I gave him a look, you know, the one that says *How do you know that? And I had better like the explanation, buster.*

"Settle down," Liam said, correctly interpreting my expression. "We dated long enough that I know her work schedule."

That made sense even though I desperately wanted to wrestle his phone out of his pocket and delete her from his contacts, along with any social media pictures, texts, emails, or you know evidence that the busty girl had ever been in Liam's orbit ever. So mature, I know.

"Okay," I said. I gave myself a mental back slap for sounding so reasonable. "Now we just have to figure out how to get into her house."

"I have a key," Liam said.

He turned onto the highway headed north. I waited until he had finished merging with traffic before I spoke. "You have a what?"

"A key to her place." Liam's eyes were on the road ahead, and I couldn't tell if he was avoiding my gaze or just concentrating on driving.

"Well, that's handy," I snapped.

Irrational much? Yeah, talk to the hand. He had a key to her place! How serious had they been?

"It was while we were dating." Liam gave me side-eye. "Are you telling me you haven't dated anyone long enough to have a key to their place?"

Landmine! I skirted it.

"That's not the point," I said. "The point is that you said you two broke up so why do you still have a key?"

"Because when I tried to give it back to her, you know, the night after I found you crying," he said. "She refused to take it."

"Oh," I said. That one I could understand. If I'd been Courtney and he'd tried to give me my key back, I'd have refused it, too.

"And isn't that a good thing?" Liam pressed.

"I suppose so," I said.

We were silent for several miles. Unable to take it anymore, I confessed, "I didn't date anyone for three years after I left you."

His head swiveled in my direction and we stared at each other for a few seconds. He nodded and then turned back to the road.

"I've dated," I said. "But no one special and nothing serious. I just couldn't find anyone that made me feel the way you did."

"And how was that?"

He glanced at me, and I shrugged. This was easy. "Loved."

Chapter Twenty-eight

Liam opened his mouth to speak at the same time that my phone chimed. He nodded for me to answer, but said, "We're not done with this conversation."

I didn't recognize the number and thought it might be a client. "Hello, Julia Blumer speaking."

"You think you're so clever," Paisley said by way of greeting.

I looked at Liam with wide eyes and he frowned.

"Yes, most of the time I do think I'm quite the smarty pants, Paisley, but how does that impact your world?"

Liam's eyes mirrored mine with the wideness and he leaned closer to hear what she was saying. I put the phone on speaker.

"You think running away is going to solve this situation just like you thought it would solve your sitch with big, tall, and hot next door all those years ago, but it won't," my cousin said.

"Paisley, what are you babbling about?" I asked. "I'm not running away. I merely ducked out to grab some coffee. I said good-bye to you on the way, sheesh, don't you remember?"

It was a brazen lie, but I was hoping my sheer confidence left her bewildered enough that she bought it at least for a few minutes. I heard some music and then laughter in the background.

"Paisley, are you having a party in my house?" I asked. "Not for nothing, but I believe that's bad form."

Abruptly, the noise got louder, and I heard Paisley snap at someone to wipe their feet, put a coaster under their drink, and for god's sake turn the music down. It went noticeably up in volume.

"I am not having a party, your sister is!" Paisley yelled. Liam and I exchanged surprised glances as she continued, "You had better rein that girl in—she is out of control!"

My cousin abruptly ended the call. I put my phone away and started laughing. This was awesome. Man, Em didn't just bust out of her shell, she freaking blew it up! I hoped she managed to do the same with her feelings for her boss, because there was no way she should be pining for a married guy.

"Another Blumer sister is going rogue," Liam said. He turned on his signal and took the next exit off the highway.

"Indeed. So, it appears Em's way of dealing with Paisley is to throw a party in the house," I said. "Genius."

"At eleven o'clock in the morning?" Liam asked. "Who is at this party?"

"Day drinkers?" I suggested. "Poor Mr. Loren has no idea what he's walking into."

He shook his head with a laugh. "More like Paisley had no idea what she was up against when she took on the Blumer sisters. Serves her right."

I grinned. The Blumer sisters. No matter what my origin story, I was still a Blumer sister, one-hundred-percent. That made me smile.

Liam drove a winding route through the Los Angeles suburbs until we were on a road that ran along the water. A sense of déjà vu hit me, and I started to suspect I knew exactly why Courtney had helped Paisley.

"We're here," he said.

He parked on the street in front of a house with a gorgeous ocean view from where it sat in the curve of a cul-de-sac named Rosemont Lane.

"No shit. Wild guess who lives over there?" I pointed to a similar house across the street.

Liam squinted at the house. "Paisley?"

"Correct," I said. "So, your Courtney and my Paisley are neighbors."

"When do you think they cooked this up?" Liam asked.

"We only found out the conditions in the will a few weeks ago," I said. "It must be recent. I'd be willing to bet it came to fruition after you dumped Courtney."

"Hell hath no fury..."

"Indeed."

He took my hand, and we walked toward the house. I had the sudden sensation I was being watched and I gave him a nervous glance.

"Are you absolutely sure she's at work?"

"Yes, she's in banking and does not have flexible hours," he said.

"Okay." I hoped he was right.

Still, the feeling persisted. I knew it couldn't be Paisley watching us because she was back at the house. I tried to look casual as I surveyed the area, thinking it might be some nosey neighbors, then I caught sight of a blue hooded sweatshirt and aviators. My stalker was here!

He was standing in the neighbor's yard peeking out at us from behind a large fig tree. Seriously?

"Hey! You! I want to talk to you!" I dropped Liam's hand and started toward the stranger with the intention of kicking his butt or getting some answers or both.

"Uh, Jules, we're trying to be inconspicuous here," Liam said as he trotted after me.

"Yeah, well, that's the guy who's been following me," I said. "At your coffee shop, at the beach, even at the art festival."

"That's him?"

"Yes," I said. "And I want to know why."

I didn't get out another word as Liam jumped over the neighbor's hedge and began to chase the strange man down. They beat feet across the yard until Liam caught the guy in a diving tackle that had them rolling almost to the rocky cliff at the perimeter of the lawn.

"Whoa, whoa, whoa!" The man jumped away from Liam with his hands in the air. "It's not what you think. I can explain."

"I'm listening," I said as I joined them.

Liam looked as if he wanted to do some listening with his knuckles across the guy's lips, but I looped my arm through his, holding him back.

"I'm a private investigator," the man said. "My name is Trent McAllister, and I was hired by Paisley to follow you and your sisters, Ms. Blumer."

"Prove it," I said.

He carefully reached into his back pocket and Liam stepped forward as if ready to take a swing at him if he did anything funky. "Easy, I'm just getting my ID out."

Liam held out his hand and Trent dropped his picture ID in it as if afraid Liam was going to take the opportunity to break his fingers. Not completely out of the realm of possibility.

"It says your office is in San Diego," Liam said. "Mission Beach."

"Yeah, I've been there for about five years," he said. "Rolled down from Los Angeles."

"What were you doing for Paisley?" I asked.

"She was referred to me by an old client. She hired me to make sure you and your sisters followed the dictates of the will, you know, that you kept the urn in the window and that you all slept in the house every night," he said. "Paisley was sure you would crack."

"So, are you the one who took the urn last night?" I asked.

"Hell, no!" Trent said. "I'm just a watcher. I don't do anything illegal. I have a reputation to protect."

"Good. Because then we'd have a problem," I said.

"Not for nothing, I'm not surprised someone took the urn from you," he said. "Paisley offered me a sweet deal, a payout to be determined if I'd do it for her. Since burglary is a no no, I refused. She didn't like that."

"What are you doing here now?" Liam asked with suspicion in his tone.

"Quitting," he said. "I went to cash the check she wrote, and it was denied for insufficient funds. That's the second time, so I came to tell her I quit."

"I think that's a good call," I said. "But she's not here. She's down at my house measuring the place for curtains."

"So, she must have found someone else to steal the urn," Trent said. "Sorry about that. That's bad luck."

"Not entirely," Liam said. "We have a pretty good idea of who did it."

Trent followed his gaze to the house across the street. "The neighbor? The one with the big...garage?"

"That's the one," I said. I jerked my thumb at Liam, "Also known as his ex-girlfriend."

Trent raised his eyebrows. "Awkward."

"I'll say," Liam agreed.

"Well, I'll leave you two to it," Trent said. He began to walk away and then turned around. "A word of advice from a pro, if you don't mind?"

"Not at all, lay it on us," I said.

"People like to hide things in their freezers," he said.

Liam and I exchanged a look.

"Thanks," I said.

"Good tip." Liam nodded.

Trent gave us a small smile and then took off down the street toward a nondescript sedan parked in front of Paisley's house.

"You ready?" Liam asked.

"As I'll ever be," I said. "My first B&E. Woo hoo!"

"We're not B-ing just E-ing," Liam said. "I have a key, remember?"

"That diminishes the excitement."

"Don't worry, I think I can come up with other ways to excite you later." He winked at me.

Oh, my!

We hurried across the street and made our way up the walkway to Courtney's house. I saw big flouncy curtains in the window and my curiosity piqued. I couldn't wait to see the inside of the busty one's home.

Liam unlocked the front door and we entered. He paused beside a keypad and entered a code. The system beeped and he relaxed.

"She didn't change the code," Liam said. "Excellent."

"You have a key, and you know the passcode to her alarm system," I said. "I know it doesn't matter now, except it totally matters to me, were you really going to ask her to marry you?"

"Truth?" he asked.

I nodded then I held my breath. I don't know why but a small part of me would die inside if he had actually thought of proposing to Courtney, which was ridiculous, I know, because I had been gone for years and it wasn't like I expected him to wait for me, but if humans were rational, there wouldn't be wars or men proposing to women who had bigger tits than brains, just sayin'.

"No," he said. "Even if you hadn't appeared back in my life, Courtney wasn't the one for me. We dated for a while, sure, but it was long distance, and we became more of each other's plus one in social situations than an actual couple with a future, at least, on my end."

At that, I hugged him hard. My man. I had a feeling Courtney didn't see it quite so casually. She'd probably thought that by giving him a key and her code, it was like slipping a light leash on him. Liam wasn't the sort to fall in with that plan. Phew!

"Let's do this," Liam said.

He hugged me close and kissed the ball cap on my head, which I found very sweet. He led me by the hand through the house toward the kitchen.

Surprisingly, other than the poofy floral drapes in the windows, the house was very plain. A few flowery prints hung on the wall, the furniture was very beige, and glass and brushed steel were the only accents. The floor was stone, the walls were shades of gray, overall, it was very *meh*.

"Start with the freezer?" Liam asked.

"Natch," I said.

We entered the large space with the typical granite countertops, white cupboards with dark pulls, and stainless-steel appliances, so boring. The only thing the room really offered was a fabulous view of the ocean. Oh, yeah, I could get used to drinking my coffee and looking at that view every day.

Liam went right to the large refrigerator freezer and pulled open the left side. He rifled around a bit and then pulled out a shopping bag from Saks Fifth Avenue.

"Wild guess here, but I'm thinking she's not keeping food in this," Liam said.

He plopped it on the counter, and I went to peer inside but then stopped.

"What if it isn't Babs?" I asked. "I feel a little bad invading her privacy like this."

"Like she did when she stole your mother's urn?" Liam asked.

"Good point." I opened the top and peered inside. Babs's sparkly urn glinted at me in the overhead light. I reached in and pulled out the mother of pearl inlaid container and hugged it to my chest. The amount of relief I felt was overwhelming. "Babs."

Liam frowned. "This is so weird."

"I know. I'm sorry my people are non compos mentis."

He tucked a wild curl behind my ear and tipped my chin up to kiss me. It was swift and sweet but still made my toes curl.

"Don't be sorry," Liam said. "I wouldn't have you any other way, which is good since we're getting married and all."

Chapter Twenty-nine

Before I had a chance to respond, which I couldn't anyway because I was sure I'd swallowed my tongue, Liam hustled me out of the house. Standing on the stoop, he took an envelope out of his pocket and once he locked the door, he put the key in the envelope and shoved it back in the mail slot. Then he brushed his hands together as if this was dusted and done.

We hurried down the walk and climbed into Soph's car. I glanced at my phone and realized I'd missed several texts as it had been on silent. Being busy doing a B and E, okay, just the E, will do that for a girl.

The texts were mostly from Soph.

Where are you? Did you find the urn?

Police cars are at the house.

Now a paddy wagon has pulled up.

Should I go over there?

The next one was from Em, using Jessie's phone.

Might need bail money. Meet us at the station.

Then Soph again.

The party is over. Em and our friends are okay.

Mr. Loren managed to talk the police out of arresting them...this time. Jules, we need to talk bout Em.

Where are you?

And then Em again.

Never mind. We're good. Party on!

I read all of this to Liam. His expression showed his concern. He wisely did not voice his worry aloud. Instead, he said, "You might want to text them that you've got the urn and Paisley's evil plans have been foiled."

"Oh, right." I set to it, trying to word the message in such a way that if our text messages were somehow subpoenaed by Paisley on a litigious rampage, then I wouldn't be disclosing the fact that I had unlawfully entered a person's house to retrieve an urn without said person's permission, even though, yeah, they stole our mom!

So, naturally, my responding text read:

Liam and I are getting married!

At this, my phone pretty much exploded.

Soph replied:

Now? Like, right now? Because we have stuff happening here.

Oh, but congratulations!

And Em wrote:

I call maid of honor! Woot!

Then it turned into a texting thumb wrestling match as Soph argued with Em over who was going to be my maid/matron of honor. I smiled at my phone and then broke into the flurry of texts.

BTW, we have "the package" fresh from its "cleaning" and will be home soon. Stall!

Before my phone caught on fire with the response from that news, I shut it off.

Putting the urn beside me on the seat, I leaned over the console and into Liam. He lifted his arm and pulled me in close. It felt right just as it always had, like two puzzle pieces that locked together perfectly.

"I hate to be a bummer," Liam said. "But by taking Babs the way we did, we can't exactly prove that Courtney took her from you at Paisley's request unless we admit our part of what happened."

"I know," I said. "I was thinking about that. It was too risky to not get Babs back. I mean, if we called the cops and Courtney dumped her somewhere to avoid being caught with her then I wouldn't be able to produce the urn and Paisley could take us to court and say I lost her and the entire estate would go to my rotten cousin."

"Unfortunately, it also means that even though Paisley lost this round, I suspect she's going to keep trying," Liam said. "You and your sisters are going to have to be vigilant and loop your attorney in."

"And we will," I said. "But today, I am going to enjoy every glorious second of our victory."

We arrived at the house shortly after that. Liam parked on the street, and we walked up the front walkway, hand in hand, noting that the front door was open.

My pace quickened. I didn't think Paisley would harm my sisters, I mean she was greedy but not unstable, or so I had thought. We heard yelling just inside the door. I jogged into the house with Liam beside me.

Paisley stood in the center of the great room. Her choppy highlighted hair was wild as if she'd been tugging at it. Her dress looked rumpled, and the hem was frayed. She only had one shoe on, and it seemed as if all of her make-up, including her false eyelashes, were dripping off the end of her chin in a bid for escape.

Meanwhile Soph and Em were sitting at the table with Dante, Jessie, and the hippie turtle rescue guy whose name I didn't know, wearing feathered boas and sparkly top hats, playing Cards Against Humanity with a big ol' pitcher of margaritas in the middle of the table. Mr. Loren was also sitting there in his impeccable suit, although he did not appear to be playing cards. His laptop was open before him.

"Jules! Liam!" Em cried at the sight of us. "You're just in time. Mr. Loren can't play because he's technically working and Paisley doesn't want to, shocker, but this game is definitely a the more the merrier type, don't you think? So join us!"

Liam let go of my hand and put it on my lower back as I sauntered by Paisley, cradling the urn.

"Sounds great!" I said. "Let's be sure to deal Babs in, too, since I just had her polished." Somehow, I managed to say that without cracking up.

Mr. Loren perked up at this. He put on a pair of reading glasses and held out his hands for Babs. I knew he wanted to verify that it was actually the original bedazzled urn with Babs's ashes sealed inside. He looked it over, nodded, and returned it to me.

"Everything seems to be in order." Mr. Loren closed the laptop and slid it into his bag. "Mr. Mahony, if you wouldn't mind walking me out, I'd like to have a word with you."

Liam looked at me in alarm and I shrugged.

"As far as I know, he's never bitten anyone," I said. Liam smiled.

"Okay, sure," Liam said.

With that, Mr. Loren picked up his bag and led the way toward the door. He paused beside Paisley and said, "You'll be receiving a bill for today's meeting in the mail."

And then he stepped outside with Liam behind him, closing the door after them.

Paisley's face went pale, then blotchy, and then it was suffused with red like she was breaking out in hives. Not a good look on her.

"Where did you get that?" My awful cousin pointed at the urn.

"Get it?" I asked. "I'm afraid I don't know what you mean. I've had it with me the whole time." Which was kind of true if you thought of space and time as fluid sorts of things.

"This. Isn't. Over." Paisley seethed.

I eyed her up and down. "Yes, it is. And now you need to leave *our* house and unless you are expressly invited, which you won't be, I do not want to see you set foot in here ever again."

Paisley stomped toward the entrance, hobbling given that she was wearing just one shoe, muttering the whole way. When she left, she slammed the door so hard it rattled on its hinges.

"Did you see her face?" Em cried. She stood up from the table and threw her arms around me. "That was epic."

"Well done!" Soph said. Then she started singing, "Ding dong the witch is dead!"

Which naturally set off the others. The next thing I knew there was a conga line weaving through the house, led by Dante, who was carrying Babs's urn, Jessie, Em, hippie-turtle guy, and Soph.

As they continued singing, Em made a take-a-picture gesture with her hands. I took several, tossing her my phone just as Soph grabbed my hand and yanked me into line.

When Liam reentered the house, we were working our way upstairs. I gestured for him to catch up, noting that he had a really weird expression on his face.

"Everything okay?" I asked.

"Oh, yeah, sure," he said.

Liam patted his pants pocket and then smiled at me and put his hands on my hips, jumping all in with the shenanigans. Man, I loved this guy. It hit me then, hard, like a punch to the chest. I loved him, I was in love with him, there was never going to be anyone for me but Liam Mahony.

"What?" he asked. Probably, because I looked like I'd been slapped upside the head.

"Nothing," I said.

I smiled as if to make it so, because I'm a big, stupid chicken, and I couldn't manage the three little words that start with "I" and end with "You" and have "Love" wedged in between like peanut butter holding the bread together. Ugh, I was such a loser.

Dante and Jessie missed their plane, the cats were not speaking to me because of the party, which apparently was a doozy and likely the conga line didn't help. They don't really like people other than me. Hippie-turtle guy introduced himself when the conga line broke up.

He was Troy, just Troy, because last names were "bad energy full of tribalism which led to isolationism, and he was an inclusive sort of guy." Okay, dude. Good thing he was nerdily cute. He was also completely enamored with Em, who seemed to think no more or less of him than any other accessory she might have like a belt or cute earrings. Given the state of Em lately, I almost took the poor boy aside to warn him off, but when I saw the way he looked at her I realized that he would heed no warnings of any kind. Poor bastard had it bad.

Hannah and Harry came to tuck their mother in, whose nerves had been soothed by three margaritas which left her unfit to tend to herself. Yes, this was Soph's first real-life embarrassing moment in front of her kids. I tried to cheer her up by assuring her there would likely be more as the twins got older. Shockingly, she was not comforted by this in the least.

I wasn't surprised that Stan didn't show up to check on his wife. Jerk. I wondered if Soph had made any decisions about him and their marriage yet. I hoped she left him. I hoped she burned his practice down and left him. Okay, maybe that was going too far. Still, a nice case of chlamydia wouldn't be out of order for the cheating prick. I could only hope.

When everyone moved to the kitchen to forage for food, Liam grabbed me by the arm and escorted me to the door.

"Where are we going?" I asked.

"My place," he said.

The way he said it made it clear that there would be no discussion. This was fine with me. I was exhausted. I waved and blew kisses at our people and then the door shut behind us and we were striding over to his house.

"How are you feeling?" he asked.

"Pretty great. We got rid of Paisley, and both Em and Soph seemed better today," I said. "Maybe we're all going to come out the other side of this grief thing."

"You will," Liam said. "You're stronger than you know."

He paused in front of his door and studied my face. "So, surfer girl, do we get to pick up where we left off?"

"You mean where you were literally picking me up? Yes, please!"

He smiled, opened the door, and we slipped inside. I made for the stairs, figuring we were headed straight for the make-up sex we'd been denied that morning, but he hooked me by the back of my baggy shorts and steered me to the back of the house. He took my hand and led me outside where we could see the Pacific sparkle in the late day sun.

"No upstairs yet," Liam said. "I need to talk to you about something first."

Oh, no. I started to panic. Had he changed his mind about us? Did he not want to get back together? We *were* getting back together, right? Oh, man, what if he'd only been kidding when he said we were going to get married and all. Ack! Why did I text that to my sisters? I felt like an idiot.

Suddenly, the lone margarita I had quaffed was making a desperate bid to come back up. I did not, not, not want to have my heart pulverized again. Was that overly dramatic? Yeah, well, Babs hadn't raised me for nothing.

We stood on the deck that overlooked the petite backyard and gave us a view of Gull's Harbor below and the sea beyond. The sun was just dipping down toward the horizon and in moments it would be gone. I thought the cover of darkness might be a good thing, especially if the big jerk was going to dump me and make me cry.

"I had an interesting conversation with Mr. Loren," he said.

I sucked in a breath. Oh, no, what did the lawyer do? Had he said something to Liam? Warned him away? Told him to run? I mean, really, who could blame him? My mind created and discarded a million scenarios all before I said, "Really? How so?"

"Do you remember the ring your mother stuck in my bag?" Liam asked.

"Oh, just a little since it's what caused me to leave you and all," I said.

"Do you remember what it looked like?"

"Yes, it was obnoxiously big," I said. "Three stones, each a carat, because my dad gave her a new diamond every time she popped out one of us girls, or, in my case acquired a baby."

"Well, did any of you wonder what happened to it when she died?" Liam asked.

"Huh." I blinked at him. I hadn't and I didn't think Soph or Em had either. "She always said we'd each get our own stone when she passed, but I guess we all assumed she put it in her safe deposit box or something. We haven't been processing very well."

"She didn't put them in a safe," he said. "She had something else done with the diamonds."

I tipped my head at him and gave him a considering look. How did he know this? "What did Mr. Loren want talk to you about?"

"Turns out Babs had another part to her will in which she left me a little something," Liam said. "In the note Mr. Loren gave me, she said she wanted to make things right."

My heart started to thump hard in my chest. When Liam moved to get down on one knee in front of me, it stopped completely. He took something out of his pocket and held it up to me between two fingers. Sparkling in the light from the setting sun was the square diamond my father had given Babs when I was born.

"Julia Blumer, I asked you once before and I meant it then, but I mean it even more now. Will you marry me?" he asked.

My face crumpled and I started to cry. I couldn't get the words out. Maybe this was what Babs had meant when she said she wished she'd had more time to make it right. Babs had done this for me. For us. For the first time ever, I felt my heart swell with gratitude for that woman. I could hardly breathe. So, I nodded and then hiccupped, "Y...Yes."

Liam slid the ring on my finger. It was a perfect fit.

"We couldn't hear her!" Soph yelled over the wall.

"Yeah, what did she say?" Em demanded.

I looked over my shoulder to see my sisters peeking over the top of the wall, along with Dante, Jessie, Hannah and Harry. I started to laugh.

"Sorry," Liam muttered. "I sort of figured witnesses might be in order this time."

"It's okay, no, it's perfect," I said. I shouted to my sisters, "I said yes!" Then I turned back to my man, dragged him up from his knees and jumped into his arms.

He kissed me as if I was everything to him, and I kissed him back just the same. When we broke apart, because oxygen is required to live, apparently, we looked at each other with matching goofy smiles.

"I love you, surfer girl," he said. "I always have, and I always will."

"I love you, too, new boy," I said. "And I'm never ever going to leave you ever again."

"Excellent." The look Liam gave me scorched. "Now we can go upstairs."

I laughed and took his hand. As we strode through the house, the light caught the diamond on my finger and I stared at it for a moment, trying to wrap my head around Babs having a ring fashioned for me and giving it to the man I love so that he could propose. It was so touching, and charming, and waaaay overreaching—in other words, so Babs.

I squeezed Liam's hand as one sly tear slipped out to glide down my cheek but that was okay. In this precise moment in time, all of the years of hurt and anger between me and Babs finally faded away.

When I glanced at Liam, I found him watching me with a tender smile on his face. He let go of my hand and opened his arms. I walked into his embrace, knowing that this time nothing would ever keep us apart.